THE
STOLEN
LETTER

BOOKS BY CLARA BENSON

In Darkness, Look for Stars

ANGELA MARCHMONT MYSTERIES
The Murder at Sissingham Hall
The Mystery at Underwood House
The Treasure at Poldarrow Point
The Riddle at Gipsy's Mile
The Incident at Fives Castle
The Imbroglio at the Villa Pozzi
The Problem at Two Tithes
The Trouble at Wakeley Court
The Scandal at 23 Mount Street
The Shadow at Greystone Chase

ANGELA MARCHMONT SHORT STORIES
Angela's Christmas Adventure
The Man on the Train
A Question of Hats

FREDDY PILKINGTON-SOAMES ADVENTURES
A Case of Blackmail in Belgravia
A Case of Murder in Mayfair
A Case of Conspiracy in Clerkenwell
A Case of Duplicity in Dorset
A Case of Suicide in St. James's

OTHER
The Lucases of Lucas Lodge

THE
STOLEN
LETTER

CLARA BENSON

bookouture

Published by Bookouture in 2020

An imprint of Storyfire Ltd.
Carmelite House
50 Victoria Embankment
London EC4Y 0DZ

www.bookouture.com

ISBN: 978-1-83888-202-0
eBook ISBN: 978-1-83888-201-3

To Lesley and Caroline, and memories of Florence.
We shall return.

Prologue

Berlin, February 1937

They came in the early evening, when businesses were shutting up for the day and most people were heading home in the winter darkness to their families and firesides. There were three of them, purposeful, businesslike. Two were dressed like any other citizen: gaberdine trench coats, woollen mufflers, hats pulled low to ward off the damp. Only the way they carried themselves, self-assured, coolly aware of their power, indicated that they were officers of the Gestapo. The third man was corpulent and comfortable, dressed in an expensive camel-hair overcoat, a soft hat and kidskin gloves – the clothes of a man who had attained a life of material ease and liked it that way. The rosiness of his cheeks gave him a deceptively jovial air, but the expression of his eyes, deep-set in folds of flesh, was hard and shrewd.

A chilly drizzle was falling. As the men paused beneath a street light, its glow highlighted the droplets which floated through the air to settle on their hats and shoulders, but they didn't seem to notice. They waited for a tram to pass, then crossed the street to stop outside a small business premises, its windows in darkness. On the frontage above, a discreet sign read 'J. Silberstein, Fine Arts'. A notice on the door indicated that the shop was shut for the day.

The man in the camel-hair coat looked up at the first-floor windows, from which lights were burning with a merry glow, and rang the doorbell. At length there came the sound of someone approaching, and the door was answered by a maid who didn't have time to do more than give a startled glance at the visitors before a man's voice called down the stairs from the flat above the shop.

'You're early – I wasn't expecting you so soon!'

The voice was followed by the sound of footsteps on the stairs, then the man himself: mid-forties, spare, his sandy hair slightly thinning, wearing his shirtsleeves and a welcoming smile, which faltered when he saw the man in the camel-hair coat, whom he recognised as a fellow art dealer.

'What are you doing here?'

'Good evening, Jacob. You won't mind if we come in, will you?' replied the art dealer.

'Well, as a matter of fact—' began Jacob, but the man had already stepped into the narrow hallway, followed by his companions.

'Are you Jewish?' said one of the Gestapo officers to the maid.

She looked puzzled, and glanced at Jacob in appeal, and he replied for her.

'No, she isn't. Go upstairs,' he said to her, and she obeyed, with a scared glance at the visitors.

The man in the camel-hair coat indicated a glass door leading off the downstairs passage, which bore the word 'Gallery' in neat gold letters.

'Let us go in,' he said.

'We're closed.'

'Open the gallery,' said one of the Gestapo men in a tone that brooked no argument. Jacob Silberstein opened his mouth to protest, but thought better of it. He produced a key from his pocket and led them into the large room that served as a gallery, turning on the light as he did so. His was a modest-sized business, but he was selective in the paintings he chose to buy and sell, many of which were highly valuable, and thanks to his acumen and hard work he had fully expected to become quite wealthy in the next few years, until the new anti-Jewish laws had put paid to it all. He stood by the door, biting his tongue, mindful of the Gestapo presence, watching as the art dealer walked around with a notebook, looking at the paintings, occasionally asking a question and making a note.

'I want to buy these,' announced the dealer at last. 'Shall we go upstairs and discuss it? It's cold in here.'

'As I said, we're closed,' replied Jacob, irritated now. 'If you want to discuss buying the paintings then come back tomorrow during business hours.'

'We will go upstairs,' repeated the art dealer, as if there were no doubt about the matter.

Jacob knew he had no choice. He led the men up and into a warm, comfortable living room. Through an open door could be seen a large kitchen, from which delicious smells were emanating. Two children, a boy of about fifteen and a girl of twelve, were sitting at a table by the window in the living room, doing their homework. Alerted by the maid, a woman, wearing a smart frock under her apron, came out of the kitchen as they arrived, wiping her hands on a cloth. She stopped as she saw their visitors.

'Go to your rooms,' said Jacob to the children. 'Or, better still, go and help your mother in the kitchen. Irma, take them. Anna, you'd better go home now.'

The maid nodded and went to fetch her coat and hat from a cupboard.

'I suggest you don't come back,' said one of the Gestapo men meaningfully as she passed him. They heard her footsteps hurrying down the stairs and the slam of the door as she went out.

'Come,' said Irma Silberstein. The children, with a wary look at the newcomers, rose and went into the kitchen with their mother. One of the Gestapo men closed the door behind them.

The man in the camel-hair coat sat down in the most comfortable chair and brought out a cigar. 'Do you mind?' Without waiting for an answer he lit it, and the room was shortly filled with the acrid smell of cigar smoke.

The Gestapo officers were standing by the door. Jacob knew he was treading on eggshells. He'd been caught employing a non-Jewish maid, and for that reason alone he could be in trouble. Of course they didn't need any real reason to persecute him – his being Jewish was enough. The man sitting in the chair was a big name in the art business, and was rumoured to have the official favour of Hitler. Jacob was certain that he'd chosen this hour to arrive and throw his weight around purely to humiliate him and show him who had the upper hand. But Jacob was still a businessman first and foremost, and if his visitor was going to insist on buying his paintings, then it was up to him to make the first offer, so he stayed silent.

The art dealer seemed in no hurry to speak, however. He sat, drawing on his cigar with great enjoyment for several minutes, then at last tapped a clump of ash onto the rug and said:

'I hear some interesting things about you, Jacob.' He indicated the Gestapo officer who was standing nearest the door to the stairs. 'Richter here tells me he has received information that you have been speaking out against the Nazi Party, and the Führer in particular.'

'That's not true. I've never said a thing against him!'

'No?' The dealer jerked his chin towards Richter, who took out a notebook and began reading.

'On October fifteenth last, you were heard complaining to a client of yours, saying that the Nazi Party doesn't care about ordinary German folk, and that Hitler will destroy Europe.'

Jacob stared.

'Nonsense—' he began.

'You also said Hitler must be given a taste of his own medicine before he goes too far,' went on Richter.

Jacob was racking his brains. Had he ever said such a thing? If he had, it had been a remark in passing, made to someone he trusted. Who had reported him?

Richter read on inexorably, a list of accusations, of statements and actions, most of them exaggerated or invented. Jacob had spat in disgust at the mention of the Aryan master race. He'd torn down posters that urged the boycott of Jewish businesses. He'd been seen associating with a group of known Communists – that was the worst one of all, because even to be suspected of being a Communist meant risking arrest and torture. Jacob denied each charge hotly as it was read out, but it was no good – it was obvious his visitors had come prepared, and that he was in great danger.

'That maid of yours,' said the art dealer, when Richter had finished. 'What are you doing employing her? You know the law.'

'She's been with us for years. She received a blow to the head as a child and she's a little simple, but she adores my wife and begged us to let her stay. She'd have difficulty getting work anywhere else, so I couldn't bring myself to fire her.'

'That's as may be. Still, as you can see, you are in trouble.' The art dealer gestured to the Gestapo men. 'All these things are enough to have you arrested and probably shot right now.'

He paused, waiting for a protest, but Jacob, increasingly angry and mutinous, said nothing. The dealer went on,

'As it happens, however, I can offer you a way out. I know Hitler would be very interested in some of the paintings you have downstairs – the Flemish ones in particular, those landscapes by Massijs and Brueghel. But naturally he's not interested in acquiring anything from a *Jew* such as yourself.' He said the word with a subtle emphasis which somehow managed to drip with disparagement. 'It will have to come from me. Now, you must have realised that you can't possibly expect to continue in business given the crimes that have been recorded against your name. Berlin isn't safe for you. Quite frankly, I don't know why you didn't leave long ago. God knows the Reich are doing their best to drive you people out of the country. But it seems many of you aren't easily persuaded. Let's see...'

He paused to make some calculations and wrote a figure at the bottom of his list, then tore out the page from the notebook and handed it to Jacob.

'Let us get down to business. I will take these paintings off your hands, and in return you shall have a week to pack up and get out of Germany. Otherwise, I will leave you to the mercies of Richter and Baumann here.'

Jacob experienced a brief surge of relief that he wasn't about to be arrested. He'd been thinking of taking his family out of Germany for some time now. This wasn't how he'd have chosen to do it, but perhaps it was the spur he needed. With the cash from the paintings he could start up in business somewhere else. He looked down at the slip of paper the art dealer had given him and his mouth dropped open in disbelief.

'This is what you're offering? You're joking, surely! This isn't even a tenth of their value.'

'Nevertheless, I think you will find it is a fair offer in view of your circumstances,' replied the man smoothly.

'I can't afford to sell them at this price. You know I can't. The proceeds won't cover the migration tax for the four of us, because they'll calculate it on the full value of the paintings. We won't be able to afford to leave.'

'You are lying. I know perfectly well you Jews all have plenty of money squirrelled away in secret places. I'm quite sure you will have no difficulty in finding the funds. It's your choice. This is not a time to be miserly. Sell your jewels or your gold or whatever and pay the tax, then get out and think yourself lucky.'

The expression on the art dealer's face was complacent, and Jacob flushed. This man had barged in without so much as a by-your-leave, and was now sitting in the best chair, scattering ash all over the rug, bent on ruining another man for his own benefit, purely because he could. It was the sort of insult Jews had had to endure for years now, the result of laws that persecuted one group of people to the advantage of another. Jacob's blood began to boil, but he remained calm.

'How dare you come in here and speak to me like this?' He spoke quietly, trying to keep his voice from shaking. 'It's obvious you're hell-bent on ruining me, but I'm damned if I'll take this sort of insult on my evening off, in my own home, in front of my wife and children. You people slither around in the dark, hiding your faces like cowards. Well, if you *are* going to ruin me, you can come back tomorrow and do it in daylight, in full view of the world, and let everybody judge you for what you really are.'

He stepped forward, fists clenched.

'Jacob!' came a warning voice. It was his wife, who was standing in the kitchen doorway, watching the scene. Behind her, the two frightened children looked on silently.

The man in the camel-hair coat stood up. He was much taller and bulkier than Jacob, and his presence seemed to fill the room. He laughed, an unpleasant sound.

'Your wife has some sense, at least. Do you think you have any rights here, Silberstein? You will take what I offer you and be thankful for it.' His face changed. It was hard, threatening, even cruel. 'And in fact, for your rudeness I'm minded to change the conditions. I'll take the paintings for nothing and you can think yourself lucky.'

'You can't do that!' exclaimed Jacob.

'Oh, but I can,' replied the art dealer infuriatingly.

At that, Jacob lost his temper. He made a lunge for the other man, catching him by surprise. The Gestapo men sprang forward, and the next few moments were confused ones. There was a sharp crack of a gun, and Jacob was on the floor. Irma screamed and ran forward, crouching over the fallen body of her husband, shot through the heart, his blood seeping into the rug. The children whimpered, terrified, clutching each other in the kitchen doorway.

'Well, I *would* have paid him,' said the art dealer. His breathing was heavy as he straightened his collar.

Irma, numb with shock, picked up the page the art dealer had torn out of his notebook, which had floated down to rest on Jacob's body. It was soaked with blood. She stared at it, then bent over her dead husband and began sobbing uncontrollably.

PART 1

Chapter One

Mr Falconetti was of the opinion that the English ladies had made a mistake in not going to see Venice. Now that September was half over, the heat and the smells would be less oppressive, he said, and the place would not be so crowded with tourists as it was in July and August. The Italian was genial, enthusiastic in his description of the Grand Canal, and the view of St Mark's Square from the lagoon, and the two ladies listened politely, since he had a strong claim on their attention – although they were keeping a wary eye out in case he began to impose upon them.

He had come to their rescue at Bologna, when they had been deserted in favour of an important local personage and his much younger wife, both of them swathed in furs and dripping with money. The porter had transferred his allegiance without so much as a backward glance, leaving the two unimportant Englishwomen surrounded by their luggage, with no other porter in sight and the train due to leave in ten minutes. Mrs Unsworth had fretted and tutted and fussed while Stella made tentative suggestions as to their carrying their own bags, but if the smart little man with his moustache and his stiff collar had not spotted them and insisted on escorting them to the right platform, fetching another porter himself, snapping out instructions and ensuring their luggage was safely stowed, they would almost certainly have missed their connection.

Having waved away their thanks, Mr Falconetti now seemed to consider them as his special charges and was sitting across from

them in the carriage, pointing out the various attractions from
the train window. Not that there were many to be seen, since the
landscape had changed all at once a short distance from Bologna,
from the flat expanse of the Po Plain to the rolling inclines of the
Apennines, and now much of the line consisted of long tunnels
that burrowed through the base of the mountains straight towards
Florence. The train was an electric one, and Mr Falconetti spoke
with pride of the opening of this new, faster line, such as they had
in other countries – America, perhaps? He remembered reading
about it somewhere. He was sure the trains in other countries were
very efficient, but nobody could do things as well as the Italians.

Mrs Unsworth, mindful of her young companion, wanted to
be only distantly polite, but his friendliness was disarming.

'You're a proud patriot,' she said indulgently, because of course
she knew England was the only country.

Mr Falconetti swelled. 'I am.' He shook his head. 'But you
English tourists, always you go straight to Florence, when there
are many other places to see.'

He himself was a native of Modena, and with the true regional
loyalty of his kind was dismissive of Tuscany as inferior to his own
homeland.

'But Florence is so beautiful,' said Mrs Unsworth.

He shrugged. '*Beh*. It is pretty, yes, but a little too loud – too
obvious. Florence is all very well, but if you come to Emilia Romagna,
you will find that the food is much better and the people are so
much more friendly. The *fiorentini*, they are not very kind. You must
be careful because they will cheat you whenever they can. They see
you are English and they will make the price double, triple. It is
not correct – this is what you must say to them. It is not correct.
And then you must leave the shop, and they will run after you and
beg pardon and say they made a mistake and ask the proper price.'

He glanced expressively at the younger of the two ladies as he
spoke. A girl she was, really, with a raw, unfinished look about her,

as if she'd just come out of school and wasn't quite sure what the world wanted of her. Not beautiful – no, he couldn't honestly say she was the type he admired – but her hair was thick and dark, and her eyes were striking: wide and deep blue, with flecks of vivid green around the pupil and a thick fringe of eyelashes. The eyes were mostly cast down, or turned away, looking out of the window, but now and again she would direct a look at him – an earnest stare that caught and held his attention until she turned back to the window or her book. She'd been reading a Baedeker's guide to Italy, consulting it at each station so as to catch as much as possible of the places they passed through, and joined in the conversation only when addressed directly. She and the older woman were not mother and daughter, as far as Falconetti could judge. Mrs Unsworth must be the chaperone. He was innocently curious to know more about them, but they had that British reserve and didn't seem inclined to unburden themselves.

The train emerged from a long tunnel and they came out into sunshine. The morning had been grey, but now the low mist had lifted and the sun drenched the countryside with colour. The train passed through several smaller stations – ugly, concrete constructions they were, but behind them could be seen glimpses of pretty villages extending up hillsides, yellow buildings with red roofs, with here and there the domed roof or proud bell tower of a church. Stella was only half-listening to the conversation. Mr Falconetti was now talking about the newspaper of which he was the editor; it was a small, local publication, but it had a long and proud history, having been published continuously since 1870, the year of Italian unification. In the early years of the current century the paper had developed Communist leanings, but after the dictator Mussolini had come to power it had been forced to moderate its tone or risk closure. Occasionally an article slipped through that might be considered subversive, but so far they had avoided trouble.

'And why should they want to harm us anyway?' said Falconetti. 'We are all proud Fascists now, thanks to Il Duce.'

Stella looked up, and he threw her an amused look, as though he had just made a joke. Mrs Unsworth had not noticed the irony in his tone, and took his words at face value.

'Mussolini has been very good for your country, I think,' she observed.

'But certainly,' replied Mr Falconetti, and again there was that note of dryness. 'He and Herr Hitler will start a war together, build us an empire and make us all rich and happy.'

'Oh!' exclaimed Mrs Unsworth. She had at last sensed an undercurrent of something and noted the creases about his eyes which spoke of concern, and in true English fashion turned the conversation to a less touchy subject. They began speaking about London, which Mr Falconetti had visited many times.

Stella's mind was drifting between the conversation and the view through the window. As far as she could tell, the train was on time, so it couldn't be long until they reached their destination. She hoped they would see Florence as they approached, and began to crane her neck for a glimpse of it. But there was nothing, only mile after mile of solid, grey railway and overhead wires extending into the distance, cutting among the hills. Mrs Unsworth's descriptions of the city dated back thirty years, and she lacked the imagination to do the place justice, but she'd dug out an old postcard, and Stella had taken it and gazed at it for hours. It was the classic view of the cathedral of Santa Maria del Fiore, taken from the Piazzale Michelangelo on the south side of the river Arno, according to the printed caption on the back. Stella had wanted to go to Stanfords and buy a map of the city to study, but for one reason or another there hadn't been time. No matter: surely Monica would have one, or if not, she could go and buy one herself.

Stella was struggling to subdue her resentment at having been packed off to Italy like a piece of unwanted furniture to stay with

Monica, of all people. Monica, the Italian beauty who had married Stella's father when Stella was eleven and Monica herself was only in her mid-twenties. Monica, who had been the reason that Stella had hardly seen her father from that day until the day he died six years later, hit by a car as he was out walking one evening. Monica, who had married a Florentine count less than a year after Raymond Cockburn's death, and was now Stella's only relation and guardian of sorts. There was a bitter irony in the fact that the woman who had torn her beloved father from her was now to be put in charge of her welfare, and Stella felt it keenly.

Mr Ellison, the solicitor who acted on behalf of the trustees, hadn't known what to do with Stella in the year since she'd left school. She'd never been the academic sort, and even if she had been that way inclined, university would have been out of the question. What on earth was the point, since she would come into her inheritance when she was twenty-one? But *something* must be done with her, and so, when a letter arrived from Monica, inviting Stella to Florence for a few months, Mr Ellison had jumped at the opportunity. If he did have any concerns about what he'd heard of anti-British sentiment among the Italians, they were soon dispelled by the reflection that Monica's husband was a senator in Mussolini's government, and would surely not have allowed the invitation had he considered Stella's presence at all unwelcome. To Florence Stella was to go, then – at least until she came of age, after which Mr Ellison's responsibilities would be at an end.

Nobody had ever asked Stella what she thought of all this, but if the trustees had ever given the matter any consideration they would have assumed she was happy with the plan. As it happened, Stella's thoughts were very much conflicted. She'd longed to visit Florence ever since could remember – but certainly not by the grace of Monica. She couldn't understand why she had been invited at all, in fact. Once Monica had come on the scene Raymond had lost all interest in his daughter, which must have been his new wife's doing, so why had Monica suddenly decided she wanted the company of a former stepdaughter she had never shown the slightest interest in up to now? In the days leading up to her departure from England, Stella had thought of many things she wanted to say to Monica about her deep-seated feelings of hurt and rejection, but in the end she'd swallowed them. What was the use? Stella had adored her father, but he'd been a busy man with an important job dealing in valuable works of art, and even in the years when she'd had him to herself she'd seen him very little. Any time they'd had together had been in the form of minutes and hours snatched from his other duties; occasional days out; the odd weekend at Easter or over Christmas. He'd done his best, but he'd never really had time for a daughter, as much as it hurt to admit it.

Stella didn't remember much about her mother; she'd died when Stella was quite small, and had almost immediately been forgotten by everyone, it seemed. Stella had spent her early years with a succession of governesses and companions, and as soon as she was old enough she'd been sent to school, and had seen her father only during the holidays – and sometimes not even then. Then had come Monica, who wasn't interested in sharing Raymond with anyone else, and so Stella had seen him even less than before. After he died, Stella had had to shed her tears in private, because nobody was interested in the feelings of his discarded daughter, who, with his death, had become nothing more than an administrative burden. Now, a year later, Monica wanted Stella to come and stay for some reason, so here she was, travelling through Italy under the watchful eye of Mrs Unsworth.

But whatever other feelings Stella might be struggling with, the foremost one at present was undoubtedly excitement. She could hardly get enough of the view through the train window, as one tantalising glimpse of scenery was rapidly replaced by another in their journey towards their destination. They had now left the mountains behind and had come out onto another flat plain. The next station was Prato, Mr Falconetti informed them. He went off to speak to the conductor about something, and Mrs Unsworth stopped fussing with her handbag and looked out of the window.

'I don't think we visited Prato last time I was here,' she said. 'What does Baedeker say? I don't suppose there's as much to see as there is in Florence and Siena.'

Stella frowned over the guide.

'They have many early Renaissance works of art,' she said. 'And the cathedral is in the Tuscan-Romanesque style.'

She would have read on, but it was obvious that Mrs Unsworth was already thinking about something else.

'Are you quite sure your stepmother knows what time you're arriving?' she said. 'Perhaps we had better ask Mr Falconetti where we can find a taxi, just in case.'

'I'm sure she hasn't forgotten. And besides, even if she has I'm sure we can find our own taxi without bothering Mr Falconetti.'

'Oh, but after what he said about the Florentines! One doesn't wish to be overcharged, even if things are so very much cheaper over here.'

'Shall you stay in Italy, do you think?' asked Stella. Mrs Unsworth was a widow whose means had become gradually straitened year by year since her husband's death, and she had been lured out to Italy by her sister with promises of sunshine, a simple life, and a much lower cost of living.

'My dear, I don't know. It's a big change, of course, but Dorothea is quite longing for company, she says, and you know she can't go back to England, as the damp would kill her. I've told her I shall give it a month or two, and then we'll see. Perhaps one could spend part of the year here and part of the year in London.'

Stella couldn't think of dull, grey London just at present – not with all these new things to look at. A little thrill went through her at the thought that here she was, in Italy, away from England and the constant talk of war. In this bright, sunny corner of the

world how could anything so ugly as war intrude? Stella wanted
to explore. She wanted to wander through the streets, haggle with
stallholders, absorb the cool atmosphere of the churches, marvel
at rich, golden altarpieces, and bask in the glorious sunshine of
this country she'd heard so much about, but up until now only
seen in pictures.

Just then the guard came to inform the ladies that they would
shortly arrive at Florence Santa Maria Novella, and Mrs Unsworth
was galvanised into a state of bustle, while Stella, her heart beating,
gathered her few belongings together and waited quietly. The train
inched into the station and at last they were on the platform and
looking about for the exit. They procured a porter immediately
and came out of the station into a wide, open piazza that was busy
with people and cars and trams and horses and bicycles. It was
three o'clock and the sun was still high, and Stella blinked at the
brightness. The air felt warm and damp; the presence of one or two
puddles indicated that it must have rained an hour or two earlier,
but the sky was clear now, a brilliant blue glaring down on the red
roof of the building opposite. The place smelled of warm cobbles
and dirt and engine fumes. The sound of voices mixed with church
bells in the distance, striking the hour, and as if in answer the bells
of the church opposite the station began to ring too. So this was
Florence. Everything was life and motion, and Stella stood very
still, trying to take it all in at once and fix the scene in her memory.

Mrs Unsworth was fussing with the baggage and keeping an eye
out for thieves, who, she was convinced, were waiting to pounce
as soon as she let down her guard.

'Which is our car, do you suppose?' she asked, although Stella
didn't hear her, as she was gazing at the church opposite, in brown
stone with a tall tower. It must be the Basilica of Santa Maria
Novella. What had the guidebook said about that?

A man approached them. He was wearing a chauffeur's jacket
and cap, but they bristled uncomfortably on him as though he'd

put them on just for the occasion. He was in his sixties, perhaps, short and strongly built, with a receding hairline, a grey moustache, and eyes that peered out from an overhanging brow.

'Villa Bruni?' he said hesitantly. 'Miss Cockburn?'

'Yes,' said Stella.

He smiled, and his face was transformed.

'I am Beppe. I bring the car for the Countess. Please, one minute.'

He indicated that they were to stay where they were and went off. A minute or two later a large car appeared, sleek and comfortable, and pulled up in front of where they were standing. Beppe alighted and began to load up their luggage.

'*Tutto fatto,*' he said at last, and smiled again. 'Now I take you to the villa.'

They waited for him to open the door for them, but he was already sliding himself into the front seat, so after a moment Mrs Unsworth opened the back passenger door uncertainly. Stella took one last glance around the piazza, and her attention was caught by a group of four official-looking men in smart uniforms with breeches and long boots. They were looking across the piazza at someone and talking in low voices. She turned her head and saw that the subject of their conversation seemed to be Mr Falconetti, who had just come out of the station. He did not see the men as they strode towards him.

'Do get in, dear,' said Mrs Unsworth.

'It's Mr Falconetti.' Stella could hear raised voices, and hesitated before shutting the door. 'Is that the police?'

'Is what the police? Shut the door.'

Stella ignored her.

'They're going to arrest him!' She craned her neck, trying to see. Two of the men had taken hold of Falconetti and he had begun to struggle. Stella gasped as one of them knocked him to the ground and kicked him viciously. Another of the men spat on him, then they hauled him up and dragged him off, still shouting and protesting.

'Mr Falconetti!' exclaimed Stella, but there was nothing she could do. Beppe had started the engine and was already pulling away. She shut the door hurriedly, and all Stella could do was turn and look behind her as the four uniformed men, dragging with them Mr Falconetti, receded into the distance until finally they disappeared altogether.

Chapter Two

Neither Mrs Unsworth nor Beppe wanted to talk about what they had just seen outside the station.

'Better to pretend nothing has happened,' said Beppe.

'But Mr Falconetti!' Stella turned to Mrs Unsworth in appeal.

'It's not for us to interfere,' observed Mrs Unsworth. 'Who knows what kind of things he'd got up to? You heard what he said about his newspaper and its Communist sympathies.'

'*Comunista*?' Beppe pricked up his ears, then muttered in Italian under his breath and shook his head. Stella knew political opposition was forbidden, even violently suppressed under Mussolini's Fascist government, but she'd had no idea she would see the evidence of it so soon. She wanted to ask questions, but she saw there was no use, so she forced her attention to the progress of their journey. Beppe had guided the car away from the station along streets that were wider than she had expected, but he now took a turn to the left. The view suddenly opened out and they were on a bridge, travelling across the Arno, and to her left, just for a few seconds, Stella could see other bridges – delicate structures arching across the water – and a grey tower peeping out from above the buildings. They drove for a few hundred yards along the Lungarno, the road running along the river, before plunging into a maze of stone streets, busy with people. Then the ground began to rise gently, and the car was squeezing along an alley, past houses with tiny gardens in front. Mrs Unsworth had been talking all the way, but even she fell silent as the houses thinned out and the car began to make its way up a dusty road that wound steeply away from the city, curving left and right as they climbed.

'*Eccoci*,' said Beppe after a few minutes. 'Here we are.'

They had arrived at a tall, iron gate set into a wall weathered with the dirt of years, on which was attached a white sign which said 'Villa Bruni' in blue writing. Beppe turned the car in and they drove up another winding road through a grove of gnarled, wizened olive trees. Then there was another gate, and they came out through the trees and at last Stella got her first sight of the villa: a large, graceful building with walls the colour of soft buttermilk and a red roof. A flight of steps led up to the main entrance, while to each side of the house protruded a smaller wing. There were shutters on all the windows, and an arched portico ran along the west side of the building, shading the lower floor from the sun.

'Well!' exclaimed Mrs Unsworth, going pink with pleasure. 'What a delightful place!'

To Stella, the comparison between the vibrant colours of the Villa Bruni and the grey and brown of London was startling, and she felt a warmth spreading through her which had nothing to do with the sun. Beppe swept the car grandly around a circular drive with an ornamental fountain in grey stone at the centre, from which water trickled disconsolately, then pulled up by the steps to the front door. Stella stepped out and gazed once more at the villa, then turned around. The main entrance to the house faced south, away from Florence, across an undulating Tuscan landscape punctuated with tall cypresses to low, blue hills in the distance, and Stella felt her hair stirred by a soft, delicate breeze.

'Welcome, darlings! Was your journey simply too foul?' came a voice just then. Stella turned as a woman strolled out through the grand front door and down the steps, and enveloped her in a perfunctory, jasmine-scented hug. 'Is that you, Stella? Well! Just let me look at you! I'd say you hadn't changed one bit, except that you're about a foot taller than when I saw you last! And you must be Mrs Unsworth. Welcome.'

Monica Carminati was no taller than Stella, but her exquisitely straight posture and her hair, which she wore in a riot of shining chestnut curls that stood out from her head, made her look it. Stella had always been awed by Monica's beauty, and she'd lost none of it since they'd last seen each other; with her high cheekbones and almond-shaped eyes of a startling light blue, there was something almost exotic about her. Although a native Italian, she'd spent much of her childhood in England and Switzerland, and had attended international schools, which had given her an almost perfect English accent, and the confident air of a woman who had slotted into her rightful place in life. Today she was dressed in white trousers with a bold striped shirt, and was carrying a tennis racquet, but even in that casual outfit she contrived to make Stella feel dowdy and shabby.

'Beastly long journey from Milan,' remarked Monica. 'And those trains are so unpleasant. I expect you'd like to wash and change. Bring the luggage, Beppe.' She raised her voice. 'Dora, where are you?'

An answering voice came from the house, and Monica turned and led them up the steps and through the door into a cool, dim entrance hall, from which several doors led. A middle-aged woman was just emerging from a side room, wiping her hands.

'Dora, show Miss Cockburn and Mrs Unsworth to their rooms, won't you?' Monica glanced at Stella's tweed skirt, causing Stella to smooth it down self-consciously. 'Come and find us in the garden when you're done,' she said, and went off, swinging her racquet.

'Please,' said Dora, and led them through a door, up a flight of smooth, marble stairs and along a corridor. 'Signorina, this is your room. Signora, if you will come this way. This bathroom between you is to share.'

As the voices of Mrs Unsworth and Dora receded, Stella closed the door and took in her surroundings at a glance. Her room was

spacious, with pale walls and terracotta tiles on the floor. A small
bed stood in the middle of the room, made up with crisp, white
linen, while against the wall were a dressing table and a wardrobe
in dark wood, which were clearly antiques. Stella pulled off her
hat, went across to the window and threw it open, and there it
was: Florence, in the valley below, with hills rising up behind it.
Or part of Florence at least; to Stella's disappointment they had put
her in the west wing of the villa, and the main part of the building
blocked the view of the centre of the city. Still, what she could see
was wonderful; the sun had that late afternoon quality to it as it
sank lower, the shadows were beginning to lengthen, and the roofs
of the buildings glowed russet and copper.

She stood at the window and stared for a while, dreaming. As
soon as they'd let her she'd go down into the city and explore. The
sound of voices from outside brought her back to herself, and she
realised she'd been dawdling. Mrs Unsworth must have already
gone downstairs, and she really ought to do the same. Beppe had
brought up her luggage, and Stella picked up her sponge bag and
went into the bathroom to wash her face and hands and tidy her
hair. Her clothes were grubby and crumpled – as Monica had
noticed – so she dug out a light frock that wasn't too creased and
put it on, then after a quick glance in the mirror went downstairs.
Dora was dusting a picture frame, and her face widened into a
warm smile of appreciation when she saw Stella.

'Better, no? Your room is comfortable, I hope? Good. *La signora*
Unsworth has gone into the garden. That way.'

She indicated a door, and Stella went through it into a huge
salone and out via a set of French windows which had been flung
wide open. Stella followed the path under another long portico
and out onto a large terrace bordered by a stone balustrade. A short
distance away she could hear voices and a tennis ball being batted
back and forth, and she headed towards the sound, down a path
that wound down a slope between formal flower beds. A stocky

young man in shirtsleeves was crouched by one of them, pulling out some dead plants. He gave her an impudent grin and nodded to her as she passed.

At length she came to another, smaller terrace with steps leading down to a large area of lawn, with a tennis court laid out on one side of it and a circular pavilion on the other. A number of people were sitting on deckchairs or on the grass, which was not as lush and green as in England. Stella wasn't looking at the grass or the people, however. She stopped and took in her breath, because here at last was the view she'd been looking for – a proper vista of the whole city: the cathedral with its vast red dome and its bell tower, just beginning to glow gloriously in the sinking sunlight; the tall, castle-like building with the square turret; and a whole swathe of lesser domes and towers that she couldn't even begin to recognise, in a sea of terracotta roofs. She wanted to stand and drink it in forever.

'That's out!' came a man's voice from the tennis court.

'No it's not!' returned Monica.

They argued the point, and the man won. From the sound of his voice he was American. Monica swiped her racquet along the grass in mock anger.

'Oh, bother! You always beat me. You won't even pretend to let me win. Not very chivalrous of you, is it?'

'If you wanted chivalry you should have played against Gerardo,' said the American. 'I like to win.'

'Even against a woman?'

'Especially against a woman.'

They left the court and came across to the group, laughing.

'There you are!' said Monica to Stella. She threw herself down into a deckchair, waved her hand around and mentioned some names carelessly. Stella couldn't possibly remember them all at once, and she was suddenly feeling gauche and awkward, so she smiled stiffly and sat down in the deckchair next to Monica's. Too late she realised the American had been about to sit in it. She jumped up apologetically, but he motioned to her to sit down, then went and threw himself down on the grass a little way away. He ran an unabashed eye over Stella, then turned to continue his conversation with Monica. Stella saw them exchange amused glances, and all at once felt deeply uncomfortable.

Mrs Unsworth had attached herself to a respectable Italian lady of her own age, and everyone else was talking about their own concerns, leaving Stella alone and silent. She felt both ignored and conspicuous. She would have joined in with Mrs Unsworth's conversation, but they were sitting at an inconvenient angle and distance, so there was nothing else to do but shrink into her stolen chair and observe the rest of the small party covertly.

From what she could overhear, the Italian lady was the widow of a cousin of Monica's husband, Gerardo, and she was telling Mrs Unsworth in halting English of a trip to Scotland she had made many years ago. Near the two women, an Italian youth in an impeccably pressed, light suit was reclining beautifully on a wrought-iron couch spread with soft cushions, addressing witticisms to a languid, bored young woman who was idly playing with a bangle that sparkled on her wrist. Monica was still flirting with the tall American, whom she addressed as Ted, and who had a shock of dark hair, a curled lip, and the air of one who'd seen it all. Stella was regretting her choice of deckchair, as she was facing away from the view. If everyone was going to ignore her, then they might at least let her see Florence, she thought. She suddenly felt tired and resentful, and was half-tempted to get up and wander off by herself. But of course she didn't; she was only just out of England, and it would have been rude, and so she sat and smiled and tried not to look too stiff and uncomfortable.

The sun was glowing orange against a sky that was slowly turning pink, and the air was still warm. After a few minutes Dora came out with a welcome tray of drinks and aperitifs and dispensed them, talking brightly all the while. She was nothing like the

silent servants Stella had known back in England, who were stiff
in uniforms, spoke only when spoken to and rarely ventured an
opinion. Dora was short and comfortable, and under her apron
wore a light frock patterned with scarlet poppies. She was affable
and familiar to everyone, but she reserved a particularly welcoming
smile for Stella, and seemed anxious to make sure that she was well
catered for. Stella smiled back and noted that at least someone
seemed pleased to see her.

'Gerardo! Marius!' called Monica suddenly. 'Stella's here. Do
come and meet her.'

Stella turned and saw two men descending the steps from the
terrace, and soon found herself being introduced to the new arrivals.

Gerardo Guidi dei Carminati, Count of Castelnuovo dei Sab-
bioni, was fifty-five or so, with sun-browned skin and thinning,
iron-grey hair which he wore scraped back from his forehead.
His position among the Italian aristocracy and friendships with
important people had given him a life of easy advancement and
promotion, and an entrée into any high-ranking job that took his
fancy. Now he was a senator, and a trusted advisor of Mussolini.
His smile was genuine as he greeted the newcomers.

'*Buona sera!* Hallo!' he exclaimed, turning from one to the other.
'Stella, yes? And you are Mrs Unsworth. I am pleased to meet you.'

He bowed over Mrs Unsworth's hand and addressed her with
absurdly old-fashioned courtesy, and she preened and fluttered.
Then he shook hands formally with Stella. His palm was warm
and damp, and he smelled of hair oil and perspiration.

'I am Gerardo. And so you have come to stay with us. I am glad.'
His English was strongly accented, and his face wore an affable
expression. 'Do you know Marius? He is the brother of Monica.'

Stella had heard vaguely of this brother of Monica's, and she
studied him curiously as he shook her hand. Marius Schwegler
was of medium height, athletically built and smartly handsome,
with light brown hair and intelligent eyes of the same startling

blue as his sister's. When he smiled there was a sudden charm to him that blazed out, catching Stella in its glow and reminding her of Monica. He talked easily, in English as perfect and unaccented as his sister's, and Stella immediately felt more comfortable. Although he and Monica were both native Florentines, their father had been Swiss, and Marius now lived mostly in Geneva. He asked about Stella's journey, and was very interested to hear about her first impressions of Italy. Polite nothings, of course, but he regarded her with a friendly interest which held a slight spark to it, and made her think that perhaps she wasn't quite as dull and plain as she felt.

'So this is the first time you come to Florence,' said Gerardo. 'It is very beautiful, yes?'

'Oh yes,' said Stella sincerely.

He and Marius Schwegler sat down and took pains to be friendly, and she immediately began to feel better. Gerardo, with a natural Italian curiosity that couldn't possibly offend, wanted to know about her life in England, and whether she'd travelled much, and what she thought of Florence, and what she wanted to see.

'Ah, you like art?' he said, when she mentioned a vague plan to visit the Uffizi gallery. 'Which is your favourite artist?'

'There are so many I couldn't possibly choose,' she replied, 'but I'd like to see them all.'

'Very good!' exclaimed Gerardo. He lowered his voice confidentially. 'But the best paintings are not all to be found in the Uffizi. I have a small collection myself, in the villa.' He glanced at Monica. 'You have seen it already?'

'No, we only arrived about an hour ago.'

'Then I shall show you.'

Marius, who had been watching Stella intently, shook his head and said:

'Never mind Gerardo's collection. If this is your first visit to Florence, then *this* is the most important work of art.'

He motioned to her to stand up, and then, to her surprise, picked up her deckchair and turned it to face the view of the city. 'There!' He turned his own chair too and sat down next to her, and looked at her to see her reaction. 'That's better, isn't it?'

Stella couldn't help taking in another breath at the sight.

'Much better,' she agreed.

Gerardo laughed.

'Ah, yes, you see her cheeks are pink now! You are right, Marius. My pictures can wait until later.'

He went off to talk to Mrs Unsworth, and Marius turned back to Stella, pointing out the landmarks of Florence, which was now bursting into a riot of purple and pink and orange against a lilac sky. The dome of the cathedral towered above the city, drawing the eye, but there were other buildings to look at, too. The tall building with the turreted tower she'd glimpsed earlier while crossing the river was the Palazzo Vecchio, Marius informed her, the city's old council building. The small dome to the left of the cathedral was the church of San Lorenzo. There was a market nearby which sold food and other things such as handmade paper and leather goods – although for the best leather she really needed to visit the church of Santa Croce, the top of which was just visible from where they sat, to the east of the city. He approved of her plan to visit the Uffizi gallery, since he himself was an art dealer specialising in Renaissance and seventeenth-century Italian art, although he'd recently begun to deal in modern works too. His conversation was so entertaining and his manners so engaging that Stella forgot her awkwardness, and they were soon talking and laughing as if they were old friends.

As the light began to fade Dora came out and began scolding them all to get ready for dinner, so they all rose and went indoors. Stella paused on her way through the *salone* to gaze back at the fading view, then headed for the stairs. On the way up she stopped to look over the banister at the hall below, just as Monica and Marius emerged into it from another part of the house. Stella caught a snatch of their conversation as they passed.

'—use that famous charm of yours that's got you so many things that didn't belong to you,' Marius was saying.

'You're too kind, darling,' Monica purred. 'I'll do my best, but you know I'm not nearly so charming as you are. Besides, you've got something I can't give her. Why don't you try using that?'

She burst out laughing, then said something in Italian. Stella didn't stop to hear any more, but fled up the stairs and to her room before they saw her. She had the uncomfortable feeling that they'd been talking about her.

Chapter Three

Stella didn't know what to wear for dinner. Most of her evening frocks would be no good at all for this kind of company: they were girlish – almost prissy, in fact – and she knew they'd bring back all her awkwardness if she put them on. Only one dress might do, a satin number in a midnight blue with a little matching cape, but even that was plain and hung too loosely in places, and it was hardly sophisticated. Still, it was the best she could do for now. She got into it, then sat in front of the mirror and tugged at her hair with a comb. Her curls were wholly natural, and nowhere near as neat as Monica's; her hair was too long, and she spent several minutes pulling it this way and that, trying to make it look like the pictures she'd seen in the magazines, but without success. She applied a little powder and was wondering whether a touch of lipstick would be too much, when there was a brisk knock at the door.

'May I?' said Monica, coming in without waiting for an answer. She looked breathtaking in a sweeping gown of rose-coloured chiffon, cut very low at the back. Her hair was a glorious halo of curls, and diamonds twinkled in her ears. 'Let me look at you.'

She spoke kindly, and seemed much more welcoming than she had earlier. Stella, feeling drab in the glow of her presence, nevertheless stood up obligingly and showed her the dress, and Monica studied it with the detached air of an expert.

'It's not bad, but it's a little loose at the waist here. Wear it tonight, then we'll give it to Dora to take in, and perhaps add a couple of decorations here and there. She's a marvel with a needle. And yes, do put the lipstick on. There! You look quite perfect.'

'So do you,' said Stella sincerely.

Monica dismissed the compliment with a wave of the hand.

'We'd better go out very soon and get you some new clothes,' she said. 'You've grown up into quite the little beauty, but these schoolgirl frocks don't do you any favours at all. I know the very place to take you. And we'll do something with your hair, too. There's plenty of it, but it's too long – it needs to be shorter, to show off that lovely swan neck of yours. Here, let me try.' She motioned to Stella to sit down again, and set to work on her hair, smoothing it down and twisting it up at the back. 'Have you some pins? There! Much better.'

Stella looked at herself in the dressing-table mirror. She looked different, older. Her hair was more fashionable now, but she wasn't sure she liked it.

'Are you going into Florence tomorrow?' said Monica. 'Marius will show you around. He's rather taken with you, by the way. I think you've made a conquest already.'

Stella stopped poking at her hair and looked up in surprise.

'Really?' She grimaced a little at her own unsophisticated response, and went on, trying to smooth it over, 'He seems very nice. Is he much older than you?'

'Darling, you flatter me,' replied Monica with a laugh. 'But do go on. We're twins – didn't you know?'

'No, I had no idea.'

'Well, now you do. What time should you like to start tomorrow? Marius can come whenever you like.'

Stella had liked Marius very much, but she was sure he had better things to do than take her around Florence.

'There's no need for him to bother, is there? I don't mind going alone,' she said.

'Nonsense. You'll get on much better with an escort, and he's perfectly happy to do it – in fact, he made a special point of claiming you. I'm afraid I haven't time to take you myself, as we're expecting some guests – just Party members, friends of Gerardo's, but I can't get out of it.'

She lit a cigarette and gave Stella another look over with the air of a professional, tweaking the shoulder strap of her gown and pulling at the seam to straighten it. Despite herself, Stella felt grateful for the attention.

'It's awfully kind of you to have me here,' she said, half-reluctantly. She'd rather not have said it, but the good manners were ingrained after five years at school.

'Not at all. I'm only sorry it didn't occur to me before.' Monica sat on the bed and gazed at her. 'I know we didn't get to know one another very well when Raymond was alive, but we have him in common, and it's not too late to make a start. I loved him dearly, you know.'

A wistful look crossed her face. It surprised Stella, and she realised suddenly that she had always assumed, without thinking about it, that Monica had never loved Raymond at all, but had married him for some purpose of her own – his money, or his position, perhaps.

'I'm sorry you never got to say goodbye to him,' went on Monica. 'It was such a dreadful pity.'

'They never did tell me exactly what happened,' said Stella. 'Just that he got hit by a car.'

'There wasn't much to tell, really – that's all there was to it. Someone knocked him down late one evening and killed him. It was rather ironic, though, since the only reason he was walking in the first place was because he'd had a near miss the day before when his brakes failed, and his car was at the garage being repaired. I know he was looking forward to seeing you though. He was planning to bring you over to Lucerne, you know.'

'Was he?'

'Well, that was the plan. But he was very busy all through April and May and didn't think it was fair to drag you out there when he couldn't pay you the proper attention. Besides, he thought it would be better if you finished school first. I don't suppose he wrote to you shortly before he died, did he? I'd have liked to hear his words.'

Stella shook her head.

'No, he didn't write. The last letter I got from him was in March last year, I think.'

'What did it say?'

'Just news about what he'd been doing. A trip he'd taken to Berlin. Nothing much.'

'Did he say anything about his work?'

'No. Why do you ask?'

Monica didn't answer straightaway, but looked at Stella as if mulling something over.

'Raymond bought a large number of very valuable paintings in Berlin a few months before he died,' she said at last. 'Obviously he left you most of his money in trust, but he left the business to me, so by rights the paintings ought to be mine. It's just that nobody knows where they are.'

'Oh.' Stella was at a loss. 'Did he sell them, perhaps?'

'If he did, then he didn't keep a record of it, and there's no trace of the proceeds. I just thought he might have mentioned it to you.'

'No. He never talked to me about his business.' *How could he have, when I hardly ever saw him?* Stella thought.

'You're quite sure of that? He didn't send you something for safekeeping, perhaps?'

'Such as what?'

Monica drew on her cigarette. She was doing her best to seem careless, but Stella noticed that her left hand was clenched tightly around the bedsheet.

'I don't know. A name, or an address, or a bill of sale, or something of the sort.'

Stella's mind darted back to the conversation she'd overheard on the stairs. Was this what Monica and Marius had been talking about? It had sounded as though they wanted something from her. Was this it? She shook her head.

'Pity,' said Monica. A thought seemed to strike her. 'I don't suppose you have the letter, do you? Would you mind awfully if I looked at it?'

The letter was one of Stella's few treasured possessions. It contained the last words her father had ever sent her, and had gone everywhere with her since he died. It was hers, not Monica's. But she didn't know how to say no without being rude, so she fetched it – two sides of cheery news and promises to come and visit her soon, much handled and cried over in the months following Raymond's death. Monica took it and scanned it eagerly.

'Well?' said Stella curiously. 'Anything?'

Monica sighed.

'No. I didn't think there would be, really.'

'Are the paintings worth such a lot of money?'

'Enough. I haven't the time or the inclination to run the business myself from here in Italy, you see, so I want to sell it, but it's taken longer than I'd hoped. The paintings would be an added incentive to a buyer.'

'Couldn't you sell it to Marius?'

'We couldn't agree on a price. I told him I wasn't prepared to let him have it cheap just because we happen to be related.' Monica stubbed out her cigarette and stood up. 'I'd better go and ask after Mrs Unsworth. Come down when you're ready.'

As she left the room, Stella went across to the bed to smooth out the creases Monica's fist had left in the sheet. Did Monica suspect Raymond had sold the paintings and put them towards Stella's inheritance? Stella didn't remember Mr Ellison's having mentioned it – but then, she wasn't due to get her money until she was twenty-one anyway, so there was no reason why he should trouble her with such details. Besides, she was more interested in Monica's claim that her father had planned to bring her over to Switzerland. Stella had never heard anything about it: as far as she knew, it had been agreed she'd stay with some friends of Mr Ellison until further notice, and she was half-inclined to suspect that Monica had invented the story just to soften her up and introduce the question about the paintings. It was obviously more important than Monica had been letting on, but Stella couldn't help her. She turned back to the mirror to examine the new hair and the dark plum lipstick, and decided she quite liked them after all. She smiled at herself, then went downstairs to dinner.

The dining room was large, its walls decorated with frescoes of scenes from classical antiquity, which according to Gerardo were the work of Luigi Ademollo. They sat at the long table as Dora served the food: little parcels of ravioli, swimming in melted butter, sprinkled with fresh sage leaves and grated parmesan cheese, followed by roast pork served with a rich sauce infused with rosemary and garlic. To Stella, accustomed to school food, the flavours were a revelation, and she ate in a kind of awed silence, thinking of nothing except the next mouthful. Fortunately, she was not required to contribute to the conversation, since everybody else was managing quite well without her. Mrs Unsworth, who had put on an evening dress in the style of ten years ago, all dropped waist and sequins, was talking in her monotonous voice to Marius Schwegler and a tall, fair German called Otto Kaufmann, who seemed to be a friend of Marius's, and was something high up in the Nazi Party. Despite what Stella had read about the Germans in the papers, he was perfectly polite and friendly. Monica and the American, meanwhile, were talking more loudly than anyone. His name was Ted Landry, it appeared, and he was a journalist who wrote for an American magazine. He and Gerardo began discussing public affairs in Rome and political matters of which Stella knew nothing.

After dinner they went into the *salone* and conversation turned to Gerardo's art collection.

'Our friend Kaufmann has come to look at one of my paintings,' explained Gerardo to Stella. 'I have a little painting by Dürer that he is very interested in buying.'

'And others too,' said Kaufmann with a smile.

'He wants my Raphael,' Gerardo confided. 'And so Marius brings him here whenever he is in Florence, and one of them talks into my left ear and the other into my right, and together they try and persuade me to sell it.'

'So we do,' said Marius pleasantly. 'One must keep trying.'

Gerardo said to Stella, 'But I haven't shown you my collection yet. Would you like to see it?'

'I'd love to,' she replied.

'Splendid! Then let us go.'

Most of the guests had already seen the collection many times and remained where they were, leaving Stella, Monica, Marius and Kaufmann to follow Gerardo into the east wing of the villa and up some stairs to a long, high, gallery-like room. One wall had windows all the way along it, but they were hung with heavy curtains to protect the paintings from the daylight. The young man Stella had seen earlier weeding the garden was here, busy with two or three flat wooden crates. Against the wall stood a painting depicting the Annunciation, the Angel Gabriel kneeling to the Virgin Mary under a loggia, holding a white flower in his hand. The paint was dark with age and the frame in poor condition, but the young man was dusting it carefully. Gerardo and the young man exchanged words in Italian.

'This painting Vittorio is unpacking is from the school of Perugino,' said Gerardo. 'Perhaps even by the maestro himself, although we will not know for sure until I have consulted an expert. After that I will have it restored. You may go, Vittorio.'

The young man went off, giving Stella another impudent grin and a wink as he passed.

'It is a pity to close off the view from the windows,' said Gerardo, 'but we must not damage the paintings.' He swept his hand around expansively. 'You see, it is not a huge collection, but all the paintings were chosen with care. These are the best ones, but others are hung around the house.'

There were about forty or fifty of them. Stella walked slowly along the gallery, examining the artworks. They covered a variety of subjects, some biblical, others more prosaic. Stella found herself drawn to a depiction of Venice in vivid colours, and stopped to examine it.

'This is my Dürer,' said Gerardo, standing by a picture of a middle-aged man wearing a tall hat. 'What do you think, Stella?'

Stella thought it was ugly, and searched for a tactful remark. Marius caught her eye and smiled.

'The young lady doesn't like it, Gerardo.'

'I do not like it much myself,' admitted Kaufmann.

'No, it is my little Raffaello you prefer,' said Gerardo. He went to stand by a painting which hung in the middle of the room. 'Now, Stella, you will see my most prized possession. It is beautiful, no?'

Stella looked at the painting he indicated. It was not very impressive in size: only about fifteen inches by twenty without its frame. The subject was a woman, sitting by a window. Her face was plump and delicately pretty, and she was dressed in robes of deep blue and coral pink, with a white shawl covering her head. The folds of her clothing were so beautifully executed that they looked almost like a photograph. In her hands she held a pomegranate, and in the background through the window could be seen a rolling Italian landscape, punctuated by cypress trees. The lines were so sharp and the colours so vivid that it might have been painted four months ago, rather than four hundred years.

'My fair *Lady of the Cypresses*,' exclaimed Gerardo sentimentally. 'The story behind the painting is a tragic one. She was the wife of a wealthy man, and she died very young, shortly after Raphael began painting this portrait of her. It is said that he completed the face from her death mask. For many years it was thought to be by one of Raphael's pupils, but I have had it examined by an expert, and he has confirmed to me that it is in fact by the master himself.'

'It's very pretty,' said Stella.

'It is, isn't it, Marius?' agreed Monica, with a sly glance at her brother.

'Did Gerardo buy it from you?' Stella asked Marius.

At that, Monica burst out laughing and Marius stiffened. Stella had the sudden feeling that she'd made a dreadful faux pas, although she couldn't think why, since it had been a perfectly innocuous question.

'No,' Marius replied shortly.

His sister came across and took him by the arm.

'I'm only teasing, darling. You don't need to look so cross. You forgive me, don't you?'

Monica flicked his cheek gently with a perfectly manicured nail. He turned his head towards her and they exchanged looks: hers amused, his guarded, less easy to read. She laughed again and dropped his arm.

'No, my dear, I didn't get it from Marius,' Gerardo said, answering Stella's original question. 'I bought it from your father.'

'My father?'

'Oh, yes. And now Marius brings people here who would like to buy it off *me*. But I will not sell.'

Marius shook his head, and Otto Kaufmann wagged his finger jovially at his host.

'One day, Carminati, I will persuade you.'

'Not today, however. But you shall have the Dürer at a fair price, and offer it as a Christmas gift to Herr Hitler. I am sure he will be overjoyed to receive it.'

Stella glanced at Kaufmann in surprise. She'd had no idea he was as high up in the Nazi Party as that. She heard something like a snort, and looked round to see that Ted Landry had come in, and was leaning against a wall away from the company, looking even more cynical than usual.

'I hope there will be no problems, as there were last time,' said Kaufmann. 'I know the Führer is impatient with the attitude of your cultural authorities. The Lucas Cranach portrait was held up for months until Mussolini overrode the ban on its export.'

'It's true our art superintendents don't look especially kindly on the removal of art from Italy,' conceded Gerardo. 'There will certainly be a few hurdles to overcome – or shall we say, formalities to complete – but Il Duce is anxious to maintain good relations with Germany, and I've no doubt he will be happy to wave it through if I speak to him personally.'

They began discussing terms. Monica was standing with them, and Stella noticed she was making a particular effort to flatter Kaufmann. Marius was standing a little removed, watching the little group as they talked, still wearing that closed expression. Stella thought he was displeased, and approached him tentatively, wanting to make amends for whatever it was she'd done.

'I'm sorry,' she said quietly. 'I didn't mean to put my foot in it.'

He relaxed visibly and turned his attractive smile on her.

'It's all right. You didn't, I promise you. Monica likes to tease, that's all.' He saw the question in her face, and went on, 'I wanted to buy the *Lady of the Cypresses* from its former owner, but your father stepped in first.'

'Oh! I didn't know. Were you very angry with him?'

'Of course not. I wasn't especially pleased about it, of course, but it's just business, and one can't win all the time. Monica was just rubbing it in. There were many times when your father and I worked together perfectly well.'

'Were you friends?'

'Friends, brothers-in-law, partners, rivals sometimes,' replied Marius. 'The art market can be a cut-throat place.'

She looked down at the floor.

'I expect you knew him better than I did. After he married Monica I hardly ever saw him.'

She tried to keep the bitterness out of her voice, but it was difficult. Monica had taken her father from her, and then married another man only a few months after his death as easily as she might have changed one frock for another.

'I'm sorry,' said Marius. 'You must be lonely without him, yes?'

She hadn't meant to bare her soul like that, and shook it off briskly.

'Not at all. I'm very self-sufficient, really.'

'Yes? And yet I think you are more sad than you like to admit. You thought you had nothing, but after Raymond died you found you had even less.'

His manner was friendly, sympathetic. She looked up in surprise, and he went on:

'But here you are among friends. There is no need to be alone.'

Mrs Unsworth joined them then, and so the subject had to be dropped, but Stella felt strangely comforted by the conversation. Marius had seemed to understand. Perhaps she wasn't quite as friendless as she'd thought.

*

After they'd seen and admired all the pictures they returned downstairs and joined the rest of the party in the grand *salone*, where the gramophone was playing. Stella immediately went across to the French windows, which stood open. Nobody seemed to be paying attention to her so she slipped out and down the path to the lower terrace. A faint evening mist had descended, and the smell of damp grass hung in the air.

'Aren't you cold?' came a voice behind her. It was Marius, who had followed her with a drink.

'No,' she replied. 'September in England is much colder.' She smiled her thanks as he handed her the glass, and they gazed in silence at the city lying in shadow below them, with the dark silhouette of the hills beyond. They talked more about her journey, and she told him, laughing, of how they'd been abandoned by the porter for the rich couple in furs, and how they'd been rescued. That brought Mr Falconetti back into her mind, and she fell silent, remembering how the men had kicked him as he lay on the ground.

'What is it?' said Marius.

She told him what they'd seen at the station.

'Do you think he'll be all right? He seemed such a nice little man, not a bad person at all.'

'One can't always tell by looking at someone whether they are bad or not,' said Marius. 'Besides, it doesn't take much to be a criminal in Italy these days. I imagine he wasn't careful enough about what he said.'

They fell silent. Nobody seemed to care especially, but to Stella the events she'd witnessed hinted at something dark under the bright surface of this beautiful country. A cool breeze had got up, and she shivered.

'Perhaps I am a little cold.' She rubbed her arms. 'I took my cape off at dinner and forgot to bring it out.'

'Let me fetch it for you,' Marius offered. He went off, and she watched him go, thinking again of the conversation she'd overheard on the stairs, and Monica's story of the missing paintings – if that was what they'd been talking about. Had Monica charged Marius with getting the information out of Stella? If so, they'd both be disappointed, because she knew nothing.

Stella put it out of her mind and went slowly down the last few steps to the lawn, where it was more sheltered. She stood gazing out at the city, lost in her own thoughts, then gradually she became aware of the sound of voices somewhere to her right – a man and a woman, she thought – coming from the pavilion. One of the voices was Monica's. Stella drifted that way idly with a view to joining them, but as she drew closer she soon realised that she'd be an unwelcome addition. The man's voice belonged to Ted Landry, the American, and she didn't know what he was saying, but the intention of it was clear enough.

'Stop it!' said Monica. 'Someone might come.'

She didn't sound particularly upset by whatever he was doing; in fact, they were both laughing. Their voices dipped to a murmur, and Stella was frozen to the spot. She was about to retreat hurriedly when there was a rustle of fabric, and Monica's voice sounded closer, towards the arched entrance of the pavilion. Stella had no wish to overhear yet another conversation, but it was impossible to run away now: she'd be seen crossing the lawn, so she ducked quickly behind one of the elegant columns. There was a creak, as of someone standing up from a wooden seat, then Ted said something she didn't hear.

'You don't give up, do you?' came Monica's voice, more clearly now. 'And I thought you were here for me.'

'I am here for you – among other things.'

'Yes, and I know well enough what those things are.' Her tone was mocking. 'Keep digging if you like, but you won't find anything – it was all quite above board. I don't know why you've got a bee in your bonnet about it.'

'No bee, just a nose for a story.'

'Well, keep your nose out of it. You're wasting your time.'

'Your name wouldn't have to appear at all, if that's what's bothering you.'

'Darling, if you think I believe that you must think I was born yesterday. I know perfectly well you'd splash my name all over the place if you thought there was a Pulitzer Prize in it for you.'

'Hmph. Well, maybe I would, come to that. But I'm going to write the piece anyway, whether you're in it or not. Wouldn't you like to see your picture in the magazine? The story could use a little sex appeal.'

Monica laughed.

'Not these days. Gerardo has a position to maintain, so I have to behave myself – in public, at least.'

'Pity.'

There was a crack and a fizz, and a brief flare in the dark, and Stella imagined Ted lighting a cigarette.

'Give me one of those, won't you?' said Monica. Another match struck, and Stella prepared to creep away while they were distracted, but found herself arrested by Ted's next words.

'What about this kid who turned up today, then?' he asked. 'Stella, is that her name? She's a queer, awkward little thing. Does she know about Daddy and what he got up to?'

'He didn't get up to anything, as I've told you. He ran a perfectly legitimate business and you'll never prove otherwise. Stella knows nothing, so just you leave her alone. She has nobody now that Raymond's dead, so I'm going to polish her up. Lord knows she could do with it.'

'What a drag for you.'

'I don't think she'll be any trouble. In fact, I think she'll turn out rather nicely. There's a pretty girl somewhere under all that starch, which is just as well.'

'Why's that?'

'Never mind. Let's just say I owe someone a favour. At any rate, from what I remember she was rather a darling when she was about eleven, although it doesn't look as though she's had much fun in the intervening years, poor thing.'

'I'll say. She looks stiff and disapproving now. You should have seen how she shied away and glared at me this afternoon when I offered her my seat – like a proper old maid. I think you've got yourself a fully paid-up member of the virgin club on your hands.'

'Don't be silly. She's fresh out of school and I dare say she's hardly ever seen a man. She'll warm up soon enough. And besides, you say that about every girl who doesn't immediately swoon at your feet.'

'You don't swoon at my feet and I'd never describe you as a paid-up virgin.'

There came a peal of laughter from Monica. 'What nonsense you talk!'

'No nonsense about it. I just know you very well, that's all.'

Their voices fell to a laughing murmur again, and Stella took the opportunity to creep away. She was confused and hurt, wishing she'd stayed on the steps. So that was what they all thought of her! Prim and proper and prudish, and someone to poke fun at. And that remark Ted had made about her – she couldn't even bear to repeat it in her head, it was so horrid. Stella was quite breathless at the unfairness of it all. She hadn't asked to come here: Monica had invited her, but why do that if she was only going to be a burden and a chore? She might just as easily have stayed in London. She was sure now that Monica's friendly overtures to her before dinner had been purely self-serving, because she'd wanted information. Stella's cheeks glowed with humiliation and anger, and she was half-minded to pack her things and leave the very next day. But she couldn't do that, of course. Where would she go if she returned to London? There she had nobody.

Besides, there was the cryptic observation Ted Landry had made about her father. What had he meant? She didn't understand it, but the implications of the conversation she'd overheard were unmistakable: her father had done something bad, and Ted wanted to put it in his magazine. What could it be? Her father had been a good man, kind, liked by everyone – as far as she knew, at least. Her heart lurched at that. *As far as she knew.* And what had she known of him in these last few years? Not much: Monica had seen to that. What could they have been referring to, then? Was it something to do with Monica's questions about these missing paintings? Whatever it was, Stella supposed she ought to be thankful that Monica was refusing to give Ted the information he sought. If her father *had* done something he shouldn't have, then at least

Stella would be spared the indignity of seeing it splashed all over the papers. But she knew she couldn't go back to England until she'd found out what it was they hadn't been telling her.

Something was clenched in her hand, and she looked down and realised it was her drink. She took a sip, thinking it might make her feel better, but it tasted sharp and sour on her tongue. She tipped it into the bushes just as Marius arrived, apologising for having been away for so long. He'd had to hunt for the cape, he explained, then Mrs Unsworth had held him in conversation.

'Not to worry, I was just coming inside anyway,' replied Stella brightly, pulling herself together with an effort.

'I want to show you something first,' said Marius. He led her along the terrace and around to the east side of the house. Here the windows were in darkness, and the city lay in shadow beyond the reach of her fingertips.

'The view is better from here,' he said, by way of explanation.

'I can't see anything.'

'Look up.'

She did, and saw the night sky arching above them, a vast and unfathomable expanse of indigo, fading to lilac at the horizon, studded with millions of stars so bright they looked as though they'd been freshly splashed on with a painter's brush. It seemed so near she might almost have put out a hand and touched it.

'I thought perhaps you were missing home, and would like to see something familiar,' he said. 'But this is all I have to offer. These are the same stars that are shining over England right now.'

'Yes, I suppose they are, aren't they? How beautiful.'

They gazed at the winking sky in silence. In London it was unlikely she'd have been able to see the stars for cloud. But here the skies were clear, the exotic scents of an Italian night-time were all around her, and the assault on her senses was new and vivid. She could hear the trickle of a fountain nearby, while from the gramophone at the other side of the house the strains of jazz music drifted round to them: the muted squawk of a trumpet and the gravelly voice of Louis Armstrong.

'I love this music,' she said.

'Why don't we dance?' he asked.

She felt self-conscious.

'I don't know. I haven't done it much.'

He smiled and took her hand.

'Don't worry, I'll lead – just follow me. You see? It's easy.'

And it was. The music played, and they danced, and Stella forgot the fatigue of the long journey, and the awkwardness of her arrival, and the hurtful words she'd overheard in the pavilion. In London she'd most likely be in bed by now. Here she was dancing to soft music with an attractive man, with the stars above her and one of the most beautiful cities in the world below her feet.

Chapter Four

Stella had forgotten to close the shutters when she went to bed, and she woke as soon as the early sun slanted in through the gauzy white curtains. For a second she wondered where she was, then her heart leapt and she slid out of bed and across to the window to look at the view. There it was, still there, and still hers. All the discomfort of her arrival and her introduction to all the new people was swept away with the possibilities of a new day, and she washed and dressed hurriedly, before running downstairs to the grand entrance hall. She looked about her. Where might one get breakfast? The sound of clinking dishes led her to the kitchen, where she found Dora and a young woman with very dark, almost black hair. The young woman threw a glance at Stella, but said nothing, then dried her hands and took off her apron, revealing a smart skirt and blouse underneath. She said something to Dora, then nodded at Stella and went out.

'You wake up very early,' Dora said, beaming at Stella.

Stella glanced at her watch, which showed half past seven. Marius was supposed to be coming for her at nine, and she wanted to be ready.

'Not so very early, is it?'

Dora shook her head. 'The Countess, she sleeps late. Now, I make you breakfast, but not here. Go and sit, I bring you coffee. You like coffee? And there is some fresh bread and jam.'

She shooed Stella out of the kitchen and pointed her towards a little room. Like the rest of the house it was tiled in terracotta

underfoot, with pale walls and high ceilings. The room faced
north and east, across the city, and light blazed in through the
large windows and the double doors which gave out onto the
terrace. A table stood in the centre, laid with a white cloth. Stella
took the seat with the best view, and in due course Dora arrived
with fresh coffee, a covered basket of bread, and a pot of apricot
jam. She waited expectantly as Stella ate. The bread was warm and
springy, and the jam was sweet and delicious. Stella expressed her
appreciation and Dora looked pleased.

'You like it?'

'Yes. Did you make it?'

Dora nodded.

'The jam, yes.' She sat down and pushed the basket towards
Stella. 'You must eat some more. You are too thin.' She shook her
head in disgust. 'The Countess tells me about the English food and
I wonder how you live. But now you are in Italy and will eat well.'

Stella laughed and accepted another slice of bread and another
cup of coffee, and Dora began to talk. She was a widow, from
Rome originally, and had worked for the Carminatis for some
years. The young woman Stella had seen in the kitchen was her
daughter, Beatrice, who had a job working at the Hotel Ambassador
in the centre of town, which was owned by the Count. Beatrice
was engaged to a very good young man called Mimmo who was
a friend of Vittorio's. Had Stella seen Vittorio? He also worked at
the villa, and sometimes in the hotel when they needed an extra
pair of hands. Vittorio had introduced Mimmo to Beatrice one
day, and that was that – they had fallen in love, and were to be
married as soon as they had the money.

Stella was still trying to absorb all this information when Mrs
Unsworth came in and immediately began talking. She was leaving
for her sister's that morning, and she had many things to say about
the management of her luggage. Shortly after she had been packed
off in great state, a note arrived for Stella from Marius to say that he

had been called away on unavoidable business at an hour's notice and wouldn't be back until later in the week, which meant he'd be unable to take her around Florence as he had promised. He was full of apologies, and promised to make it up to her on his return.

Stella's disappointment was intense. She'd been so looking forward to seeing the city, and now it would have to wait. Monica and Gerardo couldn't take her, and there was no one else she could ask. She walked across to the window and gazed out. Florence was there before her, tantalising her with its beauty. She couldn't wait any longer, she just couldn't. Suddenly she made up her mind. Why shouldn't she go by herself? It wasn't more than a mile or two, and she had her Baedeker's guide to help her. It was a bold idea, but Stella was in the mood for adventure. Before she could talk herself out of it, she hurried upstairs, grabbed her hat and gloves and Baedeker guide, then ran back down and out onto the terrace. Dora had pointed out a flight of steps which cut from the garden to the road below, and she found them and was soon walking briskly down the hill, past the houses with the wisteria, and into the streets of the Oltrarno, the district on the south side of the river, thrilled at her own daring.

It was a clear morning, but the sun, although bright, wasn't high yet, and there was still a pinch of coolness in the air. Stella passed a *panificio*, and breathed in the delicious scent of newly baked bread and cakes. She'd just eaten, but the smell was irresistible, so she stopped for a moment to look in the window at the familiar yet unfamiliar products: firm, brown crusty loaves, crisscrossed on top; little tarts, no more than a mouthful, some studded with green or black olives, others with artichokes, and still others with tomato and white, creamy mozzarella cheese. She was gazing at a cake topped with raspberries and icing sugar when a woman came out of the shop and said something to her, smiling.

'I'm sorry, I don't understand, I'm English,' she said in the best Italian she could muster up.

'*Inglese?*' The woman's smile disappeared. She looked Stella up and down and said something else in a sharp tone, making a motion to her to go away. Stella retreated and continued on her way, disconcerted, but she soon forgot about the encounter, because it was nine o'clock now and people were out and about, and it was all an exciting adventure. She heard snatches of conversation as she passed through the streets, and wished she understood what people were saying, resolving to work on her Italian as soon as she could.

At length she came into a part of town where the buildings were tall and square, and stopped at a crossroads, having momentarily lost her bearings. An elderly man approached and seemed to be offering to help her. Remembering the reaction of the woman at the bakery earlier, Stella was hesitant to speak, but he said '*Inglese? Centro storico?*' – this time without any rancour – and pointed down a street. She thanked him and hurried off in the direction indicated, through a dark archway between two buildings. Then suddenly she was at the river, and there were carts and trams and buses passing to and fro, together with the occasional car, and she could see the crenellated tower of the Palazzo Vecchio and, further to the left, the dome of the cathedral peeping out from the tops of the buildings. There were three bridges close together on this stretch of the Arno, and any one of them would take her right into the city. She was just about to set out for the nearest one when she noticed she was standing outside a little shop with a stand containing tourist maps, so she bought one and stood examining it for some minutes. Folding the map, she plunged boldly across the nearest bridge and up a street lined with elegant shops, which were just opening. She walked up the street for some way, stopping to look into the windows at the clothes on display.

But there was too much to see, too much to do, and she didn't have time to loiter. She turned into a narrower street, which as far as she could tell headed in the direction of the cathedral, and promptly got lost in the maze of alleys. She wandered happily for a few minutes, then finally took out her map, consulted it, and found she was heading in completely the wrong direction. Having righted herself, she followed the map carefully, looking about her all the while. At last she came to a halt and frowned. She ought to be nearly at the cathedral, but where was it? Then she looked up and her mouth fell open, because there it was, in front of her, its neo-gothic façade a riot of pink, green and white marble. She drew in a breath and craned her neck, following the line of the bell tower up to the sky. Surely it was wrong to cram such a magnificent building in among all these houses and shops? It ought to have been in the middle of a huge square, so as to allow one to have a full view of it.

Inside, the place was dark and almost deserted, apart from a few early-morning tourists like herself, and she spent some minutes simply absorbing the vast, cavernous interior. The interior was not as impressive as the outside, she decided, but she set out to explore anyway. She admired the inlaid marble floor, and the frescoes on the interior of the dome, and the famous painting of Dante she'd seen in a book, red-robed in the foreground, with Florence to his left and figures descending into hell and ascending to heaven on his right.

Then after she had drunk her fill she went out, consulted the map and headed to Piazza della Signoria, where the castle-like Palazzo Vecchio loomed majestically. The Uffizi gallery wasn't open yet, and besides, Stella wasn't sure she wanted to spend her first day indoors, so instead she decided to let her feet take her where they would, and passed a happy morning exploring. She stared through the windows of the jewellers' shops on the Ponte Vecchio, although without any thought of buying anything, then strolled along the river, stopping to take in the scenery as she went. By this time it was lunchtime, and Stella realised she was hungry, so she sat at a table in an open-air café and, by means of gestures and a few hesitant words, was eventually served a sandwich of sorts – a roll of moist, oily, salty bread she'd never had before, generously stuffed with ham and some sort of green leaf which on cautious investigation turned out to have a delicious peppery flavour, together with a glass of lemonade which didn't taste anything like the lemonade one got at home. She would have liked to linger over her lunch, idly watching the people passing to and fro, but the café was starting to fill up with customers, and the waiter had begun to dart impatient glances at her, so she paid and left.

The sun was high now, drenching her with warmth, and it was far too pleasant to go into another gloomy church, so Stella dawdled along the narrow streets, pausing to look in the shop windows. She would have liked to go into one or two of them, but they all seemed to be closing for lunch, so she decided to leave it until later. All roads seemed to end at the cathedral, and she soon found herself once again marvelling at its sheer immensity. The piazza was crowded with tourists, however, so she passed on, and lost herself again in the maze of streets around the church of San Lorenzo. Here there was a market, selling gifts and trinkets and other goods. One stall selling leather goods caught her eye, and she paused to examine its wares. There was a pair of dove-grey gloves in delicate, soft leather that she particularly liked.

'How much?' she said to the stallholder.

'*Settanta lire*. Seventy lire,' he replied.

She had little idea of the value of the currency, and was about to hand over a fistful of notes when a voice at her shoulder said, 'I wouldn't do that if I were you.'

She turned to see the American, Ted Landry, standing at her side. Before she could answer, he switched into fluent Italian, and began an animated conversation with the stallholder. She wanted to say something, but Landry and the other man were now haggling energetically.

'There, twenty lire,' said the American at last. 'And not worth a penny more. Here, you need this, and this.'

He took the notes from her hand, selected some and paid the stallholder, then handed back the rest of the money. 'You'd better be careful with that. The pickpockets prey on the tourists.'

The deal was done and the gloves were hers, and she'd played no part in it. She ought to have been grateful, but instead she was needled at his high-handedness.

'I didn't need your help. I was managing perfectly well by myself.' She said it more sharply than she'd meant to.

'You think so?' he replied, laughing. 'Do you know how much you nearly paid him? At ninety lire to the pound, that's about fifteen shillings in your money. Would you have paid fifteen shillings for them in London?'

He was right, of course, but still, she'd have preferred to make her own mistakes. She was annoyed at herself for having nearly been fleeced, but it was easier to be annoyed at him, especially when she remembered the remarks she'd overheard him making about her the night before.

'You couldn't possibly know what I'd have paid for them in London,' she said with cold dignity.

'Oh, I'm sorry. Did you come here especially to give the Italians the benefit of your spare cash? I beg your pardon – I guess English customs are more different from American ones than I thought.'

The mocking tone irritated her even more, but she contented herself with giving him what she thought was a freezing glare. He didn't seem to notice but instead turned serious.

'Listen, Stella, you oughtn't to be out here alone. It's not so safe for the British as it was. Mussolini's on the warpath and just looking for an excuse to throw you all out.'

Stella remembered the woman who'd shooed her away from the bakery on finding out she was English.

'I'm perfectly all right, thank you,' she replied. 'I've been here all morning and as you can see no harm has come to me.'

'Except that you might as well be wearing a sign saying "gullible tourist".' He put his hands up and took a step back. 'All right, as you wish. I'll leave you alone. But aren't you going to thank me for the gloves?'

There was something about him that positively invited rudeness, but she fought it down. After all, he *had* helped her.

'Thank you, Mr Landry,' she said instead.

He touched his forehead in an ironic salute.

'Have a good day, *Miss Cockburn*,' he replied, then turned and melted into the crowd.

Stella thanked the stallholder, who had been watching their conversation with interest, then moved away. She wanted to sit down, and she eventually found a stone bench in a quiet square with a trickling fountain, where she sat and examined her new gloves, then consulted her guide and began calculating exchange rates in her head, so as to avoid getting caught out again. After that, she looked at the map and drew with her finger the route she had taken that day. She was so absorbed in her task that she barely looked up when someone came and sat on the bench beside her. What should she do next? She remembered that the shops would be opening again soon, and contemplated a stroll down the Via Tornabuoni, perhaps with a stop for *gelato*.

She was interrupted in her thoughts by a male voice.

'English?' it said.

She looked up and saw that the man who had sat down on the bench with her was watching her. He was young, with bad skin and a cap which he wore pushed back on his head. Stella had no intention of engaging with him, so she nodded and stood up, preparing to leave. He stood up likewise.

'English, yes?' he repeated.

She nodded again and began to walk off, but he followed, talking all the while in Italian. She didn't understand what he was saying, so she shook her head and walked a little faster. He frowned and snapped something at her. The place was quite deserted, and Stella began to feel alarmed.

'Go away, please,' she said.

He darted in front of her and said something in a persuasive tone, then took her arm, turned her around and began to walk her in the opposite direction from the one she wanted.

'Stop it!' she exclaimed, and tried to tear her arm from his, but to no avail. He laughed, then pulled her to him and tried to kiss her. She wriggled free and aimed an outraged slap at him, which he ducked easily. A torrent of furious speech burst out of him, and he grabbed at her again. Frightened now, she tried to make a run for it, but his grip was like iron and she couldn't wrench her arm free. She was just making up her mind to scream when there was a shout and, before she knew what was happening, the man was hauled off her, and Ted Landry was yelling at him in Italian. Landry greatly outclassed the other man for height and bulk, and was nowhere near such an easy target as Stella. Red with anger, the Italian put a hand to his pocket, perhaps to reach for a weapon. But people had begun to come into the piazza, and he thought better of it. He gestured rudely at them both, then swung round and swaggered off, evidently determined not to lose face.

Ted picked up Stella's new gloves and her books, which she'd dropped on the ground, and handed them to her.

'Am I supposed to follow you around all day?' he said. 'When do I get to eat?'

She'd been on the point of crying, but his expression was so funny that in spite of herself she had to laugh.

'Are you okay? He didn't hurt you?'

'No, I'm all right, thanks. Just a little shaken.'

'Here, sit down a minute.'

'No, really, I'll be fine. Thank you,' she added as an afterthought.

'You're welcome. Lucky I didn't believe you when you said you knew what you were doing.'

'I do know what I'm doing,' she insisted unconvincingly.

'So do I – getting into trouble! What the hell was Monica was thinking, letting you come here by yourself?'

'She and Gerardo have things to do today, and Marius couldn't come, so I came out alone.'

'Couldn't you have waited?'

'I didn't want to. I'm perfectly capable of managing on my own, you know. When one has nobody, one learns to rely on oneself.'

She said it primly but quite unconsciously, examining her new gloves, which had picked up some dust from the ground. He gazed at her thoughtfully for a minute or two, then sighed, as if he'd just come to some decision.

'Come on. You want to get to know Florence? I'll be your guide.'

She looked up, startled.

'But—'

'I won't get in your way. You can look at things all you like and I'll stand at a distance so you can pretend you're not with me, if that's what you want.'

She wanted to say no, but she was more upset than she liked to admit by the encounter with the Italian. She'd have much preferred Marius as a guide, but he wasn't available, and in any case it was too late now: she was in debt to this brash American, much to her annoyance, and she couldn't bring herself to snub him again.

'Don't you have to work?' she asked.

He dug in his pocket and flapped a telegram at her.

'I just got fired.'

'Oh, goodness!' she exclaimed. 'How awful!'

'Don't worry. I'll get my job back. My editor likes to fire me now and again to keep me on my toes. But he can't do without me. I'm the best writer he's got, and he knows it. Four days it usually takes him to come round, so that's four days' vacation for me and good news for you. You're too young to be wandering alone, especially with things the way they are in Florence right now. How old are you? Seventeen?'

'Nineteen, if you please!' she said indignantly.

'As old as that?' He laughed. 'You're a funny kid.'

'I'm not a kid.'

'Yes you are. But you'll grow up soon enough.'

'I'm quite grown-up already, thank you. And I don't suppose you're much older than I am, for all your fine talking.'

'I'm twenty-nine, next. Old enough to know that nineteen is no age at all. Now, don't argue. You looked like a newborn lamb among the wolves just now. In a couple of weeks you'll be an old hand, but right now you're fresh off the boat and you look it. I'll take you about until your right hook's as nifty as mine.'

'What an extraordinary expression!' she said.

She was still reluctant to accept his help, remembering the dark hints he'd dropped about her father in the pavilion the night before, and the unflattering names he'd called her still rankled, but he *had* come to her rescue twice in one day. She decided to give him the benefit of the doubt, at least for now.

'All right, then, if you really mean it,' she said. 'But I warn you, I intend to walk up and down every street in Florence.'

'I'll do my best to keep up,' he replied dryly.

Chapter Five

At the Hotel Ambassador, the Saturday morning rush of people checking out had subsided and the lobby was unusually empty. Vittorio Baraldi had taken advantage of the lull to leave his post at reception and was sneaking a cigarette in a dim corner of the lobby, when Beatrice came in and began rummaging around in the papers behind the desk. It was a hot day outside, but the lobby, with its comfortable chairs and low tables for the convenience of its well-off guests, was cool and dark. Vittorio threw himself into an easy chair and watched Beatrice, admiring her smooth, dark skin and the way a glint of sunlight shining in through the window caught her black hair as she worked. As she moved a little to the left the sunbeam shone into her eyes, and she blinked and moved away. Vittorio watched it all. She was dressed in a sober blouse and skirt, her hair pinned up in a neat roll at the nape of her neck, but he was imagining her with her hair down, loose across her shoulders, and thinking about how it would feel to run his fingers through it. He let his mind wander off into a pleasant daydream. At last she glanced up at him.

'You'd better put that out,' she said shortly. 'The boss will be in soon.'

He pulled a face that indicated what he thought of Cavalieri, the hotel manager, but stubbed out the cigarette, got up and went across to the desk.

'What's this?'

He reached for one of the papers she was tidying up, and she slapped his hand away.

'Nothing to do with you. Haven't you got something you could be doing?'

'I am doing something. I'm looking at you.'

She rolled her eyes, but a smile touched the corners of her mouth.

'Well go and look at something else. I haven't got time for your nonsense.'

'Why must you always break my heart?'

'Don't be ridiculous!'

'It's not ridiculous. You know I love only you.'

He clutched at his breast, and she laughed at his mock-dramatic expression.

'Really? Is that what you said to Marianna? And Carlotta? And that girl with the red hair who came in looking for you the other day?'

'I haven't seen Marianna in months, and Carlotta got married last week. I don't know who the girl with the red hair is. Unless you mean Giulia – but I'd call her hair mousy rather than red, and I've already told her I'm not interested.'

Beatrice threw a sceptical look at him.

'Would I lie to you?' asked Vittorio, opening his eyes wide.

'Perish the thought. Anyway, I'll tell you who else is coming in soon – Mimmo, so you'd better be off.'

'Ah, Mimmo. The man you chose over me for some reason I'll never understand. I guess he's been to one of his Fascist Party meetings like a good boy. Maybe Il Duce will see him one day and give him a pat on the head for sacrificing all his principles for the sake of Italy.'

His tone wasn't humorous any more.

'I think Il Duce knows better than you do what's best for the country,' said Beatrice. 'The people love him.'

He snorted. 'Rubbish. The people are frightened of him. If the only way you can keep control of your country is by beating everybody up and carting them off to jail then you're not a proper leader. He's a disaster. He'll lead us into a war, and for what? Thousands of men will die just so we can conquer a few miles of territory and call it Italian. The Roman Empire ended over a thousand years ago, and we can't get it back, whatever Mussolini might like to tell us.'

'Hush! You mustn't talk like that. Someone will hear and you'll get into trouble again.'

'There's nobody to hear, and you wouldn't tell on me either, would you? Not even to Mimmo.'

'It's a shame you two can't get along better. You used to be such good friends.'

Vittorio grimaced. 'He changed when Mussolini hypnotised him. He used to be a sensible Communist – well, not a sensible Communist, there are no sensible Communists, but at least one could have a proper discussion with him. Now he's gone over to the other side and won't listen to reason.'

'It's you who won't listen to reason. And I agree with Mimmo. There's nothing wrong with being a patriot.'

'There are lots of ways to be a patriot without following Fascism blindly. We need a proper Socialist movement, but we're not even allowed to talk about that. Still, I refuse to keep quiet.'

'Even in front of the Count?' Beatrice threw him a wicked look. Like everybody else she'd heard the rumours that Gerardo Carminati was Vittorio's father.

'Hmph. He's a stupid old man who's looking out for himself. It's a waste of time even mentioning it to him.'

'You don't fool me – I know you're fond of him.'

'Perhaps,' he conceded. 'But I wouldn't mind so much if I thought he was a sincere Fascist. At least Mimmo believes all the rubbish he talks, but the Count – well, I'm not so sure.'

'You think he's not a Fascist?' said Beatrice curiously. 'But Mussolini is his friend.'

'Exactly! That's why he has to pretend, out of loyalty. But I've seen him shaking his head sometimes. He doesn't want war any more than I do, but he has to keep his mouth shut. We all have to keep our mouths shut. Walls have ears.'

'And so do I,' Beatrice pointed out. 'How do you know you can trust me not to report you?'

He took her hand and gazed deep into her eyes.

'Because you're beautiful both inside and out,' he replied soulfully.

She laughed and pushed him away.

'Idiot!' She glanced up. 'Shh!'

They hurriedly did their best to look busy as the heavy glass doors of the hotel opened and Monica Carminati came in, accompanied by Ted Landry and Otto Kaufmann. Monica and Kaufmann went through to the bar without so much as a glance at the reception desk, but the American saw Vittorio and Beatrice and stopped for a moment to pass the time of day. They watched him as he disappeared through the door after the other two, then Beatrice glanced at Vittorio, eyebrows raised.

'What about the Countess? Is she a dedicated Fascist too?'

'She's dedicated all right – but only to herself,' he replied. 'She'll do whatever suits her.'

'Well, it seems this German suits her at the moment. Or is it the American?'

'Both, by the looks of it. Trust her to keep her options open.'

'I wonder why the Count married her,' said Beatrice.

Vittorio let out a laugh.

'It's clear you're not a man. If you were you'd only have to look at her to see why. His wife died, and there are no children eyeing up their inheritance to stop him from treating himself to a pretty new toy. He's happy enough.'

Just then, Mimmo came in. He was taller than Vittorio, broad-shouldered with a firm jaw, and the lighter brown hair of the northern Italians. Beatrice's face lit up as she came out from behind the desk to greet him, and raised her face for a kiss.

'What are you looking at?' said Mimmo impatiently, when he saw Vittorio watching.

'Nothing.' Vittorio turned away. He would never have admitted it, but he was hurt at what had happened between him and Mimmo. They'd been friends for years, despite their very different personalities – or perhaps because of them. Mimmo was serious and focused, while Vittorio, sunny-tempered and easy-going, had always admired his friend's superior knowledge and intelligence. But in recent times a coolness had developed between them. It wasn't over Beatrice: Vittorio had frequently regretted introducing her to Mimmo, but he was philosophical enough to know you couldn't argue with love, and so was generous in defeat. No, it was Mussolini they couldn't agree on – Mussolini, who was hell-bent on driving the country to destruction. He was going to team up with Hitler and they'd start a war that would end badly. But not only could Mimmo not see it, he was supporting, even encouraging the whole thing. Vittorio often looked around him and wondered how everyone could be so blind, since to him it was perfectly obvious that Italy – and the rest of the world – were hurtling headlong towards disaster.

*

'You shouldn't be associating with Vittorio,' said Mimmo to Beatrice later, when they were having a drink together after work. 'If you ask me, Cavalieri would be better off firing him. That sort of person can't be good for a business.'

'That sort of person? He's supposed to be your friend.'

'Maybe he was once, but I'm not sure I can remember why any more. I want you to keep away from him.'

'But he introduced us. You owe him that, at least.'

Mimmo smiled. 'That's true. I'll always have that to thank him for.'

'It's a shame you fell out,' said Beatrice.

'We didn't fall out – but he won't listen to reason, and I'm not going to waste my breath trying to convince him.'

'That's pretty much what he said about you.'

'Did he? I hope you stood up for me.'

'Of course I did! He's not really bad, you know. He's just blind on the subject of Mussolini.'

Her fiancé frowned.

'I don't understand what's got into him. Can't he see Mussolini is the best thing to have happened to this country in a hundred years? Italy will be great again thanks to him. The British and the French have had things their own way for far too long. We need to expand our colonies. It's time our country took its rightful place on the world stage again.'

'Vittorio's worried there'll be a war, that's all.'

'And what if there is? We have to fight for what's right.'

Beatrice gazed at him proudly. He was so brave, and so committed to his ideals.

'Will you fight?' she asked.

'Of course I will! I'm not a coward, unlike some people. That's what it's really all about, you know. Vittorio doesn't want to join the army. He's scared to fight for his country. Can you wonder I'm not keen on his company lately?'

'Are you going to join up, then?'

She asked the question hesitantly. She wanted him to fight for Italy, of course she did, but at the same time she didn't want him to go away and leave her at home, worrying endlessly about him.

'I'll go as soon as they call me up.' Mimmo's face softened and her heart leapt, as it always did when he looked at her in that way. 'But I want us to get married first and have a little time together, so I won't volunteer unless I really have to. You still want to get married, don't you?'

'Of course I do!'

'But I want to do it properly. A man should be able to support his wife and I don't want you to be poor. We'll do it next year, for definite.'

Beatrice would have married him immediately, money or no money, but she understood why he wanted to wait.

'I can help,' she said. 'I've been putting money aside too, for – whatever might come along. And my mother has promised to do what she can, although she doesn't have much.'

'Do you think your count and countess might give us a present?' asked Mimmo, only half-joking.

She tossed her head.

'*He* might, but *she* won't. She thinks of nothing but herself and her men. They've got the English daughter of her last husband staying with them at the moment. Think of that! She has a step-daughter who's not much more than ten years younger than herself.'

'What's she like, this English girl?'

'Very stupid, as far as I can tell. She went to one of these exclusive schools where they teach you nothing except how to pick up a handkerchief elegantly. She doesn't know how to do anything, and if you speak to her she stares at you as if she doesn't understand a word. If that's the best the English can produce then I don't give much for their chances once the war starts.'

'She's not like you, then,' said Mimmo affectionately.

'I hope not! I know how to run a home, at least. You won't have anything to complain of.'

'I know that. We'll have a little house and you can look after it and our ten children, and I'll look after all of you.'

'Ten children!' Beatrice blushed.

'Of course! Then we won't have to pay income tax.'

She burst out laughing. 'That's one way to save money. But I don't know how you think I'll have time for you if we have ten children.'

He laughed in return and lifted her hand to his lips.

'You'll have plenty of time,' he said. 'We'll have all the time in the world.'

Chapter Six

The next few days passed in a whirl of activity. True to his word, Ted presented himself on Monday morning, and between then and Thursday Stella drank her fill of all the beauties Florence had to offer. She went into every church or public building of note, stared earnestly at the bronze doors of the Baptistery, studied the statue of David critically, and saw every view of the city that could be had, whether from the top of the bell tower and the cathedral, or from the distant Piazzale Michelangelo. Ted, meanwhile, who had seen all these things numerous times, accompanied her patiently through the streets, pointing out any sights she happened to miss, or sat on benches, smoking and keeping a distant eye on her, while she stared at some work of art or other and consulted her guidebook.

She still hadn't been into the Uffizi gallery, however. The queues had been long all week, and she'd been unwilling to stand and wait when there were so many other things to be seen. But by the end of the week she was getting impatient, so she persuaded Ted to come and fetch her earlier than usual on Friday morning, in order to secure a place near the front of the line. He was later than he'd promised, and by the time they arrived the queue was already getting long. He didn't seem unduly bothered.

'No matter, it won't be much of a wait,' he said.

'But I wanted to go straight in. You said you'd come at eight.' She hadn't slept well the night before, which made her cross and tired, and she couldn't help snapping a little.

'If you must know, my editor called at two a.m. to ask me back and kept me talking for a couple of hours, and then I overslept. Besides, what difference does it make if we have to stand in line for a few minutes?'

It made no difference at all, but still Stella couldn't hide her discontented expression.

'I didn't get much sleep last night either, but I was ready on time,' she pointed out.

'Well bully for you. I wasn't.' He saw she was out of sorts, and went on, 'Come on, don't take things so seriously. You have all the time in the world. Now, are we going in or not?'

He was right: they didn't have to wait long at all, but his 'I told you so' didn't improve Stella's mood. She didn't enjoy the paintings as much as she'd hoped, and irrationally blamed it on Ted's turning up late instead of her own exhaustion after a week of sightseeing.

'What do you want to do next?' asked Ted when they came out.

The sun was hot and Stella's feet were aching after the long tour. She glanced at her watch. It was already nearly three o'clock and they hadn't even eaten yet.

'I was hoping to see the exhibition at the Palazzo Pitti, but we won't have time to do it properly now,' she replied pointedly. Another huge art gallery was the last place she wanted to go at the moment, but she was still feeling peevish and couldn't help trying to provoke him. He saw it and laughed.

'Still mad because I was late, huh?'

'No,' she lied.

'Yes you are. Your mouth's turned down so far at the corners it looks like it's trying to escape from your face. Why don't you try a smile?' He put one index finger at each corner of her mouth and pushed upwards to demonstrate, and she slapped him away. He was refusing to take it seriously, which irritated her even more. She went to sit down on the edge of a fountain, and he followed. They sat in silence for some minutes, Ted resting his elbows on his knees, smoking, and Stella sitting rigidly upright, reading her guidebook and ignoring him.

'Did you know that this square, right where we're sitting now, is the site of the execution of Girolamo Savonarola?' he said, after he'd made one or two attempts at conversation and been icily rebuffed.

'Who?'

'Savonarola. He was a monk who found himself in charge of the city back in the fifteenth century. He was a fanatical puritan and didn't like fun of any kind, so naturally he made himself some powerful enemies. They excommunicated him, imprisoned him, tortured him, then hanged him and burned him for good measure. That's what you get for taking yourself too seriously,' he finished.

'I don't take myself too seriously.'

'Yes you do.'

She was still annoyed at his careless attitude, and for some reason his uncharitable remarks in the pavilion on the night she'd arrived had just come back into her mind. Before she had time to think about it, she replied:

'I'd rather be serious than shameless.'

'What the hell are you talking about?'

She hadn't meant to start an argument, but she was hot and tired after the week she'd had, and he was glaring at her now, so she had to answer.

'Don't think I don't know what you've been getting up to with Monica,' she said primly.

'What I've been—' he stared at her in disbelief. 'Okay, then, tell me, what have I been getting up to with Monica?'

She hesitated, but she'd gone too far to back out now.

'You were philandering with her in the pavilion on the first night I got here,' she said after a minute. 'Don't try and deny it.'

'*Philandering*?' He burst out laughing. 'What kind of a word is that?'

'It's true, isn't it?'

'How would you know?'

'Because I heard you.'

'Oh, so you spent your first night in Florence doing a little eavesdropping, did you?'

'I wasn't eavesdropping.' That was a lie, of course. 'I just happened to be walking past at the time and couldn't help overhearing.'

'Well, you should have kept on walking, shouldn't you?'

'How could I? You were talking about me.'

'Was I? What did I say?'

She went pink.

'Never mind – it was very rude.'

He looked at her searchingly.

'No, tell me. I want to know. What did I say about you that was so terrible? I've never been rude as far as I know.'

'Nonsense. You've been rude to me about fifty times this week.'

'Well, yes, but I meant behind your back. What did I say?'

'You called me a – a fully paid-up member of the virgin club!'

It burst out of her all at once, and she couldn't keep the indignation out of her voice.

He stared, then gave a shout of laughter.

'So I did! I'd forgotten all about that. But how could I help it? You looked so buttoned-up when you first arrived, glaring at me – just like you're doing now, as a matter of fact. You didn't take it seriously, did you? I guess I'd had a drink or two and said the first thing that came into my head. If it makes you feel better I'll apologise, although I still say that'll teach you not to listen to other people's conversations.'

'I wasn't! And in any case, what you said about me is beside the point. Monica's married to Gerardo. You shouldn't have been – doing whatever it was you were doing in the pavilion.'

'It was nothing to do with you, and it still isn't,' he said tetchily. 'And by the way, don't you think you've rather proved my point?'

'No!' she exclaimed.

'Yes you have. You're nothing but a little prude.'

'Don't call me that!'

'I'll call you that and more if you're not careful. You mind your own business and leave the grown-ups alone. Now, is there anything else you wanted to see or are we just going to sit here all day sniping at each other?'

He really was insufferably rude. They were both in a bad mood now, and she saw that matters weren't likely to improve. Besides, this was the last day of the sightseeing, and the thought of lounging in a deckchair on the terrace of the Villa Bruni with a cool drink was tempting.

'Let's go back,' she said.

Monica had visitors as usual, and Ted was immediately absorbed into the company. Dora had put some delicious *aperitivi* out on the terrace – olives, artichokes, cold sliced meats, and some chunks of warm *focaccia* bread, glistening with oil and salt – and after a plateful of food and a glass of ice-cold lemonade Stella felt better. She sat, gazing idly out at the view, but the conversation didn't interest her and she was feeling restless, and after a while she wandered inside and up to her room to look for a book to read. When she came downstairs she found Ted, standing in front of a dresser, a drawer open in front of him, rifling idly through it.

'Is it the done thing where you come from to go snooping through people's drawers?' she demanded.

'Hmm?' He was looking at some old photos, not paying attention.

'I *said*—'

But she gave it up, as it was obvious he wasn't listening. A couple of the photos had fallen to the floor and she bent to retrieve them. As she did so, a flash of recognition sparked at the sight of a snapshot of her father, sitting on a balcony, raising a glass and laughing at the photographer. She picked it up and stared at it as she rose slowly to her feet. The scenery was unfamiliar to her, and she couldn't tell where it had been taken, but it must have been within the last few years. There was the familiar close-cropped hair, worn like that for convenience because it was so thick and curly, just like hers; the wide mouth, a thinner, more masculine version of her own; the eyes that were full of humour. That was what she remembered most about him whenever she pictured him – the permanent smile and ready laugh, the easy manners that had drawn everyone to him.

A lump came to her throat, catching her by surprise, because she'd forgotten how much she missed him. She'd resented him for so long after he'd deserted her for Monica, but she'd loved him dearly, and had wanted nothing more than for him to remember she existed. If he'd only paid her a few more visits at school, taken her out occasionally, she could have forgiven him everything. But it was too late now. Blinking back tears, she glanced at the other photograph, and froze. It showed a group of eight or nine men gathered next to a rack on which were stacked a number of paintings in frames. Of the three men in the foreground, one was unknown to her; the second was her father. The third man, who was standing sideways on nearest the camera, the focus of attention, was even more unmistakably familiar.

'What's Monica doing keeping snaps of Hitler?' came Ted's voice over her shoulder. 'Don't tell me she wanted him to autograph it.' He took the photograph from Stella and gazed at it, his lip curled. 'Look at them all, cosying up to him.' He indicated one of the figures in the background, a small man with a straggling moustache who was looking at Hitler and laughing heartily as if the Führer had just made a hilarious joke. 'That's an American museum director I met when I was working in Berlin last year. Creepy little feller. He was there, fawning over the Nazis, trying to get first dibs on any paintings they didn't happen to want.'

'What do you mean?'

'The Germans have been confiscating art from museums. They call it "degenerate" – you know, modern stuff, or stuff by Jews, or anything the great and glorious leader happens to take a dislike to. They held an exhibition of it and invited everyone to come and poke fun at it.' He tapped the picture, indicating the other man she didn't know standing in the foreground. 'This fat guy's called Nicholas Honegger. He's one of Hitler's official art dealers, commissioned to sell off all the degenerate art they don't want at knock-down prices. Anything they can't sell they're threatening to burn. I don't know who the guy standing next to him is. Some other parasite, I guess, trying to muscle in on the fire sale. Well, all I can say is that they'd better hope nobody finds out how else they've been getting their paws on artworks that don't belong to them, because if it all comes out there'll be trouble.'

Stella flushed angrily.

'That *parasite*, as you call him, is my father, and I'm sure he had a very good reason for being there.'

Ted glanced up and grimaced.

'Ouch! Me and my big mouth. Sorry. So this is Raymond. Looks like you, doesn't he?'

He was frowning over the photo, deep in thought, and her mind turned to the conversation she'd overheard in the pavilion. Ted had wanted information from Monica for an article he was writing. Something to do with her father. Was this what he'd been referring to? She'd been meaning to ask him about it all week, but hadn't been able to pluck up the courage. She took a deep breath.

'Ted, what did you mean just now when you said there'd be trouble?' He looked up, and she went on falteringly, 'I heard you talking about my father too, that night in the pavilion. You were looking for a story. Was it something to do with this? You said he'd been up to something. What was it?'

He opened his mouth to reply, but must have seen the anxiety in her face and hesitated.

'I wouldn't worry about it,' he replied at last. 'I never met Raymond, and I can't say for sure he was up to anything. It was just a figure of speech.'

She met his eyes, but couldn't interpret his expression. He sighed.

'Listen, if it makes you feel any better, it's true I was digging for a story, but I couldn't get anything useful, so I let it drop.'

'For now.'

He couldn't deny it.

'For now, yes. But since you seem to have overheard the whole conversation, you'll also know Monica said there was nothing doing.'

'But—'

'And if Monica said there was nothing doing, then that's what she meant. So let's believe her and leave it at that.'

Chapter Seven

The weather had broken, and outside a steady rain was falling. In the picture gallery of the Villa Bruni, Vittorio was standing on a ladder, taking down a painting very carefully for packing. Beatrice came in and watched him curiously.

'Another one?' she said at last.

'Yes.'

She went across and stared at the picture. It was the Dürer which Gerardo had sold to Otto Kaufmann.

'It's very ugly. If I looked like that I'd never have my portrait painted. This room will be better off without it.'

He threw her a mocking glance.

'Such ignorance! He's a very important German painter.'

'Then the Germans are welcome to him.'

Vittorio set the painting down on a length of soft fabric which he had laid out on a trestle table put up especially for the purpose, then began fixing packing material around the corners of the frame.

'Is that why Kaufmann wanted it? Because the artist is German?' asked Beatrice.

'Yes. He wants to give it to Hitler as a present.'

Something in his face made her observe, 'You don't seem pleased.'

'I'm not. This painting shouldn't be leaving Italy. It's on the list of *notificati*, which means it's against the law to export it. It should stay in the country.'

'Then how come the Count sold it?'

'How do you think? If the authorities knew what he was up to they'd put a stop to it, so he went straight to his friend at the top. Il Duce wouldn't know a Botticelli from a child's finger-painting and wouldn't care even if he did. All Mussolini cares about is keeping in with the Germans, so he's not going to complain if the Count sells one or two paintings he doesn't want.'

'Why don't you say something to him if you're so worried about it?'

'It's not my place, and do you think he'd listen to me even if it was? To him all these—' he swept out an arm to encompass all the paintings '—are just playthings to him. Do you remember what we said about the Countess the other day? He likes her because she makes him look good. It's the same with these pictures. He doesn't care about keeping them for Italy – he just wants them because they're pretty and give him something to show off, and if he gets bored with one of them, well, all he has to do is sell it and buy a different one to put in its place.'

'It would be nice to have that sort of money,' said Beatrice wistfully. She nudged him out of the way and arranged the fabric neatly around the painting. 'If Mimmo and I had the price of just one of these pictures then we could get married straightaway.'

Vittorio kept his thoughts to himself and went to fetch a wooden crate which was standing up against the wall. He put it on the table and began packing it with straw from a sack, lifted the picture and laid it inside, then packed more straw around the edges until it was quite tight. He picked up a hammer and nails and began to fasten it shut. Beatrice wandered across to look at the paintings which were still on the walls. There was a rectangular space, lighter in colour than the rest of the wall, where the Dürer had hung.

'What will go in its place?' she asked.

'The Countess's brother has found something,' he replied through a mouthful of nails. 'I think a Lippi portrait of the Madonna. It's coming from Germany.'

'Is that legal?'

He shrugged.

'As far as I know. The authorities don't care about paintings coming into the country, only paintings going out.'

Beatrice walked along the wall of paintings, gazing at them with interest, then stopped in front of the *Lady of the Cypresses*.

'This is the one the Count won't sell, yes?' she asked.

Vittorio left the crate and came to join her. 'Yes.'

'I like it. It's pretty.'

'There's a story behind it, but I don't know exactly what,' said Vittorio. 'The Countess's brother and her first husband were fighting over it, and Mr Cockburn won and sold it to the Count.'

'I'll bet Mr Schwegler didn't like that. He doesn't like being crossed, that one. Mamma says he flew into a rage with her the last time he was staying here. He was late for something and told her to press a shirt for him, and she took longer than he wanted, and he smashed a vase and yelled at her.'

'Really?'

She nodded.

'He begged pardon straightaway, and was as charming as anything to her for the rest of the visit, but it's obvious he's got a temper, even if he does hide it most of the time.'

They were interrupted just then by Marius himself and Stella, who had come in to look at the paintings. Vittorio busied himself with the Dürer again, and Beatrice watched as the two newcomers strolled up and down the gallery. Marius was at his most entertaining, telling Stella about the history of some of the artworks, and she was listening, the picture of wide-eyed attentiveness. After a while they went out, and Beatrice turned to Vittorio.

'He's going to give her a private tour of the Vasari Corridor,' she said.

'I'll bet he is.'

'Did you see the way she was hanging on his every word?'

'Naturally,' he replied, and she laughed.

'Why did I even ask? She's female – of course you were watching.'

'Hey, she's not my type. But I don't think she needs to worry about making the effort to impress him – I happen to know her father left her a lot of money, and Schwegler has his eyes on it.'

'How do you know that?'

'I listen,' he replied knowingly. Her eyes were eager for more and he relented. 'I overheard him and the Countess talking. He's not as wealthy as he likes to make out.'

'Is that why the Countess invited her here? I did wonder why she bothered. It's not as if she's the motherly type, but she's certainly attracted to money – especially other people's. I guess she's looking out for her brother.'

'I heard something about some paintings too – I don't know what, exactly. Maybe Miss Stella's father left them to her, and the Countess is hoping to sell them.'

'From the amount you heard I'd say you must have been listening at the door.'

Vittorio gave her a dig with his elbow.

'As a matter of fact, they were talking about it quite openly on the terrace while I was hoeing the lower border. Anyway, this girl has spent half her life cooped up at school, and nobody's ever paid her a lick of attention so she's just ripe for the taking, the Countess said. Then she told him to snap her up before she gets her eyes on someone else.'

'Like who?'

'I don't know. The American?'

Beatrice was sceptical.

'The Countess has her hooks in him and she won't let him go if I know anything about her.'

'Maybe.'

Gerardo came in just then, wanting to know how Vittorio was getting on with the picture. As Beatrice was due at the hotel, she left. Gerardo examined the crate, then gave Vittorio a shrewd glance.

'I know you don't approve, my boy,' he said.

'I never said that.'

'I can see it in your face. And as a matter of fact I quite agree with you – we oughtn't to be sending paintings out of the country. But the fact is I need to keep on the good side of the Germans. It's politics, and we all know politics wins out over culture. Besides, we will get a Lippi in its place – a proper Italian painting, which is much more suitable. Let's keep the Italian masterpieces in our country if we can. I promise you I won't sell any of those, no matter how many rich Germans Marius brings me.'

'Good.'

Gerardo regarded him benevolently.

'You're just like your mother,' he said. 'She had principles – too many for this day and age. One doesn't get by with that sort of attitude, alas. I fear society rewards those who look out only for themselves.'

Vittorio made no comment. He didn't remember his mother, who had worked on one of Gerardo's farms, and had died when he was very young without mentioning the name of his father. Gerardo had rescued him from an orphanage, sent him to school and put him to work when he was old enough, and for that Vittorio was grateful. He was fully aware of what everybody suspected, but although the boys in the playground had taunted him and tried to provoke him into fights, he had never risen to the bait, preferring to take the matter philosophically. If it turned out the Count was his father, then that fact would bring with it all the shame of acknowledged illegitimacy without any of the benefits of the Count's money and power. If the Count wanted to tell him the truth one day, then that was up to him. For the present, Vittorio was content to accept his presumed father's assistance, and had no cause to complain of his life.

*

Stella gazed down the river at the view of the Ponte Santa Trinita, then turned to find Marius watching her. He smiled, his blue eyes crinkling up attractively at the corners, and her heart beat a little faster. She was suddenly very conscious of his presence.

'It's beautiful,' she said. 'I don't know how anybody could get tired of looking at it.'

They were standing in the section of the Vasari Corridor which crossed the river above the Ponte Vecchio. Marius had used his influence to arrange a private tour of it so she could see it properly after closing time, once the tourists had left.

'I imagine you're not the first person to say that,' he replied. 'As a matter of fact, last spring Adolf Hitler stood exactly where you are standing now, and I suppose said exactly what you have just said.'

'He came here? Did you meet him?'

'No, but I saw his motorcade as it came down Via Tornabuoni. The city really rolled out the red carpet for him – all the buildings were decked out with Nazi flags, and practically everyone turned out to watch and cheer when he passed with Mussolini. It was quite a sight, but we didn't get much of a glimpse of Hitler himself because they drove so quickly. He wanted to spend most of his visit looking at the paintings in the Uffizi gallery, you see. He fancies himself as a connoisseur of art.'

'That's why Mr Kaufmann wanted that painting, yes? To give to Hitler?'

'That's right,' he replied. 'If you want to do well in Germany these days, you have to get on the Führer's good side.'

He said it lightly, but Stella was disconcerted. Was that what her father had been doing in the photograph? Presenting a painting to Hitler to get on his good side? Or had he been buying it from Hitler's official art dealer – the man who had been in the photograph with them? The latter would certainly be the lesser of two evils. She remembered what Ted had said about the Nazis' confiscation of art from museums. It hardly looked good for her father to be fraternising with the man who increasingly looked like Britain's enemy, but surely it was better to buy unwanted paintings and give them a good home than see them burn? Stella wanted to confide her fears to Marius, but she didn't know how to begin. As if reading her mind, he looked at her searchingly, and said,

'What is it?'

She explained about the photo of her father with Hitler.

'Monica told me he bought some paintings last year in Berlin, and I wondered if that's what was happening in the picture. He was standing with Hitler and another man. Ted said he was Hitler's official art dealer – I can't remember his name. Nicholas something.'

'Nicholas Honegger, perhaps? Yes, Raymond did have dealings with Honegger last year. The Nazis aren't keen on modern art and Hitler in particular is very traditional in his tastes, so they're selling off unwanted paintings for the benefit of the Party. I know Raymond bought some of them.'

'I wish—' she began, then stopped. The Nazis had taken paintings that didn't belong to them and sold them to her father, who must have known where they came from.

'It upsets you to see your father associated with all this, yes?'

'A little.'

'It's not an ideal situation, of course, but the Nazis have threatened to burn any unwanted paintings they can't get rid of, so don't you think it's better to buy them cheaply rather than see them destroyed?'

That was exactly what Stella had been trying to tell herself. It was funny how Marius seemed to understand just what she was thinking. And it was the best way of looking at it, she was sure.

'Yes, I expect you're right. I wonder what he did with them, though. Monica said they went missing. At least, I assume those are the ones she meant. She said he bought them in Berlin.'

He glanced at her curiously.

'Ah, she mentioned the missing paintings, did she? Yes, it's a mysterious business. I don't suppose you have any idea of what your father did with them?'

'No, I knew nothing about them until Monica told me about it. She thought my father might have said something in a letter, but he didn't. I wonder where they are.'

'I expect they'll turn up,' he said.

*

It was becoming increasingly obvious, from the things Stella had overheard and the half-remarks people were dropping here and there, that there was something about her father she hadn't been told. Monica, apparently with Marius's agreement, had asked her cryptic questions about some missing paintings, and even Ted, who'd never met Raymond, clearly knew or suspected something that he didn't want to explain. Stella didn't know what it was; all she had to go on was a hint, overheard in the pavilion, that her father had been involved in something underhand. Ted had refused to elaborate when she questioned him, and it was clear nobody else was going to say anything, but she had to know what it was her father had done.

As soon as she got back to the Villa Bruni, Stella slid in quietly through a side door and crept into Monica's private sitting room, where her former stepmother kept the antique desk at which she sat to write her correspondence. It had two drawers, and several pigeonholes stuffed with papers. There must be something about her father here, surely? It wasn't the done thing to rifle through people's desks, of course, but Stella justified it by reminding herself that Monica had insisted on reading her father's last letter to *her*. Surely she had a right to read anything of Monica's that related to him?

The sound of voices drifting through from the *salone* told her she was safe for now, and she opened the first drawer and began hunting through it. She didn't know what she was looking for, but she was sure Monica must have kept letters or documents – perhaps even more photos – from her marriage to Stella's father. But the drawer held nothing of interest: just a few scattered pens, a pot of glue, a broken ruler, so she turned to the other drawer. It wouldn't open. Stella grimaced and gave a tug, but it was certainly locked, rather than stuck. She gave it up and turned to the pigeonholes, pulling out their contents, flicking through papers anxiously. They consisted of bills, receipts, invitations, thank-you notes – the normal personal correspondence of a busy woman, but nothing that mentioned Raymond.

'Who's snooping through drawers now?' came a voice behind her.

Stella gave a little shriek, shoved the papers back and whirled round to find Ted, who had just come into the room and was standing by the drinks cabinet.

'Don't mind me.' He gestured to her with an empty glass. 'I only came in for the bar service.'

She stood defensively, her back to the desk, as he opened the cabinet and took his time choosing a bottle, reading each label maddeningly slowly. She was sure he was doing it on purpose. At last he selected a Scotch whisky, poured himself a glass, took a mouthful then came across to stand in front of her.

'So, are you going to tell me what you were looking for?'

'No.'

He seemed amused more than anything else, and she glowered at him defensively, which only made him smirk all the more.

'A word to the wise. If you're going to burgle somebody, make sure you put everything back the way you found it. That letter goes in there.'

He leaned across her as he spoke, plucked a sheet of paper from one pigeonhole and slotted it neatly into another. She watched him in astonishment, but was lost for a reply.

'Touché,' he said. 'I won't tell if you don't.'

Then he chucked her lightly under the chin and sauntered out, whistling.

Chapter Eight

Winter passed, and spring was ushered in with a series of breezy days that blew away the clouds and brought with them the promise of summer. Stella had become accustomed to life at the Villa Bruni, and, whatever her reservations about Monica, they'd settled into a routine and were getting along in a reasonably civil manner. She still couldn't explain why Monica had asked her to stay, but since life in Florence was mostly pleasanter than it would have been in London, there seemed no sense in leaving, as long as the peace held – although how long it would last was anybody's guess. The international situation was becoming increasingly fragile: in September, shortly after Stella's arrival, Germany had annexed the Sudetenland in Czechoslovakia and promised peace, although few believed it. Then in November the news had come of a horrifying wave of violent attacks on Jewish homes, buildings and synagogues in Germany. Stella read the newspapers every day, keeping a close eye on the situation in case things took a sudden turn for the worse, forcing her to leave.

There had been no mention of her father for months, and since Ted was now in Spain, writing about the civil war there, Stella assumed he'd abandoned the story about Raymond he'd been planning to write. Marius, meanwhile, had returned to Geneva, busy with work. He could only come for short visits, and Stella was missing him more than she liked to admit. She frequently found herself wondering whether he had a woman in Switzerland, but equally frequently chided herself for her stupidity at even asking the question. Why would someone like Marius give her a second look, when he might choose from any number of prettier, more sophisticated women?

'By the way, I'm going up to Lucerne next week,' said Monica to Stella one day at breakfast. 'I've some matters to deal with at the gallery. Why don't you come?'

Stella had never seen her father's gallery – the gallery which now belonged to Monica. She'd known very little of his work at all, in fact.

'I'd love to come,' she replied.

'Good. Marius will be overjoyed. He'll be there next week too. He asked me to bring you specially.'

Stella's heart gave a thump, and she wanted to ask more, but Monica was already talking about the travel arrangements, the train, the hotel, the luggage.

'We must do something with that hair of yours before we go,' she said, gazing at Stella critically. 'I've let you neglect it for far too long now.'

True to her word she took Stella to her own hairdresser, ignoring all arguments. Stella sat in the chair as Monica snapped out instructions, then let out a whimper of horror as the hairdresser took hold of a lock of hair and cut off at least four inches from the length.

'That's too short!' she exclaimed.

'Don't worry, it will look gorgeous, I promise,' said Monica, and Stella had no choice but to sit and cringe in fear as the hairdresser snipped and primped and curled.

'There! You see?' said Monica triumphantly, once he'd finished. Stella stared at herself.

'It's – it's so different,' she faltered at last.

The wild curls had been tamed and smoothed, and the frizzled ends shortened and neatened off. One curl fell across her brow, and she brushed it out of the way impatiently.

'No, let it fall forward,' said Monica. 'There, like that.'

'The *signorina* is very beautiful,' pronounced the hairdresser.

Stella gazed at her unaccustomed new reflection in the looking-glass. She had to admit the new style was very flattering.

'Marius will adore it,' said Monica.

*

It was late afternoon when they reached Lucerne. The weather was chilly and gloomy; dark rain clouds hung over the lake, and an intermittent fog drifted up and down, alternately obscuring and revealing the high parts of the town. Marius met them at the station, his eyes lighting up appreciatively when he saw Stella. She felt self-conscious, but at the same time pleased that Monica had insisted on the new look. He'd arranged a car to take them straight to the gallery, and Stella gazed out of the window as the car wound its way through the streets, admiring the river and lake, the watchtowers on the old city walls, the cobbled streets and the buildings with their elaborately painted façades.

The gallery was located down a discreet and exclusive side street in the old part of town. As the car drew up outside, Stella happened to turn her head and caught some sort of telegraphed communication passing between Monica and Marius. They were wearing unreadable expressions which mirrored one another almost exactly, and at that moment looked very alike. Stella wondered briefly whether the unspoken conversation was about her, but pushed the thought aside and concentrated her attention on the visit.

They went into the gallery, passing an old man who was occupied in polishing the door handle. A smartly dressed gallery assistant greeted Monica and Marius, and extended his deference to include Stella when she was introduced as Raymond Cockburn's daughter. While the others were talking, Stella walked across to gaze at the paintings displayed on the white walls. Most of them were modern, abstract works. She was staring at one of the paintings, an angular portrait of a woman, when Monica came over to stand by her.

'Listen, darling, there's something I'd like you to do for me,' she murmured. 'Do you remember my telling you a few months ago about some paintings that went missing?' Stella nodded in surprise, and Monica went on, 'Well, it's not quite true that nobody knows where they are. At least, I don't think so. Do you see old Franz there by the door with the polish? No, don't look round yet. I'm almost sure he knows something about them.'

'What makes you think that?'

'Because he's been here for years and Raymond used to tell him everything. I've already asked him several times, but he's never been too fond of me and he denies knowing anything about them. But you're Raymond's daughter and I'm sure he'll speak to you if you ask him.'

'But what am I to say?' asked Stella, wholly mystified now.

'Just tell him you've come about the paintings. Say it confidently, as though you know he knows about them, and see what he says. But don't do it while I'm in sight, or he certainly won't tell you. I've some things to see to so I'll go into the office. Leave it a couple of minutes and then ask him.'

True to her word, Monica buttonholed the smart assistant and they disappeared through a door at the other end of the gallery. Marius was looking through a catalogue, and the place was otherwise empty apart from Stella and old Franz, who was still polishing the brass fittings on the door. Stella walked across to him, and he looked up. He had thick, unruly grey eyebrows jutting out over suspicious, deep-set eyes. Stella took a deep breath.

'Franz, isn't it?'

'Ja.'

'I'm Stella Cockburn. Mr Cockburn's daughter.'

The news didn't seem to impress him much. He merely waited, his hand holding the grubby cloth suspended in mid-air.

'I've come about the paintings. I understand you know where they are.'

He looked at her pityingly and gestured around at the walls.

'The paintings are here,' he replied, in heavily accented English.

'I meant the other ones,' she said, feeling rather foolish now. 'The missing ones. My father bought them in Berlin.'

'I don't know anything about that.'

His reply was so brusque she didn't know what to say next.

'Are you sure?' she asked stupidly at last.

'Why would I not be sure? I told *her* – here he nodded towards the office door – 'and now I tell you. I know nothing.'

He went back to his polishing with an air of finality that suggested the interview was over. Stella hesitated, at a loss now, and looked around, as if for inspiration. Marius was standing a little way away. He saw her and gave her a quizzical look.

'Well, if you do happen to remember, let me know,' she said to Franz. He grunted and went on with his work, and she retreated, feeling somewhat disconcerted, although she couldn't explain why.

Marius joined her and gave her another curious glance, but didn't ask what they'd been talking about. Instead, he took her by surprise by asking her out to dinner that evening. Stella blinked.

'Monica—' she began.

'My sister is meeting some friends, she says, so it's just you and I. You'll take pity on me, won't you?'

So this was what they'd been arranging silently in the car. Stella was on the point of stammering out something ridiculously self-deprecating, but caught herself just in time. Now was not the time to behave like an awkward schoolgirl.

'Yes, I'd love to,' she replied.

Before he could reply they were interrupted by Monica and the smart assistant, who emerged from the office. Monica threw a questioning glance at Stella, who shook her head and walked away to try and subdue her agitation at Marius's invitation, because she was sure it must be visible to everybody. He'd made it clear it was to be just the two of them. Her heart beat a little faster, and she wasn't sure whether it was out of excitement or nervousness.

The others were still talking business, so she wandered aimlessly around the gallery, although she'd already seen all there was to look at. The uncooperative Franz had stopped polishing and was now wiping the mist from the front windows in a desultory way, his back to them all. Dusk was falling outside, and the lights were on, and she could see Franz's reflection, with hers behind it, in the cleared part of the window. As she watched idly, she suddenly saw that Franz had raised his head and was staring directly at her reflection. Was he looking at her? She glanced around. The others were still talking, paying no attention. She turned her head back to Franz, who for some reason had begun drawing in the mist on the window. She watched for a moment, then widened her eyes in astonishment, because he wasn't drawing at all – he was writing a message.

She stared at the letters. '*Spr. brücke. 10 Uhr*', the message said. Franz hadn't turned round, but his eyes were still fixed on her reflection. He put a finger over his lips. She nodded quickly, and he ran the cloth over the writing, obliterating it, then went on cleaning the window as though nothing had happened.

Shortly after that they left the gallery to drive to the hotel. Stella's mind was racing. Franz wanted to speak to her privately, that much was evident. *Spr. brücke* must refer to the Spreuerbrücke, one of the wooden footbridges crossing the river. And *10 Uhr* was ten o'clock. He wanted her to meet him at the footbridge at ten tomorrow morning – yes, it must be in the morning, because they used the twenty-four-hour clock here, as they did in Italy. He had something to tell her, and he obviously didn't want her to mention it to Monica, or he'd have given her the message more openly. She was dying to know what it all meant.

*

Stella arrived at her hotel room to find that Marius had sent her some flowers, pink and white peonies and white roses, filling the room with a delicate scent. She was still exclaiming over them when Monica came in to help her dress.

'Wear the pale blue satin,' she advised. 'It will set off those lovely eyes of yours and stand out against all those horrid, drab colours the Swiss seem to be wearing this season.'

Before she knew it, Stella had been hustled into the gown in question – a recent purchase that was more sophisticated than anything she'd worn before – and was standing in front of the long glass in the hotel room while Monica looked her up and down.

'Good,' was Monica's verdict. 'Now, put this on.'

She was opening a little box as she spoke, inside which something glinted. It was a necklace, delicately wrought in silver with a cluster of blue topaz as the centrepiece. She put it around Stella's neck and fastened it.

'It looks perfect,' she said.

Stella admired the necklace, and had to admit it set off her outfit beautifully. Perhaps she wouldn't disgrace herself after all.

'Thank you,' she said. 'I'll take care of it.'

Marius arrived punctually and they went to dinner, Stella feeling not a little like Cinderella on her way to the ball.

'Thank you for the flowers,' she said once they were seated. 'They're wonderful.'

'My pleasure. You're wearing the necklace, too. I hoped you'd like it. It looks beautiful on you.'

She flushed and put a hand to her throat.

'This is from you?'

'I hope you don't mind, but Monica mentioned that you don't have much to wear in the way of jewellery, and I happened to see this and thought you might like it.'

She stammered out her thanks, but her pleasure at the gift was mixed with anxiety. She hadn't realised it was from him; Monica must have kept the information deliberately from her – understandably, because she wasn't sure she would have accepted it if she'd known. Stella was feeling a little out of her depth. It wasn't an expensive piece by any means – just a pretty trinket – but she'd always understood that women who accepted jewels from men weren't quite the right sort of women, and the idea distressed her. But it was too late now, the necklace was hers, and all she could do was comfort herself with the thought that since Monica had told her to wear it then presumably this kind of thing must be acceptable, in these circles at least.

It was a delightful evening. Stella soon forgot the necklace and began feeling more comfortable in the unfamiliar surroundings. Marius was charming and entertaining, and she basked in the glow of his attention. He had the same knack as her father of making one feel the most interesting person in the room, and she couldn't help being dazzled by him. They ate, and talked, then he took her dancing, and all too soon it was time to return to the hotel.

On the way back in the car the Cinderella spell began to wear off and Stella fell silent. It had been a long day, and she was tired, and she was thinking of her rendezvous the next day, wondering whether she'd dreamt the message on the window. It had been the strangest thing, but she could only conclude that Franz had something to tell her about the missing paintings that was for her ears only. But how was she to get away? They were to return to Florence tomorrow afternoon, but what if Monica had plans for them that would take up the whole morning? As she ruminated on various possible excuses, Marius noticed her silence.

'Is there something wrong?' he asked. 'I hope it wasn't something I said.'

'Oh, no, you've been wonderful!' she replied, then stopped and blushed, feeling stupid all over again. He laughed, but not unpleasantly.

'Well, thank you for the vote of confidence. Ah, here we are. I wonder if Monica is back.'

The car drew up at the hotel and he opened the door for her.

'I have to return to Geneva early tomorrow, but I'll be back in Florence as soon as I can,' he said. 'Will you come to dinner with me again then?'

'I'd love to,' she said sincerely.

'Then I'll look forward to it.'

She was nervous, wondering what she would do if he wanted to kiss her, but he didn't seem to have anything of the sort in mind: he merely brushed her hand lightly with his lips and went away, leaving her with confused thoughts, half-wishing now that he *had* kissed her. She touched the necklace at her throat. He was too experienced, too worldly wise for her, but for good or ill she strongly suspected that he would only have to snap his fingers and she would fall in love with him.

*

Much to Stella's relief, Monica had no objection to her going out to explore by herself the next morning, and by half past nine she was hurrying through the streets, heading down to the river and the quaint old footbridge, with its wooden sides and red roof. She arrived early, and paused uncertainly at the entrance. Which side of the river had Franz meant? It would be too vexing if they missed each other because she was waiting at one end of the bridge and he at the other. But she didn't have long to wonder, because she soon saw the old man himself, approaching along the river front towards her. He grunted in greeting, just as dour and unsmiling as he had been the day before.

'You have something to tell me?' she asked.

He nodded, a short jerk of the head.

'I could not tell you yesterday because the brother was watching and he will tell her everything. Mr Cockburn did not want her to know. If you want to tell her then that is your business. Me, I just do what I am asked – he said to give you this privately so that is what I do now.'

He rummaged in his inside pocket and brought out something, which he handed to her. It was a small key, stamped on one side with the name of a bank in Lucerne, and on the other with a number.

'Mr Cockburn, he gave it to me a few days before he died,' he explained. 'He told me that you would come, and that I was to give it to you, and that you would know what to do.'

Stella gazed at the key blankly. 'What is it?'

'You do not know? He said he was going to send you a letter. Perhaps he forgot. Maybe there will be more information in the box.'

'Which box?'

'The box. At the bank,' he replied patiently, indicating the key.

Of course – it was the key to a safe deposit box. Her father had left her the key to a safe deposit box, and he didn't want Monica to know about it.

Franz seemed to think his duty was done and turned away to leave.

'Just a moment,' she said quickly. 'My father didn't tell me anything at all about this. I didn't get any letter. Do you have any idea what it's about?'

He half-turned back and looked sharply at her from under the bushy brows, as if wondering whether to speak.

'I do not know for sure, but I think perhaps it is something to do with the paintings,' he said at last. 'Mr Cockburn took them from the Jew in Berlin after...' He said something in German she didn't understand, and shrugged. 'But that is only a guess.'

He turned and walked off, and Stella looked at her watch. She couldn't possibly leave Lucerne without finding out what it all meant, but she would have to hurry.

She found the bank without any problems, and was escorted into the strongroom. A small metal box was brought out from the stack, and she was left alone with it. Stella opened it with some trepidation, her heart beating fast. She didn't know what she was expecting to find, and was slightly deflated to discover it was only another key and a folded sheet of paper. The key was big and solid, and looked as if it belonged to a lock that was intended very firmly to keep people out. Tied to it was a tag bearing an address in a town she'd never heard of, presumably somewhere in Switzerland.

She turned her attention to the paper, but if she'd been hoping it would contain a full explanation she was disappointed. The page had been torn from a notebook, and was creased and grubby, with an irregular brown stain across the top right-hand corner, as if someone had spilt coffee over it. On it was a scribbled list in German. The handwriting was crabbed and almost illegible, and half the words were in shorthand, but here and there she saw a name she recognised: Bellotto, Van den Broeck, Ghirlandaio – all Renaissance artists, she was sure. On the right-hand side next to each item on the list was a sum, and at the bottom a total, with the letters 'RM' in front of it – for Reichsmark, the German currency, she guessed. She had only a vague idea of how much a Reichsmark was worth, but the total figure didn't seem much for so many valuable paintings, if that was what it referred to.

There was nothing else in the box. Questions tumbled one after the other through her mind. Had she discovered the missing paintings? If so, presumably they were being stored at the address on the label attached to the key – although there wouldn't be time to go and find out, since she was leaving Lucerne in a couple of hours. Also, if these were the paintings, why had her father left them to her? Monica was the one who'd inherited the gallery and all the artworks that went with it, so by rights surely they ought to have gone to *her* instead. Had Raymond left these paintings to Stella in order to add to her own inheritance without Monica's knowledge? If so, why?

Stella looked at the paper again. Here was another puzzle: why did it list Renaissance rather than modern artworks? As far as she'd been led to believe by Monica, the missing works had consisted of so-called 'degenerate' modern art that the Nazis didn't want, which her father had bought quite legally from one of Hitler's official art dealers. But according to Franz, Raymond had taken the paintings listed here from a Jew in Berlin. It was obviously a quite different collection. Had her father obtained it illicitly?

The implications were unmistakable, and Stella's heart sank. Her father had disappointed her in so many ways, and she'd made so many excuses for his abandonment of her, but one thing she'd always been absolutely certain of was that he'd been a decent man. Had she been wrong about that, too? Had she been clinging on to an image of her own making all this time?

She slammed the box shut and replaced it. The only thing she could be truly certain of was that her father hadn't wanted Monica to know about the contents of the box. Let the paintings stay where they were. If he'd obtained them through dubious means then Monica had no right to them either. Stella had no idea what to do about her discovery, but it seemed the best thing was to try and put it out of her mind, since all her thoughts on the subject seemed to lead to the uncomfortable conclusion that her father had not been the man she believed him to be.

The next couple of hours were full of bustle as she and Monica left the hotel and set off back to Florence, so Stella was easily able to keep her resolution. As the train rattled along the plains of northern Italy, however, she couldn't stop the thoughts from crowding back in. There was something she very much wanted to know, which Monica could tell her.

'What does *ermordet* mean?' she asked.

Monica looked up from her magazine and raised her eyebrows.

'Goodness, darling, what *have* you been doing?'

'I just heard it somewhere today. I think that was the word.'

'It means "murdered",' replied Monica, and went back to her magazine.

Stella bit her lip. *Ermordet.* Murdered. That was the word she hadn't understood when Franz talked of the Jew in Berlin. An image of the paper in the safe deposit box rose unbidden to her mind, and she shivered. There had been an ugly brown stain on the page. Was it coffee, as she'd first assumed, or something else? Ordinarily she wouldn't have given it any thought, but suddenly it looked much more sinister.

Chapter Nine

On her return to Florence Stella hid the key to the safe deposit box at the back of her drawer and resolved to try and forget about the whole thing. There was nothing she could do about it anyway, since her father had been quite clear that Monica must be kept in the dark, and Stella hadn't the faintest notion of how to deal with perhaps a large consignment of paintings on her own. Her father wasn't here any more, and she had no absolute proof that he'd done anything blameworthy, so she resolved to think of him as she always had – as a kind, if inattentive father – and to remember only the good things she knew about him.

Besides, there were better, brighter things to think about: Marius came to Florence as he'd promised, and she was dazzled by him all over again. They went to dinner and he gave her his undivided attention, and she gazed at him, fascinated, hardly able to tear her eyes away from his. He seemed genuinely interested in her, and if in her calmer moments she ever doubted whether she was doing the right thing in allowing herself to be taken out by a man so much older and more sophisticated than herself, she quickly shook it off. In England, of course, she'd have been shepherded about from one engagement to another by a series of Mrs Unsworths, but this wasn't England. Monica didn't seem to see anything wrong with it – in fact, was entirely encouraging – so Stella took comfort in that, and allowed herself to be drawn further into Marius's magnetic field without once asking herself whether she'd be able to pull herself away again if she got too close.

In May Ted came back from Spain. He seemed surprised at the change in Stella's appearance.

'Hey, look at you!' he exclaimed on his first visit to the Villa Bruni. 'I guess Monica got her mitts on you at last. You look almost like a grown-up. Next time we go out I'll get you a negroni instead of a glass of milk.' He looked her up and down appreciatively then stuck out a finger and flipped Marius's necklace, which she'd hardly taken off since he'd given it to her. 'Cute necklace, too. The colour suits you.'

She blushed and glanced at Marius across the room. Ted noticed it immediately and looked at the necklace again, an incredulous expression spreading across his face.

'Oh, *I* see. So Little Miss Proper isn't quite so proper after all! Which of the Ten Commandments did you have to break to get it? Or did you just shimmy round a couple?'

Clearly he hadn't changed one bit – in fact, he'd become even more exasperating, if that were possible.

'Must you be quite so coarse?' Stella said irritably. 'It was a gift, nothing more.'

'Nothing more, huh? Well, if you say so. But I'd leave it at that if I were you. He's not your type.'

'How do you know what my type is? And I shall do as I please, thank you. Now, leave me alone and go and bother Monica.'

It was a dig, because she knew Monica had turned her attention to the German, Otto Kaufmann, who was visiting the villa more and more frequently these days. Ted grimaced at her and went to talk to Gerardo, but several times she caught him looking across at her, frowning. It made her uncomfortable. Ted was the only person to have said anything about the necklace, and she couldn't deny the same thought had crossed her own mind when she'd first found out that Marius had bought it. Had she done the right thing in accepting it? And was there any truth in what Ted had said?

*

Spring and summer slid by, the weather got hotter, and Italy became more restive as talk of war grew louder. Conflict was looming, and there was a palpable tension in the air. In April Italy occupied Albania, and in May Germany and Italy formalised their alliance. Elsewhere, they heard of growing conflict in the East. Ted was spending most of his time in Rome now, but every time he came to Florence he was shaking his head, preoccupied.

'It's going to be soon,' he said, whenever Stella asked him about the war. Even now, Stella couldn't quite bring herself to believe it, but she had the sense to know she was most likely deceiving herself. The BBC talked of it constantly, and two days out of three she saw the word '*guerra*' in stark, black letters on the front page of Gerardo's newspaper.

One day in early August Stella went into Florence with Dora. Beatrice's wedding was approaching, and Dora had found some pretty lace which she thought would make a perfect trimming for her simple wedding dress. She wanted to show it to her daughter, so they stopped at the Hotel Ambassador to see her. They sought her out in her office, and found her frowning over a typewriter while Mimmo lounged in a chair. Beatrice looked up and gave an impatient exclamation.

'You too! I'll get into trouble for all these visitors.'

'It's only for a minute. I wanted to show you something, but it's not for Mimmo's eyes.'

'Well if that's not an encouragement to stay I don't know what is,' he said.

'It's for the wedding, and it'll bring bad luck if you see it.'

'Mamma, you know that's just superstition,' said Beatrice, laughing.

'Superstition or not, I'm not risking it. Out!'

Dora made shooing motions at Mimmo, and the package containing the lace fell out of her hands, spilling a length of frothy white fabric onto the floor.

'Now look what you made me do!' exclaimed Dora, as Mimmo bent to pick it up.

'Don't worry, I'm not looking at it,' he said, turning his head away ostentatiously as he handed it back to her. At that moment he seemed to catch sight of Stella for the first time. His laughter broke off and he nodded his head. It was a gesture of politeness, nothing more, but Stella felt as if he were somehow letting her know that she wasn't part of the conversation, and was disconcerted. Then the impression passed as Dora took his arm and escorted him firmly from the room, her voice going ten to the dozen as they retreated down the corridor. Beatrice had been smiling too, but now the smile disappeared and she turned to Stella.

'Why are you still here?' she demanded, her dark brown, almost black, eyes hostile. 'You had better go home to England. This is our country, not yours. I don't want my mother getting into trouble for being seen with you.'

Stella was taken aback, and didn't know what to reply, but luckily Dora returned just then, and displayed the lace for Beatrice to look at.

'See, this will be perfect for the head covering. It's much prettier than the one we already have. I'll start on it this evening and it will be ready in plenty of time.'

'Mamma, I told you not to spend any more money!' replied Beatrice, exasperated.

'But don't you think it's beautiful? See, it sits so firmly on your hair – you know I always said the other one will slip off.'

'It's very nice,' conceded Beatrice. 'Listen, we'll talk about it later. I have to get on now.'

Dora wrapped up the lace again and Beatrice ushered them out of the door. As they walked down the corridor, Stella looked back and saw Beatrice staring after her, unsmiling.

*

Dora had to return to the Villa Bruni, but Stella stayed out, thinking about what Beatrice had just said. She knew Mimmo was a loyal Fascist and could hardly be expected to have any love for the British, but Beatrice had always been polite to her, if a little distant. She'd often had the impression that Beatrice considered her to be too ineffectual to be useful – only to be expected, she supposed, given the Italian girl's eminently capable manner and the position she'd reached at the Hotel Ambassador through her own hard work. Still, Stella felt disconcerted at having been repulsed so baldly.

She wandered further into the centre of the city. The sun was beating down and the streets were unusually busy, and there seemed to be some event happening. Stella followed the crowds of people curiously, wondering what was going on, and found herself in Piazza della Signoria, where some kind of rally was taking place. Hundreds of Blackshirts, members of Mussolini's Fascist militia, stood to attention at the centre of the square while the voice of Mussolini barked out from loudspeakers. Although she'd been doing her best to learn Italian, Stella could still only understand snatches of the speech, which seemed to be about patriotic duty and the good of the country. But it didn't matter, because she was more interested in watching the crowd, who seemed rapt. At last the speech came to an end and cheers erupted.

'Are you crazy?' hissed a voice in her ear. She whirled round. It was Ted, glaring at her furiously. 'What d'you think you're doing here?'

'I'm watching the rally,' she said in surprise.

'Shh! Keep your voice down. Didn't you hear what he was just saying about the British? Look at the mood of these people. If they hear your voice there's no saying what they'll do.'

He grabbed her none too gently by the arm and hustled her out of the square. She protested, but he cut it short.

'Stella, I swear sometimes I wonder whether you keep your brain in a box under the bed and only bring it out for special occasions. Haven't you seen the posters? They're everywhere!'

'But I was perfectly all right!' she exclaimed. 'Nobody could possibly have known I was English – at least, not until you turned up and started yelling about it.'

'Listen, you need to get home. It's not safe. As a matter of fact, if you know what's good for you, you'll leave Italy altogether and go back to England.'

'But I asked Gerardo and he said there was no need for me to go.'

'That's what he's saying *now*, but Gerardo likes an easy life. If Mussolini tells him to get rid of you then that's what he'll do, so better go now while he can still get you safe passage out in a first-class carriage, rather than later, with a boot up the behind. There's going to be a war any day now and the last thing you want is to get caught up in the middle of it.'

'I'll be fine. Marius says—'

'Who cares what Marius says? What does he know?'

'Just as much as you, I imagine. And perhaps more.'

He stopped and looked at her.

'You're not really serious about him, are you? Is that wise? What kind of a man showers jewellery on a girl barely out of school?'

She bridled defensively at the mention of the necklace.

'He hasn't *showered jewellery* on me, as you put it. He happened to see it and thought I might like it.'

'That's not much better. You should keep away from him.'

'Don't be ridiculous! Why on earth should I keep away from him?'

'I don't trust him. He's cold and calculating, and he's friends with too many Nazis for my liking.'

'In case you hadn't noticed, this is Italy. Everybody is friends with the Nazis.' Her father had been friends with the Nazis too, although she didn't point that out. 'And I like him. Besides, why should you care what I do?'

'Because, strangely enough, I have enough human feeling left inside this burnt-out old carcass of mine to feel concerned when I see someone I know out of her depth.' Ted shook his head. 'If you ask me it was a mistake for you to come to Italy in the first place. You should have stayed in London and found yourself a nice English boy your own age with buck teeth and more money than you.'

She opened her mouth to reply hotly, but thought better of it. Absurd as he was, he really did seem sincere.

'Listen, I'm sure you mean well, but it's really none of your business,' she said.

He put his hands up.

'Well, don't say I didn't warn you. But if you'll take my advice you'll keep away from Marius. He's just playing with you.'

Chapter Ten

But it seemed that Ted was wrong, because the next time Stella went out with Marius, he proposed. He drove her out into the countryside for lunch, after which they went for a walk. They came upon a vantage point that gave a fine view out across the rolling hills, and there they paused, under some trees, which afforded some slight shade from the hot sun. Stella gazed out across the valley below, frowning a little.

'What are you thinking?' asked Marius.

'I was just wondering why Monica thought it was a good idea to throw a party this evening,' she replied. 'It seems an awkward time to do it, somehow, when everybody's talking of war.'

'You ought to know by now that Monica does whatever she likes.'

'Yes, she does, doesn't she? I wish I could do whatever I liked.'

'What would you like to do?'

'I'd like to stay here,' she said sadly. 'But I don't think it's going to be possible. Ted was right, drat him.' She looked up and met Marius's gaze. 'I spoke to Gerardo this morning and asked whether he was planning to send me back to England. He was very kind, but it was obvious he's starting to feel uncomfortable about having me. He didn't say as much, of course, but he said that if Mussolini gives him an order then he must obey it.' She sighed. 'I know we're not at war yet, but it's only a matter of time, and when that happens I won't have any choice.'

'Does it make you so unhappy, the idea of going back to England?'

'Yes. I've grown to love Italy, and I'll miss it. I'd go somewhere else if I could, but I don't think Mr Ellison would agree. He's been trying to persuade me to come back to London. I think he and the trustees want to keep an eye on me.'

Marius was silent a moment, then said, 'What if I kept an eye on you instead?'

Something in his tone made her glance up quickly. The blue eyes were fixed on her.

'What do you mean?'

'You could come to Geneva with me.'

'Do you want me to work for you? I don't think—'

'No,' he replied. 'I'm asking you to marry me.'

She felt suddenly breathless and light-headed, staring stupidly at him. She'd never really thought this would happen – had, despite herself, half-believed Ted when he said Marius was playing with her, because it seemed so unlikely that he would want to marry her. But here he was, proposing, and it was all suddenly very real. He seemed amused at her expression.

'You look surprised.'

'I – I am,' she stammered. 'I didn't – I mean I hadn't thought—'

'No? Haven't I made myself clear enough?'

'Well, perhaps…' she admitted, then laughed and blushed.

He took her unresisting hand in his.

'Then what do you say?'

Was he really serious? Even now, she couldn't be certain.

'Are you sure?' she couldn't help asking.

'Quite sure,' he replied imperturbably.

'Then yes – thank you, I'd love to marry you!'

There. She'd said it, and with those few simple words she wasn't a schoolgirl any more, but a grown woman, engaged to be married. Her head was whirling, and she couldn't quite take it in.

'I'm glad,' he said. He drew her towards him and kissed her very gently on the lips. She'd often wondered how it would feel to kiss him. It was an unfamiliar sensation, oddly impersonal and unsatisfying. Perhaps she needed practice. But that would all come in good time, she told herself – it was only her first kiss, after all.

'We'll do it as soon as possible, yes?' he said as he let her go. 'I'll take you to Geneva and we'll live there, and as soon as it's safe for you to come back to Italy I will bring you. Shouldn't you like to live in Geneva? It's a fine old place. I think you'll like it.'

'I'll go wherever you like, Marius,' she said.

'I know,' he replied.

*

Monica's party was that evening, and Stella dressed for it in nervous anticipation. The afternoon in the sun and several hours of mental turmoil had brought on a headache. Marius had proposed and she'd accepted, and she was going to be married. Could really it be true? It seemed unreal, somehow. She was half-convinced that when she got downstairs she'd find that the events of that afternoon hadn't happened at all, and that she'd imagined the whole thing.

She took one last look in the mirror and went down to join the festivities. It was far too hot to stay indoors, and all the guests were out on the terrace, drinking, laughing and talking. She saw Marius before he saw her and brightened at the sight of him, a handsome figure in his well-cut dinner suit, talking to a group of people. She went across to him in trepidation and smiled timidly. He claimed her at once and pulled her to his side, and a rush of relief went through her. So it was true after all. Perhaps she needed him there with her to believe it, and it was only her own self-doubt when she was away from him that made her so unsure. Well, she'd be with him all the time soon. The news had obviously been spreading, and everyone wanted to offer their congratulations. Stella was wishing she'd taken an aspirin before she came down, but she managed to paste on a smile.

It was one of Monica's better parties, and it seemed half the high society of Florence had made the effort to attend, even though it was August, when most of them went to the sea. Ted was there too, just back from Rome. He'd turned up to the party late, obviously in a bad mood, and was concentrating more on the drinks than on any of the guests. Stella, temporarily disengaged from conversation, saw the state of his temper and decided the wisest course of action was to give him a wide berth. She wandered across to her favourite vantage point on the terrace steps to admire the view of the city. The air was oppressive and sticky, and the sounds of music and laughter drifted across to her from the house. The headache was getting worse. She put her hand to her right temple and massaged it, trying to shake off an unaccountable feeling of dissatisfaction that stole across her every time she was alone, away from Marius's presence. She was supposed to be happy. She *was* happy, she was sure of it.

'Are you out of your mind?'

She jumped and turned to find Ted glaring at her. Whatever he'd been drinking didn't seem to have improved his mood.

'Were you even listening to what I said the other day? What the hell do you think you're doing, accepting Marius?'

'I accepted him because I want to marry him. Is that really so ridiculous?'

'I think you're crazy.'

'Well that's clear enough. I suppose you think he's crazy too.'

'Oh no, he's not crazy. Not at all. He knows exactly which side his bread's buttered on.'

'What do you mean?'

'Don't forget you've got money – or will have.'

Stella was astonished, then outraged.

'Are you suggesting that he only proposed because he wants… why, that's nonsense!'

'No it's not. I know a gold-digger when I see one. He wants your money and you're too blind to see it because you're so desperate for attention. He's not your daddy, you know.'

The implication stung, but she wasn't going to admit it.

'Thank you, I'm perfectly aware of that,' she replied icily.

'And you're not even in love with him,' he went on. 'He's hypnotised you so you think you are, but you're not.'

'You're talking nonsense,' she snapped. He was about to go on but she held up a hand to stop him. 'Look, I've a headache and the last thing I want is to listen to all this. Go and bother someone else if you must, but leave me alone.'

She turned away deliberately. He paused for a second then stamped off. Closing her eyes, she put her hand to her aching forehead, which had not improved with their argument, then decided to go inside and look for an aspirin. Just outside the terrace door she found Ted standing very close behind Monica, his hands on her arms, whispering something into her ear. Monica was laughing delightedly. Ted ignored Stella completely as she passed, and she felt the ire rising within her, because she knew perfectly well he was doing it deliberately to annoy her, remembering her opinions on the subject. It was wholly inexplicable, but she suddenly felt as if the devil had got into her, giving her an overwhelming urge to exasperate Ted as much as he had exasperated her. Two could play at that game, she thought. So he thought Marius was only interested in her money, did he? Well, she'd show him.

Marius was standing nearby, and she went to join him. He brightened at her approach, and she smiled into his eyes and hung on his every word. Then they danced, and she pressed closer to him than she would usually have done, and gazed at him as though she couldn't tear her eyes away from him. He returned her attention fully, as she'd known he would, and as he twirled her round she caught a glimpse of Ted, noting with grim satisfaction that he'd moved away from Monica and was watching the two of them intently, eyes narrowed. She didn't quite understand it, but she knew that in some unspoken way they were fencing, and for the duration of that dance the awareness of Ted's eyes burning furiously into her from across the terrace gave her a sensation of power she'd never experienced before.

The dance finished and Marius was buttonholed by someone else, and Stella was left alone to enjoy whatever hollow satisfaction she could from what she'd just done. The headache had returned with a vengeance, and she ran up to her room to get the aspirin. When she returned neither Ted nor Marius were anywhere to be seen, slightly to her relief. Craving fresh air and a few minutes alone, she headed down the steps to the lawn in search of a cooler spot. This part of the garden was only dimly lit, and not many people had ventured this far. A few minutes' peace in among the greenery would ease the aching in her head. But Ted had other ideas.

'Do you have any idea what a fool you're making of yourself?'

He'd followed her down to the lawn. She sighed and turned.

'I'm sure you're going to tell me,' she replied resignedly. 'But can't it wait until another time?'

He was looming over her, a solid shape in the darkness, radiating heat and anger. She put out a hand, more with the thought of warding him off than anything else, but he took her wrist in a tight grip and wouldn't let it go.

'No, it can't. Weren't you listening to what I just told you? What were you thinking, throwing yourself at him like that?'

'I didn't *throw* myself at him, as you put it. We're engaged. I talked to him and then we danced.'

'That wasn't just a dance.'

'Then what was it?' she demanded. She tried to snatch her hand away from him, but he gripped her wrist even more tightly, pulling her towards him.

'You were putting on some kind of show there. I don't know where it came from, but I know you did it deliberately just to make me mad,' he said, and she could hear his gritted teeth. 'Well, it worked – I am mad.'

'All right, then, perhaps I was doing it on purpose. But what about you? You draped yourself all over Monica for the same reason,' she snapped. 'That made *me* mad, so we're equal.'

'Are we? So that's it, is it? You're mad about me and Monica, and I'm mad about you and Marius. I guess that means something.'

They were both bristling with hostility, and yet the exhilaration Stella had felt while she was dancing with Marius had returned in full force. But this wasn't about Marius any more; she knew it, although she couldn't have put it into words. Her heart was hammering in her chest, and Ted's grip on her wrist sent a tingle of electricity along her arm that thrilled her, despite herself. There was a silence as they glared at one another furiously. Then he let out something that sounded like an impatient growl, yanked her against him and kissed her hard.

Stella's first feeling was one of astonishment, and she was far too stunned to take it in or feel anything else except for a general sensation that she'd floated away from the earth, and that he was the only thing keeping her anchored. Her mind had gone completely blank, but she came to herself to find that somehow her arms had fastened themselves very tightly around his neck as though they didn't want to let go. She stared up at him, unable to say a word. They were both breathing fast, but his anger had dissipated and he seemed amused at her dumbfounded expression.

'I'm sorry, did I spring it on you?' he said at last, although he didn't seem in the slightest bit sorry.

Before she could even begin to formulate a coherent thought about what had just happened there was a crackle in the undergrowth close by. The sounds of the evening had faded away in her ears, but now they returned in full force and she was suddenly back at the party, in the garden, kissing a man she oughtn't to have been kissing, and the world had turned upside-down. She had to get away. With a gasp she wrenched herself out of Ted's arms and darted back up the steps to the terrace and into the house, where she was immediately captured by Gerardo, who wanted her to speak to some friends of his. Fortunately Gerardo did most of the talking, which gave her a chance to calm down.

From across the room Marius gazed at her. He smiled, and she felt overwhelmed with guilt. Then Ted sauntered in, looking wholly relaxed, cocked an eyebrow at her, helped himself to another drink, and began talking to someone as though nothing had happened. Stella felt her mind churning, as thoughts chased each other through her head. Of all the feelings that were currently swirling around inside her, the uppermost was fury at Ted, who she was convinced had only kissed her to cause trouble. Well, if that was his aim, it had succeeded. Marius's kiss that afternoon had roused no sensation in her at all, but with nothing to compare it to it hadn't seemed to matter. But now it did matter, because the instant Ted's lips had touched hers she'd known that *this* was how a kiss should feel – a jolt of pure pleasure that drove away all rational thought and sent sparks fizzing and dancing throughout her body, right down to her very nerve endings. Even now she was still tingling all over at the memory of it. She was horrified and ashamed of herself, and whenever Marius looked across at her, as he did frequently, she had to avoid his eye, because she was certain that her antics on the lawn must be written all over her face. This should have been the happiest day of her life, but Ted had spoilt it for her.

By three o'clock the party was over and the last guests were leaving. Stella breathed a sigh of relief, wanting only to retire to her room and escape. She'd been pointedly ignoring Ted, and had hoped to get out of saying goodbye to him, but he sought her out deliberately. By that time she'd regained at least some of her poise.

'That wasn't funny,' she said in a low voice. She hoped she sounded dignified.

His mouth curled in amusement.

'Wasn't it? I enjoyed it. And you did too – admit it.'

The colour spread across her face. She couldn't deny it when the truth was quite obvious. She glowered at him furiously and he laughed.

'Listen, I have to go to Rome again tomorrow, but I'll be back next week some time. Don't go into the city alone.' Then he leaned forward and murmured in her ear, 'And don't marry Marius. You'll only regret it.'

The warmth of his breath on her neck sent a crackle of electricity through her that made her jump. Then he left and she went up to her room and threw herself on the bed, her mind spinning.

*

Ted departed for Rome the next day, which gave Stella some much-needed breathing space to address her confused state of mind. She knew perfectly well that Ted didn't care two hoots for her, and that he'd merely been trying to prove a point because he disliked Marius and thought she was making a mistake in marrying him. The breathtaking arrogance of the move roused her to fury all over again, and she spent half the morning running through the things she'd like to say to him if he were here – the things she should have said to him last night, in fact. The insult was inexcusable, and she'd never forgive him for it.

But the kiss – oh, that kiss! The memory of it loomed large in her mind, bringing a glow to her cheeks every time she thought of it. With that one impetuous act he'd made her question everything. If a man she didn't love could kiss her like that, what was she to think about the man she *did* love? Was the engagement all a lie? Did she really love Marius? Ted had claimed she was merely hypnotised by him, and didn't love him at all. Was it true?

Monica noticed her abstraction the next afternoon when they were playing tennis.

'Do try harder,' she said, as Stella lost her third point in a row.

'I'm sorry,' replied Stella. She must do her best to concentrate. She served, but made a bad job of it, and the ball hit the net.

'Oh, it's no use,' said Monica at last, after two more botched serves. 'It's obvious you're miles away.'

She threw her racquet down and they went to sit in the deck-chairs on the lawn. Dora had set out a jug of iced water for them, and Monica watched lazily as Stella poured two glasses.

'You seem a little below par. Is it Ted?' she asked.

'What do you mean?' said Stella quickly.

A mocking smile curled at the edges of Monica's lips.

'Oh, there's no need to be coy with me. I know quite well what was going on between you the other night. He was following you around like a dog, then you both disappeared into the garden for quite half an hour, and when you came back it was perfectly obvious what you'd been up to.'

Monica knew. Stella was horrified. Had she told Marius? As if reading her thoughts, Monica went on,

'Don't worry – I won't say a thing. I just thought we might compare notes.' She burst into a peal of laughter at the sight of Stella's face. 'Don't look so appalled, darling! It's all part of life, and quite natural, if you choose to take it that way. Still, I'm glad you've had some fun. Once you're married you'll have to behave yourself, as Marius is rather jealous and wouldn't stand for that kind of thing.'

Stella fidgeted with her napkin.

'I'm not sure I want to get married any more,' she couldn't help muttering. 'I think perhaps I'm too young.'

'Darling, if you're old enough to be misbehaving in the shrub-bery you're old enough to get married.' Monica leaned forward and raised her eyebrows conspiratorially. 'Tell me – you didn't go just a *little* further than you ought, did you?'

'No!'

Monica laughed at her shocked face.

'Well, never mind. And don't worry – it's our little secret.'

The encounter with Ted seemed to have increased Monica's respect for her, but the whole conversation left Stella feeling out of her depth. Just then, Gerardo came out onto the lawn, holding a telegram.

'It appears our friend Signor Ted is being sent to Paris,' he announced. 'He is sorry he was not able to say goodbye in person, but he asked me particularly to give his regards to Miss Stella, and to tell you to remember what he said – whatever that means. I suppose you understand him.' He raised his eyebrows humorously and glanced down at the paper. 'This is a very long telegram. Anyone would think he does not know one pays by the word.'

Stella sensed Monica was looking at her, and kept her face turned away. Now she wouldn't even get the chance to tell him what she thought of him. The anger rose in her again. She stood up abruptly and went towards the house. As she climbed the steps, she heard a voice calling her name, and looked up to see Marius, who had just come out onto the terrace. He was smiling as if genuinely happy to see her, and at the sight of him her spirits leapt. She felt a rush of affection, as the tangle of thoughts she'd been struggling with whisked away, and everything suddenly seemed beautifully clear. Ted had gone now, and she'd most likely never see him again. He'd been a disruptive influence, but it was quite obvious now that it had only been the effects of the heat and the cocktails she'd drunk that night – there'd been nothing more to it than that. But here was Marius, who loved her and wanted to marry her. And of course she loved him too. How could she ever have doubted it? She ran towards him, and it felt quite natural to go straight into his arms.

'What's this?' he asked, laughing, as she clung to him.

Stella gazed into his face.

'Let's get married soon, please. As soon as possible.'

He kissed her in reply, and she put out of her mind all memories of the other kiss, the one that had caused her so much agitation and doubt. She was going to be married. Marius loved her and they were going to be happy, she told herself.

And so, less than a week after German tanks rolled into Poland, and Britain and France declared war on Germany, Stella married Marius and went with him to Geneva.

Chapter Eleven

In the end, Mimmo wasn't called up to fight until the spring of 1940. Beatrice, who had feared he'd be drafted much earlier and sent to Albania, was secretly relieved, despite her declaration that she'd be more than happy to let him go. They were married in November 1939 and moved into their small apartment in the north-east of Florence, on the road towards Fiesole. It was a tiny place, all they could afford at the time, since Mimmo's parents had both died some years earlier, leaving nothing, but Mimmo was hopeful they'd be able to afford something better by the time their first child came along. As it happened, Beatrice got pregnant soon after the wedding, and her husband was called up to begin his military training, so the plans to move had to be put on hold. While he was away, Beatrice threw all her energies into making their home as attractive and comfortable as possible, and preparing for the new arrival. She didn't suffer at all during her pregnancy, but felt well and strong, and perfectly able to look after the apartment and keep it homely and welcoming for when her husband returned. Whenever he did visit briefly on leave, he expressed his approval.

'Your job is just as important as mine,' he told her. 'We're both fighting for Italy, but in different ways. Don't you remember what Il Duce said? The men's job is to take up arms, and the women's is to produce more patriotic Italians. Well, that's what we're doing!'

Beatrice listened to him, proud to be doing something for her country. Although she wasn't as big a supporter of Mussolini as her husband was, she was in love with Mimmo and loyal to him, and felt that his cause was her cause. Whatever happened, she would always stand by his side.

While Mimmo was away Dora came to visit regularly, full of gossip about the comings and goings at the Villa Bruni. The Countess had received a letter from Miss Stella, and had let Dora read it.

'She didn't seem to have much to say for herself,' she said. 'She talked a lot about Geneva, but you'd think she'd have said more about her husband, since she's supposed to be so in love with him.'

Beatrice was dismissive.

'What have these rich people to do with us? So Miss Stella found herself a husband willing to take her on. Good for her, I suppose, but you can be sure that whatever happens in this war *she* won't suffer – especially not in Switzerland, where there's no fighting.'

'I think you're being a little unkind. She's a nice girl. She doesn't have any airs and graces about her, at least, and she was always very polite.'

'Hmph! Perhaps,' replied Beatrice. 'But I still say she's spoilt, and can't get on without someone to look after her. Are all the English like that?'

'Now, it's not her fault if she's a little helpless. Remember she had no *mamma* to look after her and teach her things.'

'Not like me.' Beatrice smiled at her mother. 'Perhaps you're right. I expect I'd have been just as useless if I'd only had the Countess to look after me.'

'The Countess isn't exactly the maternal type,' agreed Dora.

'Exactly! She only cares for herself. I'll bet Miss Stella never saw her father either, when he was married to the Countess.'

'*Poverina*,' said Dora sentimentally. 'She was very lonely, I think. Money can't make up for the lack of a family. I hope she is happy with this Schwegler. I think he's a cold type, myself, although he's handsome enough.'

Beatrice wasn't especially interested in what the Schweglers got up to. She had better things to think about than the happiness in marriage or otherwise of two rich people. She had her own concerns, brought about by the war. Their apartment was on the ground floor, and they had the advantage of a small cellar and a little balcony on which she had a herb garden and was growing a few tomatoes. Her mother brought her what fruit and vegetables she could from the gardens of the Villa Bruni, and throughout the summer of 1940 Beatrice was kept busy making preserves in preparation for the winter – and the war against France and Britain, which had just been declared. Who knew how long the fighting would last? On the radio they talked of a quick resolution, but there was no sense in taking any chances. Plus, there would soon be another mouth to feed. But Beatrice wasn't daunted; she felt strong in Mimmo's love, and confident that she could weather whatever storms came her way.

In September Mimmo was sent to North Africa, and two weeks later Beatrice gave birth to a baby girl she called Tina. The little girl had arrived a month early, and was pale and sickly, and Beatrice worried about her and fussed over her. Dora spent as much time as she could with her daughter, and did her best to reassure her, although she, too, worried about the child.

Gradually, thanks to constant attention and care, Tina began to gain a little strength, and they started to relax slightly. She looked just like her father, Beatrice told Mimmo in her letters, and so beautiful, with her large, brown eyes and fuzzy covering of soft, dark hair. The photos she sent couldn't do the baby justice. It was such a shame the army couldn't have waited a month to send Mimmo abroad, but she would send as many pictures as she could, and regular reports of how the baby was getting on. She was careful not to mention their worries for Tina's health; there was no need for Mimmo to know anything of that – and besides, she and her mother would lavish so much attention on the baby that she would soon be as strong as any other child. Mimmo's letters in return were full of love and hopes that soon he'd be able to meet his daughter. He couldn't say much about what he was doing – or even where he was, although she understood that he was in Libya, somewhere near the Egyptian border – but he was confident that the fighting would soon be over to Italy's advantage.

Beatrice pored over his letters, and even though she herself had not told him the exact truth about the baby in her letters to him, it never occurred to her to think that he might be doing the same in his letters to her. But of course any mention of the Italian army's woeful unpreparedness and lack of equipment wasn't allowed to get through to those back home; nor was any news about the disastrous failure of Italy's attempt to invade Egypt and take it from the British. As far as Beatrice knew, the war was going well, and Italy was expected to win very soon.

One afternoon in February 1941 a telegram arrived. Beatrice had been up since very early, as she was planning a thorough clean of the apartment, so her mind was on other things when the message came. Telegrams brought nothing but bad news as a rule, but Beatrice had had a letter from Mimmo only that morning, full of cheerful stories about life in the camp, and grumbles about the food, and words of love and hope that he'd be able to get home soon and meet Tina, so she opened the envelope with no feeling of foreboding. It bore an official Italian army stamp, and said without any waste of words that it was with great regret that they must inform her that her husband, *Caporale* Domenico Fabbri, had been killed by artillery fire while defending the city of Tobruk against the British.

Beatrice's first thought was that there must be some mistake. She stared uncomprehendingly at the telegram and its bald, unemotional communication for some minutes, then frowned.

'That can't be right,' she said, at last.

She put down the telegram and, without knowing what she was doing, went into her tiny kitchen and began methodically reorganising the contents of her cupboards. When Dora arrived an hour later she found empty glass jars all over the kitchen bench, their labels picked off and put in a neat pile, and Beatrice energetically scrubbing a large pot while Tina screamed loudly in the next room.

'What are you doing?' said Dora in surprise. 'Can't you hear the little one is crying? She needs to be fed.'

She went and picked up the baby and began shushing her, then handed her to Beatrice, who took the baby mechanically, but made no move to feed her.

'What's this?' asked Dora, spotting the telegram.

'You tell me,' replied Beatrice.

Dora picked it up and read it. She put her hand to her heart and gave a heart-rending wail.

'*O Madonna*!' she cried, and began to weep. She turned to Beatrice and held out her arms. 'My poor baby! Come here.'

'Tell me what it means,' said Beatrice. She was pale, and she'd set her jaw. 'I don't understand what it means.'

Dora stared at her, shocked into calmness.

'Didn't you read it?'

'Yes, I read it, but I don't see how it can be true. Look, I had a letter from him only this morning.' She picked up a piece of paper, scrawled all over with Mimmo's distinctive handwriting, and waved it at her mother. 'See? He says he's quite well and that he's planning to go to Tripoli for a few days when he gets his leave. Of course he's not dead. There must have been some mistake.'

Dora began to weep again.

'*O cara*, there's no mistake. He's—'

She couldn't say any more, her words swallowed up by tears. She attempted to enfold her daughter and the baby in her arms, but Beatrice took a step away.

'I'll feed Tina,' she said.

She was looking about her as if she didn't know quite where she was. Then she seemed to see her mother for the first time. The tears were rolling down Dora's face, and her hands reached towards her daughter almost in supplication. Beatrice looked down at the baby, who had stopped screaming and was gazing at her mother with large, brown eyes that were so like Mimmo's. Suddenly, she knew the telegram had spoken the awful truth, and all at once there was a pain in her chest as though the ground had dropped away from her and she was falling very fast from a great height. She dropped into a chair, pale and breathless, and stared at her mother.

'What am I to do?' she whispered.

*

It seemed to Beatrice as though her heart must somehow have been encased in glass, because she never once cried over Mimmo's death. She knew logically that his loss had been a devastating blow, not only to her but to Tina, who would never now know her father, yet she felt at a distance from the whole thing, as if it were something that had happened to somebody else, somebody she could feel sympathy for in a remote sort of way. Instead of taking time to mourn, she threw herself into her housework, and dedicated all her attention to the baby, and whenever anyone tried to sympathise or offer assistance, she shook it off and rejected all attempts to help, even from her mother.

Dora, grief-stricken herself at her son-in-law's death, wrung her hands anxiously as she watched over her daughter, but Beatrice shut her out and wouldn't talk about it. Other people had lost loved ones too, she said, so why should she deserve any more sympathy than they did? There was work to be done – Tina was delicate and needed attention, and food was growing scarce now they'd started rationing everything – so this was no time for sitting about and weeping. So 1941 passed. Beatrice was thankful she'd saved up a little money before the wedding, because it meant she could buy a few essential items of food on the black market for Tina, but she worried about what would happen when the money ran out.

In October of that year Vittorio came to pay his respects. He'd been posted to Milan with the military police, the *carabinieri*, and had come to commiserate with her on Mimmo's death. Beatrice let him in reluctantly. He was dressed smartly, and wore an expression of genuine sorrow on his face, but to her mind he looked insufferably smug and well looked-after.

'I only heard two days ago,' he said, taking her hand. 'I'm sorry, Beatrice. How are you?'

She pulled her hand from his and turned away.

'Don't worry about me,' she said. 'I'm perfectly well. I see you are, too.'

She couldn't quite keep the sharp tone out of her voice, but he didn't seem to notice it. He'd spotted the baby, who was lying in her cot, asleep. Bending over the little bed, he gazed at her.

'She's beautiful,' he said at last.

'She's sick,' replied Beatrice shortly.

'I'm sorry. Can I do anything? My mother used to give me broth when I was ill.'

Beatrice impatiently straightened Tina's blanket where he'd disturbed it.

'I would give her broth, but I can't get any meat. I used up all my coupons two weeks ago and I can't get any more until next week. And black market prices are far beyond what I can afford.'

'Damn the war, eh?'

He was sympathetic, but she wasn't in the mood for it. All she could see was that Mimmo had given his life for his country, while Vittorio, who'd never wanted to fight in the first place, had got his way and found himself a comfortable job at home in Italy.

'Yes, damn the war. I see you're doing all right out of it, though,' she said, before she could stop herself.

'Is that what you think?'

'Isn't it true?'

'I didn't think so. But perhaps you're right. I suppose I am doing well compared to some.'

'Compared to all those soldiers fighting on your behalf, yes you are.'

'Do you think I'm a coward?' he said, taken aback.

'Aren't you?'

'I'm serving Italy, just like Mimmo. I know we didn't agree on politics, but we both love our country.'

'But only one of you is dead.'

'And you think it should have been me instead of him?'

She didn't answer.

'I'm sorry, Beatrice. I can't bring him back for you, but you have to believe that I would if only I could. I'm feeling bad enough because he was my friend, but it must be ten times worse for you.'

'What would you know about it?' she said bitterly. She would have gone on but just then the baby woke up and started crying. Beatrice picked her up. 'Excuse me. I need to see to Tina.'

She meant it as a dismissal and he took it as such. But two hours later he was back, bearing with him a parcel, which he held out to her.

'Meat,' he explained, when she looked at him questioningly. 'They told me it was beef, and I guess we'll just have to trust them. And some bones too, for the broth. It's all quite fresh.'

He didn't tell her the pitiful little parcel of meat had cost him all his own coupons and nearly a fifth of his weekly wage.

She hesitated. She'd called him a coward and now he was giving her gifts.

'Call it a peace offering,' he said.

*

Over the next few days Vittorio found himself turning his encounter with Beatrice over and over in his mind. He hadn't seen her since just before her wedding, when she'd come into the hotel to say goodbye to all the staff. After one look at her radiant face he'd swallowed hard and mentally given her up forever, and even now he'd gone to her apartment only in the spirit of pure friendship, to commiserate with her on the loss of Mimmo. But at the first sight of her his heart had leapt into his throat, and he'd been almost tongue-tied and unable to speak for several seconds. Then before he'd even begun to disentangle the confused thoughts that were filling his mind, she'd called him a coward, and as good as told him she wished he'd died in Mimmo's place.

Was it true? Was he a coward? He'd never made any secret of his distaste for Mussolini and his warmongering, but he'd presented himself for duty when called to do so, and was willing to do as instructed for the sake of his country – even if he did firmly believe that Italy had attached itself to the wrong side in the dispute. He was convinced that the alliance with Germany would turn out to be a mistake, but even so he had swallowed his opinions and – he hoped – shown himself to be a patriot by allowing himself to be called up to the *carabinieri*. But Beatrice thought that wasn't enough. She thought he should have joined the army and gone abroad to fight on the front lines, as Mimmo had done. Perhaps she was right. He didn't believe in Fascism – would never believe in Fascism – but still he could do more for Italy.

And so, after some little difficulty and many formalities, Vittorio Baraldi gave up his comfortable job, enlisted in the Alpini division of the Italian army, and was sent to the Russian Front. He said nothing to Beatrice, who learned of it only through one of her former colleagues at the Hotel Ambassador. She didn't suppose his decision had had anything to do with her, but her feelings became a little warmer towards him. Now Vittorio would learn what it really meant to fight, just as Mimmo had – and just as she did herself, every day, for survival.

PART 2

Chapter Twelve

It was only midday, but Ted Landry was already on his second whisky. He'd spent the morning speaking unproductively to a bland functionary of the International Red Cross Committee, after hearing that the organisation was having trouble getting parcels to prisoners of war in Italy, and had been met with a wall of polite denial from the representative, who mistrusted the press. Ted had left the Hôtel Métropole, where the organisation's records and parcels were being stored for the duration of the war, and had gone to file his unsatisfactory story at the bureau. Now he was sitting in a small café in a narrow street on the edge of the old town, not far from the Jardin Anglais. The place was panelled in dark wood, and he'd chosen a table away from the large front windows, towards the back, where the light was dimmer and he could watch the people coming in and out.

Ted preferred places buried in back streets, away from the lake front. There was something too glaring about the lake area itself, something almost too clean and wholesome, undamaged and fresh, that made him feel uncomfortable, as if by standing next to it the contrast between himself and his surroundings was too stark. From a strictly material point of view it could have been said that the war had been good to him: he was still alive, well-paid and relatively unscathed, apart from the metal pin holding his left knee together, which had given him a limp and scotched any chance of his being accepted for military service until he was fully recovered. He'd received the injury in 1940, when the Germans swept into France. He'd been attached to the British Expeditionary Force, and had insisted on reporting from the front line. All had gone well until the Germans pushed into Boulogne, and the house he was staying in had been shelled. To his fury he'd been laid up in the local hospital and missed the evacuation at Dunkirk, and, through a series of negotiations with his bureau and the local German commander, had somehow ended up in Switzerland. And now here he was, stuck in Geneva with a bad leg, feeling angry, frustrated and depressed, when he'd rather have been fighting.

He'd always considered himself far too cynical to take sides in any war, but the things he'd seen in France in 1940 had awakened in him a burning sense of the horror and injustice of it all. There had been a young mother and her two small children who hadn't managed to evacuate in time, and been cut down by a German machine gun as they ran down the street towards the quay. He'd watched it from a window, and the sense of guilt at not having been able to save them haunted him still. Even now he had dreams about it in which he ran towards them to try and pull them to safety, only to see them fall before his eyes.

And there had been other acts of violence, other needless deaths, which had made him despair of humanity. Then in late 1941 the US had been dragged into the conflict too, with the bombing of Pearl Harbor by the Japanese. The whole world was at war now, and he wanted to fight, wanted to do his bit, but he couldn't. Instead he was stuck, far away from the action, talking to complacent elderly gentlemen in smart suits who could have ended the war tomorrow if they liked, but who hedged and prevaricated, and sent thousands more young men to their deaths every day. Ted had a uniform, but it was smart and new, and made him feel a fraud. So here he was, drinking whisky at midday, because the only alternative was to rage at the skies over the awfulness of it all.

There was a girl with him, Annette, who kept him company occasionally. He knew she only went out with him because he was generous and had important connections, and he was fully aware that he was a step on the ladder to someone richer and more powerful, but she was pretty, and pretended to like him, and so he pretended to like her too, and in the meantime tried not to despise himself for his own shallowness. She was prattling to him about something, but he was only half-listening. Outside, the low winter sunshine gleamed down on the cobbles, and people scurried to and fro on their daily business, in this little Swiss oasis of calm among the warring storms outside.

He was staring absently at nothing in particular when the sunlight dimmed momentarily as a figure appeared at the plate glass door and a woman came in. She was dressed expensively in a smart blue coat with a fur collar, and an elegant matching hat. She sat down at a table near the window and ordered hot chocolate. The sunlight shone through the glass and onto her face, and Ted saw that she was younger than he'd first thought. A girl, really, rather than a woman. She took off her gloves and he saw she was wearing a wedding ring. Probably the much younger wife of some rich banker or business-man who was making a tidy profit from the war, to judge by the expensive cut of her clothes. She seemed oddly familiar, and Ted frowned, trying to place her. Had he met her at some official function recently? He ran through the possibilities in his mind, but couldn't recall. Then she turned her head slightly towards him and he got a better look at her face. Suddenly everything slotted into place with an almost audible click and he blinked.

Stella. Stella Cockburn. It must have been three years – more, even – since he'd seen her, back at the Villa Bruni in Florence, in the days when he used to visit Monica and Gerardo Carminati (what had happened to them?). It was a far-off time to him now. Things had been easier, fun. They'd all been worried about war, but the fears had cast only the dimmest of shadows over the parties, and the drinking, and the laughter, and the love affairs. An unaccustomed feeling of warmth surged through him unbidden at the memory of those times. Stella had been a sweet kid, a complete innocent when she'd arrived in Italy, as he recalled. He'd shown her the ropes and helped her settle in, which should have boosted his ego – and in a way, it had, but she'd had a way of looking at him and questioning him that had made him think that perhaps she had something to teach him too. They'd had fiery arguments over all sorts of things, and he'd infuriated her more than once by laughing at her. But they'd been friends. And they'd had a little romance of sorts, he remembered now. A sudden memory sparked in his mind, of a hot summer night in the garden of the villa, a heated row, and then a kiss. She'd been engaged to someone else, he recalled, and he'd been annoyed about it for some reason. Then the war had started and he'd been called away. It was probably for the best; he wouldn't have been good for a nice kid like her. Strange how he'd forgotten all about it until now.

He watched her for a while as she gazed out of the window. She was paler than he remembered, and the wild mane of dark, curly hair had been ruthlessly tamed into smooth, glossy rolls that peeked out from under that chic hat of hers. Her lips were painted in a neat, red bow, and her skin was smooth and clear, as far as he could tell under all the powder. Why did women wear so much make-up, he wondered. But apart from the expensive wrappings she hadn't changed much at all physically – she was still the pretty girl he'd known in Florence. She glanced up and around, and her eyes met his then slid away with no sign of recognition. He was disconcerted. Was he so unmemorable? Her head didn't turn his way again, and he wanted to go across and talk to her, but Annette was jealous and he knew she wouldn't like it. And, sure enough, she'd been quick to spot what he was doing. She demanded to know who the woman he was staring at was, and he was forced to turn his attention to her, as he knew from experience she had no qualms about making a scene over the slightest suspicion.

When he next looked up, he saw to his dismay that Stella was rising, gathering up her bag and fur-trimmed gloves and paying her bill, even though her hot chocolate had just arrived. Suddenly Ted knew he couldn't let her go just like that, but he'd have to move fast, because she'd hurried out, and the bell on the door was already tinkling as it shut behind her. He glanced at his watch and gave an exclamation.

'Hell! I forgot I'm supposed to be meeting the Austrian attaché at one o'clock,' he exclaimed. He stood up and threw some notes down onto the table. 'I'm sorry, honey. Listen, I'll see you later.'

He didn't wait for Annette's reply, although he knew he'd pay for it afterwards. He went out in a hurry and turned in the direction he'd seen Stella go. She was nowhere to be seen, but there was only one way she could have gone. At the end of the street he glanced around. To his right was a figure in blue, walking very fast away from him, and he hastened after her. The pin in his knee slowed him down, especially in cold weather, and she'd reached the lake front by the time he caught up with her.

'Stella!' he exclaimed.

She turned round, and he knew immediately that she'd recognised him in the bar. An expression of panic flashed briefly in her eyes, and she looked for a second as though she wanted to run off, then she seemed to regain her composure.

'Ted,' she said coolly.

He smiled broadly.

'I thought it was you! So you got out of Italy after all. But what are you doing here?'

'I live here.'

The sun glared off the lake, and he was forced to shade his eyes with his hand. He felt at a disadvantage, and a little taken aback at her colourless reply.

'Here in Geneva? So how come I haven't seen you around?'

'I don't know. I dare say it's because we travel about a bit on business.'

'We?'

'My husband and I.'

Of course. He'd forgotten about the ring. His eyes darted involuntarily to her gloved left hand.

'So you got married, huh? What was his name again?'

'Marius Schwegler.'

'That's right, I forgot. So you married him after all. Congratulations.'

Ted hadn't liked Schwegler much – had considered him far too smooth to be trustworthy. In Ted's opinion Marius was an opportunist, a man who would look out for himself at all costs, even at the expense of others. He was conscious of a pang of disappointment at the news. He'd thought better of Stella. He wanted to ask more, wanted to mention those days in Florence, but she was giving him no help in the conversation. She merely stood there. He didn't recognise this stiff, cold Stella, and didn't know what else to say. Then he noticed that her cool, distant manner was belied by her eyes, which were darting around anxiously. A bus was approaching along the lake front. She looked at her watch, then at the vehicle, which was just drawing up at a stop.

'I'm sorry, I have to go,' she said. 'Goodbye.'

Turning, she hurried off, and jumped on the bus just before it pulled away, leaving Ted feeling well and truly snubbed. Why had she run off like that? And why had she been so cold? That first sight of her in the café had brightened his spirits, making him hark back to a happier, sunnier time when he'd liked himself more, but her unfathomable behaviour had dampened them again. When he'd seen her an idea had half-formed in his head of spending the afternoon with her, recalling old times, but she'd seemed uninterested in him – almost hostile, in fact. If it had been anyone else he'd have let it go, but the memories of Florence were all flooding back now, and he wanted to see her again. They'd been friends – more than friends – and he wouldn't stand for being rejected.

Chapter Thirteen

Stella sat on the bus, her hands shaking and her heart beating wildly. All she'd wanted to do was to get away from Ted as fast as possible, and she had no idea where the bus was going, except that it was going the wrong way. She waited until it had turned off the lake front and gone a little distance, then alighted and took another bus back the way she'd come. Once in the centre of the city she got onto a tram which took her home to the smart district in which she lived with Marius. The apartment they lived in was grand, with high ceilings and rich furnishings – all bought with her own money – and when she got in her first thought was to find out whether her husband was in. That was the first thing she always did when she came in: find out whether Marius was home and, if he was, her second task was to assess his mood carefully and accurately, because the consequences of getting it wrong would be painful one way or the other. She did try to make him happy, but no matter whatever she did in an attempt to please him, she seemed to get it wrong far too often. That was her own fault – at least, that was what Marius said. He did love her, she told herself; he must love her, or else why was he so concerned about what she did and where she went? That was why he didn't like her to go out too much, or to have close friends. Why did she need friends when she had him, he would say.

Marius was not there, and Stella breathed a sigh of relief. She was still flustered and agitated, and she needed to calm down before he got in, or he would notice – he always noticed – and want to know the reason. She took off her hat, gazed into the mirror and touched her cheek. The powder covered up the bruise on her cheekbone nicely, and she was reassured that Ted couldn't possibly have seen it. Luckily it had only been a *little* slap, and Marius had even apologised for this one – or if he hadn't apologised, at least he'd given her an explanation of sorts. He'd had a bad day, he said – had lost out on a deal when the prospective client had cast doubt on the authenticity of the Brueghel he'd been trying to sell. The painting had come from a German collector with close links to the Reich, and if it turned out to be a fake he'd just have to swallow the loss, as it didn't do to make waves when it came to the Germans, or he could lose a lot of business. Stella had listened attentively and nodded brightly even as she clutched her cheek, then he'd smiled and told her to go and bathe it, and said she was a good girl. It was nearly better now, and hardly even hurt any more. They were due to attend an auction in one of the big hotels that evening, and she'd be on display, so with any luck no more of the same would come her way, that day at least.

She went into the bedroom and shut the door, which would allow her to prepare herself if Marius came in suddenly. Sitting down in an easy chair, she automatically glanced around the room for any mess, and tried to make sense of her confused thoughts. Of all people, why did Ted have to turn up now? As soon as she'd looked up and seen him staring at her in the café, her heart had leapt into her mouth and she'd thought of nothing but getting away from him as fast as possible.

Ted Landry. The only man she'd ever kissed apart from her husband. In the early days of her marriage she'd done her best to put him thoroughly out of her mind, out of guilt over that kiss in the garden, but once in a while he'd intruded into her thoughts and she'd wondered what he was doing now. Monica never mentioned him in her very infrequent letters, and it seemed as though he'd passed out of the Carminatis' lives. But here he was, in Geneva, out of the blue, and she'd had to flee as soon as she spotted him, because she couldn't be seen talking to him. Her husband hated it when she spoke to other men. She ought to have been flattered by that, but she knew his jealousy didn't spring from an anxiety to keep her to himself, but rather from a wish to prevent anybody else from having her.

At any rate, she hoped she'd remained calm during the encounter with Ted. She thought she had; it would have been too much on top of everything else if she'd turned into a nervous wreck in front of him. But she'd got away, that was the most important thing, and he couldn't possibly have seen which way she went, especially after she doubled back. He was working in Geneva, he'd said, and she kicked herself for not asking where, so that she might avoid that part of the city. He had a limp, she'd noticed. She hadn't even had the common decency to ask him about it. What a coward she'd turned into! She was such a fearful mouse that she couldn't even find it in her to express sympathy any more.

At four o'clock she was plumping up some cushions idly when Marius came in. She stiffened immediately, but forced herself to relax.

'Hallo, darling,' she said. 'Let me take your coat.'

He kissed her and allowed her to fuss around him.

'I think the auction will go well tonight. I suggest you wear the red dress with the diamond brooch – you know, the one in the shape of a leaf.'

'Of course,' replied Stella obediently. She'd been planning on something else but wouldn't have dreamt of arguing. She looked at the clock. 'Perhaps I'll go and have my bath now.'

He caught her wrist tightly as she went past.

'Just a moment. Not so fast. You forgot to tell me what you did today.'

She felt a stab of terror that was almost painful. Had he seen her talking to Ted? They'd been in such an exposed place that anybody might have seen them and reported back. She forced down the panic and told him she'd been walking by the lake. He smiled and relaxed his grip.

'You always take your walk along the lake front. Perhaps you ought to go somewhere else for a change.'

'Oh, but it's so beautiful down there,' she said. 'But perhaps you're right. I'll go along the river next time.'

She smiled brightly and went into the bathroom, and didn't rub her wrist until she was well out of sight.

At six o'clock the car came round, a smart, elegant Mercedes-Benz – again bought with Stella's money – and they went out into the crisp night, a few flakes of snow beginning to fall as they drove to the hotel. After the auction was over there were drinks, and many important people to speak to. Stella stayed close to Marius, and put on her usual act of nodding and smiling to all the right people. She was quite sure that everybody thought she was a complete idiot without a word to say for herself, but that was preferable to what might happen if she overreached herself and did something wrong.

Stella didn't like auctions much, because the presence of all those paintings reminded her too vividly of the unfinished business her father had left behind him. She really ought to have dealt with it by now, but the thought of discovering that he had been involved in some criminal activity had held her back. Her father had wanted her to do something. She had no idea what it was because he hadn't left her any instructions, but she knew she would never find out without first going to the address she'd found in the safe deposit box. For three years she'd told herself that she couldn't go back to Lucerne because Marius would find out and tell his sister, and her father hadn't wanted Monica to know. It was true, but she knew she was using that fact as an excuse to avoid doing it. For now the key to the box was hidden safely away, well out of the sight of her husband, who liked to search through her things every so often, looking for evidence that Stella had been disobeying him in some way. She'd occasionally been tempted to tell him about it, in the craven hope that it might stop him from laying his hands on her, but each time she'd managed to resist. It was the only currency she had, and she didn't want to waste it.

She was standing by her husband's side in among a little group of people when she happened to glance up and to her horror saw Ted, who'd smartened himself up and was talking to the auctioneer, a drink in his hand. Quickly she looked down, hoping he hadn't seen her – and, more importantly, hoping that Marius hadn't seen *him*. Her heart began to pound in her chest, and she resolved that she wouldn't stir from her husband's side all night. But it was impossible: Marius was soon drawn aside by one of his important business associates, who wanted to talk to him about a private matter, and Stella was left to stand by herself. Ted had seen her now, and she was terrified he would come up and speak to her, because she couldn't bear the thought of having him find out what a pitiful specimen she'd become. Although she was pretending she hadn't seen him, she knew he had looked over at her more than once, and would come over to her at any moment. She was feeling horribly exposed. Glancing around, she looked for even the slightest acquaintance she could go and talk to for protection, but there was nobody nearby, so in the end she made a bolt for the bathroom. She spent ten minutes in there, washing her hands over and over again until she judged it was safe, then emerged. Ted was waiting for her outside in the corridor. He stepped in front of her as she came out and she jumped.

'Stella,' he said.

'What are you doing here?'

'I looked up Marius and found out where he was likely to be this evening. I wanted to see you. Why did you run away this afternoon?'

No preliminaries, no polite niceties. Straight to the point – that was Ted all over. He couldn't even give her an easy way out by pretending he hadn't noticed, so now she had to lie to him.

'I'm sorry, but I was late for an appointment.'

'Hogwash!'

The rudeness was so like him that it took her breath away. She was looking for a suitable reply when he went on,

'I'm not stupid. You ran off like you thought I was trying to steal your purse.'

'Of course I didn't!' she said defensively. 'Why should I have done that?'

'You tell me.'

There was nothing she could say that wouldn't make her sound like a terrible coward, so she changed tack, because he was standing in front of her and there was no avoiding him any more.

'Well, I'm here now. How are you?'

'Fine, thanks. Although you might smile and sound like you were actually interested.'

He had always known how to rile her.

'Did you come here just to snipe at me?' she asked in irritation.

'No, I came to find out what's up. I wanted to say hallo, but you ran away from me twice this afternoon, and you've been trying to avoid me all evening. Not exactly friendly. I mean, we were friends once, weren't we?'

'I suppose – yes.'

'And friends talk to each other, especially when they haven't seen each other in a long time. You've done things, and I've done things, and I guess we have plenty of stories to tell each other. Look at you – you were just a kid when I left, and now you're all grown up.'

A smile curled on his lips and his eyes lingered on her. She recognised the old, practised flirtation he'd used on all the women, which had never meant anything, and turned her head away impatiently.

'Don't,' she said. He heard the weariness in her tone and was surprised.

'What's wrong?'

'Nothing.'

A painful lump had formed in her throat and she thought for a horrible minute that she was about to cry and she'd have to run away again. Just then Ted glanced at something behind her, and she turned to see Marius approaching. She straightened up and put on the mask. It was a smile she'd learned to paste on: bright, brittle, just touching the eyes briefly.

'Look who's turned up, Marius!' she said. 'You remember Ted, of course. He's working here. I hadn't the faintest idea.'

She hoped her voice held just the right amount of polite indifference. Marius greeted Ted warmly and the two men shook hands.

'Off you go and speak to the Oblingers,' said Marius to Stella. 'Mrs Oblinger wants to ask you about your dress.'

'Yes, Marius.'

Stella went off obediently. There – her husband himself had got her out of the awkward situation. If she'd spent too long with Ted, Marius would have begun to suspect that something was going on. Even though she'd never dared so much as look at another man, Marius was constantly on the lookout for signs that she might be straying.

She talked at length to the elderly Oblingers, who were among the few people Marius approved of. It was getting late and Stella knew her husband would want to go home soon. It would be a relief to escape from Ted, who seemed determined to make her feel awkward. If she could only avoid him for a few minutes more, then she ought to be safe. She glanced around. There was no sign of either Marius or Ted; presumably they were still talking in the corridor. She drifted to a corner of the room, where she felt less conspicuous and more comfortable.

'What was all that about?'

She started. Ted was standing in front of her, and now she couldn't escape.

'What?'

'You and Marius. He snapped his fingers and you almost curtseyed.'

She tried to laugh. 'Don't be ridiculous!'

'I'm not being ridiculous. I've been watching you all evening. He's done nothing but order you about like a servant.'

'That's rich!' she couldn't help exclaiming. 'You used to order me about all the time.'

'I order everyone about, but most people have the sense not to jump to attention. You never did a thing I told you, as far as I recall. But you practically grovel to Marius. He's got you trained like a circus poodle.'

Was it true? Was that what people thought when they saw her? Was that really what she'd become? The truth of it flooded in on her all at once, and for perhaps the first time she saw, in all its glaring intensity, the mess she was in and the unhappiness she'd brought upon herself. To her surprise the realisation brought with it a sudden surge of anger at Ted. How dare he turn up now, completely his old self, when her life was so very delicately balanced, to upset everything? She glared at him furiously.

'Of all the— Ted Landry, you're quite the most crass and ill-mannered man I've ever met! It's none of your business how I talk to my husband, or how he talks to me, so I'll thank you to keep your mouth shut on the subject.'

She'd expected to annoy him, but instead he laughed in genuine amusement.

'There! That's more like it. That's the old Stella I remember – not afraid to bite back. Just like old times, huh?'

She stopped short at that, as it struck her that she hadn't flared up like that in years, so complete had been Marius's defeat of her. Her fury dissipated and she stared at him desolately.

'It's not like old times at all. Don't you understand?'

'No, I don't. Why don't you tell me? Not now,' he went on, as she shook her head. 'Somewhere by ourselves. I'd like to see you, Stella.'

'I can't.'

'Why not?'

There was no sense in pretending at this point.

'Because Marius won't like it.'

'Just for coffee. He can come if he likes. Where is he? I'll speak to him.' He looked around.

'No! And please stop asking me. It's impossible.'

Her face was white and she was shrinking away from him. He looked at her thoughtfully.

'Okay,' he said slowly. 'I'll stop bothering you on one condition: that you swear to me you're happy.'

'What?'

'Are you happy?'

'Of course I—' she stopped and bit her lip.

'Say it.' He pressed on relentlessly. 'Tell me you're happy and I'll leave you alone.'

'I'm fine. There's nothing wrong with me.'

'You're lying. Now, I don't pretend to be a genius, but I can tell when someone's in trouble,' he said. 'If you ask me you could use a friend. Come and meet me. I'll wait in that same bar tomorrow at twelve and we can talk over old times.'

'I can't come tomorrow.'

'The next day, then.'

'I can't come the next day either.'

'Well, then, I'll be there every day until you show up.'

'Please.' She could see Marius moving through the crowd, seeking her out. 'I have to go.'

'I'll wait,' he said.

'You're wasting your time.'

She ducked around him. Ted made no move to stop her but watched, frowning, as she went to her husband's side and smiled nervously up at him. He kept watching as they walked towards the door together, and didn't turn his eyes away until the red dress had disappeared completely out of sight.

*

'Did you have a good evening, darling?' asked Stella as she was taking off her dress for bed. 'Mr Oblinger said the Matisse went for well above the reserve. How much were you hoping for? I can't remember.'

'If you ever bothered to pay attention when I'm talking to you then you wouldn't need to ask,' he replied coldly.

'I'm sorry, I just thought—'

'You don't think. You're ignorant and stupid. You were standing there gaping like an imbecile as usual when I was talking to Mrs Levasseur. Would it hurt you to try and show an interest in what other people are saying, once in a while?'

'I was trying, really I was. I'll pay more attention next time.'

But she knew that next time he'd criticise her for talking too much. She kicked herself for having started the conversation in the first place, but she never knew what little thing would set him off, because it could be anything or nothing. The important thing now was to remain calm and not irritate him any further.

'And you were talking to that American fool when I was speaking to a potential client and wanted you by my side,' he went on.

'Was I? I'm awfully sorry. I had no idea. I promise I'll do better in future. Here, let me take your tie.'

It was a futile gesture, because she knew the signs all too well now. It was a well-worn track. She'd apologise, smile, run around tidying up – anything to try and distract him, but it rarely worked. And it didn't this time. As she tried to take his tie he elbowed her roughly away from him, a sharp blow to the breastbone that took her by surprise and knocked her against a little table. She grabbed at it to keep from falling, but instead caught hold of the crocheted cloth that covered it, pulling it to the floor as she landed heavily, together with some books and a framed photograph, which smashed. That made him snap. He hauled her up from the floor by her hair and slammed her against the wall, and she gasped in pain.

'Now look what you've done. Can't you do anything right?'

'I'm sorry, I'm sorry,' she heard herself repeating over and over again. She ought to have learned. The more she apologised the more angry it made him, but she had never yet found a way of making him stop once he started. His hand was still clutched in her hair, and he banged her head once or twice against the wall, not enough to knock her out, but hard enough to make her see stars. She screwed her eyes tightly shut.

'Open your eyes when I'm talking to you.'

Her head hit the solid plaster again, and she forced her eyes open. His face swam before her blurred vision, implacable, remorseless. He held onto her hair, gripping tightly, until he was sure her attention was fixed on him, then let her go suddenly. She slid to the floor, her breath ragged and laboured.

'Clear that mess up,' he said, and left the room.

Chapter Fourteen

Stella turned up at the café on Monday just after twelve. Ted, sitting again at the table near the back, saw her approach uncertainly and hover by the door. A snowstorm had got up over the lake that morning and was blowing in towards the town, and he watched as she glanced behind her then down at the snowflakes that were attaching themselves to her coat, took a deep breath and came in. He raised a hand and she gave him half a smile.

'I didn't think you'd be here,' she said.

'I came Friday, Saturday and Sunday, just like I promised.'

'There was no need.'

She sat down. The waiter came up and they both ordered coffee.

'Do you come here all the time?' she said as she looked about her.

'Sometimes.'

'How long have you been in Geneva?'

'I got here in early '41, after my knee got crushed. I couldn't get the treatment I needed in France, so my bureau sent me here.'

'Your bureau? You're a news reporter now? Aren't you with the magazine any more?'

'No. Harry fired me once and for all after I told him— well, never mind what I told him. It wasn't polite.'

That made her laugh, and she began to look a little more like her old self. 'What about your knee? How did it happen? Will it mend?'

He told her about the shelling of the house in Boulogne, but didn't mention the woman and children who'd been mown down by a German machine gun. He preferred to keep that well buried.

'And now you're here,' she said. 'Do you like it?'

'It's okay, I guess. Do you?'

'It's okay, I guess.'

They both smiled.

'And you're married to Marius.'

'I am. What about you? I thought I saw a girl with you the other day.'

'Annette? She's a friend of mine.'

'One of your friends.'

'It's not like that.'

'You don't need to tell me.'

But he did want to tell her. He talked a little of Annette, and of his job, and how he'd ended up in Geneva when he'd rather have been fighting, or at least reporting from the front line. The doctors had shaken their heads at his knee and told him it would have mended more quickly if he'd come to see them sooner. As it was they thought he'd be fighting fit in a few months as long as he did the exercises, which he kept forgetting. Then he found himself telling her of his frustration at the fact that other people were doing something useful when he could only sit and watch.

'But you are doing something useful,' she said. 'People back home need to know what's going on, and you can tell them. You can influence people.'

'Me? I can't influence anybody.'

'Oh, but you can. You were always a marvellous writer – terribly persuasive. Besides, you've done a lot more than I have. I've just been here, doing nothing. I wanted to help with the refugees, but…'

'Marius wouldn't let you.'

She didn't reply, but her look was enough to confirm it.

'He seems to be doing well for himself,' observed Ted.

'He is. The art market is flourishing just now. There are a lot of very valuable paintings coming out of Germany and Austria and

Italy, and other places, and Marius is buying them up and selling them at a profit.'

'I'll bet he is,' Ted said dryly. 'At least someone's doing well out of the war.'

'What do you mean?'

'Nothing. Forget I spoke.'

She didn't pursue it and turned the subject to the wider situation. The grim news had emerged from Poland that thousands of Jews had been rounded up and sent to camps, while fighting was still fierce on all fronts, and there didn't seem much hope that the war would end any time soon, even as Churchill and Roosevelt posed for photos in Casablanca and talked of demanding unconditional surrender.

The coffee arrived and they drank it in silence. Stella was watching some people at the table opposite, and Ted watched her in turn. He thought she'd lost weight since he last saw her; her face was thinner, which made the blue-green eyes with their thick fringe of lashes look larger. She was still wearing too much make-up, he noticed. The people at the next table got up to leave and she turned her head slightly to follow them as they went out. As she did so the collar of her dress shifted and revealed a dark smudge of something on her pale skin.

'What's that?' he asked.

She saw what he was looking at, sat up and straightened her collar hurriedly.

'Nothing.'

He reached over and pulled the collar aside gently. She froze, and a silence hung between them as he stared at what he saw. Then he raised his eyes to hers.

'Dear God,' he said quietly at last. 'That explains everything. Is that what he's doing to you?'

She drew in a breath. 'No – no, of course not! It was an accident, I didn't mean—' But he was still staring. She tried again, 'Listen,

Ted, I don't know what sort of awful idea you've got into your head, but you can forget it this minute. I was wandering around in my usual daydream a couple of days ago, had an unexpected encounter with a heavy door, and came off worst. That's all.'

She was doing her best to adopt a tone of humorous exasperation, but he wasn't fooled. He tore his eyes away from her collar, which she was holding together tightly, hiding the dark bruise, and glared at her, his anger glowing hot.

'He needs a taste of his own medicine,' he said grimly.

She went pale and quailed visibly.

'No! Don't!' she exclaimed. 'I'm fine, really I am. I promise you it was an accident!'

He didn't believe a word of it.

'Stella, what the hell has happened to you? Look at you, you're white and shaking like a leaf even at the thought of me talking to Marius about it.'

But even as he said it he saw that she'd steeled herself against him and had no intention of admitting anything.

'Don't be ridiculous,' she said icily. 'Your trouble is you've been a journalist so long you automatically look for the most sensational interpretation of anything you see. Well you needn't bother – I'm perfectly well and I can assure you that whatever idiotic suspicion is swirling around that head of yours is completely wrong. Besides, it's none of your business.'

The last part of the remark didn't exactly inspire confidence, but he didn't press the issue because her eyes belied her words: they were darting from side to side again, and he could see she was poised to flee. If she went now it was obvious she'd make sure they never ran across each other again, and suddenly he knew he didn't want to lose her. Just this last half-hour with her had raised his spirits, making him feel better than he had in a long time. All right, then: if she wanted to shut him out of her private affairs that was her decision, but if he could convince her to accept him as a friend, then at least he could keep an eye on her and help her if he could. The indignation welled up inside him again at the thought of what Marius might be doing to her, and he clenched his fists under the table but forced down the words that he knew would drive her away.

They finished their coffee without speaking, but before he could suggest staying for lunch she was already looking at her watch.

'I have to go,' she said.

'When can we meet again?'

'Listen, I think it's best if we don't. You see—'

'I know. Marius wouldn't like it. But then why tell him? It's not like I'm asking you to run off with me, just come for coffee once in a while.' She was already beginning to shake her head, and he went on: 'Doesn't he ever go away?'

'Sometimes,' she replied reluctantly.

'Does he take you with him?'

'Not always.'

Ted took out his notebook, scribbled something down then tore it out and handed it to her.

'This is my number. Call me when he goes away.'

'I don't think—'

'Just if you'd like to. You don't have to promise.'

She hesitated, then took the scrap of paper and tucked it in her pocket. Pulling on her gloves she rose to go.

'Please call,' he said.

She looked at him uncertainly and gave him another half-smile, before leaving the café. He watched her go, then sat, brooding over what he'd found out and wishing there were something he could do. The expression on her face when she realised he'd discovered her secret had torn at his heart – a heart he'd almost forgotten he had – and woken something up within him. He didn't know what it was; perhaps it was protectiveness, or perhaps it was something else. All he knew was that he couldn't stand the thought of not seeing her again.

*

Stella held out for a fortnight, then one day Marius departed for Zürich, where he intended to stay overnight. It had been a tense two weeks; he'd been irritable and snappy, and she'd had to work hard not to set off the fuse. When he finally went off she did her best to ignore her disloyal sense of relief, and thought of nothing more than going out for a walk, which she hadn't been able to do lately as the weather had been unpleasant.

She looked out of the window at the street below. The snow lay on the pavement, grey and trampled, with an untouched border of white along the edges of the buildings, and the road was glistening black, scored with pulpy grey ridges of sodden snow where the cars had passed. She needed some fresh air, but it was a wet, grey uninviting day, and her mind darted unbidden to the warmth of the little café near the Jardin des Anglais. She wondered how Ted was getting on. She'd tried not to think about him for the past two weeks, but that stolen half-hour with him had raised her spirits and buoyed her up for several days afterwards. He hadn't changed in the intervening years – although perhaps he'd mellowed a little. He thought she could use a friend, he'd said, and she couldn't deny it. Marius would forbid it if he knew, but there was nothing between her and Ted – nothing her husband need worry about, anyway – so would it be so very bad if she called him and asked how he was? Drifting over to the telephone, she picked up the receiver, her hand hovering indecisively over the dial. Should she do it?

He answered at the first ring with a snappy 'Landry.' Stella jumped and almost put the phone down.

'Ted?' she managed at last.

'Stella.' His voice softened immediately. 'Just a second.' There was a muffled sound of voices as if he'd just put his hand over the receiver to talk to someone, then his voice returned loud and clear. 'How are you?'

'Very well, thank you.'

There was a pause. Now that she'd called she didn't know what to say, but he came to her rescue.

'Listen, I was just about to leave the office and have some lunch. I don't suppose you're free now?'

'Well – I could, I suppose. Yes.'

'Same place?'

'All right.'

'Great! See you in half an hour.'

She put the phone down. It hadn't been as difficult as she expected, and she felt a little thrill at her own daring. He was already sitting at his usual table when she arrived, and she smiled as she saw the familiar wave of the hand.

'So you decided to call at last,' he said, once they'd spoken to the waiter. 'I guess His Majesty's not at home.'

She knew better than to rise to the bait. Now that she was here she wasn't nervous at all. Perhaps she was less of a coward than she thought.

'No, he's not.'

'Well, it's about time.'

'What would you have done if I hadn't called?' she asked curiously.

'I don't know. I guess I'd have come and fetched you sooner or later.'

'But you don't know where I live.' She saw his look. 'Or do you?'

'I'm a reporter. Curiosity is part of the job description. I can't help finding things out.'

She shook her head.

'You haven't changed.'

'If you say so. What about you?'

She was taken aback by the question. She'd got through the past three years by not allowing herself to be too introspective.

'I don't know. What do you think?'

He gazed at her thoughtfully.

'I can't tell,' he replied. 'You've hidden it all away so I can't see it any more.'

*

And so it began. At first she only called him when Marius was away for a few days, but gradually she became bolder and they began to meet even when her husband was still in Geneva. Sometimes they met in the café, and sometimes in other places, but they always took care to avoid the northern part of the city, where Marius's art gallery and offices were located, so as to be sure not to bump into him. They'd meet for lunch, or just a coffee, and Stella would ask about Ted's work, which she found endlessly fascinating, and he'd tell her stories that made her laugh about some of the characters he'd met. She wanted to know how he'd got into journalism, and how he'd ended up in Europe, and he told her a little of his childhood, growing up in a small town about a hundred miles from St. Louis. His father, a well-off attorney, had wanted Ted to follow him into the law, but Ted had always longed for adventure and had resisted. After a short stint working as a junior reporter on a local newspaper, he'd taken off for New York and, despite his relative lack of experience, had managed to talk an important magazine into hiring him, first as a staff writer and later as a foreign correspondent. The magazine had sent him to Europe, where he'd moved from one capital city to another, uncovering important stories and developing a reputation as a talented writer. Stella listened, rapt, wishing she'd lived a more exciting life and had her own stories to tell him – although he seemed to find her company interesting enough even without them. They'd fallen into an unspoken agreement not to mention Marius any more than was necessary, but she couldn't help asking him about Annette, the girl she'd seen him with that first day. He shrugged.

'She found herself a rich banker.'

'I'm sorry.'

'No need.' He looked straight into her eyes as he said it, and she glanced away, suddenly shy. He didn't seem at all upset by his loss. Neither was Stella, although she didn't ask herself why.

Perhaps neither of them – one jaded and weary, the other lonely and neglected – were fully aware of what was happening, or understood why they were drawn to each other so irresistibly. But each looked forward to their meetings, which quickly increased in frequency to several times a week. Ted, who'd never been accustomed to examining his feelings for the various women who'd passed through his life, only knew that Stella was different, somehow. She made him feel rejuvenated, and as if he had a purpose for the first time in years. He wanted to protect her against her husband, and was determined he'd look out for her for as long as he could persuade her not to push him away. Stella, meanwhile, was emerging more and more from her shell and rediscovering her old self. Grateful for what she resolutely defined as no more than a friendship, she ignored the disturbance Ted's presence created in her, ascribing it to natural nervousness at what would happen if Marius found out about her disobedience. The consequences of anything more than that were too great to contemplate, and she wasn't ready to face the truth yet.

In late February Marius told Stella he had to go to Berlin on business. He'd been invited to the Schönhausen Palace, where works of art were stored and exhibited. Many of them were by artists proscribed by the Nazis, and available for sale. Stella told Ted about it when they next met, and his lip curled cynically.

'Your husband certainly knows how to make friends in high places,' he said.

'What do you mean?'

He was about to answer but looked at her and seemed to think better of it.

'Never mind.'

But it was obvious what he was thinking.

'You think Marius is a profiteer,' she said. 'That's what you meant, isn't it?'

'Well, isn't he?' She threw him an uncertain look, and he went on, 'Where do you think those artworks come from? At that auction the other night, the auctioneer said several of the paintings came from a dealership in Berlin. I looked at the catalogue and there were no other details given of who owned them before.'

'So?'

'If you want my guess, I'd say they were bought at a stupidly low price or even seized outright from their owners.'

Stella knew he was right. She'd thought about it herself many times but had tried to put the knowledge away from her.

'Is it so very bad?' she said. 'It's just business, isn't it? I mean, it's in a dealer's interest to get them at as low a price as possible.'

It sounded as though she were making excuses for Marius, but in fact she was thinking of her father, who had purchased art quite openly from the Germans before the war – unwanted paintings that had been taken from museums. They'd have been destroyed if he hadn't bought them and saved them. Wasn't that something?

'Well, that's between him and his conscience, I guess,' answered Ted. 'But let's not look too closely at what happened to the legal owners, right? Because we wouldn't want to make anyone feel uncomfortable.'

Stella didn't want to be made to feel uncomfortable, but Ted's straightforwardness and honesty made her feel ashamed of herself. She knew her father hadn't obtained art only from museums. She'd tried to avoid the question for a long time now, but suddenly she had to know. There was no putting it off any longer.

'Ted,' she said slowly. 'Do you remember in Florence, you were trying to find out something about my father's business dealings for a story? Will you tell me what it was?'

He gave her a wary look.

'I don't think—' he began.

'Please. I'd like to know.'

He was reluctant, but she insisted, and at last he gave in.

'All right, but remember I don't know the whole story, so it may not be what it seems. It started in Berlin before the war, when I was there writing a piece about the Nazis' peculiar attitude to art. Hitler had been storming around shouting about how you can't paint two blue squares and a green circle and call it a cow, and how Germany needed to get back to the traditional style because all this modern stuff was corrupting the nation.

'While I was looking into it I met a little Jewish art dealer called Jacob Silberstein, who didn't like the modern stuff either. He specialised in Renaissance art, and was doing pretty well with it – had a sharp eye for a good deal – until all the anti-Jewish laws came in and made it almost impossible for him to run his business. You'd think his friends in the art world would have rallied round him, but most of them turned their backs on him, and some of them even took advantage of the situation to try and pressure him into selling them his stock at a low price, but he always refused. I guess he never thought things would get as bad as they did.'

Ted stopped and looked at her in concern. 'Are you all right? Are you sure you want to hear the rest?'

Stella discovered she was hunched over, her arms crossed tightly across her stomach. She uncrossed them and took a deep breath.

'Yes,' she replied firmly.

He threw her a doubtful glance but continued.

'In February 1937 Silberstein was murdered, and all the paintings were stolen from his gallery. Whoever killed him almost certainly did it with the approval of the authorities, because the whole thing wasn't so much hushed up as completely ignored. Who cares about some small-time Jewish art dealer when they're trying to kick all the Jews out of the country anyway?

'I'd liked the guy and thought it was too bad what had happened to him, so I did a little digging, but his family had disappeared – I guess they were either taken away or escaped of their own accord – and nobody was talking. Besides, the Germans had been cracking down on free expression and didn't want foreign journalists snooping around any more, so I had to give up. Soon after that I got kicked out of the country and went to Italy.

'In Rome I palled up with Gerardo, and he invited me to the Villa Bruni. That's when I saw the painting. It was a picture of Venice, by Bellotto, in the gallery. Maybe you remember it.'

He paused again.

'The last time I'd seen that painting was at Silberstein's gallery, a few days before he died.'

'Oh,' said Stella. She looked down at her hands.

'Yeah. Some coincidence, huh? I knew Silberstein couldn't possibly have sold it in the time, so naturally I wondered how Gerardo had gotten hold of it.'

Stella swallowed, knowing what was coming. Ted seemed reluctant to continue.

'It turns out he bought it from your father,' he said finally.

'Go on,' said Stella.

'There's not much left to tell. I knew from Monica that Raymond had been in Berlin around the time Silberstein was murdered, and that set me wondering. But Monica wouldn't tell me anything about it, and I'm not even certain she knows anything, so I let the story drop. And that's all.'

So this was the truth Stella had been trying to avoid facing for so long. She hadn't known the full story, but she couldn't say it had come as a surprise to her. As soon as Franz had told her of the murdered Jew she'd known her father had been mixed up in something violent. And now she knew what it was.

'Monica does know something,' she said at last.

'What do you mean?'

There was no sense in holding back now, so she told him the whole story: Monica's search for the missing paintings, the trip to Lucerne, the key to the safe deposit box and what Stella had found inside it. Ted listened intently.

'You think the other paintings are at the address you found in the box?' he asked.

'I assume so. But my father didn't want Monica to know about them, I don't know why.'

'If they were stolen, then maybe he didn't want anyone to know about them. Maybe he planned to sell them secretly.'

'In that case why did he leave them to me?'

'I don't know.'

They fell silent again, then Stella said quietly, 'You think my father had a hand in Silberstein's death, don't you?'

'No, of course not!'

'There's no need to pretend. Do you think I haven't been wondering the same thing for years now?'

It came out more bitterly than she'd intended.

He sighed.

'Okay, I admit, maybe I did. But I never met Raymond, and you know me – I automatically assume the worst of people. He was your father, though. Does it seem likely to you, from what you know of him, that he did it?'

She didn't know what to answer. At one time she'd have been horrified at the very idea and denied it absolutely. But after what she'd found out, she didn't know what to think any more.

'I take it you didn't check out the address in the box,' went on Ted. 'Can you remember where it was?' She shook her head. 'And you say this guy Franz said your father was going to give you instructions. Maybe they're at this place. Or maybe you'll find something there that will clear all this up and prove him innocent.'

'Do you think so?' she said, suddenly hopeful.

He grimaced.

'Well, I can't say it looks like it, but wouldn't you rather know one way or the other?'

She looked down again. Could she face a harsh truth?

'Yes, I suppose I would.'

'Then let's go and see. We'll go to Lucerne, get the key and find out what's hiding at this address once and for all.'

'Go to Lucerne? With you? Oh, but I couldn't. Marius—'

'Marius is going away for five days, you said. That's plenty of time to do it.' Ted saw the fear in her face. 'Look – would he be any more angry at you for coming to Lucerne with me than he would be at you meeting me for coffee?'

'No,' she admitted.

'Then what's the problem? We could make a trip of it, stay out overnight. You look as if you could use some fresh air, and I know I could. We'll go to Lucerne and stay at one of those little chalet hotels on the way back – don't worry,' he said, holding up his hand before she could speak. 'It's all above board. We'll get two rooms – two each if you like – and we'll go out and walk in the snow and forget everything.'

He was right: there was no reason they couldn't go – none that related to Marius anyway. But there were plenty of other reasons to resist. Stella had been holding onto a memory of her father all this time that deep down she'd known to be false. She'd wanted to think she was important to him, but the fact was he'd been a hard-nosed businessman who'd preferred his new wife over her. That much she knew for certain about him; everything else had been merely suspicions that she'd tried to ignore in order to make the known truth more palatable. But marriage to Marius had introduced her to a cold, hard reality. If this was to be her life, she might as well get it all out into the open and learn how to deal with it.

'Very well, then, we'll go,' she said.

Chapter Fifteen

The address on the key turned out to be a tobacco warehouse in a small town a short distance from Lucerne. The man on the desk seemed inclined to refuse them entry even when Stella mentioned her father's name and showed him the key, but a bribe from Ted did the trick, and he suddenly became very cooperative. He led them along a passage to a room at the back of the building, then went off.

'Well, here goes,' said Ted. He fitted the key to the lock and opened the door. Inside was a large, bare room with a high ceiling and windows that had been blacked out. The floor was bare board, but pallets had been laid out, and on them were perhaps eighty or a hundred paintings, stacked leaning against the wall and each other as if put there in a hurry. Sacks had been thrown over some of them for protection.

Ted walked across and flipped up one of the sacks to reveal a landscape painting in a gilt frame. He tipped it forward and peered at the picture behind it.

'I remember this one,' he said after a minute. He lifted the landscape painting gently out of the way to show Stella a picture of the Virgin Mary at prayer, her eyes lifted piously to heaven, the drapery of her blue robe delineated in precise brushstrokes. 'Silberstein showed it to me specially. It was one of his favourites.'

He went from one stack to another, examining the artworks.

'Well, I guess we've found the paintings,' he commented at last. 'Your father mustn't have had much time, or he'd have stored them properly.' He glanced up. 'What's that you've got there?'

Stella had picked up something that had been resting on top of one of the paintings, and was staring at it. He came across to look at it. It was a dog-eared gallery brochure bearing the name 'J. Silberstein'. Ted glanced at Stella and took it, flicking through it.

'Seems like he didn't have time to make a proper inventory either.' He dug in his pocket, brought out the stained paper that had been in the safe deposit box and squinted at it. 'Difficult to make out, but I can see a couple at least that might match the names in the brochure. There's one here by Van den Broeck. I can't read the title. Is that German?'

Stella was suddenly sick at heart and wanted nothing more than to leave.

'Does it matter?' She turned away. 'We've found out what we wanted to know. There's nothing here for me, no instructions or anything, and I've no idea what I'm supposed to do with all these paintings. Let's just leave them here and go. I don't want to think about it any more.'

*

They returned the keys and the paper to the bank, then set off on the return journey. Their route back took them through Interlaken, then continued for some distance along the lake before the road turned west, winding through the valley, with mountains rising to either side of them, their graceful peaks draped with the winter's snow. Stella sat in silence for most of the way, wrapped in her own dark thoughts, despite Ted's attempts to cheer her up by pointing out the scenery along the way. Eventually he gave up and concentrated on looking for the hotel. It was a largish one – one of the few that hadn't closed because of the war. In earlier years it would have been busy with foreign tourists, in Switzerland for the winter sports, but today it had only a handful of Swiss guests. They had no problem in securing rooms, and were informed that dinner would be served shortly.

The restaurant was warm and pleasantly informal, with pine-clad walls and checked tablecloths, and was busier than they'd expected. The food was simple but flavourful, despite the shortages, but Stella wasn't hungry and merely toyed with her food.

'Why, if it isn't Stella Cockburn!' said a female voice. Stella jumped and turned to see a woman standing by their table. She was young and well-dressed, with a capable, matronly air about her.

'Enid!' stammered Stella.

'I thought it was you!' said the woman. 'I had no idea you lived in Switzerland. How long have you been here?'

Stella pasted on a smile and did her best to pull herself together.

'A few years now – since I got married.'

'Oh?' Enid looked up and her eyes took in Ted. 'Well, aren't you going to introduce me to your husband?'

Stella's jaw dropped as she suddenly realised the mistake she'd made. Enid thought she and Ted were married. She felt the colour flooding across her face, and was about to put Enid right, but Ted was already standing up.

'Ted Landry, ma'am. Pleased to meet you.'

'Enid Descoteaux. Stella and I were at school together, but I expect she's told you all about that.'

Stella sat in an appalled silence as Enid chattered away and Ted was blandly polite. At last the woman moved off and left the restaurant, and Ted sat down again.

'Why did you let her think we were married?' demanded Stella indignantly.

'Because, bonehead, I saw you were about to spill the beans and tell her we weren't, and how would that have looked?' He began to laugh. 'You should have seen yourself when she turned up. I thought you were going to make a bolt for it.'

It had been a long, dispiriting day, and this on top of everything else was too much. Stella was suddenly incensed with him.

'Why is everything a joke to you?' she snapped.

He looked at her in surprise.

'Hey, what's the problem?'

'Oh, never mind.' She stood up abruptly, left the restaurant and went up to her room. Her emotions were in turmoil; a storm cloud of anger and unhappiness and confusion was roiling ceaselessly through her head, and she wished she'd never come here. The whole thing had been a huge mistake. She'd hoped the trip might go some way towards relieving her mind, but instead the confirmation of what she'd always dreaded had only caused the unwelcome thoughts to clamour more insistently, demanding to be let in. The last thing she needed right now was to be stuck in a hotel with Ted, who only added to the disturbance in her mind.

She'd known he wouldn't let her alone, though. She'd barely arrived in her room when there was a hammering at the door. She let him in, and he stood uncomfortably just inside.

'Look, I'm sorry about the paintings, if that's what that was all about,' he said.

The muddled thought-clouds suddenly whisked together, coalescing into a bolt of anger. She was furious with her father for having abandoned her and left her his mess to deal with, and she was furious with Marius for making a coward of her. But they weren't here; there was only Ted, so she focused her anger on him.

'Sorry?' she said bitterly. 'Are you sure? Because there's a nice little story in it for you, isn't there?'

'What do you mean?'

'Isn't that why you came along? To solve the mystery of what my father got up to before the war? Well, now you know. He cheated and stole and collaborated with the Nazis and possibly killed someone, all for the sake of his stupid business. That'll look nice under your byline, won't it? I expect it'll get you lots of new commissions.'

'Is that what you think? That I came with you just to get a story?'

'Isn't it?'

'No! I came to help you.'

'I don't believe that for a minute. But don't let me stop you. My father's dead so you can say whatever you like about him. It can't hurt him now.'

'I'm not going to write about him. Do you really think I'd do that to you?'

'Why not? Why should you care?'

'Because I'm in love with you, why do you think?' he snapped.

The words knocked her sideways, and she gaped at him, unable to reply.

'Goddammit!' he said, then turned on his heels and left the room, slamming the door behind him.

She stood, breathless, for several minutes, her head buzzing. She'd never expected anything like this. The anger in her mind swirled and danced and receded, changing form almost imperceptibly into something new she couldn't have put a name to. Before she knew what she was doing she left her room, knocked on his door and went in.

He'd thrown himself on the bed, but he swung his legs off the edge and stood up when she entered. They regarded each other warily, a residual charge crackling in the air between them. When she spoke it was a kind of appeal.

'Why do you always have to barge in and upset everything?' She gestured helplessly. 'You did it before and you're doing it again now.'

'What do you mean? When did I do it before?'

'In Florence. You kissed me, and turned me inside out, and made me doubt whether I was in love with the man I'd just agreed to marry.'

He digested her words in silence.

'I'm sorry,' he said eventually.

She came closer and looked searchingly into his face.

'Did you mean what you said just now?' she asked.

'Did I mean it?' His eyes, dark and liquid in the lamplight, held her gaze steadily. 'Stella, I wanted you the minute I saw you that

day in the café, and it's been driving me crazy ever since. I want
you so badly it hurts. So yes, I guess I meant it.'

She drew in a breath.

'I'm sorry, I didn't mean to ruin everything,' he said. 'You've
got enough on your plate without that.'

Despite his words he hadn't taken his eyes off her, and now, all
at once, she knew it: knew the real reason for the tumult he caused
in her mind, the real reason she'd kept on seeing him, despite her
fear of Marius. She hadn't been angry at Ted at all, she realised
now – only at herself, and at what she'd become. Today she'd
risked everything in letting him bring her to this hotel because
she'd been impelled by some irresistible force to do it whatever
the consequences might be. That night in the garden at the Villa
Bruni they'd started something, and she'd buried it deep inside her
for more than three years. But it wouldn't be suppressed any more,
and now, as they stared at one another, it hovered tantalisingly
between them, daring them to finish what had been left unfinished.

She was almost certain she'd been the one to reach out first,
but it was his hands she felt on either side of her face, tipping her
chin up to meet him. The kiss started gently, almost hesitantly,
but rapidly deepened; it set her head spinning and sent the heat
rippling through her veins. Any minute now she'd be lost, but
she couldn't seem to draw back. Then it was too late, and she was
clinging to him, and he was gripping her tightly, kissing her more
fiercely now, running his hands down her body, burying his face in
the curve of her neck, his lips blazing hot against her skin. What
little remained of her good sense was warning her that this was
wrong, a mistake, but she ignored it, because right now it didn't *feel*
like a mistake – the impulse of the moment had overpowered her
and she couldn't help herself. The fire was coursing through every
inch of her, and she melted against him, begging him silently to
help her forget the fear and the hurt and all that had gone wrong

with her life, if only for a little while. In response he swept her up with one swift movement and carried her across to the bed, and they fumbled breathlessly with the fastenings of each other's clothes, and then they were lying, warm skin to warm skin, and his lips and his hands were on her; demanding, urgent, making her tremble, and she was returning his kisses feverishly, tangling her fingers in his hair, pulling him closer to her, wanting all of him. He was murmuring words she couldn't make out, wanting her too. All her senses were singing, and she wrapped herself around him, allowing herself to be carried away by the moment, letting the flood of pleasure sweep all the misery away.

Afterwards she lay against him, feeling the beat of his heart, slower now, beneath the hard muscles of his chest. There was no sound except an occasional muffled clanking from the hot water pipes, the creak of a floorboard somewhere, and the whisper of their own breathing. He ran his hand lightly over her arm. There were bruises on it. She'd done her best to cover them with a shawl in the restaurant, but here, where there was no disguise, the ugly blue and purple marks stood out starkly against her white skin.

'Why do you stay with him?' he asked.

'I don't have any choice, Ted.'

'Can't you get away?'

'I couldn't do that – he'd be terribly hurt.'

'Hurt that he's got no one to use as a punching bag, you mean. Damn it, Stella, you have to leave him.'

'Where would I go?'

'You have money, don't you?'

'I did, but not any more. I signed it over to Marius. He told me that was what women did in Switzerland, and I was dazzled enough by him to believe him. Tell me I'm stupid if you like – I know it well enough.'

'Don't you have friends who could help you?' he asked.

'None here in Switzerland. And besides, even if I did leave him, I'm—'

'You're what?'

'I'm frightened of what he'd do if he found me.'

He said nothing, but the expression in his eyes was soft as he bent to kiss her.

Chapter Sixteen

They left after breakfast the next morning, intending to be back in Geneva by lunchtime, but it was such a nice day they dawdled, stopping several times. By the time they entered the city a cloud of grey fog and wet sleet had blanketed the lake, making the dusk darker and dampening their welcome. The apartment was cold and empty and tidy, just as Stella had left it. She unpacked her few things and put them away, then sat looking about her.

The trip to Lucerne had forced her to do some hard thinking about her father, and to confess the truth to herself. He'd always been a disappointment and it was time she admitted it. He hadn't been the busy but honest man she'd always believed him to be, and her longing for his love had almost certainly had something to do with her marriage to Marius, as Ted had once so astutely pointed out. She couldn't blame her father for that, though; after all, it had been her own decision to marry Marius. She'd made her own bed and now she was having to lie in it.

The additional burden of knowledge she'd received the day before ought to have made her despondent, but she was still tingling all over from the effects of Ted, who seemed to have spilt pure liquid happiness into her. He loved her, and he'd promised to protect the memory of her father – inasmuch as her father deserved it. Besides, the time for writing about such things was past. Before the war the world might have been interested in hearing about the personal tragedy of an honest art dealer who was murdered for his life's work, but, now, amid wider horrors, such things were forgotten, most likely to be left buried forever. There was the ever-present fear that the Germans would invade Switzerland, and if they did then there was a good chance the paintings would be found and stolen again. If they didn't, perhaps one day she would feel strong enough to go back to that warehouse and deal with the matter herself. For now the only thing to do was to put the matter out of her head, as she'd done so many times in the past.

She sat, gazing out into the dark street, until the sound of the telephone roused her from her daydream. It was Marius.

'Where have you been?' he said as soon as she answered. 'I've been trying to call you.'

She'd almost been able to forget about him for the past few days, but now the dread and tension returned all at once, as the remains of Ted's warmth slid away, to be replaced by a cold prickle of fear. Marius had said he wouldn't ring until this evening; she'd thought she was safe, so why had he called earlier than expected?

'When did you ring?' she asked, trying to sound casual, as if it didn't matter in the least. 'I've been out most of the day.'

'I rang yesterday, four times. And last night, several times. And then this morning, and this afternoon. You must have been out a long time. Or perhaps you preferred not to answer.'

The last sentence ended on the slightest note of a question. She heard the menace and shivered.

'Of course I would have answered if I'd heard it, but the phone didn't ring at all. Now I remember – the caretaker downstairs muttered something about there being problems with the line again. Yes, of course, that's it! I tried phoning the butcher yesterday morning just after you went and couldn't get through. I thought the problem must be at his end of the line but obviously it must have been at ours. I promise you it didn't ring, Marius.'

She could hear herself beginning to babble, and had to force herself to stop talking. Marius was impatient.

'Yes, yes, always problems on the line. I'll call again tomorrow before dinner. Make sure you're at home.'

'Yes, Marius.'

Stella put the phone down. Her hands were clammy and she was out of breath. She'd arranged to meet Ted the following day, so she would have to make sure she was back before Marius called again.

The next day they met again at the little café near the Jardin des Anglais for lunch, then Ted carried her off to his apartment nearby, and there they spent the afternoon, wrapped up in their own cocoon. She was home by five o'clock as she'd promised, in time to receive the expected telephone call, and she spoke to her husband, trying to keep out of her voice the happiness that was flowing through her like a sunlit river, giving her life and hope.

*

So the affair progressed. Ted and Stella soon fell back to their old ways: he couldn't be serious for long, and he soon returned to his old habit of teasing and goading her. Stella gave as good as she got, and sometimes it would build up to a flaming row, but they could never stay angry with each other, and it would always end up with kisses and laughter, and falling into bed – which, for Stella, was proving to be a glorious revelation by comparison with the perfunctory attention she'd always received from Marius. At times playful and light-hearted, at others passionate and tender, Ted taught her the simple pleasure of making love, and she quickly discovered an eager response in herself that astonished and delighted her. They'd spend all too short afternoons together, then she'd go home, and sometimes Marius would beat her because she'd said the wrong thing, or because she'd forgotten to do something. But whenever he pulled her hair, or slapped her, or choked her, she'd remind herself through the pain that she had something of her own now, a place in her heart that could never be his. That made it a little more bearable, somehow.

April, and the arrival of spring, brought a brighter, more optimistic mood, and with it a sense of boldness. Stella and Ted began meeting in public places, in the full glare of the sunshine, and that was when they were finally spotted. It was one day when they were sitting in a little restaurant overlooking the lake front. Ted had arrived in a testy mood after a difficult morning at work, and Stella was doing her best to talk him out of it. When Marius was in that kind of humour Stella would never have dared speak to him, but Ted didn't frighten her at all. She knew he'd get over it soon.

'You seem a little out of sorts,' she observed. 'You'll feel better once you've had something to eat.'

He grunted, but ate his lunch and, as she had predicted, snapped out of his mood.

'You see? I always know how to cheer you up,' she said.

'That's true.'

She felt his hand sliding up her thigh under the table and moved her chair backwards, out of his reach.

'Stop that!'

They were laughing now, exchanging looks, excited at the thought of the couple of hours they would steal together in his apartment soon, when she glanced up and suddenly stiffened.

'What is it?' said Ted.

Stella waved politely at someone, and Ted turned to see a stout, middle-aged woman just leaving the restaurant, looking at them both with bright, sharp eyes. She bowed and smiled at him, curiosity spread all over her face, and then went out. Stella was wide-eyed and breathing fast.

'Oh, goodness, that was Gerda Buchman, Marius's secretary.'

'Will she tell him?'

'She's bound to. Listen, I'd better go home. He's going to ring me, I just know it.'

A minute ago she'd been laughing, happy, but now she was white and afraid.

'Aren't you even allowed out for lunch?'

'Not with you.'

He knew it was true, so didn't argue as she stood up and gathered her things together.

'Call me as soon as you can, okay?' he said.

She nodded, then hurried home as fast as she could, her mind racing, fearful of what Marius would do when Gerda inevitably told him that she'd seen his wife having lunch with another man. And it wasn't as though they'd only been having lunch; it must have been obvious from their manner what they were getting up to, and the secretary, who was a terrible gossip, would be only too pleased to tell Marius all about it in great detail.

Stella spent the next few hours on tenterhooks, not daring to leave the apartment again, as though spending the afternoon innocently at home might somehow atone for the wrong she'd already done him and had planned to do again. She expected the phone to ring at any second, but the longer it stayed silent the more frightened she became, convinced that her husband would do something terrible to her.

At last he came in, and to her surprise greeted her in quite his usual manner. She was chopping carrots for dinner, having spent all afternoon rehearsing what she was going to say, and for half a minute she wondered whether she'd made a mistake. Perhaps Gerda hadn't said anything at all; if that were the case then there was no need for Stella to tell her lie. But a moment's reflection told her that if Gerda hadn't said anything yet, she certainly would sooner or later, and so it was better to get her story in first. She took a deep breath.

'I bumped into Ted Landry today,' she said brightly.

Marius said nothing. She could feel the sweat prickling under her dress.

'Did you?'

He was glancing through his evening newspaper, seemingly uninterested.

'Yes. He invited me to lunch. We saw Gerda Buchman.'

He looked up vaguely.

'Oh yes, she did tell me. How was he?'

'Full of nonsense and slightly annoying.'

Well, that was true, at least, she thought with grim humour. She waited for Marius to turn to her with that cold look in his eyes that always sent a stab of fear through her, because it inevitably meant only one thing. But he didn't; merely asked her when dinner would be ready and went to change. She was disconcerted, having expected trouble, but as the evening went on it became clear that the blow wasn't about to fall. The next day it was the same. He pecked her on the cheek and went out, leaving her to feel that it had all been rather an anticlimax. The feeling of relief was immense – but still, she made a note to be more careful in future, and left it a few days before calling Ted again.

'I've been worried sick about you,' he said when they met once more. 'I was on the point of coming to get you.'

'I told you I'd call. There was no need to worry.'

'Well, what was I to think? And you say Marius didn't suspect a thing?'

'Not as far as I can tell. He didn't seem that interested when I said I'd seen you. Perhaps I've been doing him an injustice.'

'Don't kid yourself. I've seen the bruises, remember? He might be giving you an easy time now, but that doesn't mean he won't return to type.'

She supposed he was right. Funny how easy it was to forget the bruises once they'd faded. They went back to his apartment and went to bed, as they always did. Afterwards she was lying, watching the swirl of the smoke from his cigarette, enjoying the feeling of his arm around her, and thinking of nothing in particular, when he suddenly said,

'Let's get married.'

'I'll bet you say that to all the girls,' she replied idly, not taking him at all seriously.

'No, I don't. Do you know how many women I've proposed to?'

'No.'

'Exactly one. And that's you.'

'Trust you to pick one who's already taken.'

'Yeah, well, I never did like an easy life. But will you?'

Was he really being serious? She propped herself up on one arm and stared at him in astonishment.

'You don't mean it, surely?'

'Why not?'

'As I just pointed out, I'm already married. Isn't that a big enough obstacle?'

'Then divorce him.'

'I can't. It'll be impossible to get a divorce here in Switzerland. Marius will never agree to it.'

'But would you if he did? Marry me, I mean?'

She blinked. He seemed sincere.

'I – well – yes, of course I would! You know I would. But it can't be done.'

'We'll find a way. We might have to get you out of the country first. If we could just get you over to the States you could file for divorce from there.'

'And that won't be difficult at all,' she said dryly. 'Listen, it's kind of you, but—'

'It's not kind, you nitwit. I've had enough of all this creeping around. I want you for keeps. I want to be able to show you off to people, instead of hiding you away like a dirty little secret. I want to do what everyone else does – get married, have kids, and turn into a grouchy old man sitting on the porch and griping about the state of the world. And I can't do that when the only woman I want is shackled to someone else.'

Her heart had begun to beat rapidly. She'd carefully avoided making any plans for the future that involved Ted, because the reality of it was too painful to bear. But now here he was, offering her the thing she wanted most in the world but couldn't have. He stubbed out his cigarette and pulled her close to him.

'Seriously, Stella, I can't live this kind of life forever. One day the war will be over and I'll have to leave Switzerland, and I don't want to go without you.'

Then he really did mean it. Her heart sank.

'I don't want to be without you either,' she said desolately. 'But it would never work. He'll never let me go. Please, Ted, it'll only cause trouble. Just forget it.'

*

That evening Marius came home tired and tight-lipped. She'd been warming some soup for them both, and she came out of the kitchen and put on a smile.

'Hallo, darling, did you have a nice day?'

He shrugged off his coat impatiently and threw it at her but didn't reply. He was obviously in a bad mood. Under normal circumstances it would have made her wary and nervous around him, but she'd been thinking about things as she waited for him to come home, and was beginning to wonder whether, in fact, *she* was the problem. Was his treatment of her perhaps her own fault? She'd grown up mostly alone, without a mother, and had no idea of how husbands and wives normally got along, so in the early days of their marriage she'd been terribly unsure of herself and had left it to him to make all the decisions. She'd quickly found out that certain things she did made him impatient, and had learned to avoid doing those things. Then gradually the list of prohibited things had got longer and longer, and he'd become more and more impatient, and she'd shrunk away from him and learned to doubt herself.

She thought of Ted and how she teased him fearlessly. She didn't quite dare tease Marius – funny how she'd never noticed before they were married that he had no sense of humour. But there was no reason she couldn't speak to him on more of an equal footing. Ted had taught her that was possible. Perhaps Marius had only been waiting for her to wake up and stop behaving like a coward. After all, nobody liked cowards. He probably despised her, and that was what had made him hurt her. If she spoke to him confidently, like a grown woman rather than a terrified little girl, then perhaps he'd have more respect for her.

'I've managed to get some beef for tomorrow,' she said brightly, as she brushed off the coat and went to hang it up.

He still didn't say anything, but sat down, picked up the newspaper from the table and scanned it.

She bit her lip and went on. She talked to him about the beef, and about what the butcher had said, and about the weather, and about what she'd been doing that day, and about the new film she wanted to go and see, as she fussed around, plumping cushions.

Still he said nothing. She wasn't sure whether it was a good sign or not, but she decided she might as well keep going. She began to tell him about something she'd heard from their downstairs neighbour, but he cut her off.

'Be quiet. I don't want to hear it.'

'I'm sorry. Let me empty that ashtray.'

She moved to pick it up and he jerked impatiently.

'Leave it.'

'I'm sorry, I thought—'

'I told you I didn't want to hear it.'

'But—'

'*Shut up!*' he exploded. He stood up, grabbed her by the throat and pushed her violently against the wall. 'Shut up. Shut up. Shut up.'

Each 'Shut up' was accompanied by a slap across her face, and she whimpered in pain. Then he turned away abruptly. She was gasping for breath and could feel the hysteria rising in her chest, but she knew if she made another sound he'd start again, only worse this time, so she fought down her sobs, wrapping her arms around herself as if trying to hold herself upright. Marius sat down and picked up his paper again.

'How long until the soup is ready?' he asked, without looking at her.

Her face burned like fire and the blood tasted like salt on her lip. She knew it all now. Nothing she could do would ever be right, and there was no use in trying.

'Ten minutes,' she replied in a flat voice.

*

She didn't meet Ted again until the swelling had gone down, although the cut on her lip was still visible. He let loose a string of swear words when he saw her.

'Don't!' she exclaimed. 'It doesn't help.'

'Damn it! Did he hurt you anywhere else?'

She shook her head.

'He's a coward. A man against a woman isn't fair,' he said indignantly. 'Where is he now? I'm going to see to him and make sure he doesn't do it again. I'll teach him to pick on someone his own size.'

'No!'

'Stella…'

She looked down. She didn't like showing anyone the scars of her marriage any more than she could help.

'I'm all right, really,' she said at last. 'But I've stopped making excuses now. These last few days have cleared my mind, somehow. I don't know why I was so blind before.'

'Then you'll leave him?'

'I think I must. Did you mean it? What you said the other day?'

'About getting married? Absolutely.'

'Then how could we do it?'

His face broke into a grin that was so infectious she wanted to smile too, but she couldn't because it still hurt.

'I've been thinking about that. The first thing to do is to get you out of Switzerland, but it'll be difficult to do that while he's here, breathing down your neck. When's he going away next?'

'He said something about going to Florence in June or July. There are some Renaissance pictures from a private gallery he's got his eye on. It's illegal to export them, but Mussolini doesn't much care about art, and so it's easy to get them out under his nose.'

'Must be nice to have friends in high places who can get you travel permits and sell you valuable pictures.'

'Well, he spent enough time cultivating them. I do believe he saw the war coming and made plans to profit from it in any way he could.'

'He's doing that all right. He's got the Germans and the Italians practically begging him to take their unwanted artwork off their hands.'

The remark made her think of her younger self, and how she'd hung about Marius, wide-eyed, longing for him to propose to her. That was in the days before she knew about the dark side of his character.

'He can be very charming when he likes.'

'Charming enough to trick an innocent little girl into marrying him,' he said, looking at her. 'Well, if he's not going away until next month that gives me time to plan your exit route. Now listen, I've been cultivating people myself lately. There's a guy at the Red Cross who was somewhat stiff at first, but we're the best of pals now, and he owes me a favour. He's an official delegate and he goes into France all the time to look at the camps. Now, he might take a little talking round, but I think I can arrange for him to take you on his next trip as his secretary, and put you on a Red Cross ship from Marseilles to Lisbon. From there you can get to England. I'll join you as soon as I can get posted to London, and then we'll work out how to get the divorce.'

He made it all sound so easy, although she was sure it couldn't possibly be. She considered his plan. If all went well she'd have to go and see Mr Ellison as soon as she got back to England. He hadn't been at all happy that she'd got married without consulting him, although he'd come round in the end. He was the old-fashioned sort, and she wouldn't dream of telling him about Ted – in fact, she suspected he'd want to send her straight back to Marius, but of course that would be impossible once she was safely in England. Money would be a concern, but she'd left a small sum in her bank account when she departed for Florence, and she would just have to make that stretch. There were a lot of difficulties ahead, and it wasn't certain the plan would work, but Ted's optimism was raising her spirits every minute, and she felt that she might achieve anything with him by her side.

He was watching her as she considered it.

'Well? What do you think?'

'Do you think it'll work?'

'All we can do is try.'

She raised her chin, forgetting her cut lip for a moment.

'Then let's try.'

Chapter Seventeen

Now that she'd decided to do it, Stella was impatient for the day of her escape to come. She was amazed at the unexpected and enormous sense of relief that swept through her at the thought of leaving Marius, and only now did she truly begin to grasp the impossibility of her ever being happy with him. Leaving was the only option. There were difficulties in the way, naturally: it would be a long and dangerous journey back to England, but Stella found herself looking forward to seeing London again. She'd never have had the courage to leave Marius of her own accord, but some of Ted's optimism had rubbed off on her. She didn't have much money, but she'd started saving what little she could from whatever Marius gave her. Meanwhile, Ted had enlisted the help of his friend at the Red Cross, who was so far proving to be sympathetic, and had promised to ask no questions and pull a few strings to allow Stella to accompany him on his next trip.

For the next few weeks Stella and Ted saw less of each other, fearful that Marius would find them out and ruin their plans. When they did meet, it was hurriedly, furtively, in different parts of the city they knew were unlikely to be frequented by anyone they knew. At home, she did her best to behave normally and not to irritate her husband in any way. He was his normal self: exacting and distant, but he gave no sign that he suspected what was going on, being mainly concerned with preparations for his trip to Florence. There were rumours that the Allies were planning to invade Italy, and rumblings of dissent among the populace, who were tiring of the war and of Fascism, and Marius was anxious to complete his business before the situation deteriorated. At present there was plenty of opportunity to make private bargains with collectors who wished to sell their artworks, but if the pact between Italy and Germany broke down, who knew what would happen? Hitler would never permit Italy to join the Allies, and if the Germans invaded then the situation would become much more difficult.

So the day approached. The day before Marius was due to leave, Stella and Ted met in a dingy bar on the outskirts of the city to go over the arrangements for the next day. Stella had been feeling increasingly nervous, but she was comforted by Ted's continuing confidence that the plan would be a success. She was to wait until Marius had left and then pack a bag for a few days away. The day after that, she was to present herself at a certain address and meet the Red Cross representative and his driver.

'Don't pack too much,' said Ted. 'Just enough for a few days, or you'll look suspicious, and we don't want to get on the wrong side of Gersbach. He's nervous enough about taking you.'

'Is he safe?'

'I hope so. I gave him the impression that it's an intelligence matter and that you have friends in high places in London. He doesn't like the Germans, so he's willing to help, but don't scare him any more than you can help. You're meant to be his secretary, so you'd better tone down your look a little – the frumpier the better. You want to look serious and competent.'

'Oh goodness! I hope he doesn't ask me to do anything. I've never worked before. Perhaps I ought to have studied shorthand.'

'Well, it's too late now. Just do what you can. Anyway, once you've hooked up with my pal and his delegation they'll take you across the border and south to Marseille. From there he's promised to see you safely on board the ship. That passport of yours might be a problem going out of Switzerland, but you'll be going through the Italian-occupied zone, and Gersbach says he's passed that way dozens of times before and they don't raise too many difficulties if you're with the Red Cross. Just show them your Swiss residency papers and they'll wave you through.' He glanced at his watch. 'Now, listen, here's the bad news: I have to go to Bern this afternoon, and I'll be there for a couple of days, so I won't be there to see you off.'

'Oh, but—' she was dismayed.

'I know, it couldn't have come at a worse time, but I've been told to go and I can't get out of it. But you'll be okay, won't you?'

He was looking at her earnestly. This was no time to show weakness, so she nodded and tried to swallow her fear. He smiled.

'Good. Don't worry – I'll get word to you as soon as I can. It'll all turn out fine, you'll see.' He dug in his pocket. 'Here, I got you something.'

It was a ring, a slim, delicate gold band set with three small sapphires. She drew in her breath and glanced up at him. She might almost have said he looked slightly sheepish.

'Just so you know it's real,' he said.

He slid it onto her finger above her wedding ring. It fitted perfectly. Stella gazed at it and tried to stop the tears from spilling out, but couldn't quite manage it.

'Hey!' he said. 'What are you crying for? Don't you like it?'

She couldn't speak, but leaned forward and kissed him fiercely. The ring was a gesture of faith, of hope for the future, but for some reason it felt like a final goodbye.

'You'll have to keep it out of sight until he's gone,' he said. 'I guess he wouldn't like it if he saw it.'

'I'll keep it hidden in my glove and put it on as soon as I can.' She suited the action to the word, then they left the bar and went out into the street. It was getting late, and Stella's bus was approaching, so there was no time for an extended goodbye. She tried her hardest not to cling to him, reminding herself that it was only a temporary separation, and that they'd be together again soon.

'Come to London soon,' she said, as she got on the bus.

'I might even be there before you,' he replied.

He held his hand up in a wave and the bus moved off. Stella craned her neck as far back as it would go, watching him until he was out of sight, then turned and set her jaw. She was on her own now; this was her chance to prove she could be strong and brave, and look after herself, and she was determined to show she could do it.

*

Stella hardly slept at all that night. It was a long drive to Florence, and Marius was intending to leave early, so she rose at five, rushing around, preparing things for his departure. She was so nervous she spilt his coffee and was terrified for a moment, but he said nothing. *Just another hour or two and I'll be rid of him forever*, she thought, as she poured another cup with a trembling hand and gave it to him. Now that the thing was in motion she could hardly believe she'd stayed with him so long, and she was almost ready to sing for joy at the thought of the freedom that would soon be hers. She poured a cup of coffee for herself, making lists in her head of the things that would need to be done before she could leave.

'Go and pack a few things,' said Marius, breaking into her thoughts.

She looked at him uncertainly, wondering for one horrible second whether she'd been muttering aloud. How did he know she'd been thinking of what she had to pack?

'Pack a few things?' she repeated stupidly.

'Yes. You're coming with me to Florence.'

Still she didn't quite understand.

'What do you mean?'

'Didn't I say it clearly enough?' he said. 'You are coming to Florence with me, so you had better pack some clothes.'

She felt a stab of panic.

'I can't go to Italy. They won't let me in, will they? I still haven't taken Italian citizenship.'

'Of course they will. I have an Italian passport, and you are my wife. There will be no difficulty.'

'But—'

He glanced at his watch.

'And you'd better be quick about it. I want to leave in half an hour.'

Too shocked and confused to argue, Stella went off to do what he said. Mechanically she took down her case from the top of the wardrobe. If she went to Florence she would not be able to meet her Red Cross contact, and would miss the boat from Marseille, and that simply couldn't be allowed. Her mind wasn't working properly at all, but her heart was beating rapidly. Calm, she must remain calm. She threw a few things into the case at random, then opened and shut some drawers noisily, as if to drown out the sound of her mind working so that Marius wouldn't hear. *Think, think*, she told herself. How could she get away? Why hadn't Marius mentioned before that he was planning to take her? If he had, then she could have made her escape last night – could have gone to a hotel and lain low until tomorrow and her appointment with Ted's friend. She had to get away, but Marius was out there waiting for her, and she knew he wouldn't let her leave. She went out into the living room.

'I can't find my passport,' she said. 'I thought it was in my top drawer, but it's not there.'

She'd hidden the passport under her mattress some days ago, just in case he'd got wind of the plan and decided to take it away from her. She'd be in trouble, but she didn't care. All that mattered was that Marius went to Florence without her.

'I have it here,' he replied, holding it up.

She stared in dismay. How had he found it? She looked at the thin, triumphant smile spread over his face, and then it hit her.

He knew.

Of course he knew. Why should he have gone hunting for her passport otherwise? The look on his face said it all. He knew about her and Ted, and about their plan. He must have known about it for weeks – most likely since Gerda Buchman had seen them in the restaurant together and reported it to him. She'd been surprised that there had been no reprisals from that lunch, but had made the mistake of thinking it was because he had no suspicions, even though it was totally out of character for him. But now it was obvious it had been a calculated decision on his part; her transgression was such an enormity that it required him to act coldly and with deliberation. So he'd watched her and waited, biding his time, lulling her into a false sense of security while he planned his next move. And now he was taking her away with him so she could never escape. A fear ran through her such as she hadn't felt for a long time. What would happen to her now? How was she to get out of this? Why in heaven's name hadn't Ted given her the telephone number of his hotel in Bern? He'd left her on her own, and she had only herself to rely upon now.

It took only an instant for the terrible knowledge to flash through her head, but at the same time she knew she mustn't, whatever happened, let him know that she had realised what he was doing. He was watching her closely, and she said the first thing that came into her head.

'Please Marius, I'd rather not go. I don't feel too well today. I've been very headachy for a few days.'

'Then Italy will do you good,' he replied imperturbably. 'And don't you want to see Florence again? Well, now you have the opportunity. Fetch your case. It's getting late.'

It was her final gambit, and it had failed. There was nothing she could do but obey, her heart hammering loudly in her chest. She almost wished he would hit her and get it over with, because the knowledge he held over her head was more terrifying, but she could see he meant to draw it out and make her wait.

She went to fetch her case. There must be something she could do; she had to get word to Ted somehow. She ran over to the dressing table, took a sheet of letter paper and scrawled a hurried message, then sealed it up in an envelope and shoved it into her pocket.

'I'm ready now,' she said calmly, as she came out of the bedroom. They went out into the corridor and waited for the lift.

'My gloves!' she exclaimed suddenly.

'Leave them,' said Marius impatiently, but she was already dashing back in the direction of the apartment. Once she was out of sight she pulled the letter out of her pocket and shoved it under the door of her neighbour, Mme Blanchet. Then she hurried into the apartment, grabbed the gloves and returned to Marius, who was waiting in the lift for her.

'Hurry up,' he said, and she joined him breathlessly. It wasn't much, but it was the only way she could let Ted know where she'd gone. Would he be angry with her for having failed in her task? She prayed he'd understand that there was nothing she could have done.

They headed out of Geneva, Marius driving in a deadly silence which she dared not break. By the time they reached the Italian border she was almost paralysed with fear, but she was aware enough of her surroundings to be struck by how easily Marius had been able to obtain special travel papers, and how he seemed to be on good terms with the border guards. All those years charming and cultivating the people who mattered had certainly paid off. After the border she forced herself to stare out of the window and concentrate on the scenery, looking out for glimpses of Lake Maggiore in the sunshine as they travelled down towards the Po Plain. They passed through Milan, and she was shocked at what she saw. The last time she'd been here was when she first arrived in Italy, but the place looked very different now: the city had evidently suffered from heavy bombing by the Allies, because whole districts had been half reduced to rubble. Tired-looking people wandered around, their heads down, while children played in the ruins of buildings. What had happened to this once beautiful country?

They stopped for lunch in Piacenza, and still Marius said nothing. Then they were back in the car and heading for Florence across the flatlands of the Po Plain, the gentle foothills of the Apennines ahead of them. The sun was bright and hot, and Stella's mind was forced back to all that time ago, and her arrival in Italy with Mrs Unsworth. The country had seemed to hold such promise for her then; she'd had all kinds of plans and schemes, and ideas of what she meant to do. But events had overtaken her, and now here she was heading back to a city she'd once loved, in company with a man who terrified her.

'Are we going to see Monica and Gerardo?' she asked timidly at last. She'd hardly heard anything of Monica since she'd left Italy, but if they were going to see the Carminatis, then perhaps it meant Marius was intending to postpone her punishment until they were back in Geneva.

'As far as I know they're in Rome,' he replied. 'We're not going to see anybody. Or *you're* not, at any rate.'

She'd been starting to calm down a little, but at his words her fear returned. She pressed her hands between her knees to stop them trembling, as she ran over possibilities in her mind. If she could only get to a telephone box, she could place a call to Switzerland and leave a message at Ted's bureau. She had no idea what he could do from there, but it would be *something*, at least, to know that he knew where she was.

Marius said nothing more until they were driving through the suburbs of Florence, then he broke in on her thoughts and remarked suddenly:

'I didn't want to marry you, you know, but I was left with little choice.'

She turned to him in astonishment.

'What do you mean?'

He explained, almost conversationally:

'Your father and Monica lost me a good deal of money a few years ago. I had a very good opportunity with my biggest client, a German, who wanted a certain painting owned by an old man of my acquaintance. I'd taken pains to befriend this man, Johannes Stengel, and hoped he would agree to sell it to me. I knew I didn't have long, because he was sick and hadn't long to live. Sure enough Stengel died, and then I found out that Raymond, who was fond of playing little tricks, had been plotting behind my back to get the painting from under my nose, by sending in Monica to persuade Stengel to sell it. Naturally, she succeeded, and Raymond sold the painting in turn to Gerardo. You may remember it – the *Lady of the Cypresses* by Raphael. Monica never missed an opportunity to show it off and remind me how she'd cheated me. That was her mistake, and I will have the painting one day, whether she likes it or not. But it was not only that painting I lost: my German client was very upset with me, and refused to deal with me any more, and so I lost his business and that of his friends, and for some time was in danger of financial ruin.'

Marius talked on inexorably and, despite the heat of the day, Stella felt the hairs prickling on the back of her neck.

'Shortly after Raymond died my sister attached herself to Gerardo and went back to Italy with him. I visited her in Florence, and told her angrily what she and Raymond had done, and, being the kind of woman she is, she laughed. Then she saw I was serious, and told me not to worry – she would make it up to me and see that I got the money Raymond owed me. Not long after that she invited you to stay with her. When you arrived she said, "There, Marius, there's your golden goose, if you can catch it!" and laughed again.'

He glanced at Stella, who could do nothing but stare.

'I don't especially like women, and you were a particularly stupid example of the species, but Monica told me you'd been practically abandoned by your father and were very naïve, and so would be susceptible to any man who paid you a little attention. Well, it took more than a *little* attention. You were prim and awkward and shied away like a nervous horse, so I had to move slowly. Still, you came round in the end.'

Stella could feel her breath coming rapidly, but couldn't speak. It had all been a lie from the start. Marius had never loved her. All the evenings out, and the flattery, and the flowers, and the necklace – long forgotten about in a drawer – they'd all been a calculated move to get hold of her money, and presumably revenge himself on her father at the same time. And she'd fallen for it. She'd believed everything he told her, and she'd married him and put up with the beatings for nearly four years, living in a permanent state of fear, because she'd thought somewhere deep down, despite his faults, he must love her.

'God knows I'd rather have had the money some other way,' he went on. 'But this was the only option open to me at the time. However, if one really must take a wife, at least one might hope for a little loyalty and obedience from her. I particularly dislike having unpleasant news brought to me by that fat busybody Gerda Buchman, who no doubt told everyone she knew that her employer's wife was behaving like a whore. The whole thing was very distasteful to me, but still, it was necessary to act, so I instituted a few discreet enquiries, and soon heard enough to know that you were planning to leave. Landry is not a man who is very good at hiding his feelings or holding his tongue. You may not go, of course. It would create a most unpleasant scandal, and I run a respectable business.'

Stella found her voice at last.

'Please, Marius – I promise you there's nothing between Ted and me. He's an old friend, that's all, and he just wanted to be kind. He saw I was unhappy and was trying to persuade me to go, but I hadn't made up my mind to do it, I promise you.' She was telling lies as fast as she could think of them. 'I just wanted to make you happy, that's all. But it seemed whatever I did made you cross. Can't we start again? I promise I'll learn how to be a good wife to you if you'll only give me a chance.'

She despised herself for the cravenness with which she was begging him, but what choice did she have? He was wholly unmoved by her plea.

'Oh, you'll learn all right, because I'm going to teach you. You've disobeyed me, and humiliated me in front of my associates. You must understand I can't let that pass. You'll have to be punished, but I promise you, you *will* learn.'

He turned his head and the look in his eye chilled her to the bone. She began to tremble all over.

'Please, Marius, please don't. I'm sorry. I'll do anything you like, but please don't hurt me.'

She cast around wildly for something she could offer him in return. There was nothing left now except her currency of last resort.

'I'll tell you where my father's paintings are,' she burst out.

That got his attention.

'Which paintings?'

'The paintings that Monica was looking for. The ones my father got in Berlin. I know where they are.'

'Tell me,' he commanded.

'They're in a warehouse just outside Lucerne. The keys are in a safe deposit box in a bank, and I've got the key to the box at home.'

She watched him fearfully, waiting for his reaction. Would it be enough to change his mind? She could see his mind working.

'Does Monica know about this?' he said finally.

'No. Nobody knows except me.'

It was a lie, but she knew any mention of Ted would be a mistake. She waited, hoping against hope it would be enough.

'You will give me the key when we get back to Geneva,' was all he said. 'Now, here is the hotel.'

He turned the car through the big arch into the courtyard of the Hotel Ambassador. An old porter came out and took their bags, and they walked into the lobby, which was full of German soldiers. Despite her terror Stella was doing her best to appear calm, conscious that her fate was balanced on a knife-edge, and that anything she did might tip it against her. Marius hadn't said anything more, and she didn't know what to think. Perhaps he thought it was enough to hold the knowledge of her perfidy over her head. Perhaps he wouldn't hurt her at all – or at least not until they returned home. If she could only get back to Geneva she could call Ted and he'd take her away.

They entered the room in silence. The late afternoon sun was slanting through the window, and she could see particles of dust floating in the air. Marius waited until the porter had gone, then turned to face her. A trickle of fear ran down her spine.

'Now,' he said, and at that moment she knew there was no escape.

Chapter Eighteen

Stella didn't know how long she'd been lying on the floor, or even, at first, why she was there. All she knew was the cool, hard, parquet surface under her, and a square of light grey somewhere above her in the dimness. Gradually the grey square resolved itself into a pair of pale curtains, moving almost imperceptibly in the hot air that came in gentle breaths through the open window. Somewhere a clock was ticking; she couldn't see it, but to judge from the quality of the light in the room, it must be early evening. She lay there, motionless, as the memories came back in fits and starts. He'd kicked her – she remembered that much. After he'd let go of her hair, her blood running down his hand, she'd curled up on the floor, her arms around her head, lacking even enough breath to cry out as his expensive leather shoes did their merciless damage to her ribs.

Her mind was becoming clearer now. Alongside the ticking clock she noted the sound of her own breathing. That was something, at least, although she couldn't breathe deeply because it hurt too much. Their room overlooked the courtyard, and she could hear the sound of people walking to and fro, and the hotel staff calling to one another. Further away, more muffled, the sounds of the city drifted towards her. There was no one else in the room apart from herself. Marius had gone out, but when would he be back? If he returned what would he do? Would he decide to finish the job? There was nothing she could do to prevent it if that was what he intended. She'd spent her last credit by telling him about the paintings – not that it had worked – and now she was completely powerless.

Somewhere in the city a bell chimed the quarter hour. She pressed her hands against the floor and raised herself carefully to a sitting position. Her hands were sticky, streaked with dried blood, and there was a dark smear on the floor which would have to be removed or Marius would be cross. The grim irony of having to clean up the blood he'd shed wasn't lost on her. She stopped to get her breath, then rose slowly to a kneeling position and stood up, holding onto the bed for support. In the corner of the room was a washbasin with a mirror above it, and she made her way slowly and stiffly towards it. Although she knew he'd done her more damage than he ever had before, the sight of her reflection still came as a shock. The left side of her face had swollen to nearly twice its normal size, and she couldn't open her left eye. He'd burst her lip again, and there were trickles of blood down her right cheek where his signet ring had caught the corner of her other eye.

She fetched her toilet bag from her case and burrowed in it, looking for her flannel. A manicure set in a leather case fell out and she stopped as a sudden memory hit her, then opened it. Inside was the safe deposit box key that she'd told Marius was at home in Geneva. She'd completely forgotten she'd hidden it here. She tended to move it from hiding place to hiding place for safety, and this was the last place she'd put it.

Returning the key, she bathed her face carefully, and rinsed out the dried blood from her matted hair. The pain was sharp in her left side where he'd kicked her, and she guessed he'd broken a rib or two. He wouldn't be able to introduce her to any of his Florentine business associates looking like this. Just then she heard the sound of a key in a lock followed by a door opening, and she jumped violently and turned, clutching her side at the pain of the sudden movement. The noise had come from the room next door, but it took several minutes for the hammering of her heart to die down, and she found her palms had gone clammy with sweat. Even the suggestion that Marius was coming back was enough to cause panic to flood through her. She felt the nausea in her throat and all of a sudden she knew she had to get away right now, far away from her husband and the wholly rational terror he inspired in her.

His suitcase was on the luggage rack, empty. When she opened the wardrobe she discovered he'd calmly taken the time to unpack his things while she lay there on the floor. A quick search of the room showed he'd taken her passport and all her documents. Of course he had: he couldn't risk her escaping and showing the world what he'd done to her. Her gloves were lying on the bed where she'd dropped them, and she picked up the left one and felt the comforting shape of Ted's ring, where she'd hidden it inside the fourth finger. She tipped it out and slid it on. The sound of voices was approaching along the corridor and she jumped again. She had to go, and quickly. Her hat was lying on the bed where she'd dropped it when they got in. It had a small veil, not enough to hide the mess of her face, but it would have to do. The rest of her things would have to stay here.

She was just about to leave the room when she hesitated, thinking of the safe deposit box key. Why should she leave it here for Marius to find? If she'd remembered where it was earlier, she'd have undoubtedly told him and he would have taken it from her, but he believed she'd left it at home in Geneva, so hadn't looked for it. Now here was her chance to thwart him, at least in some small way. She fetched the key from the manicure case and slipped it into her pocket, her last act of defiance before she left him forever.

She put her hand on the door handle, then hesitated. She didn't know where to go. The only place she could think of was the Villa Bruni, but Marius had said Monica and Gerardo were in Rome. Perhaps Dora would still be there, and would be kind to her. She would try it, at any rate.

Stella came stiffly out of the room and along the corridor, keeping her head down, thankful for the dim light. The pain in her left side was severe, and she put a hand to it and moved slowly and carefully along to the lift. She'd been here many times in her earlier days in Florence, but she hadn't recognised any of the staff on duty when they'd come in. All she wanted was to get out of the place without being spotted. But to keep out of sight she'd have to avoid the front entrance and go out through a side door she knew of which went past the kitchen. She went past the guest lift and into the service lift instead, which was unmanned, and emerged into a quiet passageway. The sound of raised voices and clashing dishes came from the kitchen, and she judged the staff were busy with the evening meals. She crept stiffly towards the side door and slipped out quietly into the evening. As she stopped to rest and think, several soldiers in German uniform walked past, talking and laughing, and she shrank back involuntarily to escape their notice.

After a few moments she got her bearings and set off in the direction of the Villa Bruni. It was at least a mile away, and would be a slow and painful walk. The most important thing was to avoid attracting anybody's notice, and so she kept away from the main streets and took the side roads instead, heading towards the Ponte Vecchio, with its overhanging buildings, which would give her more cover than the other bridges and with any luck allow her to remain inconspicuous. The streets were busy, but nobody was paying attention to her, and she made it across the river and into the dim, narrow streets without attracting notice.

The fear had propelled Stella this far, but now, out in the hot, sticky air, the pain in her ribs was becoming sharper, and the left side of her face was burning and throbbing. Still, she ignored it and threw all her concentration into putting one foot in front of the other and getting to the villa. She didn't want to think about what she'd do if there was nobody at home; she had no money, since Marius had taken all of that as well as her passport, presumably to make quite sure she couldn't leave. Perhaps she could present herself at a hospital – she was sure she'd be looked after there, but then they'd call Marius and she'd be back where she started. All her thoughts were focused on a single idea: to get away from her husband. As long as she could do that then nothing else mattered.

Keeping to the back streets had caused her to lose her bearings slightly, but now she came out into a large piazza and saw the grand Palazzo Pitti looming up before her. The square was too exposed for comfort, and there were too many people out and about, but it was the shortest way to where she wanted to go, and she was tiring fast. After hesitating a moment she stepped out, walking as fast as she could, skirting the edge of the square and feeling horribly conspicuous. Nobody seemed to be paying attention to her, and she made it two-thirds of the way across before misfortune struck. She'd been keeping her head down, not looking at anybody, and so she didn't see the *carabiniere* until it was too late. The policeman had been gazing idly into a shop window at the edge of the square, and he looked up curiously as she passed. Suddenly it struck her that she was British, in an enemy country, without any papers to explain her presence, and if she was caught she would most likely be arrested – or worse.

She walked a little faster, trying to ignore the agonising pain in her side, but the attention of the *carabiniere* was properly caught now. He began to move towards her, and at that moment what little presence of mind she had left deserted her. She panicked, changing direction and ducking into the nearest alleyway. She heard his voice shouting at her to stop, but kept walking – limping – as fast as she could. As she passed a sad-looking grocer's shop she almost bumped into a woman just coming out, who was carrying an infant in her arms. Stella apologised hastily and pressed on. Her breath was coming in shallow sobs now, and she was starting to feel dizzy and faint, and she knew she couldn't go on much further. What was the use in trying to run away when she could hardly walk straight? It was quite futile, and she might as well give up and let the police officer catch her. If she was lucky he'd arrest her and she'd get some medical attention – if not, he'd send her back to Marius. Either way, she couldn't walk any more.

On her left was an archway leading to a little courtyard. The lowering sun didn't reach this far, and the place was in shadow, and without thinking she turned into it and sank down in the darkness of the archway, resting her back against the cool stone wall, gathering her strength for the moment when the *carabiniere* found her and she would have to summon the energy to explain herself and walk with him to wherever he wanted to take her. Every part of her body was hurting, and she closed her eyes and concentrated on breathing very carefully. The street outside was quiet, except for the sound of the policeman's footsteps approaching. It sounded as though he were stopping to check every doorway. A wave of exhaustion washed over her, and it was all she could do not to lie down. She must stay awake and explain herself. Then she heard the sound of voices in Italian, drifting towards her as if in a dream: her pursuer, presumably, asking if anyone had passed that way, then a soft, woman's voice replying. Stella sat slumped against the wall, waiting for the blow to fall, as it inevitably would. The policeman was still talking, and she heard him say, '*Grazie, buona sera,*' then there came the sound of male footsteps passing, but not stopping. She sat there for what seemed like an hour, but could only have been a few minutes, until a shadow fell in front of the archway in which she was hiding. The shadow approached cautiously, quietly, and spoke to her in English.

'Quick, come with me,' it said.

Chapter Nineteen

Ted returned to Geneva on Wednesday after two days in Bern, having been summoned to a meeting with the chief of the Office of Strategic Services, the US security service, who had found out he knew Italy and ostensibly wanted to pick his brains. The Allied invasion of Sicily from North Africa was imminent, and the purpose of the visit was to find out if he had any useful information, the chief said. Ted's knowledge was several years out of date and he told the man so immediately, but it swiftly transpired that he'd been summoned to the office for quite a different reason. The news from Italy was that there was a rising tide of anti-Fascist sentiment there, and even talk that Mussolini would be ousted at some point. Naturally, such a development could be hugely beneficial to the Allies. Would Ted be prepared to be sent into Italy to recruit groups of anti-Fascists and send back information to the OSS in that event?

'It's all theoretical at present, of course, and depends on a lot of things: the success of the Allied invasion, whether Mussolini can be toppled, whether Italy can be persuaded to change sides,' the man went on. 'And it would be risky, but you have the knowledge and contacts we need to get the thing going.'

Ted, who had more or less resigned himself to spending the rest of the war behind a desk, was surprised at the request but expressed his willingness to do what he could, as long as the OSS thought it was feasible. His interviewer seemed satisfied with his answer.

'Good. If we or the Brits go in we'll make sure your bureau assigns you to cover the Italian campaign, and we can take it from there. In the meantime I'd get that leg seen to if I were you.'

Ted left thinking that it was a hare-brained idea, but as he travelled back to Geneva he thought it over and decided perhaps it wasn't so stupid after all – and at least now there was the possibility that he might see some action at last. He was pretty sure that once the Allies had landed in Italy the Italians would crumble easily, and after that there would be a push up the peninsula towards France and Austria, and eventually Germany. If they kept the momentum up then the war might be over by the end of the year or the middle of next at the latest. It meant he wouldn't be able to meet Stella in London as soon as he'd hoped, but there wasn't much he could do about that. She'd understand that he had to do his duty.

Ted hoped she'd got away safely. He thought he could trust Gersbach to do his job, but there were many other dangers which he hadn't mentioned to her, because she was already nervous enough. Despite his confident talk, there was every chance the Italian border guards on the French side would question her papers and refuse to let her through. And even if she did make it through and as far as Marseille, travelling by boat held its own hazards. An official Red Cross ship should be able to get as far as Lisbon without difficulty, but after that there was no safe conduct agreement, and boats were in danger of being torpedoed.

Ted arrived back in Geneva in the early afternoon, and returned to his bureau, and the first thing he saw on his desk was a message. Gersbach had telephoned to inform him that the new secretary had failed to turn up at the appointed time, and he couldn't wait any longer and would have to leave without her. On reading the message Ted's heart sank. Something had obviously gone wrong, if Stella had been prevented from travelling. He didn't dare risk telephoning her in case Marius had decided not to go to Florence after all, so he waited all afternoon, sure she would call him to explain, but no message came through. By five o'clock he was getting worried, and he persuaded one of the telephonists to call Marius's company and ask to speak to him with some fictitious message. He hovered over the girl as she made the phone call.

'He's gone away to Florence,' she said briefly when she put the phone down.

Ted came away, frowning. If Marius had gone to Florence as planned then why hadn't Stella kept her appointment? And why hadn't she called? He left the office and went home to his apartment, but as the afternoon drew into evening he found himself getting increasingly agitated. He had never telephoned her before, but since he was sure Marius was away he decided to risk it. The phone rang and rang into nothingness. In the end he threw caution to the winds and went to her smart apartment building. Nobody answered the doorbell, but he managed to slip through the outer door when someone else came out. He went up to the second floor, found the apartment and pressed the button. The bell echoed, but still nobody answered. He was just about to turn away and leave when the door of the apartment opposite opened and a woman of about fifty came out.

'May I help you?' she enquired.

'I was looking for some friends of mine,' he replied.

'Are you Mr Landry?'

'Yes.' He looked at her, surprised.

'One moment.' The woman disappeared into her apartment and came out with a crumpled envelope. 'This is for you.'

He took the envelope. On it was written in French: *To Mme Blanchet: please give this to Mr Landry if he comes. Thank you, S. Schwegler.*

Mme Blanchet watched him while he opened and read it. The message inside wasn't much longer than the one on the envelope: *So sorry – I have to go to Florence with Marius. Back on Saturday. Stella.*

To judge by the handwriting she'd written it in a tearing hurry. He could only guess what state of mind she'd been in, but even so she'd had the sense not to write anything compromising in case Mme Blanchet's curiosity had overcome her and she'd decided to read it.

He thanked the neighbour and came away, exasperated that the plan had gone wrong at the last minute. Stella had been certain Marius didn't intend to take her with him. Now they'd just have to think of another means of getting her away, but it wouldn't be so easy this time, as he couldn't ask Gersbach to put himself out again.

It was a long wait until Saturday, but even then Ted knew the earliest he could expect a call was Monday, once the Schweglers were back in Geneva and Marius was out of the house again. But Saturday, Sunday and Monday passed and still he heard nothing. By Wednesday he was frantic, and went to the apartment again. Nobody was in, so he knocked on Mme Blanchet's door and she answered.

'No, Mr Schwegler is back but I have not seen Mrs Schwegler,' she answered in reply to his enquiry. 'It is a little strange, because we usually meet in the hall when she goes out.'

She was looking at him full of curiosity, but there was nothing he could tell her. Where on earth was Stella? He returned on Thursday and Friday with the same question, but still met with a negative. Mme Blanchet still had not seen her. He couldn't stand it any longer: he had to know where she was, and the only way to find out was to go and beard the lion in his den.

Marius's gallery was in a smart building in the centre of town. It was a small place, but very exclusive, with metal shutters above the plate glass windows like a bank. Ted went in and looked around. The gallery itself was a sleek, open space with white walls hung about with paintings Ted didn't recognise. The deferential young man who greeted him showed him into an outer office containing a desk at which was sitting Gerda Buchman, who glanced at him with avid, beady eyes. She spoke into a telephone and then Ted was shown into Marius's office, a plushly carpeted affair with a mahogany desk, comfortable seats and large windows giving a view over a park. In the corner of the room was a cabinet on which stood bottles of expensive whisky and crystal glasses, presumably for the purposes of entertaining clients. So this was what Stella's money had paid for, thought Ted. Marius was sitting behind the mahogany desk. He didn't bother to get up when Ted entered, and Ted didn't bother with any preamble.

'Where's Stella?' he said.

Marius gave him a long, cool stare. He was sitting in shadow, while Ted was standing in a wide shaft of sunlight that made him squint and feel at a disadvantage.

'Stella is not here,' Marius replied at last.

'I know that. Where is she?'

'Why do you want to know? What is it to you?'

'We had lunch a couple of weeks ago and I said I'd look her up again soon.'

Marius looked at him, as if calculating.

'She's gone to stay with my aunt in Zürich.'

Ted knew he was lying. If that was true there'd have been nothing stopping her from calling or writing at the very least.

'When will she be back?'

'Soon.'

Ted felt his exasperation rise up a notch.

'You're lying. I know you went to Florence and took her with you.'

'If you knew, then why did you ask?' Marius replied coldly. 'And if you will pardon me, of what interest is it to you where I take my wife?'

'I told you, we'd agreed to meet, but I can't find her.'

Marius gave the merest shrug of the shoulders. It was obvious that he had no intention of giving a straight answer, so Ted decided to lay all his cards on the table. He stepped out of the patch of sunlight, put his hands on the desk and leaned forward. He was much bigger than Marius and the move would have intimidated anyone else, but the man didn't flinch; he merely sat back in his chair and regarded Ted through narrowed eyes.

'Now listen, I know exactly what you've been doing to her,' said Ted, a dangerous note in his voice. 'Beating a woman is a low-down, dirty thing to do.'

'A man has the right to discipline his wife if she is disobedient,' replied Marius, unperturbed. 'You are overly sentimental, and Stella is a foolish girl who must be made to understand what her duties are.' He had still not stood up, but was looking at Ted with an insolent expression. 'And since we seem to be exchanging confidences, I know exactly what *you* have been doing to her, too. One might hope that you could be discreet, but no, you have to come here in this ill-mannered fashion and parade your affair with her in front of my secretary and my clients.'

Ted felt a cold stab of shock at the news that Marius knew about him and Stella. What had he done with her? Where was she now?

'It's not an affair. I want to marry her.'

'That is not possible. And even if it were, you would have to find her first.'

He was regarding Ted with that thin, complacent smile of his, and all at once Ted couldn't stand it any more. He reached across the desk in a sudden movement to grab him by the throat, but Marius pushed his chair back hurriedly and he missed.

'What have you done with her, you son of a bitch?' he demanded furiously.

'You come here and threaten me with violence?' The smile had disappeared from Marius's face, to be replaced by something altogether more dangerous. 'You think that will help you find Stella?'

He was right, of course. Ted might have a physical advantage, but Marius had the upper hand in everything else. Ted forced his temper down and held his hands up in a gesture of surrender.

'Okay, so maybe I was a little hasty. I'm just worried about her, that's all. Why won't you tell me where she is?'

The thin smile reappeared.

'Your guess is as good as mine.'

'You mean you don't know?' Ted stared. 'You're lying.'

Another shrug.

'If you say so. Still, as you have probably realised by now, you're wasting your time here.'

Ted saw it was true. There was no use in talking to Marius, who clearly had no intention of telling him what had happened to Stella. He leaned forward across the desk again.

'If you've hurt her, I'm going to kill you,' he said very deliberately.

Again came that insolent stare, then Marius pressed a button on his desk. Miss Buchman came in, her eyes darting curiously from one of them to the other.

'Kindly show Mr Landry out,' said Marius.

Ted glowered at him and turned to leave.

'I wish you good luck in your search,' came Marius's mocking voice as he went out.

PART 3

Chapter Twenty

Life had become almost impossible in Italy as the war continued. The fighting seemed to have been going on forever with little result, men were dying, and food was scarce. The north and south of the country had been bombed several times by the Allies, although Florence had been spared so far. As 1942 stretched into 1943 Beatrice found herself becoming increasingly confused, wondering what it was all for. She'd never been as strong a supporter of Mussolini as Mimmo, but she'd admired her husband for his strong principles and his willingness to fight for his country. Well, he'd done what was expected of him and died in the process, leaving behind him a heartsick wife and a frail child who were now left to make their way in the world on their own. Money was short, and there was little enough to buy with it anyway. Dora helped as much as she could, but she couldn't be spared by the Carminatis, who'd spent most of the war in Rome up to now. Beatrice would have preferred it had her mother stayed in Florence, but Gerardo paid well, and thanks to his influence Dora could obtain a few extra things for Tina which another employer wouldn't have been able to provide. Besides, it wasn't so easy to find a good job these days. So Beatrice accepted the parcels from Rome in exchange for her mother's absence. As time went on and supplies grew scarcer, the packages became less frequent and less heavy, but there was little they could do except tighten their belts and forge onwards. Beatrice longed to get a job, but without her mother there was no one she could trust to look after Tina, so she did her best to scrape by on Mimmo's meagre pension, most of which went on her daughter.

At least the day-to-day struggles helped to keep her mind off Mimmo. She'd heard a rumour, passed on via a friend whose brother Fabrizio had been injured in the same incident but survived long enough to be sent home, that her husband's death hadn't been as quick or as painless as she'd been led to believe. Through the official channels she'd been given to understand that he'd been killed instantly, but, according to Fabrizio, Mimmo had lain where he fell for several hours, and then there had been agonisingly long delays in getting him to hospital, where they'd done their best to treat his wounds until gangrene set in and his already exhausted body gave up. Beatrice wanted to speak to Fabrizio and question him about his story, but in his own weakened state he caught pneumonia and died of it that winter, and so her last chance of getting the truth about Mimmo's death died with him.

As time went on she began to question what the authorities were telling her about the progress of the war, because what she was reading didn't seem to match up with her own common sense and the evidence of her own eyes. She started to study the newspapers more closely, but also listened to the BBC on the radio. Difficult as it was to admit it to herself, it was becoming increasingly clear that the Italian campaign in North Africa had been a disaster, and that Mimmo's faith in Il Duce had been misplaced. Mussolini had promised them that they were fighting for the glory of Italy, but in reality it seemed that Italy was making mistakes everywhere it went, and the Germans had to keep rescuing them. It was hard to accept the idea that she and the rest of the Italian people had been lied to, but the treacherous thought would intrude itself into her mind, and she had to put it away from her and force herself to think of something else. If it were true – if the whole enterprise had been built on lies – then it meant that her beloved husband's

death had been for nothing, and there was no higher purpose to
this long, lonely struggle of hers.

It seemed that other people were questioning the wisdom of
the war, too. As Beatrice walked through the streets of Florence
– which was still whole so far, having not suffered the air raids
that had affected the cities in the north and the south as yet – she
increasingly noticed illegal posters and graffiti protesting the
Fascist government. In the shops, too, people had begun to mutter
discontentedly about how it was time for a new government, and
how they wished the Allies would hurry up and invade, to bring
an end to the war. Such open talk would have been unthinkable
only a year or two ago, but now it seemed people were becoming
bolder, and more prepared to express their real opinions.

In early 1943 came the news that the Italian Eighth Army had
been all but wiped out at Stalingrad. They'd been sent to Russia
to support German troops there, but had been unprepared and
underequipped for the harsh winter, and despite fighting valiantly
were overrun by the Russians. Half the men had died, and thousands
of others were injured. In spring the ones who had survived began
to arrive back in Italy in a terrible condition: sick, frostbitten and
wretched. Their appearance was a shock to those people who still
believed blindly in the superiority of the Axis powers, and caused
many more to begin questioning their loyalties. Beatrice saw some
of the returning men, and was horrified at their emaciated and
crippled state. Many of them, even if they survived, would be
wholly unfit to fight again. Still, Beatrice was reluctant to abandon
fully her faith that her country was in the right. Some good must
come of the war, surely? It wasn't right that so many people should
suffer so much for a mistake.

*

The year wore on and, on a late afternoon in July, Beatrice left her
apartment with Tina, who was now two and a half, and went into

the centre of Florence to buy food. The local shops had nothing she needed, but she'd heard of a grocer's shop in the Oltrarno where one could get cheese and olive oil and perhaps even butter without having to hand over one's ration card if one turned up at the right time – and paid the right price. By the time she got there the sun was beginning to set, and Tina didn't want to walk any more, so Beatrice picked her up and entered the shop, but to her annoyance found that the rumour was either exaggerated or untrue, because the shopkeeper had nothing to give her – or nothing she was prepared to admit to, at any rate.

Beatrice sighed and came out into the street, almost bumping into a young woman who was passing as she did so. She wouldn't have paid any attention, except that the woman was walking oddly, almost limping, her breath coming in shallow gasps, and she seemed in a hurry, glancing behind her frantically as she went. Beatrice looked at her smart clothes and hat and wondered what such an obviously well-to-do lady could be running away from, but then she saw the *carabiniere* just coming into the street. She looked for a third time at the woman, who had just ducked under an arch a little way down the street, and a memory sparked dimly. She never knew what made her do it, but without stopping to think she stepped out in front of the policeman, blocking his path as if accidentally.

'*Mi scusi*,' she said.

'No matter, *signora*. I don't suppose you've seen a woman running this way, have you? Well-dressed, wearing a hat with a veil.'

'Was she limping? Yes, she came down here and turned down that street to the right there.'

He thanked her and proceeded on his way. Beatrice waited until his footsteps had receded into the distance, then crossed the street and stood in front of the arch. There was nobody in the dim courtyard beyond, but here in the shadow of the arch itself was a still deeper shadow. Beatrice moved to one side and a thin finger of light lit up the right side of a weary face.

'Quick, come with me!' said Beatrice in a low voice.

'Who's that?' asked Stella, terrified.

'Beatrice. You remember? I am the daughter of Dora of the Villa Bruni. You are Miss Stella, no?'

There was a little sound, as if Stella had been holding her breath and had let it out all at once in relief.

'Yes. Beatrice. Of course! I was trying to get to the villa.'

'There is nobody at home and it is all locked up, or I would take you there. If you want to get away from that *carabiniere* you must come with me quickly, because he will come back soon.'

'I don't know if I can walk any more.'

'You must try or I cannot help you.'

'Yes, yes, I'll do it.'

Beatrice watched as she tried unsuccessfully to struggle to her feet, then shifted a dozing Tina onto her left hip and held out her right hand. Stella grasped it and pulled herself up with difficulty.

'*Madonna!*' breathed Beatrice as the left side of Stella's battered face came into view. 'What has happened to you?' She glanced about. The street was still deserted. 'Never mind, you can tell me later. Now we must go. Stay with me and we keep to the shade. It is more than a kilometre. Can you do it?'

The question was a doubtful one, because she saw that Stella's injuries weren't only limited to her face.

'Yes, I think so.'

They set off, but it was quickly clear that Stella couldn't move fast, and Beatrice could do nothing but hope that they wouldn't meet any more *carabinieri* between here and her apartment. As it was, they received several odd looks from passers-by as they went, which made her nervous. She was already half-regretting the impulse that had sent her to the other woman's aid, but she knew she couldn't have forgiven herself for leaving someone in such a state to the uncertain mercies of the police, so all she could do now was make sure they got home safely.

They made slow progress, keeping away from the main streets. Tina was heavy in Beatrice's arms now, and she wanted nothing more than to get home. It took nearly an hour, but at last they arrived at the little apartment and Beatrice unlocked the door. Stella had hardly said a word as they walked, and her breath had become increasingly shallow.

'I must put Tina to bed,' said Beatrice, glancing at the clock as they came in. When she came back from seeing to her daughter, she found Stella sitting on the couch, weeping silently, her hand clutching her side as if it hurt her to cry.

'I'm sorry,' she said as she saw Beatrice. 'I'll be all right in a minute.'

But it was obvious she was very far from all right. She leaned back and shut her eyes, and Beatrice saw the tears glistening on her cheeks and pitied the ravages of her face. She felt the injured girl's forehead. It was clammy.

'You must go to bed,' she said. 'I have only this couch. It will be all right, yes?'

'Yes,' came the reply, in the merest whisper. Then: 'Thank you.'

Chapter Twenty-One

It was two days before Stella was in any condition to get up, and Beatrice regretted more and more having ever brought her here. She took up the best seat and got in the way, and although mercifully she wasn't especially hungry, Beatrice's rations didn't stretch far enough for three. Once Dora returned from Rome there would perhaps be some food from the Villa Bruni, but for now she had nothing to offer. She'd initially suggested fetching a doctor, but Stella seemed so panicked at the idea that she dared not mention it again, and in any case the girl began to mend after a few days. Her face was still swollen and terrible, but she was up and walking stiffly around the house. On the third morning after her arrival she came out onto the little balcony, where Beatrice was tending to her herbs, and stood, her face turned to the sun, letting the light and warmth flood over her damaged face. As yet, she hadn't spoken about what had caused her injuries, and Beatrice was full of curiosity.

'What happened to you? Who did this?'

'My husband.'

Beatrice raised her eyebrows.

'I remember him. The Countess's brother. What's his name – Schwegler, yes?'

'Yes.'

'Why did he do it?'

'He was angry with me.'

'And you ran away from him?'

Stella nodded.

'What will you do now?'

'I don't know. I wasn't thinking of anything except to get away.'

Beatrice was nonplussed. She made an indeterminate gesture, taking in the small size of the apartment.

'I cannot keep you here. It is too small, and I don't have enough rations for another person. You don't have a card?'

'No.'

'A passport, then?'

'No. I left it behind.'

'And in any case, a British passport is not exactly welcome here. But you are a friend of the Count and the Countess. They will help you, no? They are in Rome at present, but when they return I will take you to them. Is there somewhere you can go while you wait for them to come back?'

Stella was shaking her head desperately.

'I don't have anywhere to go. Please don't send me away. I promise I'll go to Monica and Gerardo as soon as I can, but please let me stay here until then. I'm sure it won't be long. Listen, would you be able to send a telegram for me?'

'A telegram? To the Count and Countess?'

'No, to someone else in Switzerland, a friend. You remember him – he was here before the war. Ted Landry.'

Beatrice threw her a curious glance.

'The American journalist. Yes, I remember him. Do you think he will help you?'

'I don't know if there's anything he can do himself to get me out, but perhaps he knows someone who can. I'd like him to know that I'm safe, at least.'

'Telegrams are expensive and I don't have that kind of money. Have you got any money?'

'No. Marius took it all away from me.'

'Then I'm afraid I cannot help you. I'm sorry,' said Beatrice.

'Then what shall I do?' exclaimed Stella despairingly.

Beatrice looked at her. The Count and the Countess might not be back for weeks, and she couldn't let this woman, an enemy, from the side which had killed Mimmo, become a burden on her shoulders in the meantime. Why should she keep this useless person, with her fine clothes, who looked as if she liked nothing better than to sit about feeling sorry for herself, and who had no idea how much food could be bought for the cost of a telegram? There wasn't enough money or food even for herself and Tina. The easiest thing to do, of course, would be to inform the authorities of the British woman's presence – or would it? Wouldn't she be in trouble herself for having harboured her in the first place? Beatrice didn't know. She wished her mother were there to advise her, but it might be weeks before they saw each other again. Even writing to her would be a problem, as the censor would read the letter and then the secret would be out.

'Couldn't you go back to your husband? Maybe—' She stopped at the sight of Stella's face. Under the bruises and the scabs she'd gone white.

'I can't go back to Marius, I can't. Throw me out if you must, but I won't go back. He'll kill me.'

Beatrice was shocked at how Stella had begun trembling at the mere idea of it. It was obvious her husband scared her half to death. But the fact remained that her presence in Beatrice's house was a problem.

Beatrice didn't know what to do. She thought about it overnight, and decided to go and find out the situation at the Hotel Ambassador for herself. Perhaps some solution to her difficulty could be found there. The next day, therefore, she went out early, saying truthfully that she was going to buy some food. She bought her provisions – to her joy she managed to get some flour, salt and olive oil, for which she paid a small fortune – then, carrying her heavy parcels, she headed to the hotel and sought out one of the chambermaids from the old days with whom she'd been friendly. Anna was delighted to see Beatrice, who didn't even need to introduce the subject, because Anna was full of it. It seemed the hotel had been in an uproar since Tuesday, since the wife of one of the guests had disappeared – and not just any old guest: it was the brother of the Countess.

'The police have been crawling all over the place, questioning everybody,' said Anna breathlessly. 'They lined us all up and shouted and threatened, and said we'd all be arrested if we didn't tell us where she'd gone. They must think we have nothing better to do than keep an eye on the guests to make sure they don't wander off.'

'Did anybody see her go?'

'Well I certainly didn't. I wasn't even here when she went missing.' Anna glanced around and lowered her voice. 'But Gianni told me after the police had gone that he saw a woman creeping past the kitchen, who matched the description of Mrs Schwegler. He was going to tell her she shouldn't be in that part of the hotel but when he went out she'd already gone out by the side door.'

'He didn't tell the police?'

'What? And get the blame for not stopping her? Gianni said he didn't see her closely, but she was limping, as if she'd been hurt. But there's more.'

She paused importantly.

'Go on.'

Anna glanced around again.

'This Schwegler is supposed to be out of his mind with worry, but actually I think he's just very angry. I went in to clean his room on Thursday morning, and he was there, and he threw a shoe at me while I was working for no reason at all! He apologised, and said it was just because he was worried sick about his wife. He'd been walking the streets looking for her, he said, and couldn't find any trace of her. But then he started questioning me, and lost his temper again when I said I didn't know anything. He said I must have seen something. I tried to tell him I hadn't even been here when she went missing, but he shouted and swore at me. I was sure he was going to hit me, so I dodged out of the way, but he got a hold of himself and went out and left me to it, which was a relief. He seemed so charming when he first arrived, but I don't think he's nice at all. If you ask me, she got tired of him and ran away, perhaps with another man.'

They were standing in the corridor by the lift as they talked, and just then Beatrice looked up and saw Marius himself coming towards them through the door from the lobby. Anna immediately began talking of something else. Beatrice looked away in the hope that he wouldn't recognise her, but he stopped.

'Beatrice, isn't it?' he said.

Her heart sank. She was useless at deception, and had the horrible feeling that the truth was written all over her face.

'Mr Schwegler. How nice to see you again,' she replied. She knew she ought to say something about Stella, but she couldn't think what.

'Has there been any news, *signore*?' asked Anna, coming to her rescue.

He shook his head distractedly. Beatrice decided this was a good moment to leave, and said goodbye to Anna.

'Wait!' commanded Marius, as she headed towards the lobby. She froze, and he caught up with her and walked with her out into the street. 'I'd like a word with you.'

'What is it?'

He drew her under the shade of a nearby portico.

'I don't know whether they've told you, but my wife has gone missing. You remember her, don't you? Have you seen her?'

'Miss Stella? No. Why should I have seen her?' she answered quickly – too quickly. She kicked herself inwardly, but he'd caught it immediately and looked at her sharply.

'You have, haven't you?'

'No. I'm sorry, I—'

'Please,' he said. She opened her mouth to reply, but before she could say anything he went on, 'Listen, Beatrice. There's something I didn't tell the police.' He rubbed a hand wearily across his face. 'She was going to have a baby, but she lost it, quite late. It was very hard on her, and she had a sort of – a sort of nervous breakdown, I suppose you'd call it. She shut herself in her room for hours on end and wouldn't talk to me. Then a couple of weeks ago she went out and didn't come back. I didn't know where she'd gone.' He hesitated and glanced up at her. 'I got a call that evening to say she'd thrown herself in front of a train. They'd managed to drag her off the track just in time, but she hurt herself quite badly in the fall from the platform. I dare say I shouldn't have brought her to Florence, but I had business I couldn't put off, and I didn't dare leave her, and I thought perhaps a change of scene would help. But it seems I was wrong. So you see, I have every reason to worry about her. Please, Beatrice, if you've heard anything, let me know.'

His face was such a sincere picture of grief that Beatrice could see why anyone might believe him. She almost believed him herself, until she glanced up and caught him watching her closely. It was obvious he was trying to gauge her reaction. She thought of Anna's tale of how Marius had thrown a shoe at her for no reason. And she remembered the dried blood crusting Stella's swollen, battered face, and how the girl had limped, holding her side, all the way back to Beatrice's house, before collapsing on the couch. Freshly broken ribs and a smashed face weren't a sign of a mental disorder or a suicide attempt two weeks ago. Besides, Beatrice had seen the bruises on Stella's upper arms, the marks of Marius's fingers as he'd gripped her tightly in his fury.

'I'm sorry, I can't help you,' she said.

Beatrice had never been a good liar. Marius's eyes narrowed. He glanced around then moved very close to her. The sense of menace was palpable, and she wanted to back away, but he'd got her against the wall and she couldn't. His eyes bored into hers.

'Listen to me,' he said, very quietly. 'I intend to find my wife one way or the other, so if you know where she is you'd better tell me right now or I promise you you'll regret it.'

Beatrice was frightened. He seemed to be holding himself under control, but it looked as if at any moment the control might snap and he might lash out. The muscles of his jaw were tense, and his hands were curled up as if ready to bunch into fists.

'I'm sorry,' she said again, then slid away from him and walked off as fast as she could, without looking back. She turned the first corner she came to and started running, and didn't stop until she was quite sure she'd got well away from him.

*

Stella listened fearfully as Beatrice told her of her encounter with Marius.

'You won't send me back to him, will you?' she said. 'I know it's hard for you, but I'll be better soon, and I can help you around the house.'

That won't feed us, Beatrice was about to say, but Stella was already fumbling with the two rings she wore. She held one out and put the other back on.

'Look, this is my wedding ring. I don't know why I didn't think of it before, because God knows, I don't need it any more. If you sell it the money should be enough to pay for my telegram, and whatever's left you can spend on food for us all, and something nice for Tina.'

Beatrice looked at the thick, gold band. Her own had been taken by the authorities long ago for the war effort in exchange for a plain metal one. She hesitated, then took it, feeling the weight of the gold. Her hand closed around it.

'They will probably censor the telegram. It might not even get there at all.'

As she said it, she knew that in accepting the ring, she'd pledged her faith in an odd kind of way, and that she couldn't send Stella away now.

'I have to try,' said Stella simply.

*

A few days later, Beatrice returned cautiously to the Hotel Ambassador at Stella's instigation.

'Your husband has gone back to Switzerland,' she announced when she returned. 'Anna says he tried to get my address out of her but she'd already taken against him when he was rude to her, so she told him she didn't know it. The police were still there, though. I think they will send you back to him if they find you. They certainly won't let you wander around Italy without any documents.'

Stella shivered at the thought of what would happen if they returned her to Marius. Still, she was safe for the present, at least. She could hardly believe the lengths Marius had gone to in order to find out her whereabouts from Beatrice. The lie about the baby was so outrageous that it almost took her breath away. She was filled with indignation at the story he'd chosen to explain her flight, because she *had* wanted a baby, back in the early days, especially once it became clear how cold he was. A son or daughter would have given her the love she craved, but Marius had been quite firm that he didn't want the mess and fuss of a child. Then when Ted had come along, of course a baby would have been the worst thing that could have possibly happened. No – there had been no baby.

But what was she to do now? She knew full well that Beatrice had taken her in reluctantly, and that there wasn't enough food to go round. She'd also seen Beatrice casting glances at the sapphire ring she wore – Ted's ring – but she couldn't give that up, she just

couldn't. It was the only thing she had to remind her of the love
they had and the promise he'd made her. She'd been disappointed
not to receive an immediate reply to her telegram, but she was
sure she'd be on her way to London very soon, and what would
Ted think of her when they met again if she told him she'd sold it
for the sake of a few bits of bread? But she was happy to give up
anything else she could. Her expensive frock had been washed and
pressed carefully, and was just waiting to be sold. They planned
to sell her hat with the veil, too – although that would fetch less
money, being slightly stained with blood. And with any luck,
something else would turn up soon and she could stay until the
Carminatis returned and a passage could be arranged for her out
of the country. Stella was a little wary of Monica, who might want
to return her to Marius out of loyalty, but she thought Gerardo
might look upon her more kindly. He had influence, and she was
sure he'd be able to get her to England if she begged him.

But time passed and there was still no word from Ted, and,
before they knew it, three weeks had gone, and Stella was almost
fully recovered. The bruises had nearly faded and, while she still
had a little pain in her side, she was moving much more easily.
She knew that the more she improved the more likely it was that
Beatrice would want her to leave, and she had been casting around
for something to do that would make her indispensable, at least
until Gerardo and Monica returned. Without papers or a ration
card she knew she was a burden on the family, and while she
hoped Beatrice wouldn't cast her out on the streets, there was no
denying the fact that life was becoming more difficult. Sooner or
later Stella would have no choice but to leave and fend for herself,
and the thought of that filled her with fear, because she had no
one to go to here in Italy.

Why hadn't Ted replied to her telegram? It must have been
stopped by the censor, as Beatrice had said it would be, because
Stella was sure that if he'd received it he'd have telegraphed back at

the very least. She was missing him terribly and was frantic to get word to him. But even if he hadn't got it he would know by now that she hadn't turned up to her appointment with the Red Cross man. What would he be thinking? Had he gone to her apartment and got her note from Mme Blanchet? If he had then at least he would know where she'd gone, and would be wondering why she hadn't returned to Geneva by now.

Her distress at the failure of the escape plan was compounded by all kinds of other worries, of which perhaps the most illogical was the fear that Ted would forget about her. He'd wanted to marry her, but who was to say he wouldn't write her off as lost forever and move on? As the days went on with no reply she became increasingly desperate to try again to let him know she was safe. The telegram hadn't got through, but what about a letter? She made the suggestion to Beatrice, who thought for a moment.

'If they are censoring everything then we must be careful. If you write it in English it will draw suspicion because of the language and your foreign handwriting. Besides, to send a letter I will have to show them my identity papers and address, and then they will know where you are.'

'Then will you write it for me? In Italian? He understands Italian.'

Beatrice agreed, and they spent a whole afternoon pondering how to phrase it so as to let Ted know without attracting the attention of the authorities. In the end they came up with the following, written in formal Italian:

Dear Mr Landry,

I have been requested to inform you that the young friend of the Countess is so delighted with Florence that she has been persuaded to stay here for a while, at least until Their

Excellencies return from Rome and can secure her a safe
passage home. She desires me to tell you that she is well and
hopes to see you soon.

Yours sincerely,
Beatrice Bianchi Fabbri

There was enough information in it to tell Ted that Stella was
safe in Florence. They dared not add anything more for fear of its
sounding like a code but, even so, the letter was suspiciously short
for a personal note.

'It sounds like a business letter,' said Stella, reading it through.
'Perhaps we ought to add some meaningless news. Or – I don't
suppose you have a typewriter, do you? That would make it look
more official.'

Beatrice gave a sudden wide smile.

'Ah, of course! No, I don't have a typewriter, but I have a neighbour who does and might let me use it. And even better...' an idea
had struck her, and she went off to rummage in a drawer. 'See!'
With a look of triumph she brought out some rather creased sheets
of headed paper from the Hotel Ambassador. 'From my old job.'

'Perfect! With that, and Monica's name, we might just be lucky
and they won't read it too closely. You can post it later when you
go out for food.'

At that Beatrice's face fell.

'I've used up all my coupons for the week,' she said. 'I can get
a few things for Tina, but as for us two...' She shrugged. 'Even if
I had coupons there's nothing in the shops to buy. I don't know
what we're going to eat between now and Monday.'

Stella thought of her ring and put her right hand over her left
protectively. Then she looked at Beatrice, who had rescued her from
Marius. Which was more important – a tiny circle of metal and

stone that served no practical purpose, or their lives? It was only a ring. To insist on keeping it would be selfish and ungrateful. If Ted had been in the same position he wouldn't have thought twice about it. Ignoring the leaden weight that had settled onto her heart, she pulled the ring off. Her fingers had swollen in the heat and it came off with difficulty, clinging on till the last.

'Here.' She held it out. 'Get what you can for it. And don't forget the stamp for the letter.'

Beatrice took the ring. Her eyes were sympathetic, but she knew as well as Stella did that there was no other option.

'Thank you,' she said.

She went out, and Stella was left alone, staring at the groove on her finger where the ring had been. Only a few short weeks ago she'd cried and kissed him when he gave her it, and had promised to wear it always; now she'd given up her faith in exchange for nothing more than a few mouthfuls of food. She knew she'd done the right thing, and reminded herself that he would soon know she was safe, but it was poor consolation. Whatever the rights and wrongs of the situation, it felt like a betrayal, as if she were admitting to herself that she'd never see Ted again. She'd held the tears in up to now, but with that thought the dam burst, and she put her head in her hands and sobbed as if her heart would break.

Chapter Twenty-Two

A few days after Stella's arrival they'd heard that the Allies had landed in Sicily, after several months of heavy bombing of Italian cities. Florence had been spared the bombing so far, but speculation was sweeping the city as to what would happen next. Most Italians were by now heartily sick of the war, and although the air raids were causing widespread terror, there were many who hoped that with the arrival of the British and the Americans on Italian soil, things would soon improve. Stella was hoping it meant good news for her, and that the Allies would soon make it onto the Italian mainland and bring the war to an end so that she could go home.

She'd been wondering whether there was any way of getting out of the country that didn't require the help of Monica or Gerardo. Money would have bought her a false passport, but she had none and no means of getting any. She remembered with regret the paintings sitting in the tobacco warehouse just outside Lucerne. The sale of any one of them would have given her all the money she needed. Odd how easy it was to sacrifice one's principles: back in Switzerland, when she'd been well-off, she wouldn't have dreamt of selling the paintings and keeping the money, but now that she was in dire need she didn't care how her father had obtained them and would have converted them into cash without a second thought. Still, they were far away in Switzerland, and it was useless to think about it. All she could do was stay in hiding, safe for now, and wait for an opportunity to present itself.

*

In late July Beatrice found that her hospitality was about to be stretched further. It happened just as the whole country was in an uproar over the final collapse of the Fascist regime. After weeks of rumours the news had come that Mussolini's own government had turned against him, and the King had forced him to resign. He was now under arrest in a secret location. On the day the news broke Beatrice came running into the apartment with some shopping and a newspaper. Stella was on the floor, playing with Tina.

'Look!' exclaimed Beatrice. 'Il Duce has fallen!'

'Yes, I just heard it on the radio,' replied Stella. 'I was hoping it meant an end to the war, but Marshal Badoglio says Italy must keep fighting.'

'Yes, yes, but there is more.'

Beatrice dropped her bag on the floor and began turning the pages of the newspaper, searching for something. She knelt down on the floor by Stella and spread the paper out, pointing to an article.

'See? He was voted out by his own Grand Council, and the Count was one of those who voted against him!'

'Gerardo!' exclaimed Stella. The article was in Italian but she understood enough of it to see that the majority of the Fascist Grand Council had signed a motion demanding Mussolini's removal, and that Gerardo had been one of the signatories. 'Goodness me! What will happen now?'

She couldn't help it, but her first thought was how the news would affect her. According to the papers, there was to be a curfew, which would make it more difficult for her to leave. Presumably Gerardo would have to remain in Rome for now, so she couldn't appeal to him for help, which meant there was no hope of a safe passage to England for the time being. Her heart sank. She'd been trapped in Florence for three weeks already, and London and Ted seemed further away than ever. All she could hope was that despite the vow of the new leader, Badoglio, to continue the war, Italy would in reality decide to sue for peace with the Allies, and then she would be safe.

As for Beatrice, although by now she was firmly convinced that Il Duce had been bad for Italy, she couldn't help remembering Mimmo's blind faith in his leader, and thinking how disillusioned he would have been at the present developments if he'd been here to see them. As such she was unable to rejoice in the event, however hard she tried. She turned away from the newspaper, feeling suddenly sick at the waste of her husband's life and the lives of countless other brave Italians.

'I will go and make the dinner,' she said in a subdued voice, and for the next hour or two busied herself with chores around the house, which were always the most effective way to suppress her grief whenever she felt it trying to rise. More than two years after her husband's death she had still not come to terms with his loss, burying her pain deep inside herself so that it couldn't rise up and defeat her. The harder she worked, she told herself, the thicker the shell around her heart would be.

By late evening Stella had read the newspaper several times through and was frowning over it and formulating ever more unworkable plans to get herself to London. Beatrice, meanwhile, was mending a stocking, and they were sitting in a companionable silence when there was a knock at the door. Stella jumped in fright and stared at Beatrice, who stood up and went to peer out of a gap under the shutters.

'There is a man here,' she said.

'Are you expecting someone?'

'No. You had better hide, in case it is the police.' She hustled Stella out through the kitchen and through the door that led to the basement. 'Down there! And don't say a word.'

Stella needed no further telling, but disappeared, white in the face, as the knock was repeated. Beatrice went to answer the door. There in front of her was a man – or what was left of one.

He was filthy and emaciated, and was swaying on his feet. Only the battered Alpini hat with the remains of a feather in it told her that he was a soldier.

'Beatrice,' said the visitor, and at last she knew him, but only because of his voice.

'*Dio mio*! Vittorio! But what—'

She swiftly saw that there was no use in conversation, because the effort of speech seemed to have drained him of his last drop of energy, and even as she replied he slumped against the door frame, clearly exhausted. She glanced about her.

'Quick! Come in!'

She helped him into the house, and for the second time in less than a month saw an unexpected guest collapse on her couch. She stood there irresolutely for a second, then went to fetch Stella from the basement.

'Who is it?' said Stella, looking at the pitiful figure on the sofa.

'It is Vittorio. You remember? From the Villa Bruni and the hotel.'

'Goodness! I shouldn't have recognised him. He's very sick.'

'Why did he come here? You see his uniform. His regiment should be looking after him.'

'I don't know, but look at him – he's shivering, even in this heat.' Stella felt his forehead. 'He has a raging fever. He needs cooling down.'

Beatrice went off and returned with a wet cloth and a glass of water. Stella bathed his face, and he opened his eyes briefly and murmured something.

'He wants a drink.' Stella held his head up gently and tipped a little of the liquid into his mouth. There was a croaked '*Grazie*,' and he lay back and closed his eyes again. His breathing was ragged and laboured. Stella looked up at Beatrice, who had been caught off guard at this second invasion of her home, and seemed at a loss to know how to deal with it.

'Do you have any aspirin?' she asked.

Beatrice nodded. 'In the cupboard, on the top shelf.'

The medicine was brought, and somehow they managed to get it down him. After a few minutes his breathing became more regular and he seemed to be sleeping. Stella fetched a cushion to put under his head, and they watched him for a while.

'I can't throw him out,' said Beatrice. 'But where can we put him? He is on your couch.'

'Leave him there – he needs it more than I do.'

'But where will you sleep?'

'If you take Tina into your bed, then I can sleep in hers. It's only small, but it will do for now. When he wakes up we can give him some more aspirin and a little of that broth from today. He looks as if he hasn't eaten for weeks, poor thing.'

'There is no aspirin left. That was the last of it.'

'Can we get some more?'

'It's hard to come by and will be expensive.'

'Perhaps he has something we can sell, then.'

They looked in his backpack, which he had dropped on the floor just inside the door. In it were a watch, some clothes, a little food, a pair of gold cufflinks and a gun.

'That's all, I think,' said Stella, peering inside. 'It's not polite to sell his things without asking, but we might have to.'

'What about in his pockets? Is there anything else?'

They approached him cautiously. He didn't wake as Beatrice searched through his jacket.

'What's this?' She brought something out, then gasped. It was a thick wad of banknotes, dirty and much thumbed.

'Swiss francs!' exclaimed Stella. 'Praise be!'

She took the money and counted it.

'Almost a thousand,' she said in wonder.

'What is that in lire?' Beatrice wanted to know.

'I haven't a clue. Thousands, on the black market, I imagine.'

They stared at each other, then Beatrice looked back at Vittorio.

'Why didn't he spend it on food? Look how thin he is, almost starving.'

'Well, with this money we can get him some medicine tomorrow. If he lasts that long,' Stella added under her breath, because Vittorio was a friend of Beatrice's and she didn't want to upset her.

Beatrice took the money and the other things and put them away. The gun she locked away in the cupboard, just to be on the safe side.

*

Vittorio was sick and delirious for several days, but they procured him aspirin and food, and he gradually began to recover, although he was still so thin it was obvious he wouldn't return to full strength for some time to come. He said little, conserving his energy, until at last one day Beatrice came in to find him struggling to sit up. She went to help him, but he brushed her off and did it himself.

'I see you're feeling better,' she said. 'I'll make you something to eat. We have bread, and a few pickles left over from last winter. The bread's a bit stale but it can't be helped.'

She brought the food, and busied herself around him, tidying the room as he ate.

'I'm very dirty,' he remarked, looking at his filthy fingernails.

'Yes, you are, and you smell bad, too.' He grinned unapologetically, and she went on, 'If you're well enough to get up you'd better have a wash. And when you're strong enough to eat more I'll get you something good to fatten you up.'

She went across to the locked drawer, fetched the money they'd taken from his pocket and handed it to him.

'We haven't spent much, just enough to get you some medicine.' She looked down sheepishly. 'And I bought a little food for Tina. She was hungry.'

'That's all right.' He looked at the roll of notes in his hand. 'Does anybody know I'm here?'

'No, only Stella.'

'Stella?'

'Miss Stella, from the Villa Bruni. Do you remember her? She ran away from her husband and she's hiding here until we can get her back to England, whenever that will be. Do you want me to tell your regiment you're here?'

'No!' he said quickly. 'Please, not now.' He held out the money. 'Keep this, will you? For us all. Get something good for Tina.'

Beatrice took the roll of notes, and understood what he meant by it.

'You want to stay here? Hide here?'

He nodded.

'Just until I'm better. Then I'll be off your hands.'

'Vittorio, where did you get the money?'

Then he told her of the long, cold months in Russia, and how at last the Russians had overrun them, killed half the men and captured thousands of others; how he'd managed to escape, and of the long weeks hiding in farmhouses and relying on the kind hospitality of people he'd thought were his enemies. How eventually he'd made it through Hungary and into Yugoslavia, and how, hungry, footsore and weary, he'd happened upon some fighting between partisan factions in Slovenia, and had found the body of a German soldier in the woods. There was nothing he could do for the man, so he took what he could from him, including the money, and went on his way. By the time he got across the mountains into the Veneto, he was sick and couldn't eat. None of the hotels or guest houses wanted him in the condition he was in, so he made his way down the peninsula to Florence. He'd have gone straight to the Villa Bruni but by the time he got as far as Beatrice's house he couldn't walk any further.

'The Count is in Rome anyway. You were better off coming here,' Beatrice said. She looked at the money. There was no denying it would help them a lot. 'I won't waste it.'

He nodded, and with that they struck an unspoken agreement. She didn't ask him again about rejoining his regiment because, having seen the state of him, she knew she couldn't in all humanity force him to return to the fighting. Vittorio had done his duty now, and Beatrice would always respect him for that. She thought about Mimmo, who had not been so lucky as Vittorio, and who had rotted away from gangrene in a foreign hospital. Here in Florence they had little to eat, but they were much better off than the men who had been fighting a war in terrible conditions.

So Vittorio stayed. With his money they got him a mattress and some new clothes, some medicine, and food to feed him up, then when he was well enough he went to sleep down in the basement and Stella got her couch back.

The summer passed, and the situation in Italy became increasingly uncertain. The Allies were demanding unconditional surrender from the Italians, and in the meantime were still bombing all the main Italian cities. Italy was sick and tired of the war. After a few weeks Vittorio's money began to run out, and so Beatrice went back to the Hotel Ambassador and asked for work, because with two other people at home she could leave Tina now. Her old job in the office had been taken by the manager's daughter, but they offered her work as a maid, which she accepted in the absence of anything better. The work was hard but not unpleasant, and gave Beatrice the opportunity to keep her ear to the ground and find out what was going on. She noticed that the hotel was filling up more and more with Germans, who were positioning themselves in Italy in anticipation of the country's surrender to the Allies, and she feared there was little chance of the war ending soon. She also kept a careful eye on the bookings register, because every now and then Marius returned to Florence to stay at the hotel, and she didn't want him to find out she was working there. The police had lost interest in Stella's disappearance, it seemed, but she knew Marius suspected her of sheltering Stella, so whenever he did come back she was careful not to bump into him, and made sure she was never assigned to clean his room.

At home, Vittorio was gathering strength. He was still too thin, but he looked much better, and was recognisably Vittorio. His sense of humour and something of his old cockiness had returned, and he liked nothing better than to play with Tina, tossing her up in the air and catching her while she screamed with laughter. But after a while he began to get impatient at his enforced imprisonment, and began to talk about leaving them.

'Where will you go?' said Beatrice when he mentioned it one day. 'You're not going back to the army, are you?'

It wasn't really a question, and he didn't reply.

'Then where?'

'We'll see,' he said, and tapped his nose.

He'd started going out at night and receiving messages scrawled on grubby, crumpled paper. Sometimes he even received visits, late in the evening, from shadowy-looking men with drawn faces and wary eyes. On those occasions he didn't abuse Beatrice's hospitality by inviting them in, but would slip outside with them, returning to his basement room in the small hours of the morning.

'Who are those men?' Stella asked of Beatrice one day.

'Partisans,' said Beatrice. 'Resistance.'

'What are they resisting against?'

'Nothing, yet. But it looks like there will be fighting one way or another – perhaps against the Germans – and they must be ready for it.'

Chapter Twenty-Three

By the time of Italy's surrender to the Allies Vittorio was almost
fully recovered and thinking about his next steps, although it would
have been only too pleasant to stay here with Beatrice, watching
her as she moved with her easy grace around the apartment, seeing
her smile at Tina's antics and wishing she'd smile at him in the same
way. It was fortunate, perhaps, that the English woman was hiding
here too, getting in the way and seeing everything that went on,
because otherwise it would have been easy to forget himself and
blurt out something to Beatrice he might regret. She'd taken him
in and saved his life, had given him shelter for two months without
fuss, and had waved away his thanks as if it were the kind of thing
she did every day. She was the sort of woman any man would be
proud to call his own, but it was clear she had no thoughts of that
nature for him. He supposed she was still mourning Mimmo, who
had been his friend despite their differences, and who would have
looked after Beatrice and kept her happy had he lived. Vittorio
wanted to protect her for Mimmo's sake, but he suspected she
wouldn't take kindly to the idea. And in any case, his being here
would be a danger to her sooner or later. After sweeping into Italy
and taking control, the Germans had announced that all Italian
soldiers were to report for duty to continue the war – something
he had no intention of doing – so he knew he would have to leave
soon, or she'd be in trouble for harbouring him. He'd made contact
with a group of partisans who were in hiding near Florence, and
planned to join them as soon as he was fully well, which he knew

wouldn't be too long now, because he was feeling stronger every day, and was itching to do something useful.

Shortly after the armistice, Dora returned from Rome and came to the apartment. She exclaimed at length upon finding Stella and Vittorio sheltering there, but she was bursting with her own news too.

'The Count is going into hiding,' she said. 'The situation was already difficult in the summer, and he couldn't appear much in public because nobody likes the Fascists any more – even though His Excellency was one of the men who voted to get Mussolini out! But now Il Duce is back and rounding up all the people who turned against him, so it's worse now. He has even had Ciano arrested and charged with treason, and that's his own son-in-law, so you can imagine how the Count must be worrying. It is not safe for him any more.'

'Where is the Count now?' asked Beatrice.

'I don't know. Only Beppe knows.'

'He's not hiding at the villa?'

'No. That would be too obvious. I expect he will hide somewhere in the countryside, well away from the Germans.'

Stella hadn't thought about Beppe in years, even though he'd been the first person she met when she arrived in Florence. She was pleased to hear that he was still loyal to Gerardo.

'What about Monica – the Countess?' she asked. 'Where is she?'

Dora made an expressive face and looked as if she'd like to say something on the subject, but, presumably remembering whom she was speaking to, merely shrugged.

'I don't know where she is. I told her I wanted to return to Florence, and she said I could go if I liked. Beppe thinks she has gone to stay with some rich friends near Rome, to keep out of trouble.' She looked at Stella. 'So many people in hiding. *Poverina*, stuck here in Florence. You'd have done better to stay in Geneva. And you,' she went on to Vittorio. 'What are you doing here? Aren't you supposed to be fighting?'

'Yes, and I will.'

'You're going back to the army?' asked Beatrice.

He shook his head.

'Not this time. I fought for Mussolini once, and that got us nowhere, so now I'm going to fight for Italy.'

*

That night, in defiance of the curfew, Vittorio slid out into the shadowy Florentine streets and went to see Beppe, who lived alone in a flat above a garage close to the Villa Bruni. It was a warm night, and the first-floor window of the flat which gave onto the street was open. Vittorio threw a pebble up at it and waited until he saw a movement, then hissed:

'It's me, Vittorio!'

He waited until the sound came of a door being unbolted.

'Come in,' said Beppe, glancing cautiously about him. 'Were you followed?'

'No.'

Beppe led him upstairs and into his tiny, grubby apartment.

'It is Vittorio,' he announced to a man who was sitting in a battered old armchair.

Gerardo stood up. He'd aged visibly in the two years since Vittorio had last seen him, but was still his old polite, good-humoured self.

'Hallo, my boy! What a surprise! How did you know I was here?'

'Dora told me. She says you're going into hiding.'

Gerardo pursed up his lips comically.

'I'm afraid so. Such is the price of trying to do one's best for one's country. But really, you know, it was all getting too much, and we couldn't let Il Duce go on driving Italy into the ground, much as I respect the man. But I hear the Germans had other ideas, and so I must keep out of sight for a while.'

'You're staying with Beppe?'

'For the moment, yes.'

'What about Her Excellency?'

'She's gone to stay with friends just outside Rome. She'll be safe that way as long as she keeps her head down and doesn't draw too much attention to herself. Besides, I don't think she'd take well to the clandestine life, do you?' There was a glimmer of amusement in Gerardo's eyes as he said it. 'I expect there'll be a certain amount of moving from place to place. I don't even suppose I'll be able to stay here long, since it can be only a matter of time before the Germans requisition the Villa Bruni, and this place is far too close to it for comfort. Speaking of which, I'm glad you've turned up, because I need a favour, and it will be much easier with two of you.'

'What's that?'

'Why, my beautiful paintings, of course! I can't possibly leave them there in the villa. Once the Germans move in I don't give much for my chances of ever seeing them again. Oh, I know they claim to have some sort of art protection organisation, but I don't trust them an inch not to help themselves to the best ones, would you?'

'You want me and Beppe to hide them for you?'

'If you'd be so good. Beppe has spoken to the priest up in Casignano, who is going to keep them in the cellar of the church for me, but we have to get them up there first. Will you help him?'

'But there are nearly fifty of them! How will we take them?'

Beppe spoke up.

'My cousin was going to help, with his truck, but he can't get the petrol, so we will have to take his cart instead and do it in a few trips. But first we must get them out of the villa before the Germans get here. We can bring them here. Although there won't be much room for them and Your Excellency in here,' he said, eyeing Gerardo doubtfully.

'Oh, don't worry about me,' replied Gerardo. 'The paintings are the important thing. When can you bring them out?'

'We can start now if you like,' said Vittorio, and Beppe grunted in agreement.

'Good boy! I knew I could rely on you. I would come and help, but, you know…' here there was his characteristic shrug. 'At any rate, you won't find me ungrateful.'

By the time dawn broke they'd brought out eleven paintings, and Beppe had gone to speak to his cousin about the cart. Then over the next few nights Vittorio brought out the rest of the artworks, while Beppe loaded them into the cart, which was pulled by an elderly and moth-eaten mule, and drove them the ten kilometres up into the hills outside Florence to the church in which they were to be stored. It took them four nights. On the last trip, once Beppe had gone off with the final cartload of paintings, Gerardo watched them go then beckoned Vittorio back into Beppe's apartment.

'Look!' he said, pulling the old armchair away from the wall and showing Vittorio a painting which was resting there. It was the *Lady of the Cypresses*, which was small enough to be easily hidden.

'Why didn't you send it off with Beppe?' asked Vittorio.

'I don't know. Something tells me it needs to be hidden somewhere more secure.'

'Don't you trust Beppe?'

'Of course I do. But I don't know this cousin of his, so it's as well to be on the safe side. I could stand to lose any or all of them, but not this one.'

'Is it worth so very much money?'

'Oh yes, but the money isn't the point. I knew as soon as I set eyes on her that I had to have her, and I won't give her up easily. That sly fox Otto Kaufmann was pestering me for her to the last, you know. They posted him to Paris in the end and put him in charge of stealing paintings for Hitler and Goering, but I shouldn't be surprised if he or Marius turn up here again, hoping to get their hands on my young lady. Marius in particular has had an avid eye on it for years. Well, they won't get her if I can help it.'

'But the painting won't be any safer here.'

'No, of course it won't – that's why I want you to hide it for me.'

Vittorio stared at him. The rest of the collection had just departed safely in a cart, to be taken along a quiet road out of Florence and up into the hills. How could Vittorio find anywhere safer than that? And he had no transport, so how was he supposed to smuggle it out? He was convinced the old man had lost his mind, but Gerardo was looking at him with such a serene expression of confidence that he hadn't the heart to point out the dangers. Besides, there were bigger things to worry about than the paintings, not least the fact that if the Count were found then he would be arrested for treason and possibly shot.

'All right,' he said at last.

Gerardo beamed. 'Splendid! I knew you'd think of something.'

Vittorio hadn't thought of anything yet, but he didn't see the need to tell Gerardo that. Truth to tell, he didn't think it would be possible to keep the painting hidden from a really determined searcher, but if it was the most valuable of them all he supposed he could see the wisdom of keeping it separate from the rest of the collection, especially if there was a chance that Beppe's cousin might talk.

'I'll take it now, before Beppe gets back,' he said. 'But I'd better go quickly – it'll be getting light soon.'

Gerardo dropped his hand lightly onto Vittorio's shoulder.

'Thank you. Your mother would have been proud of you.'

Vittorio smiled uncertainly and went out, but he didn't go very far, because he realised, if Gerardo didn't, that to carry a genuine Raphael in its frame through the streets of Florence would be foolishness to the point of suicide. Instead, he walked a few hundred yards down the lane in the direction of the Villa Bruni, keeping to the shadows as much as he could, and knocked on the door of Dora's house just outside the gates.

At last the door opened a crack.

'Vittorio? What are you doing here?'

The door opened wider, to reveal Dora in her dressing-gown, and Vittorio stepped inside quickly and shut the door. He explained the situation in a few words.

'He seems to think I can hide it better than Beppe can, but I don't know where to put it. Is there room here?'

Dora frowned anxiously.

'Yes, but it will easily be found if someone comes. We must think of a better place, but in the meantime it can go in the attic.'

She fetched a torch from a drawer and led him upstairs to a tiny attic room in which all he could see in the darkness was a sloping ceiling and two small windows at floor level. Dora switched on the torch.

'These windows face the garden and no one will see,' she explained.

Vittorio looked about him. On one side of the room, below the slope of the roof, a little bed and bedside table stood where the eaves had been walled off. He went and knocked on the wall. It was hollow.

'We can put it behind here. Would you mind?' She hesitated, and he went on: 'Look at it this way, *signora*, if they catch the Count and shoot him, we'll be set for life – if we can sell it, that is.'

'Ah, and that will be child's play of course. All right, I'll keep it if I must. But you don't really want them to shoot the Count, do you?'

'No, of course I don't.' He slid the painting under the bed. 'Leave it there for now. I'll come tomorrow and do the work. Don't say a word to Beatrice. It's just between you and me.'

She promised, and he slid out into the darkness again, but returned the next day as he had said. By the time he'd finished walling up the painting in Dora's attic, Gerardo had already gone into hiding.

Chapter Twenty-Four

As Gerardo had predicted, the Germans requisitioned the Villa Bruni. Dora came to deliver the news, bristling with indignation.

'I saw it this morning when I arrived. I went up to see that all was well, but they were there, with their Nazi flags and their big cars and their salutes and their *Heil Hitlers*. I told them I will keep coming to make sure they are looking after it, and they'd better behave themselves. They think I'm a foolish old woman so I can say what I like, but they'll have me to deal with if they break anything.'

'Then they're keeping you on?' said Vittorio. 'That's good news. You can keep an ear out and bring us any news you get.'

'Just as long as nobody thinks I approve of them,' she said. 'I'm only there because I care about the house, not because I care about the Germans. Oh, goodness, what will the Countess say if they wreck the place? She ought to have come back to Florence with the Count.'

Not long after that Vittorio left them to join the partisans. He packed his few belongings, and the gun he'd brought back with him, then threw Tina into the air one last time and went to bid Stella and Beatrice goodbye, his eyes lingering longest of all on Beatrice.

'What are you going to do?' she asked. 'You can't fight the Germans.'

'Maybe not, but we can fight the Fascists and destroy them once and for all,' he said.

'You will be careful, won't you?'

He nodded, then before she could stop him kissed her hand and left in a hurry.

'He's in love with you, you know,' said Stella, as Beatrice stood in the door, watching him go.

'Oh.' Beatrice shrugged it off. 'I'm not interested in that any more.'

Stella hoped she would come to change her mind, because she liked them both and wanted to see Beatrice happy. Stella had spent the summer doing her best to put her own troubles out of her head, but there had been some vicarious pleasure in watching Vittorio and Beatrice and hoping something would come of it. Now it looked like they wouldn't see Vittorio for a long while. She was sad at the thought, as he'd been an entertaining companion during the long, dull days when Beatrice was at work, and since he hardly spoke a word of English she'd found amusement in practising her Italian on him. She'd been stuck in the apartment for nearly three months, craving a taste of the fresh air, hoping for Gerardo to return or for some other way to get out of the country. Now the Germans were here, and Gerardo was powerless to help her, and all she had to look forward to was yet more long days hiding indoors, missing Ted, until the war was over. The nights were already long and dreary enough; many a night she'd dreamt of him, only to wake up to a wave of desolation and emptiness as the truth rushed in all at once. And now, without Vittorio, she'd have nothing to do in the day either, except fill her time with thoughts of Ted, and painful memories of the all too few months they'd had together, when she'd known for the first time in her life how it felt to be loved.

*

If staying cooped up at home was dull and frustrating, it was preferable to what came next, because in late September the Allies finally bombed Florence, and their apartment was destroyed. The first bomb hit without warning, three streets away, and shook the house so hard that several plates fell off the table. Tina began howling, and Beatrice grabbed her, and all three of them went to cower in the basement – just in time, because the next bomb hit the building next door to them. Had it been a direct strike they'd all have been killed outright, but as it was it destroyed the roof and one wall of their building, and blew all the windows out. The raid seemed to go on for hours, and they could do nothing but sit in the darkness and pray it would come to an end soon, but at last it was over, the all-clear went, and they emerged cautiously and surveyed the devastation. It was early evening, and they went to see if they could help the people in the next building, but it quickly became obvious that there was little that could be done: what had once been a handsome block of flats was now not much more than a heap of rubble, and many people were already at work in the ruins.

Beatrice, still holding tight onto Tina, went to speak to a neighbour she recognised, while Stella looked around in helpless shock. It seemed as if, during those months she'd been indoors, Florence had turned into a kind of hell. The air was thick and gritty with dust particles, making her cough, and she felt for her handkerchief and put it over her face. All around her were screams and cries and the sound of shouted instructions, as willing helpers, together with those who had emerged relatively unharmed from the wreckage, desperately shifted piles of rubble and tried to see if anyone had survived. A bell began to ring somewhere, tolling for the dead and wounded, just as a woman was brought out on a stretcher. Stella knew she was a woman because she was wearing a dress, but other than that she was unrecognisable: a twisted mass of blood and bone that had once been a human being. An old man was weeping, shouting her name, being held back by some of the onlookers as he tried to reach his dead wife. Stella wanted to do something, anything, but she felt powerless. The dead woman was carried off, and the old man followed, the tears running down his cheeks, leaving tracks in the thick dust that powdered his face. As he went by Stella pressed her handkerchief into his hand. It was all she could do. He put it to his face and the grim little party passed on.

Darkness was falling now, and the air was getting cold. Stella turned back to look at their own apartment, which was badly damaged but still in a better condition than the building next door. The windows had all gone and the door had been blown off its hinges. Inside, the floor was scattered thickly with broken glass, and the whole place was coated with dust. She ventured in through the gaping wound of the front door and was joined by Beatrice, who had been providing what aid she could. They walked round the flat, Beatrice still holding tightly onto Tina. Many things were beyond repair, but there was much that was salvageable.

'What are we going to do?' asked Stella. 'We can't stay here.'

'We must go to my mother,' replied Beatrice. She was staring at a pretty jug that had been a wedding present, and which had been broken in two by the force of the explosion. She put Tina down and sat down heavily on an undamaged chair, as if her legs had just given way under her. Stella saw she'd gone white in the face, and felt her forehead.

'You poor thing. I do believe you're in shock. If we were in England I'd give you some hot, sweet tea, but I don't know…'

'I'm all right. I'll be fine. It's nothing.'

'No, don't get up – stay there until you feel better. Once you've recovered a little we'll set off for your mother's.'

'We can't both go and leave the place open like this,' objected Beatrice. 'All our things will be stolen.'

'Oh, goodness, you're right. Well, then, you and Tina stay here, and I'll go and tell her what's happened – or would you rather go?'

'You go, please. If you wait here you'll be caught when the authorities turn up – *if* they turn up – but if you go now nobody will see you in the dark and my mother will keep you safe. I'll stay here and clear up, and put Tina to bed. The bedroom isn't damaged, thank God. It's too late to bring our things out tonight, but perhaps Mamma can get help by tomorrow.'

'Will you be all right?'

Beatrice nodded, and Stella hurried off. In all the confusion she'd forgotten her own situation, and it wasn't until she was a hundred yards down the road that she realised how dangerous it was for her to walk through the centre of Florence. Still, this was no time to be fearful; she'd just have to keep her head up and walk confidently as though she had a perfect right to be there. The curfew would be soon, so she couldn't afford to dawdle.

She hurried through the streets, shocked at the damage the bombs had caused. The bombers had obviously been aiming for the Campo di Marte railway station, but they'd missed it and hit the surrounding streets. Everywhere she looked were pitiful scenes similar to those she'd already witnessed that afternoon. The streets were full of people, and she felt horribly exposed, hoping that nobody would speak to her. With her dark hair and in Beatrice's old frock she could pass physically for any other Italian, but she knew her accent would immediately reveal her as English, and since the Allies were responsible for the damage she now saw around her, she couldn't expect anybody to take her nationality kindly.

She dared not go through the very centre of the city but instead took a circuitous route, using the dome of the cathedral and the tower of the Palazzo Vecchio as landmarks. It seemed like a lifetime ago that she'd wandered these streets freely, happily, out in the sunshine. Now the city was a dark, foreboding place, a place of terrible danger. Once she was at Dora's she would be safe, but she had to get across the river first.

As she arrived at the bridge she saw German soldiers stationed at the entrance, and her heart sank. The area was busy with people hurrying to and fro across the river, trying to get home before the curfew, but the soldiers weren't checking everybody's papers, so

Stella hoped they would overlook her. She stood a few minutes, watching from a shop doorway, trying to pluck up the courage to move forward, waiting for the right moment. There seemed to be a problem with the papers of one man, and he was arguing with the soldiers. Stella took her chance while they were distracted and walked boldly forward and onto the bridge, her heart racing, her palms clammy. For a few seconds she thought she might have got away, but then a figure stepped out in front of her and she jumped.

'You, Miss,' a voice snapped in German. 'Where are your papers?'

Stella's heart was in her throat and she knew her fate was balanced on a knife-edge. If they found out she was English she would be taken away and interned, perhaps even sent to a camp in Germany. With a silent prayer and gathering all her strength she burst out into a torrent of the best Italian she could muster, put her hands together as if praying, gestured desperately to the sky, and talked of the bombs and the American *bastardi* who had destroyed her apartment. Of course she had no papers – they were buried in the rubble along with all her possessions. Her husband was away fighting, and now she had nothing and nowhere to live, and wanted only to go to her mother. Then she burst into tears.

It had been an emotionally wrenching few hours, and her sobs were real, but as it turned out, crying was the best thing she could have done. The German soldier recoiled in alarm from the weeping woman before him, and waved at her to pass on. She thanked him fervently through her tears, and needed no further encouragement to get across the bridge and out of sight of the Germans as quickly as possible.

She slipped across the river and into the narrow streets of the Oltrarno, keeping to the darkest areas, then followed the road that led up into the hills and to the Villa Bruni. Her heart beat rapidly as she approached Dora's little house. The Germans were at the villa, not a hundred metres up the lane. If they caught her again she couldn't dare hope she'd get away with it a second time.

She knocked on the door, and Dora answered, gave a muffled shriek and hustled her inside.

'What's happened to my baby? I heard the bombs drop but they wouldn't let us through the checkpoints, and then the curfew came. Please tell me they're all right!'

Stella hastened to reassure her. Once Dora had calmed down and been brought to understand that Beatrice and Tina were both perfectly safe, she threw herself into action.

'We must get the cousin of Beppe and his cart, and bring them back. They are not expecting anyone until tomorrow, you say? Very well. Tomorrow we will arrange everything, and in the meantime, Miss Stella, you must stay upstairs and not show your face. Here it is pleasant, though more dangerous, but we must hope that the Germans will not suspect a thing. They know me, so there is always a good possibility that you will not be found.'

That night Stella slept in a proper bed for the first time in three months, upstairs in the cosy attic. The next day Dora, true to her word, went to Beppe's cousin, and by that evening all three of the refugees, together with as many things as could be saved, were installed safely at her house. It was cramped in the small attic, but not uncomfortable. The house was too close to the Germans at the Villa Bruni for Stella to feel quite easy, but there was nowhere else for them to go. Besides, there was some consolation in knowing that by moving to the south of the river, they were closer to the Allied lines, since the news had come through that the people of Naples had risen up against the Germans, allowing the British and Americans to enter the city. The closer they got, the more hope there was that she'd be safe. Another good thing was that Dora was still working at the Villa Bruni, and was able to smuggle out fruit and vegetables from the garden, and so they had a little more food coming in than they had before.

So, as autumn passed into winter they settled down in a state of reasonable comfort. Stella was by now resigned to a long stay in

Italy. She and Beatrice had talked many times about whether she ought to give herself up, but they'd always decided against it. She might have put up with being interned, but the fear that they would merely send her back to Marius always held her back in the end. She could bear anything but that. And there was nothing Ted could do to help her – she'd accepted that, although he was never far from her thoughts, and even in his absence he brought her some degree of comfort. Time and again she relived her memories of him: their first meeting in Geneva and his insistence on seeing her again; the trip to Lucerne, when they'd discovered her father's guilty secret and spent their first night together; the day they'd kissed goodbye. All far in the past now, but memories to be cherished, along with the fervent hope that one day they'd be reunited.

Besides, for the first time in her life she was enjoying the feeling of being useful. By looking after Tina she'd allowed Beatrice to get a job and earn some money, and she'd helped in caring for Vittorio when he was sick. If they hadn't taken him in he'd most likely either have died or been sent back to his regiment, but now he was fit and well and off fighting the Fascists and the Germans.

Vittorio himself turned up one evening, and was as surprised to see them as they were to see him. He was living nearby but wouldn't tell them exactly where, as it was safer that way, he said. He was more serious than they'd ever seen him, and was also cagey on the subject of what he'd been doing. Dora took him into the kitchen and they talked in murmurs while Stella and Beatrice exchanged questioning looks. At last he went away, and Dora went on with her ironing as if nothing had happened, seemingly without having any intention of mentioning why he'd come. But Beatrice wasn't going to stand for that.

'I didn't know you were in touch with him,' she said. 'Why did he come here?'

Dora wavered a minute, then took another frock and applied the iron to it.

'He comes here for information, of course.'

Beatrice stared.

'You're a spy!'

'What an idea! Do I look like a spy?'

'But you're passing on information from the villa?'

'Only a bit, and only because he asked. Not that I can give him very much, because I don't understand German very well, and in any case they don't talk about important things in front of me, but I can tell him little things now and again.'

'But that's dangerous!'

'Do you want the Germans here forever?'

'No, but—'

'Well, then,' said Dora, as if that settled the question. 'We have to do what we can.'

Beatrice was silent while she digested her mother's words.

'Who are the Banda Carità? I heard you talking about them?' she asked.

'Oh, *those*.' Dora pressed her lips together. 'They're devils, that's what they are. Haven't you heard about them? They're the new Fascist SS, just set up a few weeks ago. They're arresting people and torturing them to make them talk. One of Vittorio's friends was taken away three days ago and they don't know when – or if – he'll come back. It's a dangerous job those boys are doing.'

*

Vittorio's friend did return, in a terrible state, and very early one morning Vittorio brought him to them. His name was Franco, and he was barely conscious, and he needed a place to stay just for a few days. He'd been arrested by the Banda Carità for what they called interrogation, but it was easy enough to see what they meant by that. He'd been badly beaten; his face was barely recognisable as human and his right hand was crushed and mangled. They stared at him in horror, as Vittorio pleaded for his friend. They had nowhere else to put him until he was well. Please would the ladies help? No decent person on looking at Franco could have refused to assist. Somehow they got him down into Dora's basement, where they'd stored Beatrice's couch on which Vittorio had slept when he first returned from Russia. They laid Franco down and made him as comfortable as possible.

'He needs a doctor,' said Stella.

A doctor was brought – a thin little man with sharp eyes and the air of being unshockable. He did what he could for Franco, but came out shaking his head.

'He's lost a lot of blood, and he's very weak,' he said when he came out. 'And he won't be using that hand again. Keep him quiet and change his bandages when you can. The next few days will tell.'

They watched over Franco and gave him what care they could, but they could see him weakening before their eyes, and he slipped away from them three days later. Stella wept, but Beatrice was dry-eyed. Throughout the long hard years since Mimmo's death she hadn't cried once. The war seemed to have taken away her capacity to mourn, she thought, and she felt nothing except a sort of distant sadness for this young man who'd come here to die. When Vittorio and two of his companions came to take Franco away, Vittorio's face was set and determined. Beatrice was struck by the change in him as he looked down at Franco's battered body.

'Is this what the Fascists are doing?' she said. 'This isn't what we were supposed to be fighting for.'

He looked up at her, and she went on:

'It was meant to be about a strong Italy, and about finding our place in the world. It wasn't meant to be about...' she gestured helplessly at the dead man on the couch.

'No, it wasn't.'

'Why did they arrest him?'

'Because he sold me a can of petrol and they thought he had information.'

'Then he wasn't even one of you?' She hesitated. 'This could happen to you too, couldn't it?'

He nodded.

'If they catch me. But they won't. Listen, I shouldn't have brought Franco here. If it was just your mother living here – she's strong, and she knows what she's getting into. But now you've come—'

'What makes you think I'm not strong?'

'You are, but you have Tina. They are cruel, bad people and won't hesitate to harm a child.'

Franco's mangled body made that clear enough, and the thought of what they might do to Tina chilled Beatrice's heart. Still, she couldn't stand by while people were being tortured and murdered.

'Some things are important.' She looked down at Franco again. 'If my mother is willing to take risks to get rid of these – these animals, then I am too. And I'll die before I let them hurt my daughter.'

And I'll die before I let them hurt you, his eyes said. She saw it and turned away in confusion, the heat rising to her cheeks, although she didn't know why.

They'd brought a makeshift stretcher to put Franco on, and they lifted him onto it gently and covered him up.

'His mother lives in Pistoia,' said Vittorio. 'Someone will have to get word to her. I will go today.'

'You will be careful, won't you?' The words escaped her almost involuntarily.

He gave her a flash of his old impudent grin.

'Anybody would think you cared about me.'

'Of course I care about you. You're Mimmo's friend.'

'And yours. Always,' he said.

Chapter Twenty-Five

It was a cold winter that year, and as they entered 1944 the snow fell, blanketing the cathedral and the rooftops with white, and camouflaging the scars of the war-ravaged city. Stella was growing increasingly bored and frustrated hiding in Dora's house. She wanted to get out and do something, but she didn't know what, and since she had no papers and no ration card, she couldn't even help by getting provisions in. She was feeling useless, and in those dark days struggled to keep herself cheerful and optimistic. The longer her enforced imprisonment went on, the more she found herself casting her mind back to the stolen hours she and Ted had spent together, and remembering the happiness she'd felt. After the long years of her lonely childhood and cold marriage, Ted's love had blown in and enveloped her like an unexpected breath of warm summer air, giving her the promise of life and joy. She missed him more than she could say, and ached to know what he was doing, and whether he thought of her. Beatrice had been keeping an eye on the post at the hotel ever since she'd sent her letter all those months ago, but there'd been no reply – and in any case, there was no mail into or out of the country since the Germans had taken over, so she couldn't even be sure he'd received her message. It seemed only reasonable to assume that he'd given her up for dead by now. Had he already found solace for her loss with someone else? The idea tormented her, and she shed many tears in her bed at night at the thought that he might have moved on and left her in his past. There was companionship of a sort with Beatrice and Dora, but they were committed to the war in a way she wasn't. They wanted the Germans gone so they could clear up, mend their city, and go back to their old lives as best they could. Stella, without roots in Italy or anywhere else, had no such future to look forward to – only the painful prospect that when she finally made it out of Florence Ted wouldn't be there to meet her, and she'd have to take her next steps alone.

The harsh winter passed, and they all longed for spring. Before the snow had quite melted they received a visit from Vittorio. Mindful of the trouble they could be in if the Germans or the Fascist militia discovered them, he'd taken care to keep away from them, and they hadn't seen him for several months. But one day in late February he turned up again, on his best behaviour and with an apologetic grin. He hated to ask them for a favour in these dangerous times, he said, but he'd found himself with a problem on his hands in the shape of two former British POWs.

Italy had been full of escaped Allied prisoners ever since Mussolini had been ousted from power in July of 1943 and the prison camps had been opened. Many of them had been rounded up again when the Germans arrived, but thousands of them were still in hiding, or wandering around Italy, trying to avoid capture and reunite with their countrymen. Vittorio had found these two up in the hills near Fiesole, hiding in a ruined shed with only half a roof. They didn't speak a word of Italian, but as far as he could gather they'd been there for weeks. One of them had a nasty flesh wound from a bullet, which wasn't healing properly, the other had possible pneumonia, and they both had frostbite. At Signora Dora's house there was a warm cellar and blankets – and also Miss Stella, who could speak to them and translate for them, and make them feel at home for a few days, just until they were well enough to move on. Here he gave them his most engaging grin. Stella wondered how Beatrice, to whom he addressed himself, could resist his charm, but she merely nodded seriously and said:

'Very well; Mamma will be back soon and if she agrees then we will take them.'

Dora had only one thing to say when she returned. She'd been outraged by Franco's death and was becoming increasingly determined that she would do anything she could to get one over on that pack of murderers, as she called the Banda Carità. If that meant helping the partisans, then so be it.

'Of course we'll take them!' she exclaimed. 'Why do you need to ask?'

So it was agreed. Vittorio had decided Dora's basement was not well enough concealed for safety, so one night he and some of his associates came and blocked up the door, then cut out a small panel in the new wall that was just big enough to crawl through.

'There,' said Vittorio. 'You see, we put the panel back into place and put in front of it this chest of drawers, and if the Germans come to look they will not find anybody. You too, Miss Stella: you can go there if they come and search.'

The British men arrived: one tall and one short, and both very blond. They'd escaped from a camp near Verona, they said, and at first had tried to get across the mountains into Switzerland, but had been arrested again and sent to another camp outside Bologna. From there they'd escaped and were trying their luck heading south this time. They were astonished and delighted to find an Englishwoman living in their refuge, but were both too tired to say much that first night. Once their various injuries and ailments had been attended to, Vittorio showed them how to get into the secret room, and they crawled in and collapsed on the mattresses that had been made up for them.

'It's not exactly the Ritz,' said Stella, peeping through the hole at them. 'But it's the best we can do, I'm afraid.'

They assured her they were more than happy with their accommodation, and she left them to sleep. She was strangely cheered by the presence of two of her countrymen in the house, even though they were no better off than she was – still far from the Allied lines and with no immediate prospect of escape.

The Englishmen stayed longer than they'd expected, because soon afterwards the weather took a turn for the worse, and there was no possibility of sending them out into the snow. They spent much of their time in their cellar, playing cards and smoking the few cigarettes that could be got for them – and of course talking to the pretty English woman whenever they got a chance. They were both missing their families: the older one was married with three children, and was only too happy to show the photos which he carried with him for the ladies to coo over. The younger one had a girl waiting for him in Plymouth, and when he made it back to England he was planning to ask her to marry him. They were both curious to know what Stella was doing in Florence. She couldn't tell them the whole story, so merely said she'd been living in the city before the war and had ended up trapped. It was near enough to the truth.

By early March the weather had improved appreciably and the British officers were desperate to move on. All radios had been officially blocked by the Fascist government, but Dora hid hers down in the basement, where it was still just possible to get a signal, and every evening they all went down there to listen to the BBC. The Allies had landed at Anzio just south of Rome, but were making painfully slow progress up the peninsula, as the Germans were fighting back with everything they had. There was much anger on the part of the Italians when the Allies destroyed the abbey at Monte Cassino in an attempt to break through the German lines, but even that hadn't helped them make any progress, and it seemed they would be stuck in that part of the country for some time to come.

'They might get a move on,' said the younger officer, who'd told them to call him Leslie. He and Stella had struck up something of a friendship. 'But if they're going to take their time then I think we'll have to try and meet them halfway. We can't stay here for the rest of the war.'

'But you'll never get through the German lines,' objected Stella. 'It's impossible.'

She'd heard many stories of escaped prisoners trying to get across the lines only to be scooped up and sent to camps in Germany. It didn't seem worth all that effort if it would only end up in their being captured again. The British men seemed to accept her words with resignation at first, but after a few days she saw they were becoming increasingly restless and unwilling to remain at the house.

'Wait until Vittorio comes back at least,' she said. 'He'll be able to help you get out of the city.'

But Vittorio had concerns of his own. Several of the men in his brigade had been killed in a shootout with the Banda Carità, and a number of others wounded, and the leaders were planning to lie low for the next few weeks. He came to them one night on a rare, quick visit, to ask if Dora had any information for him about German troop movements.

'Not that we have time to fight the Germans,' he said in frustration. 'The Fascists have been keeping us busy enough. They know we've been active in the Santo Spirito area so we're having to keep off the streets for now. I can't stay here more than a few minutes.'

The officers, who'd emerged from the cellar briefly to stretch their legs, were listening uncomprehendingly to the rapid flow of Italian.

'Ask him when we can leave,' they said.

'They want to try and get across the lines,' Stella told Vittorio. 'They were hoping you'd be able to lead them out of the city.'

Vittorio grimaced and shook his head.

'It can't be done at present. They'll have to wait. Tell them we'll get them out as soon as possible. Maybe in a few weeks.'

'He can't help you yet,' Stella translated, although they'd already understood Vittorio's meaning from his expression.

'If you give us directions we'll make our own way out,' said Jimmy, the older officer.

This was conveyed to Vittorio, who eyed them doubtfully.

'There are checkpoints all over the place just outside Florence, they don't know the way and I can't spare them a map.'

'I could take them,' Stella heard herself saying.

'You?' Vittorio laughed.

'It's not far, is it?'

'It's far enough if you get caught.'

'I won't get caught. If all it involves is showing them the road south then I can do it. We used to drive around these roads all the time before the war, so I know the way, but you'll have to tell me where the checkpoints are.'

She didn't know why she was being so insistent, except that Vittorio's disbelieving laugh had nettled her, and she knew that the two British men were in a state of mind to leave right now without any assistance at all if nobody could be found to volunteer help. She felt oddly protective of them and didn't want to send them out into the night alone. At last Vittorio seemed to understand she was being serious.

'You'll need to take them at least as far as Galluzzo, but there are sentries on all the bridges there, so they'll have to take their chances in the river. After that they're on their own. Take the San Michele road and then cut across country. There's a little *osteria* on the corner where it turns off. Do you know it? It's called Da Paolo.'

'Yes, of course I know it. We went there lots of times before the war. I know the way you mean.'

He was looking at her assessingly now, sizing her up for the task.

'It's a long way, about ten kilometres there and back. Do you think you can do it?'

'I don't see why not. All I have to do is avoid being caught, and I suppose I can do that just as well as you can.'

A grin spread suddenly across his face.

'All right, then, if you want to. Show me how brave the English women can be.'

Stella didn't feel brave at all. In fact she was already regretting her offer, convinced she'd bitten off more than she could chew. But it was too late to back out now, because Vittorio was shaking the hands of the British officers and slapping them on the shoulder, and indicating with clear gestures and a few references in broken English to '*Mees Stella*' that they'd found an escort.

'I'll come back as soon as I can, to find out how you got on,' he said as he was about to leave. He gave her a serious look. 'But be careful – if you're caught they'll torture you and worse. Remember Franco.'

'I will,' she promised, and he disappeared into the night.

'Have you taken leave of your senses?' hissed Beatrice, once the officers had retreated to their cellar. She'd been listening to the conversation in alarm. 'What are you thinking? What if you get caught?'

'I'll just have to try not to,' replied Stella. Having committed herself to this possibly foolhardy course of action she wasn't about to show how frightened she was. She'd wanted a chance to prove herself – well, here it was. She would lead the British men out of Florence and point them towards where they wanted to go. And then she would come back here and never volunteer to do anything so ridiculous again.

The moon was invisible behind clouds the next night when they set out stealthily from the little house and into the street. Stella was glad of it – it would be difficult to see in the pitch darkness, but at least there was less risk of them being seen themselves. She'd warned the officers to be as quiet as possible for the first part of the journey, since the gates of the Villa Bruni were very close by, and there were guards placed just inside. They slipped silently up the road away from the villa, then began the walk along the lane which led out of the city. There was a high stone wall to one side of it, and they kept in the shadows, not talking, only the sound of their breathing breaking the silence.

It was a walk of about three miles along narrow roads through quiet countryside, and for most of the way they met nobody. After a while the clouds cleared somewhat and the moon appeared at intervals, showing them the outline of the nearby hills, punctuated by the tall, slender shadows of cypress trees. At length they began to pass houses, and the road widened and they came into civilisation. If they were going to meet a patrol then it would most likely be here. The clouds had fully dispersed now, and the moon was straight ahead of them, shining brightly, giving little shadow for them to hide in, but they did their best to keep out of sight, pressing themselves to the walls of the houses that lined the street.

'Shh!' whispered Stella, stopping suddenly as she heard a noise. She didn't know what it was, but there was no time to waste. They'd just passed an open gateway, and she turned and pushed the two men through it. They stood silently, holding their breath and listening as the sound of footsteps approached. It was two sentries, walking along the centre of the road towards them. The Germans stopped just opposite the gate to light cigarettes, and the hiders pressed themselves as far into the shadows as they could. Then the soldiers continued on their way. Stella peeped out, her heart beating rapidly. The Germans had disappeared around a corner.

'Now, quickly. Just across there.'

She led the way and the three of them ran as swiftly and silently as they could across the road, then turned onto a narrower road lined on both sides with trees. Here the moon couldn't penetrate and it was almost pitch black. Stella gestured to indicate that they should take cover under the trees.

'This road leads to the bridge,' she whispered. 'But there'll be a roadblock there.'

She led them further into the trees, bearing away from the bridge. The sound of the damp foliage slushing under their feet seemed very loud, but it was gradually drowned out by a louder sound further ahead, and soon they came upon it: the river, swollen with melted snow, rushing and tumbling headlong past them.

'You see it bends here, so we're out of sight of the bridge,' said Stella, as they stood looking at it. 'It would be much easier to cross in summer, but I'm afraid it can't be helped. It'll be freezing cold, but it can't be much more than waist-deep. Once you're on the other side keep to the hills and avoid the towns if you can. It'll take you a few days, but with any luck the weather will hold.' She held out a hand to Jimmy. 'Good luck!'

They all shook hands.

'Don't you want to come with us?' asked Leslie.

She shook her head and pointed out her thin shoes.

'I'm not equipped, and I'd only slow you down. I'm not much good at this sort of thing, in any case. But you might mention I'm here if you do get through. Now, quietly does it.'

The men slid down the bank and entered the water. As Stella had said, despite the rapid current it was shallow enough for them to wade across. She watched as they pulled themselves out on the other side, scrambled up the bank and disappeared with a wave. She hoped they'd make it across the lines, although she thought it was unlikely.

Returning to the main street, she listened out for the sentries, then hurried up the lane that led into open country and back home. The return journey was quicker because she was on her own and had only herself to worry about, and almost before she knew it she was slipping through the shadows and letting herself softly into Dora's house. Beatrice was still awake, even though it was three o'clock, and demanded to hear how it had all gone. Stella was filled with a sense of exhilaration she hadn't felt in a long time. She'd done something truly useful at last! She'd risked her own life to help others, and finally she felt she had a purpose. The adventure had been easier than she'd expected, and now she knew she could do it she wanted to do it again.

Vittorio managed a quick visit the next day, and she told him of
the success of her mission, trying not to look too proud of herself.
He seemed impressed – and even more so when she told him she'd
be happy to do it again.

'You want to help us?' he asked. 'Then you shall.'

Their next visitors were three South Africans. They stayed
only a week before Stella escorted them along the same route
and across the river. After that came a steady stream of escaped
prisoners of war – British, Canadian, American and many other
Allied nationalities – all wanting to go south and get through
the German lines. By now Dora and Beatrice had become quite
accustomed to the idea of sheltering people in the basement, and
all three women took turns at escort duty – although Stella did
it most often, as she didn't have to go to work during the day. By
now she was familiar with several different routes out of the city,
while Vittorio and his men kept an eye on German movements
and checkpoints, and warned her of them in advance. After her
first two or three outings, Vittorio gave her an automatic pistol
and showed her how to use it.

'A rifle would be no use to you. You can keep a pistol hidden,
and it will kill a German or a Fascist just as well. Besides,' he went
on practically, 'if you are cornered it is much easier to turn a pistol
on yourself than a rifle.'

She drew in her breath at that. It had seemed like a game so far,
but now she realised it was deadly earnest. She took the pistol and
kept it close to her. She didn't know whether she could use it, but
she knew the time might come when she had no choice.

Chapter Twenty-Six

Wherever Ted turned in his search for Stella, he hit a brick wall. Although Marius obviously knew what had happened to her, it was equally obvious he had no intention of divulging the information to Ted, but whether it were out of spite or for some more serious reason Ted didn't know. He feared the worst, and was determined that if Marius had harmed Stella, then he wouldn't get away with it, and to that end he made some discreet enquiries with a friend of his in the Swiss police. But all he could find out was that Marius had certainly taken Stella into Italy in early July, and had returned without her, although he had not reported her missing. When asked where she was, Marius told the police they had had a disagreement, and that she had chosen to remain in Italy with his sister and her husband. This could not be verified at present, since the Count and the Countess could not be reached. However, since there was no suggestion of anything untoward having occurred on Swiss territory, there was nothing Ted's police friend could do at present, he said, except institute enquiries with the Italian police, and Ted must understand they were unlikely to be very helpful given the current situation in that country.

Ted had already telegraphed to the Carminatis, but received no reply. He hoped Stella was staying with them, because if she wasn't then she had most likely been arrested and interned. If that were the case presumably she'd be expelled from Italy sooner or later, and with any luck would be sent to England. In that event all he could do was wait until he heard from her. That was the way

his mind ran in his more rational, optimistic moments, at least
– although he couldn't push away the little voice that whispered
continually in his ear, telling him that if she were really safe, then
surely she would have communicated with him by now. But he'd
heard nothing. Why hadn't she telegraphed?

Weeks passed and still he heard nothing, either from London
or from Monica and Gerardo, and he couldn't shake the fear
which had taken hold of him that Marius, having found out
about their affair, had decided to punish Stella in some terrible
way. Ted's frustration at his own powerlessness was acute, and the
only way he could work it off was to take long walks along the
lake to exercise his leg as he'd been instructed – partly because he
felt in some obscure and illogical way that had he been fully well
Marius wouldn't have succeeded in taking Stella away from him.
Besides, if something had happened to her, and he never saw her
again, then at least with a fully functional leg there was a chance
he would be sent into action, and could find an outlet for his grief
and rage that way.

July and August passed with no news, and it wasn't until early
September that a glimmer of light dawned – but even then it
was very little. It came in the form of a letter which arrived in a
cheap envelope, but which was typed on the expensive headed
paper of the Hotel Ambassador in Florence. He stared at its
contents for a few seconds in perplexity, but gradually it dawned
on him what it must mean, and then his heart leapt. Although
the message was cryptic, it was obvious it must refer to Stella.
She was safe, then! Relief flooded through him, and he read the
letter over and over again, trying to make more sense of it. It was
dated late July, about three weeks after she must have arrived in
Italy, and a few days after he remembered telegraphing to Monica
and Gerardo. If Stella had subsequently found her way to them
then surely she would have telegraphed as soon as she arrived, to
let him know she was safe? But instead all he had was this barely

comprehensible letter, which must mean she wasn't staying with them at all. Where was she, then?

The letter was signed by a Beatrice Bianchi Fabbri. The only Beatrice he knew was the daughter of Monica's housekeeper. He remembered her – a dark-haired girl who'd worked at the hotel. Was Stella staying there, then? The letter was cagey about giving her name, but that was understandable given that everything going out of Italy was censored. He gazed at the letter as if he hoped it would reveal more secrets the longer he looked at it, but that was as much as he could glean. The whole thing was still somewhat of a mystery, but he was partly reassured that Stella was alive and well – or had been six weeks ago, anyway. He was desperate to get a message to her, but by now communications with Italy had been cut off, and there was no way he could send a letter or a telegram through. He would just have to trust that she would come to no harm until she could be got out of the country.

There was no question of his applying for a transfer to London now, however. On the contrary, Ted was eager to join the Allied forces in the liberation of Italy – although they weren't liberating it very fast at present, having encountered more resistance from the Germans than they'd expected. He'd heard from the OSS, who instructed him to stay put until his leg was fully well, and he spent the autumn and winter chafing with impatience in Geneva. At last, in early January, he received word from his bureau that he was to be sent to Italy to report on the campaign there, and at the same time he heard from the OSS that he was to accompany the troops, do his job as a war correspondent and await further instructions. He left Geneva without much regret, and embarked upon his new job, pleased to be doing something at last.

So it was that he witnessed the Allied landings at Anzio, and sat in a cold, muddy ditch watching the destruction of the abbey at Monte Cassino, writing pithy reports that were syndicated all over the US and read avidly by the people back home. The job was difficult and uncomfortable, but he was happy to be doing some active duty at last, although when he saw soldiers of his own side risking their lives every day for the war he still wished occasionally that he might join them.

Then one day he was summoned to the army headquarters at Caserta, where a cheery OSS man told him he'd heard from the chief in Bern, who wanted to know if Ted was willing to do something a little more dangerous than sitting in a tent with a typewriter. It swiftly turned out that the job would be *much* more dangerous than sitting in a tent with a typewriter: if he agreed to do it, Ted would be landed by boat far behind the German lines, carrying with him a portable radio transmitter, where his objective would be to get into communication with Italian agents in the field and groups of partisans in the countryside to the north of Rome, transmitting information back to Allied headquarters about German troop movements and the state of readiness of the various partisan brigades, among other things.

Ted accepted the job without hesitation, and almost before he knew it he was sitting on the deck of a torpedo boat on a freezing cold night in early March, heading for a deserted beach a few miles north of Civitavecchia, carrying a rucksack full of supplies that would almost certainly get him shot if he were caught with them. Despite his fake papers and his fluency in Italian, he and his superiors knew that with his height and build he looked far too much like an American to pass as a native, and so his instructions were to stay out of sight and only travel by night. It was too dangerous for him to try and get into Rome itself, which had checkpoints all around, but he would be taken to a place to the north-east of the city, where he was to establish radio contact with headquarters and wait for an OSS agent to communicate with him.

The landing occurred without incident, and he was met by a car, which drove him twenty miles inland to a house, where he spent the night and all of the next day. From there he was taken, again at dead of night, across country and south-east, avoiding Rome, then up into the hills to a house owned by a surly old man who didn't seem very keen on having him. Ted was put in a cold shed with only a straw mattress which, it appeared, was to be his accommodation for the present, and spent the first night thanking his lucky stars he'd brought his own provisions with him, because the old man didn't seem to be in a hurry to feed him. He established radio contact with Caserta, as he'd been told, then settled himself to wait for the OSS man to turn up: a senior agent who'd been organising partisan resistance in the hills nearby. It was freezing in the shed, but Ted dared not come out, and so he spent the next two days kicking his heels and wondering whether all intelligence work was as dull as this.

On the third night he was sitting in his shed at about ten o'clock when an urgent radio message came through. He wrote it down and his heart sank as he deciphered it. The agent he'd been waiting for had been caught and shot in Rome. Someone had betrayed them. This was a blow, but, worse still, HQ now warned him that they couldn't guarantee the safety of his current accommodation, and instructed him to evacuate with all speed. Cursing the incompetence of the organisation, Ted hastily packed up his equipment and prepared to leave. He had a sneaking suspicion the surly owner of the house had had something to do with the betrayal of the agent in Rome – there had been something about the man which had aroused his suspicions from the start – and if that was true, then he'd better leave with as little fuss as possible. He took a quick look around him to make sure he hadn't left anything, and slipped out of the shed.

There was no way to the road without going past the house, which was in darkness. Treading as lightly as he could, he was just passing the building when a light went on downstairs and the old man came out. Ted flattened himself quickly against the wall, out of sight, but the old man didn't seem in any hurry; he stood in the doorway, smoking a cigarette, making it impossible for Ted to get past without being seen. He was just wondering whether to make a run for it anyway, when he heard the sound of a car engine approaching up the hill and his heart sank. He knew with a dull certainty that the car was here for him, but there was nowhere he could retreat to except back to the shed, and if he did that he'd be trapped. If they caught him he'd be arrested, and almost certainly tortured and shot as a spy. He had no choice but to risk it.

There was a wall about five feet high on the other side of the road that passed in front of the house, beyond which the ground fell away steeply and was shaded with thick woodland. Quick as lightning, ignoring the shout of the old man, he made a bolt across the road, getting caught for an instant in the car's headlights as he did so, then vaulted across the wall, backpack and all. But he'd misjudged the drop on the other side and landed badly. An agonising pain shot through his bad knee and he collapsed onto the ground, clutching at his leg and stifling an exclamation of pain.

The car had stopped now. From his position behind the wall Ted heard doors opening and closing, and judged that there must be at least three of them. They didn't say a word – confirming his suspicions that this was no ordinary visit – but instead the darkness grew a little paler, and Ted imagined they'd switched on torches. The beams of light grew brighter, flashing to his right and left above him. He had to stay low – which would be no difficulty as he knew he wouldn't be able to stand up anyway – but the men would be over the wall and looking for him any second, so ignoring the pain he slithered down the hill as speedily and silently as he could. The ground underneath him was wet, soaking him as he went, but he ignored it and kept on going, his heart racing. When he'd slid far enough down the hill to put some distance between himself and his pursuers, he stopped and looked back. He could still see the light of the torch beams flashing here and there through the trees, but they didn't seem to be coming any nearer. At last they retreated and disappeared altogether. Ted didn't blame them, since a heavy rain had set in now and it was no weather to be blundering about in the dark. He wasn't much enjoying it himself.

Now he needed somewhere to rest for the night. A little way away was a tall shrub with wide spreading branches, which he thought would offer some shelter, and he dragged himself under it and examined his knee by the light of his torch. It was painful and swelling rapidly, and would need to be rested for a few days – but that was just what he couldn't afford to do. Still, he couldn't get any further tonight, so he remained where he was, curled up under the bush, using his rucksack as a pillow. It was freezing, and his clothes were drenched, and rain was dripping on his neck, but at least he was safe for now.

As the thin dawn broke the next morning, after a shivering, sleepless few hours under the bush, Ted took stock of his situation. When he stood up cautiously he found he could put a little weight on his knee – which was a relief – but not enough to do any strenuous walking. Had it not been for the knee he'd have made his way further up into the hills, hoping to meet with one of the bands of partisans he knew were operating in the area, but he was in no condition to go tramping about in the mountains. Besides, the weather was getting worse, and he knew he wouldn't last long without provisions or shelter. He was already chilled to the bone and didn't want to die of exposure, and he needed a couple of days to rest his leg, so he bound up his knee as best he could and continued through the rain, limping, down the hill, keeping a north-westerly course, hoping to reach civilisation. He'd have to trust someone sooner or later, and he knew many peasant farmers had been sheltering escaped Allied prisoners of war, so he kept his eye out for a likely house from which he could beg some food and a night or two in a warm barn or outhouse. Once his leg had recovered he'd ask to be put in contact with the local partisans.

To his relief, he soon reached a road. It was too early for traffic, but set back on the other side of the road was a cottage with a wooden lean-to at the side of it, which looked as though it would provide decent shelter, at least. No other houses were nearby, and Ted was soaked and flagging rapidly, so this would have to do. He didn't want to turn up at the door carrying a rucksack full of radio equipment in case the inhabitants of the house turned out to be untrustworthy, so he shoved the bag under a hedge a little way off the road, making sure it was well concealed and completely protected from the weather, then approached the cottage. Nobody answered his knock, but a brief investigation showed him that the door to the lean-to was unlocked and unoccupied. Ted's knee was throbbing unpleasantly and he didn't think he could walk much further, so he decided he was going to rest there for a few hours whether the owner of the house liked it or not. First he had to retrieve the radio from its hiding place across the road and let HQ know he was safe.

But in his tiredness and relief at finding shelter he'd forgotten the need for caution. He stepped out through the gate and the first thing he saw was two German soldiers, walking along the road towards him. His heart almost stopped. His first instinct was to turn and run, but his knee was useless, and besides, they'd already drawn their guns. There was no escape. He put his hands up.

'Don't shoot,' he said.

*

As March stretched into April and the weather grew warmer, Stella was still doing escort duty, accompanying stray Allied soldiers out of the city and directing them south. She was accustomed to it now and had lost her fear, proud to feel like she was doing something for the war effort. Thanks to Vittorio she had information about checkpoints and patrols, and so far there had been no trouble.

One night she had two young South Africans to escort away from Florence. The river was lower now that the weather was dry, and it was easier to cross, so they used the Galluzzo route as much as they could. The trip across country passed without incident, and they were just about to leave the road and start threading through the trees down to the river when they saw a patrol of four German soldiers just ahead of them, approaching round a bend. It was a bright, moonlit night, and the soldiers spotted the little party immediately.

'Halt!' shouted one of them.

Stella went cold. The Germans didn't usually come along here at this time. They must have changed their patrol. But there was no time to think – they had to act fast.

'Quick! This way!' she hissed.

Without stopping to see whether her companions were following, she darted under the cover of the trees, the sound of gunshots ringing out behind her. She scrambled through the undergrowth, her breath coming fast, heedless of the noise she was making, trying only to put some distance between herself and her pursuers. She ran and ran until she couldn't go any further, then paused at the edge of a clearing and took cover behind a tree while she got her breath back, reassured that the sounds of voices and tramping feet were still some little distance away. At last the beating of her heart subsided somewhat, and she was preparing to move on when there was a crash of undergrowth nearby, and she almost jumped out of her skin with fright. She was about to flee, but it was only one of the South Africans, who'd emerged into the clearing. He'd lost his beret in the chase, and a finger of moonlight lit up his fair hair.

'Psst!' she hissed.

He gave a start and whirled round, then came to join her behind the tree.

'Where's your friend?'

He shook his head.

'They got him.'

His breath was coming in short, ragged bursts, but whether it was from the flight or his distress, she didn't know. Stella felt a rush of grief for a dead man she'd hardly known, but there was no time to stop and mourn, because she could see torch beams bobbing about, and the sound of voices was coming closer.

The adrenaline was pumping through her veins, and she was hardly thinking of the danger. She didn't know what had possessed her; all she knew was that she was responsible for these soldiers, but one of them was dead and she'd failed him. She couldn't fail the other one too. They'd come this far, and the river was so close that it would be a terrible pity to retreat now. If she could get her remaining companion across the water he'd be safe.

'Do you see that fallen trunk over there?' she whispered. 'Get down behind it. I'm going to make some noise and try and lead them away. Once they've passed, you double back very quietly and try to get across further upstream that way. The overhanging growth will give you cover.'

The South African was young – not more than eighteen – and scared, but trying not to show it. He nodded. The torches were coming closer.

'Now, stay down,' she whispered.

He swarmed into the space behind the tree trunk. She stole away silently until there was a fair distance between them, then gave a cry of pain, as though she'd just caught herself on a sharp twig. Then she began to push forward through the brush, which was dry after a few weeks without rain, making as much noise as she possibly could. She permitted herself a brief glance back, and saw that the torch beams had changed direction, pointing towards her. Someone shouted and she broke into a run. There was a darker patch of woodland just ahead, across another clearing. She darted out, but in the moonlight the clearing was almost as bright as day, making her clearly visible. She heard another shot, and the whine of a bullet as it sped past her ear, and at that moment she tripped and fell heavily into the darker undergrowth, tearing her frock and scraping her knees and hands.

She could hear the sound of voices behind her; the Germans had evidently decided they could catch her easily, and had opted to plough openly after her rather than stopping to listen. Picking herself up as quietly as possible, she crept on. Her breath was coming in sobbing gasps now, but she forced it down. She'd certainly managed to attract enough attention; the South African would just have to look after himself now.

The trees thinned out and suddenly she was at the edge of the road. She glanced quickly in both directions and darted out. She slipped along the road back in the direction she'd come, keeping to the shadows, such as they were, making for the crossroads that would lead her back across country and into the outskirts of Florence. But to her dismay she found that her German pursuers must have split up, because just then two of them emerged from the trees just ahead of her. They weren't looking in her direction, and she had just enough time to dart in through the same gate she and the British officers had hidden behind on the first night she'd done this. In the little front yard was a bin, and she crouched down behind it, breathing a prayer, as the Germans drew closer. She could hear their voices. They were still looking for her, although she couldn't know she'd made it as far as the road, surely?

The sound of footsteps approached slowly. They were pushing open gates and looking over walls as they went. Stella's blood was roaring in her ears, and she was sure they must be able to hear her heart beating. Then she remembered the little pistol in its holster around her waist. She always carried it on these nocturnal outings, more from habit than anything else, but she'd never thought she'd have to use it. Could she do it? A pistol wouldn't be much use against several German soldiers with rifles. She brought it out and set her jaw. She'd go down fighting if she had to. The footsteps came closer, then paused at her gate. Concealed in the shadows behind the bin, the gun warm and solid in her hand, her finger resting lightly on the trigger, she held her breath.

The torch beam played slowly over the wall to her right, and she shrank further into her hiding place, trying to make herself as small as possible, not daring to breathe. After what seemed like a century, the torch flicked off and the footsteps continued on slowly, retreating along the road until they passed out of hearing. Stella let out her breath very quietly and waited for the hammering of her heart to die down. Once she'd gathered her courage together she emerged silently into the dark street and set off back across country towards home.

PART 4

Chapter Twenty-Seven

Things were getting harder by the day in Florence. In spring and early summer the Allies bombed the city several times, with the aim of destroying the marshalling yards and disrupting the German supply lines. German soldiers were stationed at checkpoints scattered everywhere around the city, and were rounding up young men to be sent away to labour camps, or forcing them to join the army and fight with the Fascist side. Food and medicines were scarcer than ever – the Germans were taking what little there was for their own troops – and there were disruptions to the water supply, which made the city smell and meant that everyone had to fetch their water from public fountains. Bands of armed Fascist thugs roamed the city, looting and raping at will, and rumours had begun to circulate that the Germans were planning to blow up the bridges to hold back the Allied advance, and that they would seize hostages to take with them in their retreat. The weather was getting hotter and hotter, and disease was beginning to spread, but faced with the almost unbearable conditions, most of the population could do little more than grit their teeth and wait for the Allies to arrive. The Americans had marched into Rome in early June, but their advance had been slowed again, and it was anybody's guess when they'd make it as far as Florence.

Meanwhile, the women at the little house outside the gates of the Villa Bruni carried on grimly. They had no food to spare for escaped prisoners now, and could do little for them, but Stella continued her nightly outings, escorting men of many nationalities to the edge of the city and directing them across country. She had no idea whether any of them ever made it into Allied territory, and she had to use another route now that the Germans were wise to the river crossing, but since the battle lines were slowly drawing closer, at least there was comfort in knowing that the escaped prisoners had less and less distance to travel these days. One day in July Dora came home from the Villa Bruni with news.

'That German, Kaufmann, is here. Do you remember him? He used to come here before the war and buy pictures from the Count. They have put him in charge of protecting all the art in Florence.' She snorted. 'I could tell him how to do that! Send the Germans home and there'll be no need to protect anything.'

She was addressing Vittorio, who had come bringing a toy for Tina and some food. He made some reply, and she looked at him curiously.

'Where did you put the Count's paintings, by the way? Kaufmann was asking about them.'

'It's best you don't know – that way you can't get into trouble.'

He went out of the room to give the toy to Tina, and Stella, who had been reading a newspaper he'd brought, glanced up.

'The paintings?' she said. 'Do you mean Gerardo's art collection?'

'Yes,' replied Dora. 'The Count asked Vittorio to hide them, because he didn't trust the Germans not to take them. That's wise, if you ask me.'

Stella's mind was driven back to another cache of paintings in a warehouse in Lucerne. Switzerland was still resolutely neutral, so presumably they were still there. One day she wouldn't be able to avoid the issue any longer – she'd have to decide what to do with the pictures and finally confront her past and the implications of what her father had done. She turned back to her paper. There was no guarantee she'd get out of Florence alive, so what was the use in thinking about it now?

*

Tina loved her new doll and wanted Vittorio to play with her, and he sat on the floor obediently as she thrust her old toy rabbit at him and showed him how to tuck it up in bed.

'See? This is how to do it,' she said, demonstrating on the new doll. She shook her head at Vittorio's attempts to put the rabbit to bed. 'No, like this.' She pushed him out of the way and did it to her own satisfaction, then once the toys were settled Vittorio sang them a lullaby, and Tina did the same. Then she decided they'd had enough sleep and it was time for them to get up, so she got the toys out of bed again and took them upstairs to show them her own bedroom in the attic.

Beatrice had been watching the game, smiling.

'She looks more like Mimmo every day,' said Vittorio from his place on the floor.

'Yes, she does.'

He stood up.

'There's fresh pasta today,' he said. 'I gave it to your mother.'

'Thank you. You're so kind to us always – I don't know why, when you have so many other things on your plate.'

'It's nothing. And you know why.'

He was wearing his usual light-hearted expression, but his eyes were serious. They were always serious when he looked at her these days, but this time she felt the danger. She looked away.

'Don't!'

'Why not? It's not as if I've ever made any secret of it. I've loved you as long as I've known you, Beatrice, and I don't know how to stop.'

She felt a pang of something – she might almost have said it was her heart leaping, but she knew it couldn't be. Mimmo had died and she hadn't even cried for him, which meant that her heart was cold and she was a bad person, and if she forgot about him and began thinking about Vittorio then surely that made her even worse? Amid all the chaos of war she couldn't begin to think straight. She shook her head, her eyes meeting his in appeal. He understood what she meant and smiled to show he wasn't offended.

'I'm sorry,' she said.

'It doesn't matter. I just wanted you to know.'

But it did matter. She made a wild gesture and cried out:

'I hate all this! We're trapped in the middle of it all – in the middle of this terrible joke that no one's laughing at. Mimmo was trapped too, and look what happened to him. And Franco, and all the other thousands and millions of people. And Tina – you see her, how delicate she is. Every day my heart is in my throat looking at her. I'm terrified she'll fall ill, or that we'll be bombed, or that I won't have enough food to give her, and if anything should happen to her I couldn't bear it. How can anyone think of normal things while this is all going on? It's impossible!'

He watched her as she said it, and all she could see in his eyes was sympathy. Suddenly she felt weary, as though she could sleep for a week. She put a hand on his arm and met his eyes, wanting him to understand.

'You're strong, Vittorio, but I'm not. Not any more. Please don't ask me to think of you when I have barely enough strength to think of my own daughter.'

He couldn't argue with that.

'Of course I won't ask anything of you. But always remember I'm your friend. If you need me, I'll be here.'

*

When Beatrice arrived for her shift at the Hotel Ambassador the next day she found the place abuzz with news.

'The Countess is here!' exclaimed one of the other maids, as Beatrice was stacking her trolley with sheets.

'The Countess?'

'Yes. She came last night from Rome, and she's staying in Cavalieri's apartment. He's had to move into one of the small rooms on the fourth floor. You'd better go and see if she wants anything. She's been complaining ever since she arrived, but I guess you know better than the rest of us what she needs.'

Beatrice went up to the apartment. The place was on the top floor, and was usually occupied by the hotel manager, who was no doubt highly disgruntled at having been thrown out of his home for the benefit of the owner's wife. Monica was still in bed when she went in, sitting propped up against the pillows, alternately reading a magazine and filing her nails. She was dressed in a silk negligée that was frayed at the hem, and her face was drawn into a frown that formed a deep line between her brows. Her once glossy hair was dull, and dry at the ends, as though she hadn't had it seen to in a while. She looked older than when Beatrice had seen her last; closer to her real age. She glanced up and threw Beatrice a languid greeting, but didn't mention Mimmo, although she must have heard about his death from Dora. Then she tossed her magazine aside and yawned.

'This place is even worse than Rome! I thought perhaps there would be more food at least, but it seems there's nothing to eat here either.'

'Have you been in Rome all this time?' said Beatrice.

'Mostly. But it's a hellhole and getting worse all the time, and they've frozen Gerardo's bank accounts and I can't even live decently. And then the friends I was staying with went away, and the Americans decided they wanted my house, so I had no choice but to come here – and in the most uncivilised fashion, too, bumping about in an appalling heap of rusted metal they had the cheek to call a car. And of course one can't travel in the day for fear of being bombed, so we had to do it in the dark, and I was horribly frightened all the way. Ugh!' She shuddered. 'I thought I'd never make it here. This whole thing is a terrible bore, and with no money it's even worse. I only hope Gerardo will come up with the goods.'

'Are you going to see His Excellency, then? But he is still in hiding, isn't he?'

'Yes, unfortunately. Although I wonder whether it's really necessary at this point. Surely Il Duce isn't still looking for revenge after all those people he had shot in January? Tell me, how are the Germans treating the Villa Bruni?'

'My mother is taking care of it,' replied Beatrice. 'She is making sure they don't damage anything.'

'I suppose I ought to go and see them. Perhaps they'll let me take some of the antiques to sell. My clothes are all in rags and anything decent to eat costs a fortune, and God knows nobody needs wobbly old chairs and china vases these days.'

'My mother says Mr Kaufmann is there. Perhaps you can ask him.'

Monica perked up immediately at that.

'Otto?' A smile spread across her face. 'How delightful! Then I shall certainly go up to the villa today. One might as well take advantage of one's friends in high places.'

She swung her legs off the bed and sat up, then went across to the dressing mirror and examined her reflection. From what Beatrice could see, she looked very pleased with herself.

Beatrice reported the new arrival when she got home. When Stella heard the news, her heart leapt. Here at last was her chance to get out of Italy. Monica knew important people; surely she could arrange something?

'Did you tell her I was here?' she asked eagerly.

'No. I didn't think you'd want me to. What if she tells your husband where you are?'

That was a concern, of course. Monica and Marius had an uneasy relationship, but they were brother and sister after all, and there was no reason to suppose Monica wouldn't reveal Stella's whereabouts to him. He was still in Switzerland as far as Stella knew, but the danger was still there. How could she be sure Monica would keep quiet?

Stella's hand was fidgeting with something at her throat as she pondered, and she looked down and realised what it was. It was the key to the safe deposit box, which she'd been wearing on a string around her neck for safekeeping ever since their old apartment had been bombed. She wasn't sure why she'd held onto it so carefully; perhaps she felt she owed something, on behalf of her father, to the little Jewish art dealer who'd met a terrible end in those dreadful days when the dark heart of the Nazis' wicked plans had begun to reveal itself. But Silberstein was long dead, and Stella was still alive and in danger, and the paintings were the only bargaining chip she had. She'd used them once and could use them again. She'd offer the paintings to Monica in exchange for a passage out of the country and an assurance she wouldn't send word to Marius.

'I don't know why he'd be here now, given the state of Florence at the moment, so I expect he's still in Geneva,' she said. 'But you might check the register first, just to be sure, and ask Monica whether she knows where he is. I'll make sure she doesn't tell him about me.'

The next day Beatrice arrived at the hotel to find Monica up and dressed, and looking much better than she had the previous day. She'd seen to her hair and put on make-up, and she looked much more like the old Monica. She was sitting in an armchair, smoking and flicking through the same magazine she'd been reading the day before.

'Clean those ashtrays first, would you?' she said without looking up. 'It's a pity you couldn't get some fresh flowers. I suppose they'll be able to send up drinks, at any rate, although I doubt they'll have anything decent.'

'Are you expecting someone?' asked Beatrice. 'Your brother, perhaps?'

'Marius? He's in Geneva as far as I know. No, Otto is coming. I couldn't get up to the villa yesterday but I managed to put a telephone call through. He was terribly pleased to hear from me and can't wait to see me. It'll be quite like old times! He wants to see Gerardo. I expect there's something he can do about unfreezing our funds, and goodness knows it'll be about time.'

From what Beatrice had seen of Monica up to now she hadn't changed a bit, and she hesitated once again at the thought of telling her about Stella. But Marius wasn't here, and they'd agreed to it, so she took a deep breath and broke the news that Her Excellency's former stepdaughter, Miss Stella, had been hiding in Florence for almost a year now without papers, unable to leave. At her words Monica went stock-still for a moment and stared at her in amazement. Then her lips curved in that self-satisfied smile of hers.

'Well well! So she's been here all this time, has she?' She let out a sudden loud laugh which rang through the room. 'Tell her to come and see me.'

'It's too dangerous.'

'Well, I'm not walking all the way up to see her – and I suppose she wouldn't want me to go in the car, as it's bound to draw the Germans' attention to the place. I'm sure you can find a way to get her here. I'd like to see her – and besides, if it's true she wants to get out then I might be able to do something for her.'

Beatrice went away with many misgivings, and reported the conversation to Stella.

'I'd stay here if I were you,' she said.

But Stella was thinking of Monica's important friends, who might be able to help her. Would the Germans give her safe passage through the lines? It didn't seem likely, but at this point anything was worth trying. She was as sick of the war as everybody else: Florence was hot and sticky, they were all starving, and she longed for a good wash and a change of clothes from the old ones of Beatrice's she'd been wearing for months. There were fewer escaped POWs to help these days – the battle lines were drawing close, so it wasn't safe to travel across country any more – and she was starting to feel a burden again: just another mouth to feed. Before the war she'd protested at the idea of returning to England, but life was hard, and now she'd have welcomed it.

'I could slip in through the side door after lunch,' she said. 'Things will be quieter then. If you get me a maid's uniform nobody will give me a second look.'

'Well, if you're sure,' said Beatrice doubtfully.

It was easier than they'd expected. As Stella had predicted, nobody looked twice at her in her maid's uniform, although she had to remind herself to walk through the streets as though she had every right to be there, because looking furtive was the surest way to attract suspicion. A few months earlier she'd never have dared come out into the streets in broad daylight, but she'd grown bolder since then, even though it was more dangerous these days. There were far too many Germans around for her liking, but she and Beatrice slipped in through the side door without attracting any attention, and up the back stairs to the manager's apartment.

'I'll come back in few minutes,' said Beatrice.

'I'd rather you came in with me,' replied Stella, suddenly nervous again, although she didn't know why, given the dangers she'd just run in getting here.

They knocked on the door and went in. Monica was sitting in a chair in the living room, her legs crossed, a cigarette dangling from her fingers. She looked up as they entered. Stella took a deep breath.

'Hallo, Monica,' she said.

'Well, and so here you are!'

Monica put out her cigarette, stood up and came forward, looking Stella up and down assessingly as she had on that first day at the Villa Bruni, before the war. Stella felt shy, as though she were an awkward nineteen-year-old again.

'Beatrice tells me you've been hiding here for months. Well, much good it's done you! I see war agrees with you as little as it agrees with me.' She smiled and drew Stella into a hug, then pushed her away to look at her again. 'So it's really you! Tell me, what have you been doing? Sit down. Cigarette? Ah, you still don't smoke? It's probably for the best. What about a drink, then? Or is it too early?'

This was Monica at her most charming, and Stella felt a rush of relief. She realised she'd been scared for some reason, although she couldn't have put her finger on why. She sat down as instructed, while Monica sent Beatrice off to fetch drinks then lit another cigarette, talking all the while. It seemed she'd been moving from place to place, staying with various friends. Stella, reading between the lines, got the impression that she'd remained at each place until she'd exhausted the hospitality and patience of her hosts, before moving on.

'It's all been a dreadful bore since the Nazis turned up and started throwing their weight around,' Monica continued. 'One can hardly live in decent comfort these days.'

'I expect other people have had it worse,' replied Stella, thinking of Beatrice and their struggles, and the poverty and hunger she'd seen all around her in Florence. But Monica had no idea of poverty, and could think only of concerns that directly affected her.

'Oh, yes, poor Gerardo! At least I haven't been stuck in a cramped little attic for months. So horrid for him, the poor dear.' She perched on the arm of a chair and gazed at Stella thoughtfully. 'But let's not talk about that any more. Why are *you* here? Why aren't you in Geneva with Marius?'

Stella hesitated. This was the difficult part. She didn't know how Monica would take the news that she'd left Marius, but she was almost sure that Monica's love of money was greater than her loyalty to her brother, and she had a collection of valuable paintings to bargain with. She was just about to begin her explanation when there was a knock at the door. It must be Beatrice, returning with the drinks. Monica went to open it. Stella's back was to the door, so she didn't see who it was.

'You're just in time,' Stella heard Monica saying. 'I've a surprise for you.'

Stella's skin prickled cold all over.

Marius.

With the instinct of a split second, she knew. Her heart gave a sudden, painful thump, but it was too late. She stood up and turned as Marius entered the apartment. He stopped dead when he saw her, and for one seemingly endless moment his eyes bored into her, narrowed and calculating. Then he turned his head slowly to Monica and raised his eyebrows in query. She was looking from one of them to the other, amused curiosity written all over her face. It was clear she was enjoying herself hugely.

'I thought your little wife was back at home in Geneva,' she said. 'And yet here she is in Florence – has been for months, apparently.' She saw Stella's hurt look and shrugged. 'Don't look at me like that, darling. I had no idea he was in Florence until yesterday evening. But I couldn't not tell him you were here, could I?'

Stella's idea of bribing Monica with the paintings had been based on the assumption that Marius was in Geneva. But here he was, standing in front of her, and in the space of an instant all her hopes and plans went out of the window. She couldn't move, couldn't tear her eyes away from her husband – her husband, who'd beaten her hard enough to break bones, who'd made her life a living terror for months and years, so that constant danger and near-starvation were preferable to a life of comfort and ease with him. She could feel, just as if it were happening now, his hand tight on her throat, the blood running down her battered face, and the stabbing agony in her ribs that were her last memory of him. And here was Monica, treating it all as a huge joke. She felt the nausea rising, and forced it down. Apart from that initial reaction he'd shown no sign of surprise or anger at her presence, and in fact was looking at her with interest.

'Hallo, Stella,' he said.

'What are you doing here?'

It was no good, she couldn't quell the fear, and the question came out as a whisper.

He was smiling, just as he used to before they were married – before she'd found out what he was really like.

'Why, I—' he stopped, then his smile broadened and he came forward before she could retreat, resting his hands lightly on her arms and kissing her on the forehead. Then he stepped back and looked into her eyes, and she saw only concern in his face. 'You're here! I thought the worst had happened.'

Her mind was buzzing confusedly, and she couldn't think.

'But why are you here?' she repeated stupidly.

'I'm here with Kaufmann – you remember him, don't you? He's working for the Kunstschutz, the German art protection unit, and they've given him the responsibility for protecting all the artworks in Florence. He invited me to come and advise, so I thought I'd better do it. Better that than leave the Germans to trample over everything – you know what they're like.'

After that first instant of surprise and calculation his manner was friendly, humorous, and he seemed quite like the Marius Stella had known and liked before it had all gone horribly wrong. He went on:

'But never mind that – it's not important. The important thing is that I've found you at last. You know I've missed you terribly, don't you? I'm sorry you felt you had to leave over a misunderstanding, but there's no need for you to stay away now.'

His bright blue eyes were looking deeply into hers and she stared back, almost hypnotised, almost believing him. She had to make the effort to remember what he really meant by a misunderstanding. His hands were on her arms again, and he was speaking softly, soothingly.

'Where have you been staying? Look how thin you are! You must be very tired. I'm staying with the deputy superintendent of the Uffizi. Why don't you come back there with me? There's food, and it's comfortable, and we can get you some new clothes.'

His voice flowed on, beguiling her, drawing her in. He was talking about the war, and how it would soon be over, and how sorry he was that he'd neglected her for his business in the past, but he wouldn't do that any more, and they'd go back to Switzerland and be happy. After a year hiding in cramped rooms in Italy the idea of comfort and food and – yes, even a hot bath – was ridiculously tempting. But while he talked she was watching a little vein as it pulsed in his temple. Whenever he'd hit her in the past she'd always noticed that vein pulsing, and she knew that despite his kind words he was very, very angry with her.

At that she came to herself and shook her head, stepping back.

'No,' she said. 'I don't think I will, Marius. I'd prefer to stay in Florence, if it's all the same to you.'

It was the firmest thing she'd ever said to him, and she felt her heart hammering as she marvelled at her own daring.

'Goodness me!' drawled Monica maliciously. 'I see your wife would rather starve to death in Florence than come back to you. For shame, Marius! Didn't you treat her nicely? Did you reveal your true colours in front of her? You really ought to learn how to be kind to a woman.'

Marius ignored Monica and seized Stella by the arm, his fingers pressing painfully into her flesh. The mask had slipped and this was the Marius she remembered from Geneva. The violence was bubbling up to the surface, and she felt the familiar prickles of terror all over her skin.

'I wasn't asking,' he said softly. 'Did you think you could just run away and do as you like? I'm your husband and you'll do as I tell you. You're coming back with me whether you like it or not.'

Stella was sure the presence of Monica was the only thing holding him back from hitting her right now, and in spite of her fear she felt bold enough to shake her head. Even that small act of resistance was enough to provoke him. He jerked her closer and grabbed a handful of her hair, his other hand raised, about to strike. Stella cringed, screwing her eyes shut in anticipation. But the blow never came, because just then there was a sound, like a shocked gasp, from the direction of the door. Marius let go of Stella suddenly and swung round. Beatrice was standing there with a tray of drinks, her eyes wide. Marius loosened his grip on Stella, who seized the opportunity to wrench herself away.

'Here are your drinks, Your Excellency,' faltered Beatrice. She put the tray down, eyeing Marius warily as if she thought he might explode at any moment.

'Stella!' snapped Marius commandingly.

But Stella was shaking her head again and backing towards the door. She turned and stumbled out. Beatrice and Monica were both calling her, asking her to wait, but she couldn't, she had to get away. She ran down the stairs, out through the side door of the hotel, and didn't stop running until she reached home.

Chapter Twenty-Eight

It was midday, and the low rumble of the guns could be heard from Arezzo, fifty miles to the south-east, when Vittorio knocked on the door of the farmhouse in the hills where Gerardo was lying low in a little room upstairs. The Count had lost a lot of weight in his months in hiding, and it didn't suit him: the skin hung in folds from his cheeks, and his clothes were too loose. He was getting arthritic and had lost most of his hair, and his face wore an unhealthy pallor from lack of sun. Still, he greeted Vittorio with his usual bonhomie.

'What news, my boy?' he asked, as he sat down stiffly on the bed from which he'd risen with difficulty.

'The Countess is back in Florence,' replied Vittorio briefly.

'Ah! Is she? I take it Rome didn't agree with her.'

'I guess not. She turned up here on Friday night and is staying at the hotel. She's in contact with Kaufmann at the villa, and seems altogether friendly with the Germans in general. Beatrice says she has no money.'

'Then I expect we'll see her here sooner or later,' said Gerardo resignedly.

'Do you need to stay in hiding? You could be living in comfort at the hotel by now if you liked.'

'My dear boy, never underestimate the capacity of Mussolini to exact his petty revenge on those who cross him. If he can have his own son-in-law shot, then he can certainly do the same for me. When I voted him out I was doing what I thought was best for the country, as I assumed was his wish, but it appears that what he *really* wanted was for me to do what was best for Mussolini. No, from what you've told me the Fascists are still roaming too wild around Florence for my liking. I'll stay here for the present, if you don't mind.'

'As you wish.'

'Now, I have something I want you to do,' went on Gerardo. 'Father Filippi tells me he's received some more paintings from the wife of a collector who got into a dispute with the Germans and came off worst. She wants to keep them to sell once the war's over, but they arrived in the back of a butcher's cart in rather a hurry, and could do with a little attention. Perhaps you wouldn't mind going up there and taking a look. I gather there are one or two nice Mannerist pieces that might be worth something if the offal hasn't spoilt them.'

The church was only a few minutes away, and Vittorio was in no particular hurry.

'I'll do it now,' he said.

He was preparing to leave when there was a hammering at the door. Both men froze. Vittorio advanced cautiously to the window, looked down at the street and swore.

'Fascists! We must get you out. Is there a back door?'

But it was too late. The thumping of fists had turned into the sound of blows with feet, as the door was kicked down and the intruders thundered through the house and up the stairs. There were five of them, armed to the teeth with rifles and pistols, and they hadn't come to talk. They hauled a protesting Gerardo to his feet, and three of them marched him downstairs while the other two seized and disarmed Vittorio, following behind. As they emerged from the house a car drew up, with three people in it. Vittorio recognised Monica, Otto Kaufmann and Marius Schwegler. Monica was wearing a light blue summer frock and an elegant hat, and looked for all the world as though she were on her way to a tea party. Kaufmann stepped out of the car in a hurry and surveyed the scene with displeasure.

'What's this?' he demanded. 'Your orders were to wait.'

'Never mind our orders,' replied one of the Fascists sullenly. 'This man is a traitor and must be dealt with.'

'You shall deal with him as you like afterwards, but I want to speak to him first. Take them back inside. We don't want to make an ugly scene in the street.'

Monica was looking shocked.

'Just a minute. Who are these men? They weren't supposed to be here. Otto? Marius?'

They both ignored her. Gerardo and Vittorio were bundled roughly back into the kitchen, then Gerardo was thrown into a chair, while two men pinned Vittorio's arms behind his back.

'Otto!' exclaimed Monica. He didn't reply, and she turned to Gerardo. 'Gerardo, I didn't do this, I swear!'

'Silence!' snapped Kaufmann.

'Be quick,' said the Fascist leader.

'I want the paintings that were hanging in the Villa Bruni,' said Kaufmann to Gerardo. 'The pictures are to be taken away for safekeeping. Official orders.'

Gerardo, pale and sweating at gunpoint, was nevertheless imperturbably polite.

'I thank you,' he replied. 'But they are already quite safe, so there is no need for your organisation to disturb itself.'

There was a swift, brutal movement as one of the Fascists smacked him across the face with the butt of his rifle. Monica cried out and darted forward, but was held back.

'Not too hard, you fool! I need him conscious,' said Kaufmann. 'However, you're right – we don't have time to waste.' He stepped up to Gerardo, who had been swept half out of his chair by the blow, and held a pistol to his head. 'Tell me where the paintings are.'

'Otto!' cried Monica. She turned desperately to her brother. 'Marius, stop him! Why don't you stop him?'

Marius ignored her, and she began to wail. Gerardo's mouth was bleeding freely, but there was still a touch of defiance to him.

'So this is how you repay my hospitality to you,' he said to Kaufmann. 'I always knew the Germans had no manners. But it seems I have no choice. Very well, they are in the church at Casignano. Tell them I sent you.'

'How far is it?' demanded Kaufmann.

'Five minutes from here,' replied one of the Fascists.

Kaufmann lowered his gun and nodded at Marius, who went out. Monica, still sobbing, hung on Kaufmann's arm.

'Otto, what are you doing? This isn't what we agreed. You said you wanted to buy the paintings. You said you'd pay a fair price.'

He shook her off roughly, and she ran to Gerardo, threw herself at his feet and clutched at his hand.

'I'm sorry Gerardo, I didn't mean this, I promise!'

He eyed her wearily and mumbled something.

'Get her off him,' said Kaufmann impatiently.

One of the Fascists grabbed Monica by the sleeve of her dress, which tore, and threw her roughly across the room. She hit the floor hard and her hat came off. The man aimed a kick at her and she scrambled away from him, then went to crouch in the corner, smoothing at her torn sleeve, her breath coming in rough hiccups.

The wait seemed interminable, the silence in the farmhouse broken only by Monica's sobs. Kaufmann sat down and lit a cigarette.

'Any chance of a smoke?' said Vittorio lightly to one of his captors, who replied with a sharp blow to the side of the head and something unrepeatable.

In reality Vittorio was deadly serious and thinking rapidly, formulating various means of escape. He'd recognised one of the

Fascists as being from the Banda Carità, and he knew they'd show no mercy. If he didn't escape they'd take him to their headquarters at the Villa Triste for interrogation, and who knew if he'd ever come out alive?

At last Marius returned, and nodded at Kaufmann.

'Yes, they are all there – apart from one.'

'Good,' said Kaufmann. 'We will take them for protection, on behalf of the Kunstschutz.'

'You don't want to protect them at all, do you,' said Gerardo dryly. 'The Kunstschutz doesn't operate at gunpoint as a rule. If you were to ask me I'd say you were operating on your own initiative and for your own benefit.'

Marius now approached Gerardo.

'Where is the Raphael? The *Lady of the Cypresses*?' he asked.

Gerardo shrugged.

'Isn't it there with the others?' he replied politely.

Marius hit him hard across the face, leaving an ugly cut across Gerardo's left eye that began to bleed.

'Marius!' cried Monica.

'Where is it?' Marius's voice was soft, sinister. 'Tell me. I want it. It's mine.'

Something like a gleam of insolence appeared in Gerardo's one good eye.

'Then you will have to look for it yourself,' he replied.

'Give me your cigarette,' Marius said to a Fascist, who had just lit up. 'And hold him.'

The man handed over the lit cigarette, and Marius brought it close to Gerardo and held it close to his face. Gerardo didn't flinch.

'Tell me,' whispered Marius, and put the cigarette to Gerardo's neck. Gerardo let out a strangled shriek of pain, and Monica screamed.

'Gerardo, tell him!' cried Monica. 'Marius, stop it!'

She began sobbing again.

Marius ignored his sister. He applied the cigarette again, and there was another yell. Vittorio couldn't stand it any longer.

'I'll take you to it!' he shouted. 'I hid it. The old man doesn't know where it is. Leave him alone!'

Gerardo's eyes darted towards him.

'Don't tell them, my boy,' he slurred exhaustedly. 'It won't do any good.'

Marius came across to Vittorio and regarded him through narrowed eyes.

'Is this true?'

Vittorio glared back at him defiantly. The leader of the Fascists was looking at his watch.

'Look, we haven't got time for all this. You have all the paintings you need. Let's go.'

Marius whipped round.

'Just a minute,' he began. But he didn't have the same authority as Kaufmann, and he was forced to submit as the Fascists hauled Gerardo up from his chair and bundled him out of the house.

'You, up!' ordered one of the men, gesturing with his rifle at Monica, who was still on the floor.

Monica wasn't one to go down meekly.

'It's *Your Excellency*,' she spat.

'Very well, Your Excellency,' he replied mockingly. She stood up and brushed herself off.

'Give me my hat.'

'You won't need that.' He motioned with his rifle again. 'Get going.'

She drew in her breath.

'You'll be in trouble for this,' she hissed. 'I know important people. I know Il Duce himself. Wait until he hears of this!'

'Who do you think ordered it? Traitors are always punished.'

'I'm not a traitor! What have I done?'

'Not you – your husband.'

CLARA BENSON

'He's not a traitor either!'

'Then he has nothing to worry about, does he? Don't worry, we'll give him a fair trial and he can speak for himself.'

He threw back his head and laughed unpleasantly as he pushed Monica before him out of the house. The three prisoners were marched down the road, Kaufmann and Marius following behind. After a hundred yards or so they were taken through a gate into an olive grove. The sun was hot, and the footsteps of the party crunched through the long, dry grass as they walked. Monica, lurching and tripping in high heels, had begun to sob again. Gerardo, his hands fastened behind his back, kept falling to his knees, and each time was yanked roughly to his feet. On the other side of the olive grove was a patch of woodland, which they entered. It was a relief to be out of the scorching sunlight, although it hadn't escaped Vittorio's notice that they were now out of sight of the road. The sweat was prickling on his forehead, and he glanced from side to side as they marched, looking for any opportunity to make a break for it.

At the edge of the wood was a stately old oak tree with wide, spreading branches, by which they came to a halt. The two men escorting Gerardo seemed to need no instructions. They pushed him up against the tree and tied him to it. Gerardo must have been fully aware by now of what they intended, and he stood straight, looking calmly ahead. The leader of the Fascists began to speak. He had been charged by his superiors with the task of seeking out all the enemies of the new Italian Fascist state, especially those who had committed shameful treachery in July 1943 and attempted to oust Il Duce from power. It was known that the Count was one of those enemies – they had proof of it in the signature he had given, demanding Mussolini's removal from office – and for that there could be only one punishment.

Monica's sobs had intensified as she understood what was about to happen to her husband. She turned to her brother, who was standing close by with Kaufmann.

'Marius!' she cried. 'Stop them!'

Marius paid no attention. He and Kaufmann were talking. The German was impatient.

'We have not time for this nonsense,' he said. 'I have a meeting at two o'clock and it will take us that long to get back to Florence. Let us leave them to it. We have what we came for.'

'You might,' replied Marius, 'but I want the Raphael. They've hidden it somewhere, and if Gerardo won't tell me where it is then I will make this fellow talk.' He stepped up to Vittorio and stared at him with cold menace. Vittorio glared back at him but didn't flinch.

'Leave it,' said Kaufmann. 'There are plenty of other beautiful paintings in Florence.'

'But I want this one. I've waited a long time for it, and I'm not letting it go now.'

'Look, take my word for it, he'll be much more likely to talk if you wait a couple of days and then go and see him at the Villa Triste. I can guarantee that once the Banda Carità have been let loose on him he'll be in a much more amenable frame of mind. Now, what about your sister? I don't suppose they plan to shoot her, but they will probably interrogate her to find out whether she has anything to tell them. Would you rather we took her back with us?'

Marius turned to Monica and looked her up and down with deliberation.

'No,' he said coldly. 'I owe her a favour or two. Let them do what they like with her. She might even enjoy it.'

At that, Monica let out a shriek of rage and fear and tried to wrench herself free from the Fascist who was holding her. He pinned her wrists and slapped her across the face, and she let out another shriek. Marius and Kaufmann turned to walk away.

'Marius!'

He turned round. Monica's hair had come loose from its carefully pinned coils, and there was an ugly mark on her cheek where the

Fascist had hit her. She was panting, transfixing him with a look of utter hatred.

'If you leave me here now, as God is my witness I promise that I will kill you the next time I see you,' she said in a low, shaking voice.

He smirked and turned away quite deliberately, and he and Kaufmann walked off. Monica shrieked and struggled again as the sound of their voices receded into the distance, but there was nothing she could do. She collapsed once more into loud sobs.

Now that Kaufmann and Marius had left, there were only five men remaining. Three of them were occupied with Gerardo, while one was covering Monica and another had hold of Vittorio's arm, holding his own pistol to his head. Vittorio looked out for his chance. The Fascist leader had now finished addressing Gerardo.

'Have you anything to say in your defence?' he said.

'What is there to say?' replied Gerardo. 'It's quite evident you've made your mind up. But I'm in rather a lot of pain, so I'd take it as a favour if you'd get on with it.'

'As you wish. Have you any last words?'

Gerardo looked at Vittorio and gave him the ghost of a smile, then turned to Monica, who had sunk to her knees.

'Forgive me, Gerardo,' she wept.

His face softened.

'I forgive you, my dear.' He turned to face forward. 'Whenever you like,' he said firmly.

The firing squad raised their rifles. Vittorio stood helplessly and swallowed at the sight of Gerardo's calm dignity and courage. He wanted to cry out, shout at them to stop, but he knew it was useless: there was nothing he could do to help the man who everyone thought was his father. Gerardo had never admitted to the relationship, but he'd looked out for Vittorio and had given him assistance and employment. Vittorio had been fond of the old man, but had never had the chance to say it. Now he never would.

But if there was nothing he could do for Gerardo, there was at least one last thing Gerardo could do for him. Heart thumping in his chest, Vittorio muttered a brief prayer and waited for his opportunity. His captor, watching the scene with avid pleasure, had lowered the gun and was momentarily off guard. Nobody else was looking. The captain shouted, 'Fire!' and the rifles discharged. Vittorio didn't even wait to see Gerardo slump forward: as quick as lightning he twisted his captor's arm up his back, grabbed the pistol from his hand, hit him hard with the gun and threw himself towards a deep thicket. He'd reckoned on having a head start of about five seconds, but he didn't stop to time it. Instead he ran and ran, ploughing doggedly through thick brush, ignoring the sound of shouts behind him, concentrating on putting as much distance as possible between him and his pursuers. He heard no more gunshots, only the sound of twigs snapping and foliage brushing, and his own laboured breath as he fought his way through the trees, heedless of razor-sharp leaves and thorny branches which scratched and tore at his skin and smacked his face and ripped at his clothes. It didn't matter: the trees were shelter, protection, his salvation, and he battled his way through them, taking a circuitous route into the thickest part of the wood, bearing north-west away from the road.

After a long while he paused to get his breath back and listen, but heard only the thundering of his own heart and The sound of grasshoppers chirruping in the afternoon sunshine. Had the Fascists come after him? There were five of them, but they had the Countess to take care of – and the Count, poor devil. A dart of pain went through him, and he was surprised to find tears rolling down his face, but there was no time for that now, if he was to escape. His intention was to hide in the woods as long as necessary, then make a break for it across country. He shook the tears off and pushed onwards, looking for a place that would give him cover for the next few hours, then stopped again as he heard something. It was the sound of a car engine, unusual in these days of fuel shortages.

Marius and Kaufmann had left some time ago because Kaufmann had to be somewhere at two o'clock, so it couldn't be them. It was most likely the Fascists, taking the Countess away with them. Or had they executed her too? Vittorio hadn't heard any more gunshots, so perhaps Kaufmann was right and they'd taken her away for interrogation, which would be bad enough.

Vittorio remained hiding in the woods until the sun went down, after which he judged it was safe to come out. He knew this part of the country like the back of his hand, and he headed across the fields, keeping away from the roads and checkpoints, walking through sparsely populated areas. It was pitch dark and he was exhausted by the time he came to the little house by the gates of the Villa Bruni. He ought to have kept well away from the place given that the Germans were so near, but he knew Dora would have to know the news – and besides, he was weary and heartsick, and needed the sort of comfort and consolation he could only get from the women – Beatrice especially. Now that the immediate danger was over, the memory of the Count tied to the tree, and of the Countess on her knees, supplicating him for forgiveness, played in his mind over and over again, a burning image imprinted on his brain like a brand. There was nothing he could have done for either of them, but he knew the guilt would live with him forever.

Chapter Twenty-Nine

Ted spent two months kicking his heels in a prison camp near Avezzano – and kicking himself for having let himself be caught so easily, before he'd even been in the job a week. He ought to have been making himself useful to the Allies, but instead he was whiling away his days playing cards with the other prisoners and waiting for his knee to mend again. The conditions in the camp were harsh, but there was one thing to be thankful for at least: he'd managed to hide his rucksack with the radio before he'd been captured, so they'd found nothing on him that marked him out as a spy. If they'd discovered the equipment he'd brought with him he'd have been tortured and shot. As it was, his smart mouth had already got him into trouble with the camp commanders on numerous occasions, and he'd been put in solitary confinement more than once.

The weeks went by, and the thought of the radio, lying useless under a hedge fifty miles away, filled him with frustration. If only he could get out of here, he'd make straight for it and get back to the job he was meant to be doing. He felt just as powerless as he had in Geneva – although at least there he'd been doing something productive, instead of rotting away slowly in a camp. And he'd had Stella. But she was gone now, missing somewhere in this godforsaken country, and whatever ideas he'd had about getting to Florence and finding her were now nothing more than smoke in the wind.

One day the word came that they were to be evacuated and taken to camps in Germany, and it didn't take too long for the rumour to go around that the Allies had pushed through and were only a few miles away – a positive development all told, but of little comfort to the men who were about to be whisked away before they could be rescued. The next night they were all lined up and loaded onto trucks, which set off in convoy in a westerly direction, as far as Ted could judge. They hadn't been told anything, but he assumed that at some point they'd all be unloaded onto a train and sent north. In the back of the truck with him were a lot of men he didn't know. It was late, and most of them were sleepy and silent, but one of them was from London: a talkative sort, who kept on talking despite all invitations from his fellow passengers to shut up. Ted closed his eyes and tried to doze as the man's voice droned on about his home, his garden, and every member of his family. He had three brothers and a sister, it seemed. The sister was called Stella. Ted's eyes snapped open at the familiar name.

'I know a girl called Stella,' he murmured, almost to himself.

'So do I,' said his neighbour opposite.

Ted glanced up at the speaker. He was a South African, and very young – much too young to be so far from home, fighting a war. He felt a twinge of sympathy.

'Is that your girl?' he asked.

'No. I don't really know her. She was just someone I met in Florence a couple of months ago. English, I think.'

Ted was suddenly wide awake, all thoughts of sleep forgotten.

'An English girl? What'd she look like?'

At his urgent tone the South African looked at him in surprise.

'I don't know. Brown hair, curly. Just a girl. Kind of pretty. She got us out of Florence.' He looked down at his knees. 'Or she got me out, anyway. My pal got shot.'

Ted hardly heard what he said about his friend, because his mind and his heart were racing. An English girl in Florence called Stella. It couldn't be a coincidence.

'She got you out of Florence? How come?'

'I think she was working with the partisans,' replied the boy.
'Was she all right?'

'What do you mean? Do you know her? Is it the same Stella you know?'

'I don't know. Maybe.'

The South African shrugged. 'I wish I could help you, but I can't tell you. She led the Germans away from me so I could escape, then they started shooting at her. She saved my life but I think they might have shot her. I don't know. I didn't hang around long enough to see. I'm sorry.'

Ted felt suddenly cold, but he'd hardly had time to take in the South African's words when there was a sudden roaring overhead, and a series of thunderous explosions all around them. They'd been caught in an Allied bombing raid. Everyone threw themselves to the floor.

'Not us, you idiots!' shouted someone uselessly.

Then everything began to happen very quickly. Ted, on the floor with the others, was aware of another explosion. He felt the ground shake, and clung on for dear life as the truck swerved sharply. It careered off the road and went over the edge of a low bridge, rolled over several times and came to a stop in a dried-up riverbed. Once the noise and the shaking and the banging stopped, Ted opened his eyes to discover that he'd been thrown clear of the truck along with several others as it went over.

He lay, winded and dazed, for several seconds, then sat up slowly and felt himself all over. Miraculously, apart from a few cuts and bruises, he seemed to be more or less unhurt. Someone was lying a little way away from him. It was the young South African, who hadn't been so lucky. It looked as if he'd broken his neck when he landed, and he was lying, his eyes staring unseeing into the darkness. Ted felt a pang of pity, but there wasn't time to stop and think, because here was his opportunity to escape. All around him was confusion: fires were burning on the road, lighting up the darkness, and there were shouts and gunshots a little distance away as the Germans tried to round up those who had escaped the bombs. Ted didn't give much for his chances if he was caught, and it looked as though the men from his own truck who'd survived the crash were thinking the same way, because they were scattering in all directions, many heading into the nearby hills. Ted did likewise, and spent an uncomfortable night out in the open in company with a small group of survivors, listening for approaching search parties. But it seemed the Germans weren't especially interested in rounding them up, because nobody came.

The next morning he took leave of his companions, who were heading south to try and cross the Allied lines. They'd invited him to travel with them, but he had other plans. He was going to find his radio and finish the job he'd come here to do two months ago. Fortunately the convoy had brought him several miles in the right direction, and as far as he could work out he couldn't be more than about twenty miles from the place where he'd left his rucksack. He hoped it was still there.

The next two days were miserable ones: the weather was warm and dry, but he had no tent, no provisions, and no map, so he couldn't stray too far from the road, and had to rely on such road signs as there were. Added to that was the disturbing news he'd had about Stella, and her uncertain fate. She was working with the partisans, the South African had said. The idea was strange to Ted. He'd always thought of her as the kind of woman who needed protecting, but if this was indeed his Stella, then it looked as though she'd somehow involved herself in something active, even dangerous. He remembered the South African's words. Stella had saved his life, and then the Germans had shot at her. Perhaps she was dead. Ted's heart plummeted at the thought. The fear that he'd lost her forever would be an additional burden to carry until he could get to Florence, but he wouldn't give up hope – not now that he'd come this far.

In the meantime his chief concern was to retrieve the radio, then find somewhere safe where he could re-establish contact with HQ. He ploughed on, usually at night, taking a generally westerly direction, keeping to the hills. He knew the partisans mostly hid in the mountainous areas, and his hope was that he would come across a group of them sooner or later, but so far he'd seen nobody he dared approach – and in fact, he was taking care to keep out of sight, because he knew he looked conspicuous and distinctly un-Italian. He slept the whole of one day in a recess under some rocks, and the next in a tumbledown pigsty from which the pigs had long gone.

By the third day he was exhausted, hot and famished, and ready to approach someone for help, so he carried on walking by daylight. It was a sparsely populated area – wild hill country, punctuated with the occasional village – but there would surely be people who were prepared to shelter Allies and partisans? He didn't know whom to trust, that was the trouble, and so he walked on, keeping to the trees and looking out for a barn, or a shed, anywhere he might settle down for a day or two, with perhaps some food he might steal.

Darkness came and no shelter presented itself. He'd had nothing to eat for nearly three days now, and his stomach pinched painfully, but he had no choice but to carry on. He'd been walking along the side of a road for some hours, keeping to the shade of the trees, even though not a single car had passed. The road wound upwards through the hills, and he ploughed on doggedly until he saw a light a little way ahead and to the left. His spirits rose cautiously. Where there was light there would be shelter. He changed direction and left the road. The ground underfoot was uneven, covered with long brush, and he struggled to get through it. It was too dark to see where he was going, but he had to keep moving. Suddenly he gave an exclamation as the ground gave way under him and he found himself up to his knees in a freezing cold ditch. He swore, and floundered forward to where a tree stood, its branches forming a spiky silhouette against the dim light from the nearby house. Reaching up, he grasped at the nearest branch to pull himself out of the water. Then a voice came suddenly in the darkness, almost causing him to lose his grip and fall back into the ditch.

'*Chi va là?*' it rapped out sharply.

A torch came on suddenly, blinding him. He was hanging from the branch, half in and half out of the water, and couldn't see a thing, but he could hear the presence of two or three people, and the ominous sound of a rifle being cocked. He held up his left hand, since the other one was still clinging to the tree, preventing him from falling.

'Don't shoot!' he said in Italian. '*Americano.*'

'*Americano!*' exclaimed the voice.

The torch was lowered, and a hand reached out to grab his and pull him up the bank. He stood there, dripping, and took them in by the dim light. There were three of them, all wearing uniforms of sorts, although they were clearly not Fascists. Despite the rifles two of them were pointing at him, they looked as though they were finding the situation very amusing.

'What sort of time is this to go for a swim?' said the one who'd spoken first.

'I got lost,' replied Ted.

They seemed impressed that he spoke Italian.

'Where did you come from?' asked another. 'Did you escape from one of the camps?'

'Yes. I'm looking for some food and somewhere to stay.'

'Well we can give you something to eat but you can't stay here. They'll be looking all over for you and you'll just be a liability.'

'I won't be a liability, I promise. I was sent here to find you. It was just my bad luck I got picked up by the Germans first.'

They looked him up and down doubtfully.

'You were sent to find us? Why, what can you do for us?'

'I know where there's a radio,' he replied.

At the magic words all three faces spread into broad grins, and they came forward and shook his hand. The first man slapped him on the shoulder.

'Come inside!' he said. 'You're just what we've been looking for!'

*

Glad to be doing something useful at last, Ted spent spring and early summer being smuggled from safe house to safe house by the partisans, always heading further and further north as the Germans retreated gradually up the peninsula. At length he fell in with a band of guerrillas who were occupied with arranging ambushes on German lorries driving between Rome and Florence, and reported back to HQ on their capabilities. It was dangerous work, not least because the various groups of partisans had the tendency to fall out among themselves, while some of them were little more than bandits, using the war as an excuse to extort money and food from civilian homes. And all the while there was the danger that his radio signal would be detected by the Germans, and he'd be caught and shot.

The weather grew warm, then hot, and in early June came the news that Rome had fallen to the Allies. But the Germans were still fighting every inch of the way, and it was increasingly clear that Italy would not be liberated any time soon. Ted had heard of atrocities happening everywhere: murders, assassinations, reprisals, rapes and hangings, as the country descended into little less than civil war. Italy was an incredibly dangerous place at present, and Ted had to force himself not to think of Stella too often, because whenever he did he was gripped by the conviction that she must surely be dead. In spite of his attempts to remain hopeful, he couldn't help remembering the South African's story. How could she have escaped the Germans' guns? Thoughts of her only filled him with despondency, so he shut his mind to her possible fate, set his jaw grimly and pushed on with the job he'd been given. At least he could say he was doing his duty.

In early July he found himself staying at a smallholding in
southern Tuscany. He'd been there a couple of weeks, listening to
the sound of the guns as the battle lines followed close behind him.
He was stranded there for the present, picking up what news he
could and sending it back to headquarters in Rome. The partisans
brought him information and he relayed news to them in turn.
He was staying in an old tumbledown barn, part of which had
been used to keep goats, although the family had been forced to
slaughter them when they'd run short of food. Now he was sharing
his accommodation alternately with rats and roving groups of Allied
POWs, who were trying to get through the lines. The farm was
owned by a family consisting of an elderly couple, their daughter,
and the daughter's two children, whose father had been forcibly
rounded up and packed off to a work camp in Germany. They
were struggling by as best they could, sheltering as many people as
they had room for, and hoping, like everybody else, that the war
would end soon and that they could begin to rebuild their lives.

One afternoon Ted came out of his barn and went into the
kitchen yard to fetch some water. It was a blazing hot afternoon,
the sun scorching the flagstones of the tiny yard outside the modest
home in which the family lived, and the air was still, with not
even a breath of wind to disturb the trees. The place was deserted;
presumably they'd all gone out, or perhaps they'd gone upstairs to
sleep as they waited for the heat of the day to die down. He filled
his little pail at the rusty old pump, glancing idly round as he did so.

Then he heard something: it sounded like a muffled shriek, and
it was coming from the open kitchen door. Then another sound:
a thump and a scrape, like a foot striking against wood, perhaps a
table. He frowned and went across to the door. Inside the kitchen
a struggle was taking place as the daughter of the house, Maria
Luisa, fought desperately with a German soldier. He had forced her
up against the wall, and she was fighting to free her wrists from his
grasp, as his other hand fumbled with his clothing. It was obvious

what was going on. Ted didn't stop to think: he strode forward and wrenched the German away from the girl, catching him by surprise. He threw the man out into the yard, then, while he was lying sprawled on the ground, pulled out his Beretta automatic and shot him clean through the head. The sound rang out, echoing sharply into the afternoon stillness. The German hadn't had a chance to say a word.

Maria Luisa came out and stared down at the dead man, smoothing her clothes, her breath coming rapidly. Ted felt an obscure need to apologise.

'I'm sorry,' he said. 'It was unavoidable.'

She looked at him, her eyes cold.

'I'm only sorry I didn't shoot him myself,' she replied.

Then she spat on the German and went back inside.

They took the dead man's money and his few possessions and buried him in a shallow grave in the woods, in case anybody came looking for him. It was the first blood Ted had drawn and he was surprised at how little it had affected him. War hardened all hearts, he supposed.

*

In Florence, the battle was approaching fast, and everybody felt it. Every morning German batteries opened fire on Allied planes flying overhead, and rumours intensified that the Germans would lay waste to the city as they retreated. The buildings on the south bank of the Arno were increasingly exposed to shelling from Allies ranged in the hills to the south, and it became almost too dangerous to go out. Dora had been told she was no longer needed at the Villa Bruni, as the Germans were preparing to leave, but she continued to go there every day and see to the gardens, which she'd been tending as best she could, so that they'd have fruit and vegetables at least once the occupiers were gone – always assuming the Germans didn't steal them. She'd been busy making enquiries as to what had happened to Monica, but to no avail – they had no idea whether she'd been shot or merely taken away for interrogation.

Stella had wept when Vittorio brought the news of Gerardo's execution, and told how Monica had unwittingly led the Fascists to him. She could hardly believe what her former stepmother had done. Stupid, selfish Monica, so blindly concerned with her own comfort and pleasure that she hadn't considered the danger she was putting her husband in. And poor Gerardo! Stella remembered how kind he'd always been to her. There'd been nothing malicious or evil about him; he'd been a harmless bon vivant who liked to surround himself with beautiful things, and who'd wanted nothing more than to enjoy his prosperity and good fortune in peace. He hadn't deserved to die like that. And it looked as though Monica had been punished for it too, one way or another.

Stella was horrified at Marius's role in the proceedings. That was the worst thing of all, somehow. She'd known for a long time that there was something not quite right about him, but to abandon his own sister to the Fascists in cold blood like that, just out of petty revenge for some imagined slight! Ever since the unexpected encounter with him at the hotel, Stella had lived in fear that he would turn up at Dora's house, looking for her. She knew Dora and Beatrice would never give her away, but still, every time there was a knock at the door she jumped and her heart began racing. Where was he now, she wondered. He'd told her he was staying with the deputy superintendent of the Uffizi gallery. Presumably he hoped to pick up as many cheap paintings as he could under the guise of working for the Kunstschutz, buying them – or stealing them – from desperate people. Kaufmann had left the city, Dora told them, almost certainly taking with him Gerardo's precious art collection. Marius had no doubt been promised a fine fee for his help, but it was obvious he still fiercely coveted the *Lady of the Cypresses* above all, since he'd been prepared to torture Gerardo to make him give up its hiding place.

The more Stella thought about it, the more she wondered why she'd ever married him. At one time she'd thought him charming, kind, pleasant – but of course that was what he'd wanted her to think. He'd needed her money, and so had kept the true darkness of his soul well and truly hidden within him, hoping to fool her into marrying him. Well, he'd fooled her all right, but he hadn't been able to keep up the deception for long. And now he'd shown himself to be more wicked than she'd ever imagined. She shuddered. Whether she ever found Ted or not, one thing was certain: she never wanted to see Marius again.

Chapter Thirty

They had no news of Monica until the end of July, when Dora came hurrying home to say the Countess was back at the hotel, keeping to the apartment on the top floor and refusing to see anybody.

'They say she's in a terrible state,' she said. 'I don't know where she's been, but Anna says they took her to the Villa Triste first for interrogation, then threw her into the prison at Santa Verdiana. Her lawyer had to get the Cardinal himself to intervene and get her released. If you ask me she's feeling ashamed of herself, that's why she won't come out of her room. And quite right, too!'

She had more news the next day when she came back.

'I saw her. She stays in bed all day with all the blinds down. She made me clean the place in the dark. I don't know what's wrong with her, but she looks terrible. Whatever they did to her at the Villa Triste must have driven her out of her mind. She was talking like a crazy person and pulling her hair. I was frightened and came away as quickly as I could. She wants to see you, Stella.'

'Me?'

Stella was astonished. The last time Monica had asked to see her she'd confronted her with Marius, but she couldn't mean to do the same thing again, surely? No, of course she didn't. Marius had not only ruthlessly tortured Gerardo, but had left his own twin sister to her fate without so much as a backward glance, so it was highly unlikely that she was feeling well-disposed towards him, to say the least. Stella found herself feeling an unwilling sympathy for Monica. She'd done a terrible thing in leading Gerardo to his death, but it

had been out of selfish foolishness rather than outright malicious-
ness. Monica had never learned to think of anybody but herself,
and it had cost her dearly in the end. She'd lost her husband, and
had herself fallen into the hands of the Fascists. Despite Monica's
unkindness the last time they'd met, Stella found herself wanting
to see her, to hear from her own lips what had happened.

'All right, I'll go,' she said. 'But don't tell her I'm coming.' She
didn't say it out loud, but there was still a residual fear that she'd
bump into Marius.

It was early on Saturday evening when Stella left the little house
and headed down the hill to the river. There were people about but
she wasn't so scared of being stopped any more, since the Germans
had other things to occupy their attention now. Even though the
sun was sinking the air was still stiflingly hot, and the few people
in the streets moved listlessly, as though all hope were gone and
they were only waiting for the end. As Stella walked she saw that
notices had been posted on all the buildings, and she went to read
one. It was an order to all residents living within two hundred
metres of the Arno, instructing them to evacuate their homes by
the next day. So it was true! They were planning to blow up the
bridges, and soon. Stella came to the Ponte Santa Trinita and saw
that here, unlike everywhere else, people seemed to be in a hurry,
rushing across the river as if they were late for something. German
soldiers were stationed by the bridge, ordering the passers-by to
keep moving, and she hesitated, wondering whether to turn back.
Then one of the Germans shouted at her and gestured at her to
move along, and without stopping to think she ran onto the bridge
and crossed the river.

She saw no more Germans, either in the street or at the Hotel
Ambassador. They must have already left. The notices to evacuate
were posted here too, and, as she entered the hotel through the side
door, she saw one or two kitchen staff scurrying about in a state
of agitation, seemingly preparing to leave. She hurried up to the

apartment on the top floor and knocked. There was no answer, so she tried the door. It was unlocked, and she went in. Monica was in bed, lying in the dark.

'Who's that?' she said. 'Oh, it's you, Stella. I wanted to see you, didn't I?'

'Monica, we have to go. The Germans have given the order to evacuate. I think they're going to blow up the bridges.'

There was a foetid odour in the room, like the smell of broken drains, overlaid with the acrid tang of cigarette smoke and stale alcohol.

'Why should I care what they're going to do?' replied Monica. 'It's all the same to me.'

She was slurring her words. Stella pressed the light switch, forgetting there was no power, then went to open the shutters. When she turned back to the bed she gave a gasp. Monica's face, bare of its usual careful make-up, looked drawn and sunken in the natural light. A beam of the sinking sun threw into sharp relief the deep lines on her forehead, and at the corners of her eyes and mouth. She was wearing the same negligée she'd been wearing last time Stella had seen her, but it was all twisted round to one side as though she'd been tossing and turning, trying to get comfortable. It was a low-necked affair, and as Monica turned towards her Stella saw weals and scars across her breast, standing out starkly purple and red against her pale skin. They were healing now, but the sight was still ugly and shocking. Stella clapped her hand over her mouth.

'Good God!' she exclaimed. 'What did they do to you?'

Monica winced and made a half-hearted attempt to pull the nightdress across it to hide it.

'Never mind.' She pulled herself unsteadily up against the pillows and reached for her cigarette case, taking out a cigarette and lighting it. 'I can't remember what I wanted to say. Come back tomorrow.'

She was obviously very drunk. A nearly empty bottle of whisky stood by the bed, surrounded by about twenty carelessly discarded cigarette stubs.

'I can't come back tomorrow,' said Stella. 'Don't you understand? You have to get out!' She turned to an armchair where a heap of discarded clothes lay, pulled out the first frock she saw and brought it across. 'Quickly! Get the dress on. You can come to Dora's until it's all over. Don't argue!'

She didn't know how she managed it, but somehow she got a resisting Monica into some clothes and bundled her out of the door and into the street. She was unsteady on her feet, but Stella gripped her arm firmly and got her as far as the river. There they were stopped by two German sentries.

'The bridge is now closed,' one of them said. 'Nobody is to pass. This area is to be evacuated. Go back.'

Stella looked about her. Sure enough, the Lungarno was now deserted, with not a civilian to be seen, only German soldiers.

'But where are we to go? We live south of the river.'

He shrugged.

'That is not my problem,' he answered. 'But I advise you to stay indoors.'

There seemed no choice but to do what he said. The manager, Mr Cavalieri, was just coming out as they arrived back at the hotel, looking very harassed, a big bunch of keys in his hand.

'Everybody has left now, Your Excellency. I'm going to lock up and hope for the best. With any luck we'll be able to reopen in a few days.'

'Give me the keys,' said Monica. She seemed to have sobered up slightly.

'But Your Excellency—'

'Never mind that!'

She took the keys, against the objections of Cavalieri and Stella.

'Where else are we going to stay? This is the best hotel in Florence. If they're going to destroy the city then we might as well be comfortable while they do it. Go, then, if you must,' she said to Cavalieri.

The hotel manager needed no further encouragement, and hurried off.

Once they got back to the apartment Monica sagged again, and collapsed tiredly into a chair.

'I need a drink,' she said.

'Oh, no you don't!' Stella took the remains of the bottle of whisky and put it out of reach. 'You'll already feel dreadful enough tomorrow. Look, is there any drinkable water here? Any food?'

'There might be something left in the kitchens,' replied Monica. She sounded drowsy.

It looked as though they were stuck in the hotel for the time being. Stella searched the cupboards of the apartment but found nothing useful.

'I'm going downstairs to see what they've got,' she said, but Monica had already dozed off.

The corridors were eerily dark, deserted and silent, while downstairs in the restaurant the tables were bare except for the tablecloths. Stella went into the kitchen and tried one of the taps. A thin stream of water came out, presumably from the tank on the roof, and she shut it off immediately so as not to waste it. There wasn't much in the way of food: mainly dried ingredients that weren't much use without gas to cook with, and that had gone off some days ago. Stella foraged and brought out what she could, then filled an empty wine bottle with water and took it upstairs. She poured a glass of water for Monica, who was bound to be thirsty when she woke up, then sat and ate a frugal meal. The shadows lengthened and the sun went down, and Stella sat, waiting for the dreadful blow to fall and the earth to shake, but the night passed and all was silent.

The next day she went downstairs and peered out into the street to see what was happening. The hotel was on the very edge of the evacuation zone, and many people in the surrounding buildings had remained in their homes, leaving only to fetch water. Stella stopped a man who was passing with an empty petrol can, and asked him if he'd heard anything, but he hadn't.

'It's in the hands of God now,' he said philosophically, and hurried on.

The wait seemed interminable. One day stretched into two, then three. Monica did nothing but sit in her chair, smoking and staring into space. Stella had refused to let her have any more whisky in case they had to move in a hurry, and it seemed she didn't have the energy to go and fetch any herself. She'd hardly said a word since that first night, but was wrapped up in herself, hardly noticing Stella's presence at all. Was she thinking of poor Gerardo? Stella wondered how Beatrice and Dora were getting along. If Dora had tried to return to work at the hotel, she'd have been turned back by the Germans, and so they must know by now that Stella was trapped on this side of the river. She was bored and restless, stuck here in the deserted hotel. She wanted to talk to Monica, and ask her about that dreadful day a month ago when the Fascists had come, but she couldn't bring herself to do it. She'd made one or two tentative remarks, which were ignored. Whatever Monica had wanted of her, it seemed she wasn't prepared to say now. It looked as if she'd retreated into herself to battle her demons alone.

Chapter Thirty-One

On the morning of the 3rd of August Stella was awoken suddenly by a series of low rumbling thuds. She sat up, her heart thumping, listening. Was it the bridges? The explosions continued at intervals, and she lay down again. The sound wasn't near enough to be the bridges, she decided. It must be shelling. The Allies were very close now. The heat that day was almost unbearable. Even with all the windows thrown wide open the place felt like an oven. The afternoon wore on, and as the sun began to sink Stella went to the window, seeking even the tiniest breath of a breeze, but there was none. She was still looking out into the quiet street when she heard a sound, the buzz of a voice through a megaphone in the distance, coming slowly closer. She remained at the window and watched as a German military vehicle approached, repeating the announcement over and over again. A state of emergency had been declared, it said. All citizens were to go inside immediately and stay there, preferably in a basement, keeping away from windows. Anyone who failed to obey orders would be shot. The catastrophe was imminent, then; this confirmed it.

'Did you hear that?' Stella demanded. Monica looked up vacantly. 'They're going to do it soon. Is there a basement here?'

'There's a wine cellar,' replied Monica dully.

'Then let's go there. Quickly!'

Stella rushed around, collecting things they might need. She found a torch in a drawer, and they went downstairs. Monica seemed resigned, watching passively as Stella filled several bottles with water, and fetched breadsticks and some shrivelled lemons, which were the only fruit she could find, out of the store cupboard. The cellar consisted of two rooms, one containing rows of much-depleted wine racks, and the other a smaller space where bits of broken furniture and other odds and ends were kept. It had barred windows at pavement level which gave out onto the deserted street. The place looked eerie in the dim, late afternoon light. An old, worn mattress was standing against one wall. Stella dragged it across the floor to the safest-looking corner, and they sat down to wait. It was stiflingly hot down here, and Stella could feel the perspiration running uncomfortably down her back, soaking into her frock. She knew she ought to eat something, but she wasn't hungry. Instead she took a sip of water from the bottle.

Monica had run out of cigarettes, and was fidgeting.

'I wish they'd get it over with,' she said.

'So do I. I'd like to get out of this hotel. Who knows, perhaps once the Germans have gone we can go back to the villa,' observed Stella.

Monica gave something like a little sigh, but didn't reply.

The evening drew on, the dim light faded into dark, and they sat in silence, waiting.

'I never meant it to happen, you know,' said Monica at last.

'Never meant what?'

'Gerardo. I never dreamt – only I was so terribly tired of having to live in such dreadful conditions, without good food or new clothes…' She trailed off. 'I know it doesn't sound like much of an excuse,' she went on defensively.

It didn't, but Stella said nothing.

'I couldn't get any money, and I knew Otto would be more than willing to take the paintings off Gerardo's hands at a fair price. Or that's what I thought. And I missed Gerardo, too. I don't suppose you'll believe me, but I was awfully fond of him, and I wanted to see him, and I thought it couldn't do any harm.'

There was a pause.

'Otto and I were friends!' Monica burst out suddenly. 'Why did he report Gerardo? He betrayed us, just so he could steal the paintings.'

'Was it he who did it, or was it Marius?'

'Marius!' spat Monica with sudden savagery. 'He's always hated me, ever since we were children. I'm the eldest, you know – just by five minutes, but that was enough to make him ferociously jealous. He thought I'd taken his birthright somehow, although of course I hadn't, because *he* was the boy. He didn't lose out on a thing for being the youngest, but it always ate away at him.'

The shadow of a smirk crossed her face. 'I used to rub it in, rather, and he *hated* that! He couldn't stand it when I beat him at anything. And when I married your father and started helping him in the business – the same business that Marius worked in – it almost drove him mad. If Raymond wanted a painting and Marius knew I was helping him get it, he'd go to any lengths to stop me. The *Lady of the Cypresses* was rather a coup of mine. I stepped in and got it from under my brother's nose, and he loathed me for it, and Raymond too. Well, he got his revenge on me. I'm only surprised he didn't try and revenge himself on Raymond as well.'

She shifted slightly and the mattress creaked under her. Stella turned hurt, reproachful eyes on her.

'But Monica, why did you encourage me to marry him, if you knew what he was like?' she asked.

'Because you were a little lost waif, and looked as though you needed it, and I thought it might mellow him a little. Besides, he was bothering me about losing money on the *Lady of the Cypresses* and you were about to come into your inheritance. I didn't mind beating him to a painting, but I didn't especially want to see him ruined either. If I could have found Raymond's paintings I'd have given them to him, but I never did. So he got you instead.'

Her total nonchalance as she said the last sentence took Stella's breath away. Marius had got her instead: Stella Cockburn, the daughter of his business rival, who'd never realised she was being traded about like an old painting nobody wanted to buy. She ought to have been filled with resentment at them all, but the implications of what she had just heard were unmistakable. It was true she'd been treated badly by everyone, but had she, ultimately, been the cause of her own misery? Would Marius have wanted to marry her in the first place if he'd had Jacob Silberstein's paintings? Stella had thought she was doing the right thing in keeping their whereabouts a secret all this time, but if she'd spoken up when she first learned of it, would things have turned out differently? Had her loyalty to her father turned her into an unwitting sacrifice, offered to heaven in atonement for his sins?

She fingered the key to the safe deposit box, still around her neck. The missing paintings. Had Monica known where they came from? Did she care?

'These paintings,' she began. 'The ones from Berlin. My father stole them, didn't he?'

'What makes you think that?'

'I don't know. I just got that impression from the way you talked about them.'

'No, he didn't steal them. He took them for safekeeping after an art dealer friend of his was murdered. Raymond had been invited to dinner at the man's flat one evening, but when he turned up he found that the Gestapo had been there first and shot his friend dead, and were planning to come back for the paintings. The man had a wife and children, and Raymond gave them money to get out of Berlin, and promised to store the artworks for them. He took the paintings away in a truck overnight, brought them back to Switzerland and put them somewhere for safekeeping. He died without telling me where they were, but I was sure you knew something about it.'

Stella's heart was racing. Her father hadn't killed anyone. He hadn't stolen the paintings. He'd taken them to keep them safe.

'I found them,' she said.

'Did you? Where?'

'Near Lucerne.' She wasn't going to say any more than that. 'But I didn't know what I was supposed to do with them.'

'It was all in the letter,' said Monica.

'Which letter?'

At that, Monica seemed to realise what she'd just said. She hesitated.

'I don't suppose it matters now,' she said at last. 'Raymond wrote you a letter. He was on his way to post it to you when he died, and the police gave it to me and I opened it. He wanted you to take care of the paintings in the event of his death, and see they were returned if possible. You were to come to Lucerne and speak to old Franz at the gallery, who would tell you where to find them. Franz denied knowing anything about it when I asked him, but I thought perhaps Raymond might have mentioned his trip to Berlin in an earlier letter to you, and given some hint as to where the paintings were. I asked you about it when you first arrived in Florence – I don't suppose you remember – but the letter you showed me said nothing about it, so I came to the conclusion that you didn't know a thing, and that Franz had been instructed to keep quiet. That's why I asked you to speak to him when we went up there.' She looked at Stella with interest. 'So, you managed to wheedle the information out of him behind my back, did you? Oh well, I tried my best, but it seems I underestimated you.'

'Why didn't he leave the paintings to you?' Stella wanted to know.

'Because he knew I'd want to sell them, of course.'

'But they weren't yours to sell.'

'Their owners were Jews. It's all very unfortunate, but do you really think they'll be coming back for them? And I thought someone ought to benefit from them, so why not I?'

They fell silent, Stella trying to take in all the information. Monica had wanted the paintings for herself, and had kept back the letter which would have told Stella that her father wasn't a thief or a murderer. She supposed she ought to feel relieved, but she wasn't sure what to think any more.

'Do you still have the letter?' she asked.

'Not here. I gave it to my lawyer to keep.'

'I'd like to read it.'

At that, Monica gave a hollow bark of laughter.

'You can read it and welcome – always assuming the Germans don't blow this place up with us inside it.'

Her remark jolted Stella back to the reality of their situation. It was very dark now, and the heat was oppressive. How much longer would they have to stay here?

'Was Marius very unkind to you?' asked Monica, after a while.

'You might say that,' replied Stella bitterly, thinking of the years in which she'd crept around him like a terrified mouse, all the times he'd cuffed her almost casually and drawn blood. And of that final, dreadful encounter here in the hotel when he'd beaten her half to death and she'd fled for her life, only to end up trapped in the middle of a battlefield, far away from the man she loved.

'I suspected as much. I'm sorry. I expect you hate me for it, do you? Well, if it helps, I hate myself just as much right at this moment. I know everyone calls me spoilt and selfish, and perhaps I am. I invited you to Florence to let Marius have you, and I can't honestly say I gave you much thought then; you were just a useful way of getting him out of my hair. But I've seen what he's really like, now.' Her voice cracked. 'This is more than jealousy on his part. I really believe he's evil. I'm sorry he hurt you. He's hurt me too, now. You saw a little of what they did to me at the Villa Triste. Three days and three nights they kept me there. They cut me and burned me, and did unspeakable things to me, and they laughed when I screamed in pain and begged them to stop, and just tormented me all the more. Then they threw me in jail. That was Marius's doing. He might not have hurt me with his own hands, but he's responsible for it, and I swear I'll make him suffer for it one day. And Gerardo…'

The tears had begun to roll down her face. 'He was cruel to my poor Gerardo, who loved me. I loved him, too, I promise I did! He was kind, and decent, and honest, and he cared for me. Nothing was too much for him. And I was a good wife to him, right up until the last – until I made that one stupid, stupid mistake. How can I ever forgive myself?'

*

They'd been in the cellar so long now that Stella began to wonder whether the Germans had had a change of heart. But then, at just before ten, it happened. They heard it and felt it at the same time: an almighty explosion that deafened them temporarily and caused the whole building to shake. The windows blew in, scattering shards of glass everywhere, while the piles of old furniture were sent flying, and from the next room there came the harsh sound of glass shattering as the remaining wine was thrown to the floor. Stella had been in the act of standing up to stretch her legs, but the thunderous blast threw her backwards and against the wall, knocking the breath out of her. She lay sprawled for several minutes, gathering her thoughts, as the sounds of destruction died away and all became quiet again.

'Stella!' came Monica's voice in the darkness. It was a sob. 'Are you there?'

'Yes, I'm here.' She sat up gingerly. She was bruised and shaken, and she'd bumped her head against the wall, but she didn't seem to have broken any bones. 'Are you all right? You're not hurt?'

'No,' quavered Monica. 'But don't leave me. I don't want you to leave me.'

'I won't leave you.'

Stella could see her arms reaching out in the darkness, hands groping. She crawled across to the mattress and Monica grasped eagerly at her, gripping her arm tightly. They clung together on the mattress, Monica shaking violently. Stella was really afraid now. Was this what death felt like, she wondered.

A while later the second explosion came, just as violent as the first, and just as shocking in its intensity. This time they were ready for it, sitting with their backs against the wall, away from anything that might fly across the room and hit them. All the piles of furniture had already toppled, so there was less danger, but they felt the enormous pressure of the blast through the open window. Stella crouched low, her hands over her ears, until the noise died down. It left a ringing in her ears that continued for several minutes. Monica was whimpering next to her, and Stella put her arms around her again and they clung together, waiting for the next one. It came, as did the next, and the next. When would the night end? Had the Germans decided to destroy the whole city?

The last three explosions came towards dawn, and they were the worst of the lot because they were the nearest. The whole building shook as one deafening blast after another split the air. By this time they were both crouched in the corner, clutching one another as though their lives depended on it, crying out in fear. But at last the roar faded and all was silence.

'That was the Ponte Santa Trinita,' whispered Stella.

The darkness had begun to lift slightly, and she could see the outline of the overturned furniture. That must be the end of it, surely? They waited, but no more explosions came. After a while the dawn broke, but they dared not come out yet. Stella was exhausted and desperate to sleep, but she knew she couldn't. All they could do was wait.

Chapter Thirty-Two

On the morning before the Germans demolished the bridges, several Allied shells hit buildings in the Oltrarno, and the Villa Bruni was one of them. Beatrice and Dora were safe inside their house, but they felt the thud as the shell exploded, far too close for comfort, and hurried down into the basement with Tina. After a little while they judged it was safe to come out, and were debating whether to go and assess the damage, when the German order came that they were to remain indoors and go back down into the basement until further notice. They obeyed, and spent a terrified night huddled in the darkness, listening to the destruction of the bridges, feeling the house rock and wondering whether the world was about to end. The house was further away from the explosions than the hotel was, but even from where they sat, huddled together in the darkness, the sound of the blasts was tremendously loud, and the earth shook beneath violently them.

The next morning Dora came up from the cellar cautiously, to see whether the house was still standing, and discovered that several of the windows had been blown in. She clicked her tongue in annoyance, and was about to start clearing up the broken glass, when she heard a commotion out in the street. Opening the door she found people running up and down, shouting, 'The Americans have arrived! The Americans have arrived!'

Dora's heart lifted with joy. Could it really be true? Had they been liberated at last?

'Beatrice!' she called. 'Quick! Come up at once! They're saying the Americans have come!'

Beatrice came up from the cellar, holding a very tired and fractious Tina in her arms.

'Are you sure?'

'Let's go and see,' said Dora.

They weren't Americans at all, as it turned out, but South Africans and New Zealanders, who drove down the streets, seemingly astonished at the welcome they were receiving. Men ran up to shake their hands, while women kissed them and wept. It didn't matter who they were, the important thing was that the Germans had been driven out – from the Oltrarno area at least, although the word quickly went round that they hadn't retreated from the north side of the river yet.

'Perhaps we'll have something to eat at last!' exclaimed the ever-practical Dora.

The sleepless night and the noise of the crowds greeting the arriving Allies had all been too much for Tina, and she was howling.

'She's tired,' said Beatrice. 'I'm going to put her to bed. In the meantime why don't you go and see if the Germans left anything at the villa? There might be something in the garden they didn't take with them. Be careful!'

Dora went off, but was back half an hour later, wringing her hands.

'Half the place is destroyed!' she exclaimed. 'The west wing is nearly gone, and part of the front wall. But the east part is still whole. I didn't dare go in, but from what I could see the Germans have taken a lot of stuff. I expect most of the antiques will have gone.'

'What did they leave to eat? Anything nice?' asked Beatrice hopefully, looking at the bundled-up apron in her mother's hand. Dora grimaced and opened it to show her.

'They've dug up everything from the garden. All I could find were a few apples and pears.'

'Better than nothing, I suppose. I'll stew the pears for Tina later.'

That afternoon, Vittorio arrived, much to Beatrice's relief. Franco's death had brought home to her the dangers Vittorio had been running, and she'd found herself worrying about him more and more lately, and about what might happen to him if he were caught.

'The bridges are gone,' he said grimly. 'They bombed them all to stop the Allies following them. The only one left is the Ponte Vecchio, but we can't cross that one either because they bombed all the buildings nearby to block the entrance.'

'What about the city?' asked Beatrice. 'The cathedral, and the Palazzo Vecchio? Are they still standing?'

'Yes, thank God. They only demolished the bridges, but even that's bad enough. There are terrible scenes down by the river – corpses lying everywhere, and people wandering about in the rubble.'

'Is there anything we can do to help?'

'Better not,' he replied. 'It's still not safe. The Germans might be gone from the south, but the Oltrarno is still overrun with Fascists. They've got snipers stationed in windows, and they're picking people off in the streets as they walk by. Stay indoors for now, and I'll come and tell you when it's safe to come out.'

'What are you going to do?' Beatrice wanted to know.

He gave her a flash of his old cocky grin.

'I'm going to root them out,' he replied.

She put her hand on his arm as he prepared to leave, her expression full of concern.

'Be careful, won't you?'

'Of course.'

'I'd hate anything to happen to you.'

It was the first time she'd ever told him her fears for him in so many words, but she wanted him to know how important he was to her. His eyes softened, and he lifted his hand and just touched her hair, then left. Beatrice watched him as he sauntered off down the street with a cheery wave.

'He's a good boy,' said Dora, who had been following the progress of their friendship with pleasure.

'Yes.'

'We must look after him, for the Count.'

The mention of Gerardo reminded Beatrice that Stella had gone away to see Monica and had not come back.

'I hope Stella is all right,' she said.

'I'm sure she is. I dare say they found somewhere safe to shelter.'

'But the Germans are still on the north side of the river.'

'They've got better things to do right now than to arrest English women.'

Beatrice's brows drew together. She'd sheltered Stella for so many months that she felt responsible for her. Besides, they were friends now.

'I hope you're right,' she replied.

*

Ted rejoined the Allies shortly before they arrived in Florence, and drove into the city alongside them, to find the bridges shattered and all the buildings by the river reduced to great heaps of smoking rubble. The water and gas mains were broken, and the city stank of death and disease. Somewhere in among the dust and the dirt and the hopelessness was Stella – or someone who must know what had happened to her. The first thing he did was to go to the Villa Bruni. The gates were locked but the outer wall had fallen into disrepair in places, and he had no trouble in climbing over it. The place looked as normal as he approached from the east side, but as he came closer the damaged part of the building came gradually into view.

He stopped, taking in the gutted west wing, of which little more than a couple of walls remained standing, and the main section of the house, one front corner of which had collapsed. Then he walked slowly around to the other side, past the kitchen gardens, which had been dug up, and round to the terrace and the lawns. The grass was yellow and parched, the tennis court had great gouges in the ground, and there was graffiti all over the pavilion. He slowly mounted the steps to the terrace and looked out over Florence. A great cloud of dust hung over the city, but the towers and domes of all its most historic buildings still stood out proudly against the skyline. At least the Germans had had the decency to leave those.

He didn't stay long, since Stella was obviously not here, and neither were Monica and Gerardo. The next place to try would be the hotel, he supposed, but he couldn't go there until it was safe to cross the Arno, because the Germans still controlled that part of the city. He left the villa and walked down towards the river. Despite the threat of snipers, a fair number of people had emerged and were hurrying anxiously through the streets, some laden down with possessions, others carrying water cans, all looking tired and dusty. The sound of sporadic shelling could be heard from German artillery up in the Fiesole hills, but people were ignoring it.

Close to the river the scenes of devastation were horrific. Piles of rubble stood thirty feet high, and people were tearing at them in a desperate and hopeless search for survivors, while others tried to retrieve what they could from the ruins of their former homes, and men with picks and shovels cleared paths to allow a way through. Ted passed two dead bodies lying half-buried by fallen masonry. Who knew when they'd be removed?

He stopped by one of the flattened buildings to light a cigarette, then glanced up and saw one or two of the diggers staring longingly at the packet in his hand. He went across, offered the cigarettes around and lit them for the men, and they nodded their thanks, too weary to say much. Leaving them to their work, he went to clamber up one of the heaps of rubble, from where he could get a view of the river. The bridges had collapsed, while rubble and masonry from the buildings they'd bombed near the Ponte Vecchio had slid across the embankment and into the river, which had turned into a ribbon of brown sludge. The smell was unbearable here, and after a while he clambered back down, disheartened by the wanton destruction of such a large swathe of the city.

But there was no time to waste on regrets, because he had a job to do. The Germans might be gone from this part of Florence but the Oltrarno was still a dangerous place. Fascists and partisans were occupied in house-to-house fighting, and the sound of sporadic gunshots echoed through the still afternoon air. The OSS wanted him to make contact with the partisans in this part of the city, and so he was heading for an address he'd been given by the band of guerrillas he'd been working with in southern Tuscany. The place turned out to be a bar which was closed. Ted banged on the shutters, looking around warily, because it was broad daylight and he felt like an easy target. He waited, then heard an exclamation from somewhere above and looked up to see a head just being withdrawn from a window overhead. After a few more minutes the shutter came up a little way and a hand came under it and beckoned to him. He ducked down and slid underneath and into the bar, which was dark after the brightness of the day. As his eyes got used to the dim light he saw that several men were there. They'd been expecting him, it seemed, and listened as he gave them their instructions and told them where to report. Then a young man came forward and gave him a grin. Ted thought he looked familiar.

'Eh, I thought it was you. Welcome, Signor Landry. Remember me? Vittorio, from the Villa Bruni.'

'Vittorio!' exclaimed Ted, as they shook hands. 'I just went to the villa, but it's been shelled.'

'Ah, *sì*,' said Vittorio with an expressive gesture. 'It's a pity.'

'Was anybody living there? I take it the Count and the Countess have gone?'

Vittorio's normally cheerful face fell.

'The Count was taken by the Fascists,' he replied. He pressed his lips together and shook his head soberly, leaving Ted in no doubt as to Gerardo's fate.

'Damn it! That's terrible.' Ted was more saddened than he could have imagined at the news. 'And Monica?'

'She was taken away too, but they let her go in the end.'

Ted hesitated. He had to ask, although he wasn't sure he was ready to hear the answer.

'There was an English girl – Stella…'

Vittorio's face cleared.

'Miss Stella, yes! Of course, she is here. A very brave woman.'

Ted's heart soared. He grasped urgently at Vittorio's arm.

'Where is she?'

'That I don't know. She was staying with Dora and Beatrice, but she went across to see the Countess at the hotel a few days before they blew up the bridges, and didn't come back. I imagine she took shelter at the hotel, but it won't be possible to cross the river until the Germans have gone.'

Ted gave an impatient exclamation. So near and yet so far! But he felt a lightness of spirit he hadn't felt in months. So Stella was still here, in Florence, alive – or at least she had been until a few days ago. The Allies had captured the south bank of the city and they'd soon capture the northern part too, and when that happened he would go and look for her.

He left the bar and set off on the return journey to HQ, heading back through the streets of the Oltrarno, seeking out the shadier alleys where there was some respite from the stifling heat and less danger of being shot at. As he came out into a small piazza he saw women gathered around a fountain, collecting the water that issued from it in a desolate trickle. He also saw a man standing in a doorway, unnoticed by them all. The man had a rifle to his shoulder and seemed to be trying to decide upon a target. The rifle moved around, and at last came to a stop, pointing directly at a boy of about seven or eight, who'd separated himself from his mother and was idly pushing a football around a tree with his foot.

Ted had a sudden flash of memory, as the mother and her two children who'd been cut down by machine-gun fire in northern France darted into his mind. He was a good twenty feet from the sniper, who was facing away from him, and he knew his aim wasn't good enough to hit him, but it might be good enough to distract him. He pulled out his automatic and fired. The bullet hit the doorpost next to the sniper, who jumped and turned. There were screams, and everyone scattered. Out of the corner of his eye, Ted saw a woman drag the boy away, as he barrelled towards the sniper and shot again. This time he hit the man's arm. The rifle clattered to the ground, and a third shot dispatched him permanently. Ted stood, getting his breath back, the dead man crumpled at his feet, then judged it better to get away as quickly as possible, before more Fascists turned up. The square had emptied in a trice, and Ted felt a sense of satisfaction at what he'd done. Perhaps he'd sleep a little more easily tonight. And tomorrow or the next day, as soon as it was possible, he would go and find Stella.

Chapter Thirty-Three

Now was the time for the partisans to come into their own. The Germans had gone but there were still plenty of home-grown Fascists in Florence who were determined to throw as many obstacles as they could in the way of the Allies. The partisans had taken it upon themselves to clear the ground to help the Americans and the British get through, and the sound of gunshots rang out in the streets of the Oltrarno as partisans and Fascists took part in fierce house-to-house fighting.

On one particular day Vittorio's brigade had spent several hours clearing out a small band of Fascists who were holed up in a convent. The partisans had the advantage of surprise, and after a pitched battle all the Fascists lay dead or had escaped, and the partisans paused under a cloister to get their breath and regroup as they prepared to make their retreat. One of the brigade, Antonio, eyed the body of a Fascist, who was lying in a patch of sunlight a few feet away, his bandolier nearly full of cartridges.

'This one has plenty of ammunition,' he said.

He went to bend over the dead body of the man and began unbuckling the bandolier. As he did so Vittorio, who was standing in the shelter of a pillar a couple of yards away, about to reload his rifle, glanced up and was puzzled by a glint of light moving across the wall in front of him. He put his head around the corner of the pillar and saw a man standing in the shadow of the cloister opposite, aiming his rifle directly at Antonio. There was no time to think, only act.

'Antonio!' shouted Vittorio.

He darted out from the pillar, intending to drag Antonio into the shadows, but at that moment the sniper fired. Vittorio felt as though he had received a punch to the stomach. He twisted and was thrown against the wall, as Antonio raised his rifle and fired back at the sniper, killing him instantly.

The pain in Vittorio's left side was like fire, and he clutched at it, staggering, feeling his knees buckling under him, as sparks danced before his eyes, clouding his vision. He was dimly aware of shouts all around him, and then someone was at his right side, speaking urgently to him, telling him to hang on. Vittorio felt his arm being pulled around someone's shoulder – he wasn't sure who, but he thought it was Claudio – and the next thing he knew he was being helped out of the convent and into the street.

His thoughts weren't too clear, but as far as he could understand they were taking him back to the hideout, from where they could call the Americans for help. Just ahead of him one of his comrades, Giorgio, was keeping an eye out for any stray Fascists, while Claudio was still supporting him and urging him on. Vittorio was concentrating very hard on remaining conscious, because it wouldn't do to pass out. He didn't want his comrades to have to carry him, so he gritted his teeth and willed his legs to keep walking, although the pain in his side was exquisite.

'Not far now,' came Claudio's voice. 'Keep going.'

All Vittorio had to do was keep going. Just a few hundred metres more, and then they'd be back at the hideout, and he could lie down, and somebody would radio to the Americans, and they'd come and fix him. Just a few hundred metres more. He could do it.

Then there was a blinding white flash and it seemed as if all sound had been blanked out. The deafness lasted for what seemed like years – although in fact it was only a couple of seconds – and when Vittorio's hearing returned he was on the ground, and there were more shouts and cries, and Claudio and Giorgio weren't there any more; they'd been replaced by two twisted heaps of rags. Vittorio couldn't feel a thing, although he didn't understand why. He lay, helplessly. Just a few hundred metres and he'd be safe, but he couldn't move. Antonio was bending over him, saying something, but he couldn't understand what it was.

'Beatrice,' said Vittorio, then blacked out.

*

Beatrice and Dora had managed to get some bits of wood and were busy boarding up the windows of their house when they saw a figure coming up the road towards them, whom they recognised as a partisan belonging to Vittorio's brigade. He was dirty and dishevelled, and his face was covered with cuts and grazes. Before he even had a chance to say a word, Beatrice went white, because she knew something terrible had happened.

'What is it, Antonio? Where is Vittorio?' she demanded.

'You must come,' said the man. 'He's asked to see you.'

Her heart was in her throat, and she tried to swallow it down. 'Of course I'll come!'

She looked at Dora, who said, 'Go with him – I'll look after Tina.'

'Do you have bandages? Or any medicines?' asked Antonio.

'No medicines, but I have bedsheets. Will that help?'

'Yes, if that's all you have.'

Beatrice didn't even stop to think. She ran inside and collected what was left of the linen she and Dora had made for her wedding, which she'd rescued from the old apartment when it had been bombed. She'd had to turn most of it into skirts and dresses, but there were still a couple of sheets left that she'd been planning to use for winter clothes soon. Then she followed Antonio as he headed down the hill, turning right and left as if avoiding certain streets.

'What's happened to him, Antonio? Please tell me. How is he?' she asked breathlessly, as she tried to keep up with him.

'There was a fight, and he was shot, and when we were retreating we set off a mine that the Germans left. Giorgio and Claudio are dead. Vittorio didn't get caught by the full blast but his leg is all smashed, and there's a bullet in his side.' He shook his head. 'It looks very bad. I hope we can get there in time.'

Beatrice drew in her breath.

'Please, let's hurry!'

They slipped quickly through the streets towards the river, and came to the brigade's hideout. The shutters were half-open today, and they ducked underneath them and into the bar. Inside it was dark, and it took a moment or two for Beatrice's eyes to adjust. The place was stiflingly hot, full of noise and activity, because several of the other partisans had been hurt. One man was wincing in the corner as he tried to extract bits of shrapnel from his own leg, while another was holding a blood-soaked handkerchief to the side of his head. Somewhere, someone was groaning in pain.

Vittorio was on the floor in the corner, on a bed made of seat cushions. He was lying quietly, his eyes closed. They'd done their best to bandage his middle using an old flour sack, but Beatrice could see the blood seeping through. His left leg was a dreadful tangle of blood and shredded fabric. It was obvious he'd been terribly wounded.

'Vittorio!' She threw herself down on her knees at his side.

He opened his eyes and turned his head slightly. His face was grey and haggard, but when he saw her it broke into a shadow of his old smile.

'Beatrice.' It was a whisper. 'I wanted them to bring you, and here you are.'

'Of course I'm here! What happened?'

'I thought we'd got them all, but it turned out we hadn't. And then there was a mine those blasted Germans left when they went.'

He tried to shift himself, and winced.

'Don't try to move! We have to get you well. This is no place for you.' She began tearing up one of the sheets quickly. 'And that sack is no good for a bandage. We need to try and stop the bleeding.'

She busied herself, trying to stem the flow of blood as best she could, focusing all her attention on Vittorio. She wouldn't let him die as Mimmo had died. But there was so much blood, and she didn't know what to do. She had no training in this sort of thing.

'He needs to get to a hospital,' she said, and heard the high, frightened note in her own voice. The heat was unbearable, and everybody was making so much noise, while Vittorio bled slowly to death in front of her. Why couldn't they be quiet and let her concentrate? She fought down the panic, because it would do him no good to hear it. The chaos and the confusion and the voices were just a distraction, and she told herself she'd lived through worse, even though she knew it wasn't true. She'd never had to tend to a dying man before, especially one who meant so much to her as Vittorio did.

There was a rattle of shutters behind her as someone arrived.

'What happened here?' came a voice. It spoke Italian but with a foreign accent, although Beatrice hardly registered it until a tall man in an American uniform came and crouched down beside her.

'Please,' said Beatrice. 'We need to get him to a hospital.'

In among all the noise her mind couldn't take in very much, and she could only focus on Vittorio, and the fact that his lifeblood was draining away before her eyes.

'Please,' she repeated.

She had a vague sense that the man with the American accent was promising something, but she didn't know what, then he went away. Whatever he was going to do, it would be too late, she knew it would be too late. She concentrated on willing Vittorio to live. Some time later – she didn't know how long it was – there was a shout and a bustle and people began talking. Beatrice heard only the word 'ambulance', and then she was gently shoved out of the way and Vittorio was being raised onto a stretcher and carried out into the street. She followed, and saw the dull green truck with its red cross emblazoned on the side. Vittorio was lifted in carefully, along with another man. Beatrice pushed her way forward.

'You can't come, ma'am,' said a different American voice, in English.

'Please.' She turned a beseeching eye on the first American who spoke Italian.

'Let her come, Joe,' he said. 'It can't do any harm.'

The man addressed as Joe shrugged and went to get into the driver's seat. Beatrice climbed in, knelt on the floor between the two wounded men, and felt Vittorio's forehead. The tall American got in the back with her and they set off at a breakneck pace.

'Where are we going?' she asked.

'To the evacuation hospital.' The tall American seemed familiar. 'You're Beatrice, aren't you?'

'Yes.' She suddenly remembered who he was. 'Mr Landry, isn't it?'

'Ted. You sent me a letter.'

'Did I?' she said blankly, then her brow cleared. 'About Stella. That was a long time ago. I'd forgotten. Have you found her? She went to the hotel.'

'Not yet. Haven't been able to get across the river yet.'

'I hope she's all right.'

'Me too.'

Her attention was taken then by Vittorio, whose eyes were growing heavy, she noticed, and she felt an instant of panic, because she was almost certain that if she let him fall asleep he'd never wake up again. She took his hand very carefully and stroked it, and he made a little sound, like a sigh, and his eyes opened a little.

'It really is you, isn't it? I'm not dreaming?'

She shook her head. 'No, it's me. Don't dream. Don't fall asleep.'

'I won't, not if you're here. Talk to me.'

He winced as the ambulance jolted over a bump in the road, and she drew in her breath at the thought of the agony it must be causing him. The pain was coming slowly back to her, too; it was an unaccustomed feeling, after so many years of burying it deep within. It started as a little knot in her heart, then grew hotter and

hotter and radiated upwards from there into her throat. She felt
it pricking at her eyes and stabbing like sharp knives at her brain.
But this was no time for weakness; she had to hold things together.
She must shake it off, as she had done ever since Mimmo had
died. The Americans were taking Vittorio to hospital, and they'd
operate on him and look after him and he would be well again.
So she talked to him. She told him of something funny Tina had
said that morning, and how, now the Germans had gone, they
could start thinking about the future. Perhaps the Countess would
give Beatrice her job back at the hotel or at the Villa Bruni – and
Vittorio too, once he was well. The villa was in a sad state but
perhaps the Americans would help them rebuild it. She talked at
random about anything that came into her head, because she saw
the sound of her voice gave him comfort.

The journey passed as if in a dream. At some point along the way
the other man they'd brought died, but Beatrice was hardly aware
of Ted's hurried exchange of remarks in a low voice with the driver.
All her mind was focused on keeping Vittorio alive. Then – it might
have been an hour or a day or a week later – they arrived, and there
were more men in uniforms, and loud voices, and tents, and activity,
and a general sense of purpose, and Vittorio was lifted out and taken
into the receiving tent, and from there sent to another tent to await
surgery. Beatrice wanted to follow but was stopped by a nurse.

'You can't come,' she said.

Beatrice protested, but the nurse was firm.

'He's in good hands now, but you won't do him any good by
hanging around.'

Beatrice saw the nurse and Ted exchange glances, and felt a sudden
certainty that Vittorio was already dead and they hadn't told her.
She'd promised to stay with him, and she couldn't leave him now.

'Let me just say goodbye,' she said, and ran after the stretcher
before they could stop her. To her relief Vittorio's eyes were open and
there was still a light in them, although it was growing a little dim.

'I thought you'd gone,' he whispered.

'No, I'm still here. They're going to operate now, and then you'll get better.'

'Good. Will you wait for me?'

'I'll stay as long as you like, Vittorio. I won't leave.'

She gave him one last squeeze of the hand then turned away as he was taken off, because she didn't want him to see her pain. She hadn't felt pain for so many years now; when Mimmo had died she'd warded it off by shutting down her feelings and refusing to admit it. Then she'd buried herself in work to keep it at bay and prevent it from finding even a chink through which it might enter. But now it dawned upon her that the pain had been inside her all the time, walled up in her heart, and a crack had formed through which it had begun to escape. The crack was threatening to get wider, and if she wasn't careful she knew she'd lose all control over herself, and this was no time to do that. She had to be strong one last time for Vittorio.

She didn't know when she'd begun to love him; it must have stolen upon her very gently – perhaps it had been there all along, even, she couldn't tell. All this time she'd put up a brick wall between herself and her feelings in order to distance herself from them and get through this terrible war, which seemed interminable. It had been her way of coping, because she couldn't afford to break down, not with a delicate child to look after, and until now it had worked well enough: she'd got by, and had even been able to spare attention for other people – Stella, for example, and Vittorio himself when he'd turned up on her doorstep that night, sick and exhausted. But she'd had no room for either pain or love until now, when there was a very real likelihood that Vittorio was going to die – and it was the prospect of losing him that revealed her own heart to her. What would she do without him? He'd stood loyally by her, congratulated her when she'd married another man, and looked after her and Tina without any thought of reward. She'd never appreciated his love before, but now, just as it looked as if she was going to lose him, she finally understood just how much he meant to her.

There was a large tent in which she'd been told to wait, and she sat through the night, heedless of the noise and bustle that was going on around her. She'd heard of the darkest hour before the dawn, but had never given it any thought before, until her name was called and she was granted a couple of minutes' audience with a kind but very busy army surgeon.

'It's touch and go,' he told her gently. 'We've amputated his left leg below the knee – that was a clean job – but the bullet in his middle is another matter altogether. The next few hours will tell, but you should prepare yourself for the worst. Pray for him, if you think that will help.'

'Thank you,' she replied calmly.

Beatrice didn't go back to the waiting tent, but instead went outside to feel the cool air on her face. The dawn was just starting to break, but the camp was still active with medical personnel wandering to and fro, ambulances arriving and departing, and civilians wandering around just like herself, as if in a dream. She sat down on a pile of tarpaulins. The doctor had told her to pray; well, there was nothing left but to do that. She sat in the grey dawn for a very long time, looking for the words she wanted to say. Then just as the first gleam of sunlight was peeping above the horizon, the dam suddenly broke, and she put her head in her hands and sobbed her heart out. She wept for Vittorio, and Mimmo, and Gerardo, and Franco, and for all those whose lives had been cut short by this terrible war. But most of all she wept for herself, because right now she felt utterly alone, with no one to ease the terrible aching in her heart.

Chapter Thirty-Four

The Germans finally pulled back from the centre of Florence on the 10th of August, although they were still holding the northern suburbs. On that day Mr Cavalieri braved the dangerous streets and returned to the Hotel Ambassador, anxious to see the damage and start putting the hotel to rights, because there was a good chance the Allies would want to base themselves here soon, and they needed the custom. He clucked and tutted at the sight of the toothless, gaping windows – not a pane of glass had survived apart from the ones in the thick entrance doors, which were merely cracked – and exclaimed in horror at the destruction of all the wine bottles in the cellar, but after he'd been around the hotel and taken note of the damage, he became much more sanguine.

'Once they've restored the water and the gas, and if we can get some food and some kitchen staff, then I think we will get on reasonably well,' he observed. 'I don't know how long it'll take to get new windows, but it's not as though we need them in this heat. For the rest, the beds are the most comfortable in Florence, and we have some of the best views – or we did, at least. When we'll have them again is anybody's guess. Have you seen the river yet? The place is a wasteland, and all the bridges are gone.'

'We haven't been to look yet,' replied Stella. 'It was too dangerous. Is it possible to cross? And is it safe?'

'You can cross at the Ponte alle Grazie if you don't mind clambering about on a great pile of rocks. As to whether it's safe – I wouldn't go that far, but the partisans have taken control in that part of the city, so it's not as dangerous as some other places.'

'Did you hear that?' Stella said to Monica. 'You can go back to the Villa Bruni today and see what state the Germans have left it in.'

'I don't want to go by myself!' exclaimed Monica in alarm. Her experiences of the last few weeks seemed to have damaged her in ways that weren't just physical. She was no longer the careless, confident Monica she had been, but someone altogether more nervous and disturbed. One minute she'd retreat into herself, seemingly uninterested in what was going on around her, then the next she would snap and lash out at anything Stella said. She'd spent the past few days alternating between apathy and tears, building to the occasional fit of hysteria, which was the most disturbing of all, because when that happened there was nothing that could calm her down, and the only thing to do was to wait until it burned itself out. Stella wondered whether the damage was permanent. For the moment at any rate Monica was her responsibility, and she knew she couldn't leave her.

'I'll come to the villa with you,' she said. 'But first we must go and see how Beatrice and Dora and Tina are getting on.'

They left the hotel early, before the sun got too hot, and followed the trickle of people who had begun to emerge tentatively from their various refuges, emboldened by the presence of the bands of partisans who were roaming the streets. Many of the streets were impassable, piled high with the remains of destroyed buildings, and they were forced to take a circuitous route to the Arno, where they stopped and gasped. The scenes of destruction were breathtaking. How could this part of the city ever be rebuilt as it had once been? It was unimaginable.

'The bridges have gone,' said Monica, staring at the devastation as though she'd only just understood the reality of it. 'How are we to get across?'

Access to the Ponte Vecchio was completely blocked, but a thin file of people were clambering laboriously over the remains of the Ponte alle Grazie, much of which remained above the water.

'That way,' replied Stella, indicating it.

Monica took some persuading, but eventually they joined the people who were scrambling across the fallen stones as best they could, hot, dusty and tired. It was hard work but at last they made it across, and Stella hurried Monica through the streets of the Oltrarno, because she'd overheard people talking about snipers, and she knew the Germans might start shelling again at any moment. Monica clutched at her arm, her eyes darting right and left, terrified that they might encounter a band of thugs. After what the Fascists had done to her, Stella couldn't blame her.

Dora was overjoyed to see them.

'Stella!' she cried, embracing her. 'Thank God! We have been so worried about you. And Your Excellency. Come in, quickly. The Americans are here, but there is still danger, so better not linger outside.'

She hustled them in and shut the door. Tina was there, playing on the floor, but Beatrice was absent.

'Where's Beatrice?' asked Stella, noticing Dora's worried expression.

Dora wrung her hands.

'It's Vittorio. They have taken him to the army hospital, and Beatrice has gone with him.' She shook her head. 'I haven't heard anything for two days. I think it is very bad.'

'What happened to him?'

'I don't know, exactly – he was shot, and I think there was also an explosion that killed some of the other men. Antonio said there was a lot of blood.'

'Oh, goodness!' exclaimed Stella.

'He said the Americans came and took charge, and got an ambulance for him, and they would let me know as soon as they had any news, but I haven't heard a thing. *Povero* Vittorio, he has been such a friend to all of us, and he's almost like a son to me. I am so afraid I won't see him again. And what will happen to

Beatrice? He's been so good to her, and so loyal, and it will be too much, after Mimmo.'

Dora began to sob into her apron. Stella put her arms around her.

'Hush, now, you mustn't talk like that,' she said, although she felt close to tears herself. 'If he's gone to a proper hospital with doctors, then I'm sure they're doing everything they can to look after him. We'll just have to hope and pray very hard that he pulls through.'

'But—'

'If you haven't heard anything for two days then that must be good news, because if he were— if anything had happened, then surely Beatrice would have come back by now.'

Dora looked up hopefully.

'Do you think so? Yes, yes, that's true. We must keep praying for good news. Surely good things must begin to happen soon, after all this time. They will, I feel it!'

Stella could only hope she was right. Dora dried her tears and busied herself with the chores that needed doing, while Stella saw to Tina, who was hungry. She'd half-forgotten Monica, who had been looking on silently, but at last she remembered what they were supposed to be doing.

'We'll go to the villa now if you like,' she said.

'Oh!' exclaimed Dora, upset. 'I completely forgot. That's another thing, on top of everything else.'

Stella exclaimed in dismay when she heard what had happened, and Monica closed her eyes briefly as Dora described the state of the house and its collapsed west wing.

'Some of the rooms are quite whole, though,' she finished. 'I didn't go in, because I was mainly looking for food from the gardens.'

'It sounds as though we'll have to stay at the hotel for the present,' said Stella, 'but we'd better go and take a look at the villa since we're here.'

'Must we go now?' asked Monica fearfully. 'What if there are unexploded shells? What if there are snipers hiding in the ruins?'

'I don't know about shells, but there were no snipers there yesterday,' replied Dora. 'Most of them have been caught, and the ones who are left are down in the Oltrarno, where the people are.'

'I think we ought to go,' said Stella to Monica. She wanted to be busy, wanted to do something to keep her mind off poor Vittorio. 'We'll need to see if there's anything worth salvaging. If there is then better we take it than some passing thief. Who knows when you'll be able to get at your bank accounts? It might be weeks or even months, and you'll need money in the meantime.'

Monica wrinkled her brow worriedly, but said, 'I suppose so. If we must, we must. But you are coming with me, aren't you? I'm too frightened to go alone.'

'Of course.'

Stella cleared the remains of Tina's meal away. Monica began opening drawers and cupboards.

'Do you have any cigarettes?'

'Not here, I'm afraid,' replied Stella, coming back into the living room. 'Shall we go?'

Monica was staring into a cupboard, and Stella had to repeat her question.

'Yes,' Monica replied at last, glancing at Stella. 'Where are Dora's keys? I don't know where mine are.'

Stella left Monica gazing into the cupboard and went to fetch the keys from a hook in the kitchen, then they went out. The villa was exactly as Dora had described it, and yet it still came as a shock to see it, glaring starkly at them in all its broken beauty. Stella and Monica stood on the drive, under the blazing midday sun, gazing at the ruins of the west wing and the collapsed front wall. Several large stones had landed in the ornamental fountain and badly damaged it, but that was nothing to the damage done to the building itself. The front wall had a great, gaping hole in its left side, while the west wing had been reduced mostly to rubble. Here and there they could see bits and pieces of smashed furniture sticking out from the heap, or a dusty strip of fabric that might once have been a curtain. Pipes that had once been plumbing protruded in various places, while on top of it all a white object painted with blue flowers proved to be a china jug that had miraculously survived the explosion, losing only its handle.

'*Madonna!*' muttered Monica. 'What have they done to it?'

They advanced cautiously, clambering across piles of fallen masonry. The steps up to the front door were undamaged, but where the front door had once been there was now nothing except a fallen lintel and some splintered wood. They stepped inside carefully, keeping a wary eye out for anything that might fall on them or give way under them. Where they stood had once been the entrance hall, but it was now practically unrecognisable. The plaster had fallen from the walls in great chunks, and the floor clinked and crunched underfoot, covered with broken glass and broken tiles. The air was thick, floating with dust, which attached itself to Stella; she felt it gritty against the damp palms of her hands; it got into her shoes and coated her hair. The hall seemed bigger than she remembered, and oddly shaped. Then she realised that the shell had destroyed the wall which separated the hall from the kitchen, and that the dust-coated object she'd been staring at, puzzled, for the last minute, lying on its side on the floor, had once been the kitchen sink.

There was nothing salvageable here. Stella looked to her right. The door to the stairs was hanging off its hinges, but the marble stairs up to the next floor and the east wing were still whole. She moved towards the back of the hall and went through the doorway to the *salone*. This room had suffered no shell damage, but it bore the marks of the Germans' occupation of it. They'd stripped it completely bare of furniture and left it full of rubbish. Incomprehensible graffiti was plastered all over the walls, and the place smelled unpleasant. Stella wandered across to the French windows, which were still mostly intact, and gazed out over the city, then went into the breakfast room. This, too, had been stripped of its furniture, but at least they'd left the frescoes in the dining room alone. She went back and found Monica in the *salone*, picking through the rubbish to see if any of her possessions remained. She'd entered the villa fearfully, gripping Stella's arm, but as they toured the house and saw the dreadful devastation caused by Allies on one side and the Germans on the other, she became more and more angry.

'Look at what they've done to my beautiful villa,' she muttered repeatedly through gritted teeth. 'They're no better than animals!'

Stella followed her into the little sitting room in which Monica had been accustomed to read and write letters. It didn't overlook the city, but it had pleasant views over the gardens at the side, and had been one of Monica's favourite rooms. Here not everything had been taken: they'd left the antique writing desk and a little drinks cabinet, although they'd taken all its contents. But it looked as if someone had deliberately taken an axe to both of them: the surface of the desk had several deep gashes in it, and the door of the cabinet had been hacked to pieces, while a glass lamp Monica had been particularly fond of lay shattered on the floor in a thousand pieces. There was rubbish strewn about in here, too, and the whole place was filled with the unmistakable smell of human waste.

Monica surveyed the ruins of her room. Her rage was growing hotter. She kicked at the broken glass.

'If I could kill them, I would!' she spat suddenly. She turned on her heel and stalked out. 'We'd better go and see what a mess they've made of upstairs.'

The situation there was little better: in each room they entered they saw the same evidence of wanton destruction. In one of the bedrooms a washbasin had been pulled off the wall, while in another more human waste had been smeared over every surface. Monica marched from room to room, increasingly angry, noting down things that had gone missing or been smashed. Stella suddenly felt she couldn't stand it any more. Her own bedroom had been lost with the collapse of the west wing, but the state of the remaining rooms, once so beautiful, was almost too much to bear.

She left Monica and went downstairs and outside. The flower beds were untended and unkempt, and the lawn was as dry as straw, but at least the grounds were still dimly recognisable as the attractive haven they had once been. She spent some time gazing out over the city, then descended the steps to inspect the damage to the pavilion and the tennis court. After a while she turned to look back at the house, thinking she ought to go and find Monica, who had mentioned going into the gallery – although of course there were no pictures left there now: Vittorio had hidden them for Gerardo, until Monica had unwittingly given the game away. Now the paintings were in the possession of Otto Kaufmann, who had taken them under the pretence of protecting them, and who knew whether they'd ever be seen again?

Stella walked across the lawn, feeling the grass crunch underfoot, then returned up the steps to the terrace and round to the east side of the house. Several of the windows had gone from the gallery, blown out by the force of the explosion.

'Monica?' she called up, but there was no reply.

She went along the terrace, in through the French windows and into the hall, wondering where Monica was. She looked into all the downstairs rooms but saw no sign of her. Then she heard a sound coming from the door that led to the stairs. Monica must be coming down now. Stella went through to meet her.

'There you are,' she said brightly, then jumped.

Because it wasn't Monica at all. It was Marius.

Chapter Thirty-Five

Marius's foot was on the bottom stair; he'd obviously been just about to go up. He looked at her for a long moment, then stepped back from the stairs and came towards her. Stella backed away into the hall, and he followed.

'What are you doing here?' she said. Despite her attempt to speak firmly her voice sounded wobbly and uneven in her own ears.

He didn't answer, just continued staring at her. Even after all this time, after all the things she'd done and the courage she'd found within herself while hiding in Florence, the sight of him made her skin turn to ice. He saw her fear and his mouth turned up slightly at the corners. It was a complacent look – the look of a man who knew he was in control. This was the man who'd had no qualms about beating and burning his own brother-in-law to get what he wanted, and who had left his own sister in the hands of ruthless torturers. He was dangerous, possibly even a little mad, and Stella's mind told her to run from him now, just as she had the last time she'd been confronted with him at the Hotel Ambassador. But as his eyes looked her up and down, the thought of Gerardo and his kindness came into her mind, and caused the chill to evaporate suddenly, driven out by the blood that coursed white-hot through her veins, as all the pent-up anger of years rose to the surface at once.

He'd destroyed so many lives – Gerardo's, Monica's, her own. He'd starved her of affection, driving her into someone else's arms, then out of pure spite had torn her away from the man she loved and stranded her here in Florence, cut off from everything. And now here he was, standing amid the ruins, cool and unperturbed, with that amused, superior look on his face, as though nothing had happened. Stella had never hated anyone as much as she hated Marius at that moment. She straightened up and lifted her head. She wouldn't cower in front of him any more.

'Why didn't you bring your German friend?' she asked disdainfully. 'I assume you're here to see if there are any of Gerardo's paintings you missed? Well, as you can see, there aren't.'

He was silent for a moment, watching her carefully.

'As a matter of fact, the Americans have asked me to assist the superintendent of the Uffizi gallery with a few things,' he said.

'Oh, you're on our side now, are you? I understood you were helping the Nazis loot all the art they could get their hands on. They must be losing if you've switched your allegiance to the Allies – you always did know which side your bread was buttered on.'

She said it deliberately to sting him, but he merely shrugged.

'It's business.'

'Is it? Is that all it is? Was Gerardo just business to you?'

He said nothing. He was as cool and imperturbable as ever, standing there in front of her, looking at her through narrowed eyes. She wanted to shake that self-possession of his, show him at last that she was the one who had the upper hand.

'Well, Gerardo's dead, and this is what remains of his life.' She swept an arm around, indicating their surroundings. 'Feel free to go digging in the rubble. There's lots of stuff here – you know, bits of furniture, possessions, things that used to mean something to somebody. Do you care about that, Marius? You don't, do you? All you care about is yourself and getting what you want, and you don't give a damn how many people you trample over along the way. You trampled over me, and you trampled over Gerardo just for your own selfish ends.'

Now she'd started she couldn't stop. She was saying all the things she'd wanted to say to him for so long, and it was an enormous relief. She couldn't harm him physically, but she'd do her best to hurt him with words. She glanced at him in disgust.

'Have you ever done anything brave, Marius? I don't suppose you have. You've never been a patriot, have you? You don't give a damn about Italy, or your fellow Italians. The only thing you're loyal to is yourself. I despise you.'

He took a step forward and his hand jerked a little, as if to strike her. She stood her ground and laughed, and with that laugh felt her power growing. Why had she ever been afraid of him?

'What are you going to do to me? Beat me again? Burn me with cigarettes as you did Gerardo? Or kill me, as you did my father?'

There was a long silence as the suggestion hung in the air between them, floating in among the clouds of dust, and suddenly, with a certainty she couldn't explain, Stella knew that she'd hit upon the truth. It had been a wild accusation, made on the spur of the moment, but all at once the truth flooded in and everything made sense. A remark Monica had made long ago came back into her head: the only reason Raymond had been out walking on the evening he died was because the brakes on his car had failed the day before. It had happened only a few weeks after Marius lost the *Lady of the Cypresses*, and more than anything Marius hated to be crossed. He'd had his revenge on Monica when he sent her to the Villa Triste, but had he revenged himself on Stella's father too? Had he tampered with the brakes on Raymond's car, then come back for a second attempt when the first one had failed? She stared at him incredulously as the certainty solidified.

'You did, didn't you? He beat you to the Raphael, and you can't stand being beaten, so you saw to it he couldn't do it again.'

Marius's brow twitched, and she knew her accusation had hit home.

'Your father nearly bankrupted me,' was all he said.

'So you killed him, just as you tried to kill me.'

'You'll never prove it,' he replied.

'Won't I? No, I expect you've covered your traces well enough. But even so, I can still make your life awfully difficult. I wonder what the Swiss police will say when your own wife reports you on suspicion of murder. Will they take it seriously, do you think? Probably not, if they're already satisfied my father's death was an accident. But what about your friends? What about your clients? Rumours spread fast and can get out of control, you know. Reputations can be tarnished. Will respectable people want to do business with you once they know what you've been accused of?'

Stella had the satisfaction of seeing a flash of anger cross his face at that.

'Enough!' he snapped. 'You dare to speak to me in this way?'

She lifted her chin.

'I'm not afraid of you any more, Marius. For a long time you frightened me, because I thought I was the one getting it wrong. I thought if I tried harder then you'd be kinder to me. But it was never enough, was it? Nothing I did could ever have been enough, because you had no intention of ever being kind. Your cruelty had nothing to do with me, and everything to do with you. I see you now for what you really are – selfish, cold-hearted and vicious.'

'But I am still your husband.' He said it very softly, and again she saw the vein pulsing in his temple. He took a step towards her and still she stood her ground. 'And you are still my wife. That counts for something, doesn't it?'

'Not any more. You never cared a thing for me. All you wanted was my money, and the satisfaction of revenging yourself on my father for whatever bad turn you think he did you. How you must have hated him!' She gestured wildly. 'How can you live like this? Always so eaten up with hatred and vengefulness against anybody who thwarts you. You're sick and twisted inside, and I want nothing more to do with you. Don't call me your wife. I'm not yours, and never have been.'

'Perhaps not. But you'll never be anybody else's either. If you think I'm going to give you a divorce you're mistaken.'

'Do you think I care? I'd rather be alone forever than spend another minute with you.'

Finally she'd said it all, everything that she'd been bottling up inside herself for so long. She drew herself up and stared him down contemptuously. 'Go away, Marius, and don't come back. I never want to see you again.'

She turned away, intending to put distance between them and get him out of her sight, but he wasn't having that. His hand darted out and he grabbed hold of her arm, wrenching her round to face him.

'Not so fast!'

She struggled to free herself, but his grip was like steel. She wasn't frightened in the least, only very angry.

'Let me go!' she exclaimed. 'Weren't you listening?'

'Yes, I heard what you said,' he replied. Both his hands were on her arms now, and he advanced, pushing her backwards until she felt her back meet the wall. He held her there, and she felt the rough surface of the damaged plaster digging painfully into her, and the pressure of his fingers gripping her arms. 'I was listening very carefully.'

He let go of one arm, and she immediately raised her hand to push him away, but he clamped both her wrists together in one hand and pressed his body against her, trapping her against the wall.

'Do you think I will let you go as easily as that?' he said. His face was thrust up close to hers, and she could feel his breath warm on her face. His right hand brushed her cheek softly, then she felt his fingers slide around her neck, exerting a gentle pressure.

'What's this?' His hand had found the string holding the key to the safe deposit box. He pulled it out and looked at it. 'Ah,' he said with dawning realisation. 'So this is the key you begged me to take in exchange for my forgiveness for your infidelity. These are Raymond's famous missing paintings, yes? No wonder I couldn't find the key at home. I should have known you were trying to trick me, you devious little bitch.'

At those last words he gave a sharp tug and she gasped in pain as the string burned against her neck. It snapped on the second tug and he put the key in his pocket. The pressure returned to her neck, more tightly this time.

'I never finished punishing you for what you did, did I? You ran away before I could teach you a proper lesson.'

She glared at him, still too angry to be afraid.

'Go on then,' she said defiantly. 'Strangle me if you like. Much good it'll do you.'

'I won't strangle you. Not yet. That would be far too quick. You need to feel the pain first.'

His voice was soft, almost loving. She felt his grip tighten a little more, his hand hot and clammy around her throat. She was beginning to feel light-headed.

'I've already felt plenty,' she replied through gritted teeth. Her voice was tight and hoarse. 'Do you think this will make any difference?'

'Let's see, shall we?'

He fumbled in his pocket with his other hand, still keeping her pressed against the wall with his body, and brought something out. It was a cigarette lighter. He flipped it open with his thumb and clicked it on, then held the flame up so she could see it. She willed herself not to show any fear, because she knew if she did she was lost.

'Just a little taste.' He brought the flame very close to her face, and she felt herself jerk back involuntarily, but his grip on her throat was inexorable. 'Are you sure you wouldn't like to come back to me?' he said mockingly. 'We could have such fun.'

She could feel the heat of the lighter flame close to her cheek. She closed her eyes.

'*Marius!*'

The voice rang out sharply from behind him, and he let go of Stella and turned around. It was Monica, who had just come down the stairs. Stella gasped as Marius's hand released her, and she darted well out of his reach, taking in gulps of air and massaging her throat. Marius closed the lighter and put it back in his pocket, Monica's eyes on him all the time. She hadn't given Stella so much as a glance; all her attention was focused on her brother. They faced one another, their eyes narrowed, both looking very alike at that moment.

'Well, well. And so my little brother dares to turn up here, after all he's done!'

'What have I done?' he asked offhandedly.

She took a step forward.

'You ask me what you've done?' she hissed. 'Have you forgotten already? Do you think I don't remember every single thing you said and did that day? Do you think I don't remember how you told Otto to let the Fascists take me and do what they wanted with me? How you'd have let them kill me without a second thought?'

'But they didn't,' he pointed out. 'You're standing here now, alive and well, so don't come to me for sympathy.'

'Alive and well? Do you call *this* well?'

She made a sudden movement, pulling aside her dress to reveal her scars. Even in this dim hall they looked terrible. Marius flicked a glance over them expressionlessly. Monica bared her teeth in a snarl and advanced slowly, her eyes boring into him.

'Believe me, if I could do to you right now exactly what they did to me then I would – blow for blow, burn for burn, cut for cut!'

'I know it only too well,' he said. 'And I also know you'd have done exactly the same to me if the boot had been on the other foot.'

She drew back.

'Is that what you think? You think I'm as bad as you are? Do you think I'd have dreamed of telling Otto about the paintings if I'd had the faintest idea of what he'd do? You beat Gerardo and burned him with cigarettes, and then you handed us both over to those *bastardi* – never mind that I was your sister, who cared for you, and played with you, and stopped Papà from beating you when he found out some of your nastier habits!'

She'd begun to shake, Stella noticed, and her voice was rising to that hysterical note again.

'You've always had a vicious streak in you, haven't you? You kept it under wraps long enough, but you've stopped hiding it now, and it's there for all to see.'

Monica felt in her pocket for something and brought it out, then began circling him slowly. Marius turned, watching her warily. Stella, standing away from them, still catching her breath, didn't understand what was happening until she saw with a sudden shock what Monica held in her hand. She gave a gasp. It was the gun Vittorio had given her. She'd never used it in the end, and had put it safely away in the cupboard, out of reach of Tina. Presumably Monica had feared they'd meet trouble while they were out, and had taken the gun while Stella was fetching the keys to the villa.

'Monica!' she exclaimed, but Monica wasn't listening. She continued, her eyes never leaving her brother:

'Do you remember what I said to you, when Gerardo was tied to that tree? When you and Otto calmly discussed whether or not you should leave me to my fate? When you smirked and said you thought I might enjoy it? Do you remember? I remember. I promised then that I'd kill you if I ever saw you again. So tell me why I shouldn't shoot you right now.'

'Don't be stupid,' Marius replied. 'You're not thinking straight. Put it away.'

She took a step towards him, jerking the pistol upwards, and he flinched. Stella could see Monica getting increasingly agitated, and was dreadfully afraid she was working herself up into a full attack of hysteria.

'Monica, please don't!' she begged, but the plea fell on deaf ears. Monica was still circling Marius, and he was turning with her, always keeping his eye on the gun. She was berating him in rapid Italian.

'You've always hated me, always been jealous of me underneath it all. You couldn't wait to stick the knife in as soon as you got a chance, could you? But what harm did Gerardo ever do to you? You betrayed us for your own selfish ends. You killed him.'

'I didn't kill him.'

'You might as well have. Just because you didn't do it with your own hands doesn't mean you weren't responsible. Give me one good reason why I shouldn't pay you back in kind here and now.'

She was brandishing the gun wildly at him, and Stella as well as Marius was watching it carefully in case it went off, because Monica didn't seem to have much control over it. Brother and sister were staring at each other, their eyes locked together in a battle of wills. Monica seemed to have the advantage, but Stella knew not to underestimate Marius, and something about his stance put her in mind of a panther waiting to spring. She recognised that look: whenever she'd seen it on him during her marriage she'd taken care to avoid him. It meant danger. But Monica was so distracted with her own grievances that she'd lowered her guard and hadn't noticed. She continued to talk, and Marius crouched slightly, ready to pounce. Any second now he'd get the gun, and then they'd be in trouble.

'Monica! Watch out!' Stella cried out, just as Marius made his move. He sprang forward and made a grab for the pistol. Monica gave a shriek. Stella watched, horror-struck, as they tussled. It couldn't have lasted more than a second or two, although it seemed like hours, before the gun went off – a sharp, ugly sound ringing out into the dead afternoon air. Stella cried out in shock and watched as Marius staggered backwards, clutching his stomach. He fell to his knees, his breath coming in laboured, wheezing gasps. He raised his eyes to his sister.

'Monica,' he said faintly.

Monica stared at him coldly for a long moment, then lifted the gun deliberately and fired again.

'For Gerardo,' she said, as Marius crumpled to the floor.

The gunshots had disturbed the dust, which danced and swirled through the air, before settling slowly back down into drifting lethargy. Monica seemed to have calmed down all at once. She saw her brother lying dead and dropped to her knees.

'*Dio mio*, what have I done?' she cried, and burst out sobbing.

Stella stared, horrified, at the scene before her, and suddenly felt a great weariness settle over her. She couldn't take anything in, couldn't feel anything, couldn't think. Leaving Monica, who was now cradling her brother's head in her arms, she turned and walked, with dragging footsteps, into the *salone* and out through the French windows onto the terrace. Outside the sun shone, and Florence stood, proud and resplendent below her, ready to heal its wounds and rise again, but for the moment Stella felt no relief, no comfort, no hope. There was nothing to do now but wait for the future, and whatever it might hold, to come and meet her. And so she sat on a wall and waited.

Chapter Thirty-Six

On the day the Germans pulled out of the centre of Florence Ted finally made it across the river via the Vasari Corridor, which had been pressed into service by the Allies, and found scenes of devastation similar to those he'd witnessed on the south bank. He headed for the Hotel Ambassador, half-fearing that it might have collapsed in the explosions, but was relieved to find it was still there, seemingly whole, although without any windows. He entered through the cracked glass front doors.

'Hallo?' he called out.

There was nobody in the lobby, so he went into the bar and then through to the dining room, looking for signs of life. He eventually ran Cavalieri to earth in the kitchen, where the manager was busy making lists. He was very pleased to see Ted, who he thought had come to arrange billeting for his fellow officers, but was still happy to be of assistance when he found out he was looking for Stella.

'Yes, the English miss is staying here with the Countess,' he said. 'They took shelter from the bombs. Now they have gone to the Countess's villa over the river. I don't know when they'll be back.'

Cavalieri would have taken the opportunity to offer the use of his hotel, but the American had already thrown him a hasty thanks and hurried off, so he shrugged his shoulders and returned to his lists.

Ted lost no time in returning across the river, and hurried through the streets of the Oltrarno, desperate to get back to the Villa Bruni before Stella left again. His spirits were in turmoil: he was half-convinced that Cavalieri and all the other people who'd mentioned her must have been talking of another English woman called Stella, because it hardly seemed possible that after so long apart from her she could be still alive. He'd spent so many months thinking of her, keeping her fresh in his memory, picturing her face, serious in repose, but ever ready to break into a smile or a laugh at something he said, recalling things she'd said that made him laugh in turn. There was a particular look he remembered: a diffident, hopeful sort of glance she gave him whenever he told her he loved her, as if she didn't quite believe it could be true after so long stuck in a cold, cruel marriage. He'd meant to take her away from all that. They'd have got married, and he'd have loved her and treated her well, and they'd have been happy. But the war – and Marius – had come between them, and he hadn't seen her for over a year. Throughout all those months fearing for her he hadn't even had a photograph to remember her by, and he'd been so dreadfully afraid that one day the picture of her he held in his mind would fade away altogether.

He quickened his pace, remembering the condition of the villa when he'd seen it the day before. She might have already seen it and come away, and then he'd have no option but to go and wait at the hotel until she returned, and he'd be late for a meeting with the OSS, who wanted to speak to him about going through the lines again and liaising with the partisans further north. What if he was sent out of Florence tomorrow and missed her altogether? He wished he'd thought to leave a message – although he was sure Cavalieri would pass on the news that an American had come looking for her.

Ted climbed over the wall as he had the day before, and headed up the path towards the east wing. The sound of gunshots rang out from somewhere close by, and he paused a second, then carried on. Presumably it was a sniper firing from a window in one of the streets nearer the river. When he arrived at the house he paused to listen, but could hear nothing; no sound of voices anywhere. Had they come and gone already?

He went around to the terrace, then stopped short as he saw a young woman sitting on a wall, staring out across the city, lost in her own thoughts. She was wearing a worn, filthy print frock and shoes that were falling apart. Her face was streaked with dirt, and her dark hair was coated with so much dust that it looked almost grey. At first he didn't recognise her, and thought only that she might be able to tell him where Stella was, until she glanced up, alerted by the sound of his footsteps. She saw him and her eyes widened, and he recognised those eyes and knew who she was at last. For several long seconds he stood, rooted to the spot, as she rose from her seat and took an uncertain step towards him, then another. Without conscious effort he moved forward, and they came to meet there on the terrace.

For a moment they did nothing but stare at each other. She seemed to want to say something, but no words came out of her mouth. He had a thousand things he wanted to say, too, but he was struck just as dumb as she was. At last he raised a hesitant hand and gently brushed away a streak of dust from her cheek, then another, and then suddenly he couldn't stop stroking her face, touching her hair, because if he stopped then it might turn out she was a figment of his imagination and she would disappear in a puff of smoke, but as long as he could feel her under his hands then he knew she was real. Her hand was reaching up to him, too, her fingers running over his cheek, light against his warm skin, while her other clutched convulsively at his sleeve as if she had had the similar thought that he might disappear at any second.

She might have whispered something, he couldn't be sure, because suddenly the spell of that suspended moment was broken and she was in his arms, and he was crushing her to him so tightly that she could hardly breathe, and he could feel her trembling under his hands and her heart beating wildly against him. Then her voice, muffled, sobbing his name, 'Ted... Ted... Ted...' over and over again.

'I thought I'd never find you,' he said at last, his own voice breaking slightly. 'Don't you ever run off like that again, do you hear?'

They stood like that for a very long time, holding each other, his face in her dusty hair, murmuring words that didn't mean anything but at the same time meant everything. Then he held her away from him and looked into her eyes in deep concern. She was thin and worn-looking, and her brows were drawn together in a permanent frown.

'Are you all right?' he asked. 'You're not hurt, or anything?'

'No, I'm fine.' She gulped, and her face broke into the ghost of a smile. 'Is it really you? I'm not dreaming, am I?'

'It's me all right. I've been looking for you ever since you went away. I'm only sorry it took so long to find you.'

He pulled her close again and she nestled against him, feeling the rough cotton of his shirt under her cheek.

'You're so thin,' he said. 'Are you sure you're okay?'

'Yes. I'm just so awfully tired. The last few days have been… very difficult, and now there's – oh!'

She broke away and gestured towards the house. He misunderstood her.

'The villa? That's not something you need to worry about. I guess they'll rebuild it sooner or later.'

'No.' She put her hand to her forehead, rubbing it as though she were trying to erase an unwelcome thought. 'You'd better come and see. I don't know what to do.'

She turned away and led him in through the French windows. Puzzled, he followed her inside and into the remains of the entrance hall, and stopped dead at what he saw. Monica was sitting on the floor, among broken tiles and chunks of plaster, by the dead body of a man he recognised after a shocked moment as Marius. Blood had seeped out from under him, and was soaking into the dust that coated the floor, while Monica hugged her knees, staring at him as if she expected him to wake up. The gun was still in her hand.

Stella crouched down by Monica.

'Monica. Ted's here. You remember Ted, don't you?'

Monica looked up and registered Ted's presence with uninterested eyes, then turned her gaze back to her dead brother.

'Listen,' went on Stella. 'We can't stay here much longer. It'll be getting dark soon, and we ought to get back to the hotel, or at least to Dora's.'

Ted was taking in the scene, astounded.

'What the hell happened here?'

'The gun went off accidentally,' replied Stella. 'He was trying to get it from her.' She didn't mention the second shot which had been wholly deliberate. She took the gun from Monica's unresisting hand.

'We'll say we found him like this, and they'll think he was shot by Fascists or partisans. The gun can go in the river. It'll be less complicated that way. We'll have to get someone to come and remove the body. I'll speak to Dora. She'll know someone who can take him away.'

She was talking soothingly, as a mother to a child. Monica was quite docile and made no argument.

'Come on, you can't stay here,' Stella went on briskly, and held out a hand. Monica took it and stood up. She looked around her as though she'd just realised where she was, then pulled herself together visibly and patted at her hair, in something of her old manner.

'Yes. Take him away. I had to do it, you know.'

'I know,' said Stella. 'He would have killed you if you hadn't.'

'Do you think so?'

'Or he'd have killed me. I'm glad you turned up just in time.'

Monica put a hand to the ruined plaster of the wall, glancing around.

'I'll go to Dora's and see about getting this place cleared up,' she said. 'We must start rebuilding as soon as possible.' Then she stepped over Marius as if he wasn't there and gave them both an uncertain smile. 'Ted, how nice to see you.'

She looked as if she were about to offer him her hand, but then thought better of it and turned away, picking carefully through the debris on the floor and out via the hole in the wall that had once been the front door. They watched her go, then Ted turned a questioning gaze on Stella.

'What did I miss?'

'It's a long story.' She looked down at what had once been Marius. 'I ought to feel something, but I can't. I don't know if I can feel anything normal any more.'

Ted was still trying to digest the strange scene before him, and this new Stella, who'd ordered Monica about while standing over the dead body of her husband. He couldn't quite take it all in. A sudden thought struck him.

'It was Monica who killed him, wasn't it?' he asked hesitantly. 'It wasn't you?'

She turned eyes on him that were suddenly hard.

'No, it wasn't me, but I might have done it if I'd been the one with the gun.' Then the hardness left her and she seemed to sag. 'Oh, Ted, I'm so glad you're here.'

She put a hand to her eyes as the tears started, and he took her in his arms and held her.

Chapter Thirty-Seven

It was nearly sunset on the day after they'd brought him to the hospital that Vittorio drifted gradually into semi-consciousness. He felt very comfortable, and for a good few minutes he thought he was in his old bed in the attic of the Villa Bruni. But the ceiling above him was made of canvas, and there were poles holding it up, and there were people, men and women, wandering around in medical uniforms. This couldn't be the villa, then. Where was he? The answer wouldn't come, so his sleepy mind abandoned the matter for now, and slid to the question of why he couldn't move. Hazy visions that didn't seem to belong to him drifted through his mind, of shouts, and gunshots, and then a blinding light, and at that moment his memory came back to him all at once, and he wondered idly for a few seconds whether he were dead. Then he heard what sounded like someone crying very quietly somewhere close by, and turned his head slightly to see Beatrice sitting by his bed. Her eyes were pink-rimmed and glistening with tears, and she looked completely exhausted. Vittorio thought he had never seen anyone so beautiful.

'Hallo,' he said, but it came out as a croak. He swallowed and tried again. It was difficult to speak. 'You're still here.'

'I told you I'd stay,' she replied. She was smiling and crying at the same time.

'I dreamed about you,' he murmured drowsily. 'At least, I thought I did. But perhaps it was really you all along.'

She gave him her sweetest smile, and after a while he drifted off again. The next morning he woke up and she was there again, still sitting by his bedside. This time he felt much more alert – and a lot less numb. It wasn't pleasant.

'What time is it?' he asked.

'About half past seven, I think.'

'Have you been here all night?'

'No. I wanted to, but they sent me away to get some rest. Not that I could sleep.'

'Don't wear yourself out on my account.'

'Don't worry, I won't.'

A nurse came up, brisk and efficient.

'You're awake,' she said. 'That was quite a nap you had.'

She busied herself about him, then looked at Beatrice doubtfully.

'May I stay a little while?' asked Beatrice.

'All right, just a few minutes. He needs rest. Don't let him move.'

'Am I still alive, then?' asked Vittorio as he watched the nurse's retreating figure.

'It looks like it.'

'Everything hurts. What have they done to me?'

'They've patched you up. No, keep still,' she admonished, as he tried to raise his head and look down at himself. 'You heard what the nurse said.'

'Did they fix my leg?'

Beatrice had never been any good at telling lies, but it was important not to upset him.

'In a manner of speaking,' she replied carefully.

He looked at her, but her eyes slid away from his.

'I'd laugh, but it hurts too much,' he said after a short silence. 'Still, spoken like a true diplomat. *Brava!*' There was another silence, as he considered the matter. 'In any case, how many legs does a man need? Some people might say two were too many.'

'You're still here.' Her voice came unevenly and her eyes were bright with tears again. 'That's all that matters.'

*

The next morning Vittorio woke up feeling pain in every part of his body. He looked for Beatrice but to his disappointment she wasn't there. Then the nurse came to pass on the message that Beatrice had gone home to see Tina, but that she'd be back very soon. And she was: by the end of the day she returned to his bedside to find him wide awake and flirting with the nurse in very bad English.

'You're on the mend, I see,' commented Beatrice. She sat down close to his pillow and he held out his hand for her to take.

'Here is the chief doctor,' he said. 'I won't get well without you.'

'I think you'll do fine. How are you feeling?'

'Terrible,' he replied cheerfully.

'That's only to be expected. I imagine you'll be in pain for a while yet. But it will get better. As soon as you're well enough you can come home to us. It's not exactly comfortable at the moment, but it's no worse than anywhere else. And you'll have at least two women running around after you, if not three.'

'This is my dream,' he said sincerely, and she laughed.

He still couldn't exert himself without pain, so he didn't talk too much. She had things to tell him about what had been happening in Florence, but thought it better to leave it until he was stronger, because she didn't want to agitate him and set back his recovery. He was still very sick, and a relapse or an infection would be dangerous in his weakened state. As for Vittorio, he was content to have Beatrice sitting by his bedside, giving him all her attention for once.

'I wonder what it'll be like to have a false leg,' he said after a while. 'I imagine it will feel strange.'

'Mamma's cousin lost his leg at Caporetto and got a false leg, but you would never have known. He hardly even had a limp. He said he'd forgotten what it was like to have a real one.'

'Is that right? Still, I think I'd prefer my old one back. Do you think they could sew it back on?'

'I don't think there was much of it left. That's the price you pay for being brave.'

'I'm not brave.'

'That's not what Antonio said. He said you took the bullet that was meant for him.'

'Hmph. If I'd known how much it was going to hurt I mightn't have bothered.'

But Vittorio didn't really mind her thinking he was brave.

They stayed together, Beatrice holding his hand and occasionally stroking his head, until the shadows began to lengthen.

'I'll have to go soon,' she said. 'I can't leave my mother to do all the work. There's a lot of clearing up to do, and Tina to look after.'

'When will you come back?'

'I don't know. That depends on Mr Landry. He's been getting them to give me a lift in the ambulance, but I can't expect them to do it all the time.'

'These Americans – always so busy.'

'You should go to sleep,' she said, seeing his eyes growing heavy as the light faded. 'Don't mind me. I'll stay until you doze off if you like.'

They were silent for a few minutes as he began to drift off. Beatrice thought he'd gone to sleep, but then he suddenly opened his eyes and remarked, 'This partisan life isn't much fun. When I get out of here, and once the war's over, I'm going to settle down and get a steady job.'

'What would you like to do?'

'I don't know. Gardening, maybe, like I did at the villa. Or perhaps I'll start my own car repair business. Something in the practical line, anyway.'

'That sounds nice.'

'It does, doesn't it? And I'll buy a house, a little *casetta* just outside Florence, maybe up near Fiesole or Settignano, where the air's healthier, and I'll grow olives and lemons and artichokes and broad beans. Maybe we could even have a little vineyard and make our own wine.'

'We?'

'Did I say we?'

'Yes, Vittorio, you did.'

She felt his hand tighten around her fingers.

'Maybe I'll have a wife by then. There must be some girl out there who won't turn me down.'

'There must be lots.'

'But I only want one.'

'Do you? Is there anyone you have in mind?'

'Well, there is a girl I like, but I'm not sure she'd be willing.'

He held her gaze.

'Tell me about her.'

He expelled a long breath, like a sigh.

'What can I say about her? She's beautiful, of course – that goes without saying, because Italian girls are the prettiest in the world. She has black hair and brown eyes, just like you, and a perfect nose and mouth.' He lifted his hand and brushed her lips lightly with his fingertips. 'She doesn't smile much, but when she does it lights up the whole room. Sometimes I like to just watch her, waiting for that smile, because it's so rare and special. She's a hard worker, and strong, and doesn't suffer fools gladly, but she's also the most kind-hearted woman I've ever met. Any man would be lucky to have her for his wife.'

'Then why do you think she wouldn't want you?'

'Because she's told me so, many times. And because – well, because I'm not exactly in the best shape just now. I wouldn't want her to say yes just out of pity.'

'It wouldn't be out of pity.'

'Are you sure?'

'How could anyone pity you? You're strong and courageous, and you fought for your country like an honourable man should.

And you nearly died saving someone else's life. Mimmo would have been proud of you.'

'Do you think so?'

The tears came to her eyes so easily now. She nodded.

'Yes. And I am too.' They gazed at each other, then she whispered, 'Ask me if you like.'

'Then will you, Beatrice? You know how much I love you.'

He said it in a low voice that was barely audible above the hum of voices all around them, but Beatrice heard it clearly.

'Yes, Vittorio, I know, and I will.'

'Beatrice!' He tried to sit up but subsided with a groan of pain.

'But if you don't keep still I'll change my mind,' she said firmly.

'What sort of proposal is this if I can't even kiss you?'

She leaned forward and kissed him gently, and he sighed with pleasure.

'Now, go to sleep, and I'll come back as soon as I can. But you must get better for me, because I can't do without you.'

'I will, I promise.'

The exertion had tired him out, so she stayed with him until he fell asleep, and long after that sat watching him, her eyes soft, until it grew dark and she could no longer see him clearly.

Chapter Thirty-Eight

Some of Vittorio's partisan friends came to take Marius away, and didn't ask any questions. There was no wood to be had for coffins, so bodies were being laid out in the public gardens of the city until they could be properly buried. Monica seemed to have put the incident out of her mind altogether, perhaps as her way of dealing with what had happened – because God knew they all had enough on their plates right now – and was refusing to have anything more to do with the matter. Stella, for her part, didn't know how she should feel about Marius's death. She knew she ought to hate him for having killed her father, and perhaps she did, but for the rest there were mingled feelings of horror, sorrow and relief at how it had all ended up – with an additional touch of guilt at her own conduct.

She knew now that she'd married him for all the wrong reasons: she'd been too young, and had been looking for something he couldn't provide. Admittedly she'd been encouraged – even tricked – into it, but she felt that if she'd been a stronger person none of it would have ever happened. She'd been too unsure of herself, too easily swayed, too lacking in self-reliance. Well, a year hiding in Florence had changed all that. She'd had to learn strength, and now *she* was the one who took charge, the one who made all the decisions about what to do about Marius's death. That first shot by Monica had been accidental and, while the second one had been wholly deliberate, it couldn't be denied that Marius had brought it on himself. There was no sense in reporting it to the authorities, as it was just one more distraction in an already broken city, and Stella couldn't see how it would serve the ends of justice to have Monica taken in for questioning about it, when she was already so physically and emotionally damaged by her recent experiences. No – far better to let the incident pass unnoticed in a sea of other, similar incidents. Florence was full of dead bodies, and Marius was just another addition to the total. Once upon a time Stella might have left it to Ted to make these decisions, but she was a different person now. It had been a hard year, but her time in Florence had allowed her to discover what she was capable of alone.

Late in the evening, once the question of Marius had been dealt with – temporarily, at least – Stella and Monica returned to the Hotel Ambassador with Ted. Ted couldn't stay, but promised to return the next day.

'Keep an eye on Monica, won't you?' he said, as Stella clung to him. 'And don't run off again.'

Stella promised, and he kissed her and went away reluctantly, leaving her alone with her own thoughts. The whole day had been unreal, somehow. Up to now she'd been thinking of Marius's death in terms of its immediate effect, but now it slowly began to dawn on her that she was free of him at last.

*

Over the next few weeks the people of Florence slowly began to pick up the pieces of their lives. The situation could hardly be called normal, but water and power were gradually restored, paths were cleared through the devastation, and a temporary bridge was thrown over the river where the Ponte Santa Trinita used to be.

Beatrice had returned from hospital with cautiously good news about Vittorio. He was getting better all the time, and was now sitting up a little in bed and telling his usual bad jokes. The main danger was infection, but they had penicillin at the hospital, and it was hoped he'd be well enough to be transferred to another hospital soon, nearer Florence, to convalesce. The radiant look of relief on her face brought hope to them all, and it seemed like a new Beatrice who hugged Tina very close, and shed tears easily now. It wasn't that Mimmo meant any less to her; rather that her capacity to love had expanded to include both Mimmo and Vittorio. Mimmo was far away and would never come back, but Vittorio was here, and had showed every day how much he loved her, and now she knew she could love him too.

There was no time to rest in those weeks. The staff of the Hotel Ambassador were trickling back, and there was work to be done to get things in order for the Allies, who, as expected, wanted to take over the place. The city was still desperately short of food, but the Germans hadn't succeeded in requisitioning the whole harvest before they went, and people brought out stores that they'd managed to keep hidden, so supplies gradually began coming into the city.

If Stella had expected any sort of reaction from Monica to what she'd done, she was disappointed, because with the arrival of the Allies at the Hotel Ambassador Monica had smartened herself up and attended to her hair, and was once more doing what she did best – charming everyone around her into doing what she wanted. She'd been to the bank and the lawyers and had at last managed to get them to release some funds, and she had Cavalieri working hard to restore normal service at the hotel. Nobody had time for mourning, because there was a city to rebuild and food to be got, and anything beyond immediate necessities would have to be postponed to the future – or relived in bad dreams at night, when all was quiet and the mind had full rein.

One day Stella was in Beatrice's old office at the hotel, trying to bring some order to all the piles of papers that had built up, when Monica came in with some letters in her hand.

'Here, these are yours,' she said, tossing them at Stella.

There were two envelopes, one addressed to Stella in her father's writing, and another with a United States postmark, addressed to her father in handwriting she didn't recognise. Both had been opened. Stella looked up at Monica in surprise. She didn't exactly look uncomfortable – that wasn't Monica's way – but there was a certain self-consciousness to her manner. She gestured at the letters in Stella's lap.

'I dare say you'll blame me, but one has to look after oneself, and when your father died I had no idea Gerardo would come along so soon. Still, I suppose there's no harm done in the end,' she added, as she went out.

Stella opened the letter from her father first. It was dated the day of his death in May of 1937, and was very different from his usual breezy, chatty communications. After the greeting and some general pleasantries it went on:

I wasn't intending to write until next week, but I had a near miss with my car brakes yesterday that shook me up rather, and set me to thinking about some unfinished business I have that needs dealing with. I don't suppose for a minute that you'll need to bother your head about it, unless I'm particularly unlucky and something carries me off in the near future, but I'm leaving you the details just in case.

It's not a pleasant story, but it has to be told. You'll remember in my last letter I mentioned a trip to Berlin. What I didn't tell you was what happened during my visit. I was there because the Nazis had some art they wanted to sell off, and it looked like a good opportunity to pick up a few good pieces cheap. One can't buy anything without going through their official dealers, and the one I spoke to on this occasion was a chap called Nicholas Honegger. I've known him a few years and never liked the fellow much, although we've always been on civil terms, and on this occasion I bought some good modern pieces off him that would most likely have been destroyed otherwise. (I met Adolf Hitler while I was there, incidentally. Odd little fellow – very sure of himself.)

The night before I was due to come home I'd been invited to dinner at the house of an old pal of mine, Jacob Silberstein. I turned up as instructed, only to find his wife and children weeping over his dead body on the hearthrug. It turns out Honegger and a couple of Gestapo thugs had arrived at his door just before I got there and demanded his paintings off him with menaces. He didn't take it lightly, things got nasty and they shot him and left, saying they'd come back the next day.

Irma Silberstein was terrified and wanted to get herself and the children out of Berlin immediately before anything worse happened to them, but they had no ready money. They weren't especially keen to see Honegger get his hands on Jacob's paintings either, but they didn't think they had much choice. As it happened I'd arranged a truck to bring my own acquisitions back to Lucerne the next day, so I offered to take Jacob's artworks with me, and keep them until the Silbersteins got to safety and sent me further instructions. I gave them some money to get out of Germany, but Irma insisted I take one of the paintings in exchange, so I took one I knew I could sell easily to an Italian count of my acquaintance who considers himself a bit of a connoisseur.

We got the paintings out in the middle of the night, and smuggled them through customs, hidden in among all the official purchases. I'd offered to take Irma and the children too, but she said she wanted to go to her family in Hamburg. I haven't heard from them since, but I dare say they have other things on their mind at present and Irma will write as soon as she can.

Now, I haven't told Monica about these paintings, because I suspect if I leave them for her to deal with after my *death she'll sell them and keep the money. Your stepmother's a delightful woman in many ways, but to her business is business, and she'll see these paintings merely as a stroke of good fortune that's landed in her lap. I took the paintings in a hurry, you see, so there's no official proof of provenance, and given the current climate in Germany she could easily make a case that she has the perfect right to keep them. However, I made a promise to Irma, and I intend to keep it. Besides, I don't like the thought of that crooked brother of Monica's muscling in and demanding a share of the proceeds if she does sell them. But someone needs to deal with all this if I'm not here, and there's no one I'd rather trust than you, Stella.*

So, then, to business: the key to the place where I put the paintings is in a safe deposit box here in Lucerne. According to my will all the paintings in my possession ought to belong to Monica, and if I leave the key to the box with my lawyer he'll simply give it to her, so instead I've given it to old Franz, the doorman at the gallery, with instructions to pass it on to you when you turn up (as I assume you will if anything happens to me). There's also a scrap of paper with Honegger's handwriting on it that I thought might be useful to keep as evidence in case he ever comes to trial – although I doubt that will ever happen, given the way things are going at present.

I have an address for Irma's sister in Hamburg, and I'll write to her with instructions of how to get in touch with you in London if necessary. It's all a bit unsatisfactory, I know, but it's the best I can do in a hurry. I'll put a more permanent arrangement in place as soon as I can, but I wanted you to have the information just in case – God forbid – something happens to me.

By the way, I've been thinking about your future. You'll be leaving school later this year, and I'd like you to come out to Lucerne after that. I realise the business has occupied me rather too much in recent years, and I haven't seen you nearly as much as I'd have liked to. I expect you have lots of friends at school, and don't care much to see your dull old father, but there's lots to do here in Switzerland, and I'd like to show you the place properly. And perhaps I might show you a little of how the business works too. I think you'll enjoy it – one's forever meeting fascinating people. Do come.

I'll finish now, as I want to catch the post, but I'll write again next week as usual, by which time I should have organised this business with the Silberstein paintings, and then you can tear this letter up if you like.

Love,
Dad

The other letter was from Irma Silberstein. The date on it was early 1938, several months after Raymond's death. It was in German, but the address was New York, and as far as Stella could make out it said the Silbersteins had now settled there and Irma was hoping to make arrangements for the transport of the paintings to America. Presumably Monica had ignored the letter. Had Irma suspected Raymond of withholding her possessions from her deliberately when he didn't reply? Stella put a hand to the key around her neck. She'd had the presence of mind to retrieve it from Marius's pocket before the partisans took him away. When the war was over she'd write to Irma and assure her that Raymond had done his best to keep the paintings safe, just as he'd promised.

She turned once more to her father's letter and sat, reading it over and over again. It was his last message to her, the letter he'd written on the day he died, spurred on by a premonition that something was about to happen to him. Had he suspected Marius in particular of wishing him harm? From the letter it didn't sound like it. But he hadn't had the chance to write again, because he'd been killed on his way to the post, and Stella had never received his letter because Monica had kept it and opened it, and found out about the paintings. Then she'd tried to deceive Stella into finding out their whereabouts for her when she knew full well they weren't hers. It had been a bold move, but it hadn't come off. Stella was glad of it – not least because she was sure her father was right, and that Marius would have got his hands on some of the proceeds one way or another. She still wasn't sorry Marius was dead, but she thought she could forgive Monica. Self-centred and amoral as Monica was, she wasn't evil, like her brother. She'd suffered for her mistakes, and deserved a second chance, Stella thought.

She read the last paragraph of the letter again with sadness. It looked as if her father had finally realised he'd been neglecting her, and had planned to spend more time with her in future – a future that had been brutally cut short. The tears rolled down Stella's cheeks at the thought that they'd never have the chance to get to know one another better now. Still, there was at least some consolation in among the sadness: she was finally free of the hurtful suspicions that had dogged her for so long, and she could restore him to his rightful place in her memory.

*

Now that Ted had found Stella at last he wasn't about to let her go again, and he went about things in his usual direct manner. With Marius dead there was nothing to stand in the way of their getting married, so he spent several days yelling at people to complete the formalities and get him the necessary documentation, ignoring Stella's protestations that there were more important things to do at present.

'Nothing is more important than this,' he said, then hesitated. 'Unless you've changed your mind.'

There was a note of uncertainty in his voice that was so unlike him that Stella stared.

'Why do you say that?'

'I mean, before all this you were escaping from something. Now you have nothing to escape from.'

'You think that's the only reason I agreed to marry you in Switzerland? To get away from Marius?'

'Wasn't it?'

He gazed at her searchingly. She put a hand to his cheek.

'No,' she said softly. 'Ted, it's you I want – it's you I've always wanted.'

A smile spread across his face.

'All right, then what are we waiting for?'

If she'd ever been worried that he would forget her, the past few days had eased her fears. He still wanted her, and she still wanted him, and although she'd been a little wary of marrying him just now, thinking that it might look insensitive when so many others had lost loved ones in the carnage of the past few weeks, she understood his unwillingness to wait any longer.

So they were married one morning in the English church, in a service conducted by an army chaplain, Ted in his uniform and Stella wearing a dress borrowed from Monica. Scarcely able to believe it was really happening after so many months of misery, Stella felt light-headed and was fighting the urge to giggle, and throughout the ceremony the two of them were so preoccupied with gazing at each other that several times Ted had to ask the chaplain to repeat himself. They got through it at last, and Ted didn't need to be told twice to kiss the bride. As they came out of the church, Ted gripping Stella's hand so tightly it almost hurt, they bumped into an American of Ted's acquaintance.

'Hey Louie, I got married,' said Ted cheerfully.

Louie gave Stella a startled glance.

'But you just got here,' he replied, evidently taking Stella for an Italian woman Ted had just met.

Stella hadn't laughed properly for at least a year, but now she couldn't stop, so Ted had to break off in the middle of his explanation and kiss her again to shut her up. Then he carried her off to the Hotel Ambassador, where he'd managed to wangle them one of the best rooms, and there they stayed for a day and a half. If the OSS wanted him they could come and find him, he said.

The last time Stella had been a guest here Marius had half-killed her and she'd fled, terrified, into the evening. Now she was here with Ted, who loved her and wanted only to protect her – in fact, was already doing his level best to persuade her to leave Italy for her own safety.

'Don't be silly,' she replied. 'You tried to send me away once before and look what happened. No,' she went on, as she saw him about to interrupt. 'You're not getting rid of me. I'll stay here and wait for you. Besides, what would I do stuck in London? I'd feel useless, but here I'm needed. There's so much to do at the moment – I could work at the hotel, or help Dora organise the clear-up at the villa. And Beatrice will have her hands full with Vittorio and Tina. It'll be far better than sitting about moping without you.'

He saw the set of her jaw and gave up.

'You never would do anything I said, would you?' he demanded.

'No, and I'm not going to start now, so you'd better get used to it.'

They both knew he would have to leave Florence soon, pushing further north to link up with other groups of partisans, until the Germans had been driven completely out of Italy. Until then all they could do was make the most of each other's company, because it was uncertain when they'd meet again.

Chapter Thirty-Nine

It was a long, cold winter that year, but it passed, and spring blossomed, just as it always had. After a hiatus, the Allies resumed their offensive in April and, after fierce and bloody fighting, the Germans were at long last driven out, and Italy was liberated. It was good news, although the Italian people were by now too exhausted, picking among the ruins of their country, to feel much like celebrating for now. There was too much to rebuild, but at least the country was finally free of its occupiers.

On a warm afternoon in early May, Stella arrived at Santa Maria Novella station after a journey from Rome which had taken much longer than it should have, given the damaged lines and shortage of rolling stock. She had only a few things in a light bag, so she threw it over her shoulder and set off on the walk to Dora's house. Beatrice was at home, hanging some new curtains.

'The place needed brightening up,' she said when Stella admired them.

'They're nice. And with any luck you won't need to turn them into frocks again.'

'How was Rome? I wish I could have come with you.'

'Still standing, more or less. And it's taken nearly two weeks of badgering the British embassy, but I have a proper passport at last. The Swiss embassy weren't much use, though. They say they can't do anything from Italy, and it would be much better if I went back to Switzerland in person. I pointed out that if I could have gone back in person I wouldn't have bothered coming all the way to Rome, but it didn't seem to help.'

'Now that Hitler is gone it can only be a matter of weeks before the war's finally over, then you can go where you like,' observed Beatrice.

'I'm not sure it'll be that easy – at least, not for a while.'

'Do you think there will be any money left for you?'

'Who knows? Marius never told me what he was doing with it, and I was always too scared of him to ask.'

'You don't seem particularly bothered.'

Stella smiled, and put a hand to her stomach.

'It doesn't matter now. I have everything I wanted. If there's any money left, then so much the better, but if it's all gone I won't waste time wishing.'

Dora came in, with Tina. The little girl ran to Stella and held out her arms to be picked up, and Dora clucked.

'No, no, she can't pick you up! Stella, sit down.'

'Of course I can pick her up,' said Stella, and did so. 'Goodness, Tina, I think you've grown two inches in ten days!'

Dora was fussing around her.

'Did you walk from the station? You shouldn't be walking.'

'I'm fine, honestly. I feel perfectly well.'

'And you shouldn't have gone to Rome alone. What if the baby decided to come?'

Stella laughed.

'As you can see, it didn't, and I'm here now. Truly, Dora, there's no need to worry.'

'When is Ted coming?' asked Beatrice, shaking her head at her mother.

'Not till this evening, or perhaps tomorrow, depending on how the roads are. He said he'd wait for me at the hotel.'

Stella hadn't seen Ted in over a month. He'd been up in the north on OSS business, but now that the war was coming to an end she was looking forward to being able to spend more time with him.

Beatrice stepped down from the chair and looked at the new curtains critically.

'They'll do,' she said.

'Where's Vittorio?' asked Stella.

'At the villa. He was supposed to come back for lunch but I guess he lost track of time. I'm going to take him some food. Do you want to come with me?'

Some of the rubble had been cleared from the damaged part of the Villa Bruni, but it was still a shell of its former self, as it was too soon to start rebuilding. They found Vittorio clearing a corner of the garden which had become overgrown. He hailed Stella cheerfully. He was walking a little stiffly, but he was looking well, and the way Beatrice gazed at him warmed Stella's heart.

'Did Beatrice tell you the news?' he asked.

'What news?'

He glanced at Beatrice mockingly.

'What kind of a woman are you?'

'It wasn't my news to tell,' said Beatrice.

'Well? Don't keep me on tenterhooks!' exclaimed Stella. 'Is this about the letter you got from the lawyer?'

Vittorio waggled his eyebrows significantly and seemed inclined to draw out the suspense for as long as possible, but eventually Stella got out of him that Gerardo had left him a sum of money in his will – not a huge amount, but enough to buy a small house with some land, or perhaps a business. When Vittorio would get the money was anybody's guess, and he was about to launch into a long diatribe about the crookedness of lawyers when Beatrice interrupted him.

'Never mind that. That's not all the Count left,' she said to Stella. 'You remember the Count's favourite painting?'

'The *Lady of the Cypresses*? Yes, I remember it.' Stella was astonished. 'He left you that? But didn't the Germans take it?'

Vittorio shook his head.

'No. The Count wanted to keep it separate from the others, so I hid it somewhere else, and forgot about it until a couple of weeks ago. Then I took it to the superintendent of the Uffizi gallery, and he went white in the face and had to sit down,' he finished with some satisfaction.

'I'm not surprised – it must be worth a fortune. Did Gerardo only leave you that one? What about the rest of the paintings?'

'Those are for the Countess, if the Americans can get them back. But he left the Raphael to me because he knew I wouldn't let it go outside Italy.'

'But what will you do with it?'

'Well, I thought of putting it on the wall in our little cottage, but for some reason Beatrice thinks that is a very stupid idea, so perhaps I will let the Uffizi gallery keep it for now. It's much safer there.'

'Will you sell it?'

'Not just now. The money the Count left us will be enough to let us get married.' He put his arm around Beatrice and she smiled into his eyes. 'I will keep the Raphael as insurance, in case Beatrice runs away and I need the money to hire someone to bring her back.'

Stella smiled at the two of them, thinking how Beatrice had been transformed in the past few months. Vittorio was walking so well now, and was full of plans, and she knew they would be happy.

'Come and see how the vegetable garden is looking,' said Vittorio.

Stella had suddenly discovered she was more tired than she thought, after her long journey and the walk from the station, so she excused herself and said she would rest on the terrace for a few minutes. The other two went off, Vittorio whispering in Beatrice's ear and Beatrice giggling, and Stella sat on the bench on the terrace, looking out over Florence, still stately and beautiful despite all that had happened. She was thinking back over the past few years and how things had changed. Many things had been lost in the chaos of war, but other things had been gained.

Despite what she'd said to Beatrice, she hoped to get back to Switzerland to have the baby now that the Germans were no longer standing in the way. There was a lot of work to be done in Geneva: most of her possessions were still there, and if Marius hadn't left any money she hoped at least to sell the apartment and recoup some of her losses, since there would soon be another mouth to feed. It would be a difficult journey, given the state of the roads and the railways in Italy, but Monica had agreed to go with her if Ted couldn't get leave. After that night in the hotel, when they'd clutched each other as the Germans bombed the bridges, they'd formed a friendship of sorts. Stella was glad of it, as she felt it gave her some sort of connection to her father's memory. She wasn't as naïve as she had been all those years ago when she'd first come to Florence, and she half-suspected that Monica was still interested in the missing paintings, but she was determined not to let her get her hands on them.

Stella had written to Irma Silberstein as soon as some semblance of a postal service had been restored, to let her know the artworks were still safe. Then in early spring she'd received a reply, full of commiserations for Raymond's death, and joy that he had kept his promise despite everything. Even in the darkest days of the war Irma's faith in him had never wavered, she said. He'd been a good friend to her husband, and she would always remember with gratitude how he had saved her and her children in their time of need. The paintings could wait for now, but if Stella was ever in New York, she would be more than welcome as a guest at the Silbersteins' home. The letter was a comforting reminder to Stella that whatever his faults, her father had been a good man at heart.

She felt a kick and her hand moved to her rounded stomach as she gave silent thanks that with just over two months to go she was still feeling so well. Given the energy and determination with which the baby had been battering her insides lately, she suspected it would be a boy, probably just like Ted, and she wondered how she would cope with two of them. She smiled at the thought of the exciting new adventure that lay ahead of her.

She was sitting there in a daydream when a voice called her name, and she turned. It was Ted himself, approaching along the terrace, smart in his uniform, just as he had on that day last August, when they'd found each other after a long, painful year apart. Her heart leapt at the sight of him.

'I thought you said you were going straight to the hotel,' he said. 'I was waiting for you, but then Monica said the train must have arrived hours ago, so I figured you'd probably come here.'

He sat down next to her on the bench and kissed her, then put a hand on her stomach.

'Did you walk here? I'll bet you did. You know what I said.'

'Don't start that again. I'm perfectly all right, and so is the baby.'

'Still trying to kick his way out?'

'Pretty much. How was Milan?'

'Don't ask. Let's just say it makes Florence look like a day at the races. Still, at least the Germans are gone for good. They're talking about a full surrender within days.'

'I hope so,' she said fervently. 'I'm so tired of war.'

'Me too. It'll be good to get back to normal at last.'

'By the way, have you heard Vittorio's news? Gerardo left him the *Lady of the Cypresses*.'

He raised his eyebrows.

'A whole Raphael? Well, why not? I guess he worked hard enough for it.'

'Did you find out anything about what happened to the other paintings?'

'Not yet, but I heard they found about a thousand paintings in a building just outside Bolzano. We'll just have to wait and see whether Gerardo's are among them.'

'It would be nice to get them back. Gerardo would have hated to lose them,' said Stella.

'Don't you think Monica will sell them as soon as she gets her hands on them?'

'She might, but if she does I'll try and persuade her to keep them here in Italy.'

He slid his arm around her, and she leaned her head against him, and they sat comfortably, their hands clasped lightly together over her stomach, looking out over Florence.

'Are we going to live in Italy when the war's over?' she said at last.

'I don't know. I will if there's a job for me. I'd like to go back to the States for a while first, though. What do you say?'

'Yes, why not? I'd love to go to America with you.'

He sat back and looked at her in disbelief.

'Are you kidding? When did you ever do what I wanted?'

'There's a first time for everything,' she replied, and laughed happily.

A Letter from Clara Benson

Dear Reader

Thank you for choosing to read *The Stolen Letter*. If you enjoyed it, and want to keep up to date with all my latest releases, sign up at the following link. Your email address will never be shared and you can unsubscribe at any time.

www.bookouture.com/clara-benson

A long time ago I spent a period of several months in Florence. This year (2020) I'd intended to return, but a certain global pandemic put paid to that, so I had to make do with revisiting the place in my imagination. Looking at photos of the city today, serene and beautiful, it's difficult to imagine what it must have been like during the dark days when World War Two was at its height, although so many other towns and cities were completely flattened by bombs that I suppose we can only be thankful that Florence escaped the worst of the damage. It is true that the bridges were blown up as the Germans retreated, but as soon as they could the Florentines rebuilt them painstakingly, brick by brick, and today you'd hardly know that the city was once so deeply scarred by war. If you've never been to Florence, I hope this book inspires you to visit, because it really is one of the most beautiful places in the world.

I hope you enjoyed *The Stolen Letter*. If you did I'd be very grateful if you could write a review – even just a sentence or two will do. Reviews are incredibly helpful to authors, and they're also useful for readers looking for new books. And if you'd like to drop me a line you can find me on Facebook, Twitter, Goodreads and my website.

Thanks for reading!
Clara

clarabensonbooks

clarabooks

clarabenson.com

Acknowledgements

Once again I'd like to thank my husband Paul, who patiently answered questions like 'What do you call those shoulder-strap thingies with lots of bullets in them?' without rolling his eyes (at least to my face). Thanks, too, to Laura Dinale and Silvia Da Pozzo for their thoughts on Italian names. I'm sorry Zvonko didn't make the cut.

And of course, a big thank you goes to the team at Bookouture, especially my fantastic editor Christina Demosthenous, for doing such a sterling job and helping me make the book the best it could be.

Printed in Great Britain
by Amazon

54159519R00224